A
KILLER'S
DAUGHTER

A
KILLER'S
DAUGHTER

JENNA
KERNAN

bookouture

Published by Bookouture in 2021

An imprint of Storyfire Ltd.
Carmelite House
50 Victoria Embankment
London EC4Y 0DZ

www.bookouture.com

ISBN: 978-1-80019-271-3
eBook ISBN: 978-1-80019-270-6

For Jim, always

PROLOGUE

Couple one

I'm not a monster. But I do kill people, have been for more than two decades. Mostly, I'm doing the world a favor.

Sitting in my kayak, hidden in the mangroves, I wait for the lovers to arrive. I've watched them before; their affair so old it has become routine. Their other partners wait at home as they "work late" every Saturday night. She'll arrive on her paddleboard; he'll arrive on foot from the parking lot with wine and the blanket.

The scrape of her board on the sand gives me a rush of power and foresight. Beyond the Intracoastal Waterway, lights from the million-dollar homes wink on, most set on timers in the summer months as their owners are back up north. The view from that private key is spectacular, with the sunset already in progress, but from their shore, this barrier island and the adulterers are invisible against the dark greenery of the city park. Most of the boaters have already headed to their moorings or berths. The few people left here are on the Gulf side of the point, watching the sinking sun. Sunset is an event here every night, weather permitting. And today, the weather is perfect.

I retrieve the rope and fish-filleting knife, then slip on my latex gloves as the lovers embrace. Lifting my paddle, I leave the tangled roots of the mangroves and cross the inlet.

Before today, I feared I faced the impossible. But now I recognize the point is not about being in total control. It's about legacy. What lives on after we are gone.

It's also about commemorating a master. And she was that. What I admire best about this killer's trail of death is how simple she kept it. The water concealed the bodies, washed away the blood and gave her time to flee.

The challenge, the risk and the start of a journey combine in a heady rush of pleasure. I've never taken one outdoors before. I'm aroused at this new challenge and lick my lips, anticipating, exhilarated, feeling younger and, oh, so very alive.

A knife isn't my weapon of choice. The death it brings is usually too quick for my liking, but this is an homage, re-enacting her creations with an added purpose beyond meeting my own needs. And I admit that a kill by knife has a simplicity, an elegance.

This pair is so like Gail and Charlie. Those two cheated on their spouses in the back of the carpet warehouse, screwing on a bed of foam instead of sand. The similarities are important; otherwise, how will she know?

They are in a hurry, dropping to their knees, face-to-face as they tussle with unwanted clothing. I beach the kayak. I'm so close to them now, close enough to smell the sweat on their bodies and hear their sighs. The woman senses me and opens her eyes as I reach out and slice through both his Achilles tendons. I hit one hamstring on the return stroke.

He cries out in pain and turns, looking at his legs. I grip the knife, now slick with blood. Confusion blankets his flabby face. In the twilight, his blood is dark.

He falls from her arms into the sand. Her eyes dart from him to me. She sees but doesn't understand, the shock blinding her. She lifts her hands in defense.

Why doesn't she scream? I like to hear them scream. But she seems paralyzed, mouth gaping. Meanwhile, his words are a jabbering garble of cries and pleas as I open an artery.

I look him in the eye as I cut again, a long slice down his upper arm. Was this what she felt, carving into the one who betrayed her? Did she experience this rush of power and appreciate that the killing is the point?

Another sweeping arc and slice, her this time. The blade is so sharp that the laceration across her abdomen doesn't even seem to break the skin. The line of red is razor-thin—at first. Then the pain receptors register. She screams at last. The sound carries across the water, but who is to hear? The boaters over the roar of their motors? No, her scream is just for me.

She presses her palms to her stomach, and I slice the vessel at her neck.

He's struggling to his knees. He roars with fury and lunges for the knife. So, I give it to him, swinging wildly across his wrists and forearms. He recoils, falling to his seat, opening the opportunity for me to slice his femoral artery just below his junk.

The blood sprays across the sand and blanket and me. She's reaching for him, calling his name.

"David! David!"

Her hero, only he's not. He's a butcher at a local market.

Who's the butcher now?

A panicked look blankets her face as she sucks in a breath. She sways as her blood spurts, pouring down her naked torso. Her final scream is a gargling yowl.

I grab his arm and drag him to the water. He struggles and ends up facedown. I lift his wrist and make a final cut, then return for her. She's holding her belly and her neck. Her face is pale as moonlight.

"Did you find everything you need today?" I ask.

Her eyes widen as she recognizes the words that she has spoken to me dozens of times from behind her register, never really seeing me. She sees me now.

I clasp her wrist and slip on the noose. She's too weak to struggle. She leaves a wide trail in the sand as I drag her to the shore. The gentle waves wash over his face as I tie the other end of the rope to his wrist. Can he still see us? The possibility thrills.

I cut a strip of skin from his finger and his hand twitches. Yes, he still sees me. I give him a final triumphant smile, then turn to her, squatting to carve the letters in her flank, enjoying the twitch of her muscles as the blade cuts deep.

She struggles as I yank off her wedding and engagement rings. She doesn't deserve them. She moans as I cut, then tug away the skin around her finger and flick it into the water. When I roll her into the current, her mouth opens. She breathes in seawater. The convulsions are fascinating.

The rope pulls tight, tugging his wrist, and I heave him after her. For several moments, they roll and drag along the shore. Then the tide takes them. His head bobs like a coconut. I wade in after them to wash.

And so it begins, this new adventure. The initial step toward making her mine. I have gone to great lengths to bring her here. She is the reason that the hot blood now drips from my fingers.

"Do you feel my presence yet, my dear? Can you hear us calling you?"

I glance down the empty shore between the mangrove forest and the channel. Everyone is on the opposite side of the park, a half mile away, on the Gulf beaches, watching the setting sun paint the clouds the same color I have painted the sea.

I can't see the couple anymore. I turn and retrieve the crushed seltzer can from my rear pocket and drop it on the blanket, wondering where the bodies will land. But I am already losing interest. The tingling excitement fades, turning me sullen. I make my exit shortly after the lovers have made theirs, heading to my watercraft, carrying an unopened bottle of wine.

CHAPTER ONE

In over your head

The 6 a.m. news opened with a breaking story. Two bodies were recovered from the water in Sarasota's Bayfront Park. The correspondent reported from beside a kayak rental that the identities of the victims were being withheld, pending notification of the families. Law enforcement offered a big "no comment" on the cause of death.

Dr. Nadine Finch reached for the remote and flicked off the television as if it were a screaming smoke alarm. The forensic psychologist stared at the dark screen, struggling to control her breathing as sweat beaded on her forehead.

Bodies in the water. She shuddered. The sense of familiarity from these murders stirred. Two people found together in the water—it brought to mind the murders that still haunted her. But this had to be a coincidence.

A bird crashing into her front window startled her from her musings. Nadine stood up and stared out at the sunny summer morning, and watched the seemingly lifeless creature right itself and fly off. Then the alarm on her phone blared, warning her she would be late if she did not leave right now.

Her hands trembled as she collected her bag, then headed out into the oppressive July humidity. Inside her Lexus, the AC pushed away the heat as she drove to the Sarasota City Courthouse. There, she spent her morning trying to shake off a sense of dread, while administering a battery of tests to an elderly man who had starved his wife of forty-five years to death.

When she finished, Nadine motioned to the guard who stepped forward to take custody of Mr. Swineford.

The old man tried and failed to rise with her.

"Can I see my wife now?" he asked.

Her heart gave a sharp pang at his guileless expression as she considered her response, settling on, "Not today."

Mr. Swineford began to cry. Tears welled in her eyes in response.

"I don't like it here," he said.

Nadine's hand went to his forearm and she squeezed.

"I'm sorry," she said, and assisted him to his feet.

She would use her influence with the court to keep this man from prison. A plea deal including placement in a geriatric facility was all that was needed to protect society. Prison would serve no one, least of all this helpless aging veteran who could not care for himself, let alone a wife with dementia.

"Thank you for your cooperation, Mr. Swineford."

He patted her hand. "You're a nice lady."

The officer handcuffed his spindly wrists before him and assisted him out of the interview room. Nadine wiped at her eyes before gathering her things and heading out.

She passed through the lobby of one of Sarasota's most beautiful buildings, designed in Mediterranean Revival style. Colorful mosaic tile brightened the central tower, courtyard and exterior. Most days Nadine lingered to appreciate the statues, fountains and reflecting pool in the inner garden. But today, gray-bottomed thunderclouds billowed skyward, threatening rain, so she hurried along one of the interior corridors adjoining the gardens. She passed several city employees, who did not even glance in her direction.

Nadine stood only five feet two inches on a small frame, and had been told by more than one detective that she wasn't very imposing. In much of her work, this was an advantage. Her pale complexion swung between rosy and florid depending on the heat index. Her hair was shoulder-length and a forgettable brown. While working, she mirrored a submissive posture. Most people never noticed her hazel-green eyes, because she limited direct eye contact to avoid appearing a threat. But appearances were deceiving. Her mother had taught her that.

Being overlooked and underestimated were two of her super-powers, which was why hearing someone shout her name startled Nadine.

She found Dr. Juliette Hartfield heading in her direction.

Juliette was a new hire and one of two medical examiners in their district. The medical examiners' offices were three miles south, though Juliette was occasionally in court as part of her job.

She'd only started here one month ago, and Nadine hadn't figured her out yet, but there was a connection forming that went past the workplace. She was becoming a friend, which was concerning. Nadine didn't let anyone get too close. It wasn't safe.

"I was about to text you," said Juliette. She lifted the seltzer and drained the can's contents.

"Oh?"

"I just testified for the first time." She sagged in mock exhaustion.

She'd forgotten Juliette had mentioned her first court appearance.

"How did it go?" asked Nadine.

"Easier than expected."

Her golden complexion and brilliant blue eyes would have been Juliette's most distinguishing features, if she did not dye her hair platinum-blond and spike the five-inch strands in every direction, so it bristled about her. Despite the use of sunscreen, her skin was perpetually tan.

"You just missed Officer Dun." Her grin was conspiratorial.

"The creepy lurker?" Nadine made a face.

You would assume the forensic team would be creepy, taking apart bodies day after day. But the one who gave her the willies was a court security officer who always managed to be in the same courtroom as her, and always stood a little too close.

"Nathan isn't creepy. He's sweet on you and a little awkward." She tossed the empty can in a recycle bin with the proficiency of a basketball player.

"I'm not getting that. He's always watching me. It's disturbing," she said.

Juliette grinned. "Because he's attracted and too shy to speak to you. I think it's cute."

"He isn't shy. In fact, I have to make excuses to get away from him."

"Anyway, he's gone."

Nadine ceased scanning the corridor and blew away a breath, then turned back to Juliette, who was holding a grin.

Getting on so effortlessly with Juliette made her cautious. But she and the new ME were both single and new to Sarasota, so exploring together seemed harmless, if it only went so far. Acquaintances. Never friends.

She remembered the old joke about not wanting to join any club that would have her as a member. That was how Nadine thought of friends. If they wanted to connect, there was something wrong with them.

Still, she longed for true companions, family and all the normal things that seemed too dangerous to pursue.

As a girl, she knew never to bring friends home. And now she was grown, if the loneliness and isolation weighed heavily, she reminded herself what had happened when she had tried in the past to connect with people. Once she told them the truth about her past, they never looked at her the same way again.

Who could blame them?

"I've still got work to finish up," Nadine said, thinking Juliette was looking to catch lunch together.

"Me too. I have three today and the court thing really set me back."

Three, meaning three bodies and their autopsies. How Juliette kept so cheerful when she spent much of her day up to her elbows in noxious bodily fluids and decomposing corpses, Nadine would never understand.

Were any of her "three today" the victims recovered from the bayfront that she'd seen on the news?

"Were you on hand for the two found this morning?" Nadine swallowed and repressed a shiver despite the July humidity.

Juliette's brows lifted. "You heard?"

"Morning news."

"Ah. I saw the reporters there."

"Was it a drowning?" asked Nadine. Did she sound hopeful?

Juliette held her gaze as she gave a slow shake of her head. "Nope. Papers might report it as a drowning because I haven't released the cause of death yet."

"Why not?"

"Well, first off, autopsy's pending. But I also have orders from above." Juliette pointed to heaven.

"Is that normal?"

"I haven't been here long enough to know. My supervisor said it's all right to hold the death certificate pending toxicology results. That gives us a couple of weeks."

Which made Nadine wonder why they needed to hide a cause of death for a period of weeks. For the sake of the homicide investigation? She wasn't sure.

There was no way to know it was homicide. Two victims. That was all. She didn't even know if they were a male and a female. That would mean another similarity. Another red flag.

"One male, one female," said Juliette. "Sliced up like a Sunday ham. We have a wacko." She glanced at Nadine. "Sorry. Disturbed individual."

Nadine focused on Juliette's mouth. She was speaking, but the ringing in Nadine's ears distorted her words.

"… Stabbings… Multiple lacerations."

Nadine squeezed her eyes shut, imagining the blood, so much blood. Juliette kept on talking as Nadine swayed.

She was sure she knew these two deaths. Intimately. They'd have been married, engaged in an illicit affair. The woman would have taken the brunt of the attack.

But wait. She didn't know that for sure. The only parallels were the two victims, and a stabbing. And the water…

"… called our guys to process the scene… turned up on bayside. Right next to the tiki bar. Some kid found them near the kayaks. Can you imagine?"

She could. Vividly.

"Anyway, it's got the lab buzzing. And we can't determine where they entered the water. The Coast Guard is helping investigators to figure that, but I can't zero in on the time of death any closer than five hours, and the tides change every four, so…" Juliette frowned. "You okay?"

Nadine resisted the urge to ask if the victims were tied together at the wrist with a length of cording. Did the female have long hair, dark eyes and a slim build? Nadine's face heated.

"You okay?"

"Okay?" she repeated, giving herself processing time and landing on a redirection. "It looks like I won't beat the rain." She motioned to the first large droplets splattering sidewalks in the courtyard.

Juliette peeked out of one arched opening to stare at the approaching storm.

Stabbing deaths. She had a special horror of those. Nadine crossed her arms over her middle, flashing a defensive posture because Juliette was suddenly a threat. The urge to run nearly overwhelmed her. These deaths were all too familiar.

"Lead detective wants a profiler for this one," Juliette said, still looking skyward.

"Did you suggest me?" Nadine heard her voice squeak as she strained to maintain control of the terrified creature writhing inside of her.

"No," Juliette assured. She waved her hands and made eye contact now.

"I'm not a profiler."

"But you could be," she said.

"I help *after* arrests. That's what forensic psychologists do, help the police *after* they catch the bad guys. Work with suspects, inmates. Assessment of mental state, interviews, sentencing recommendations." She glanced up to see Juliette looking at her as if she'd stepped off the deep end. Nadine realized she was babbling and reined herself in. "What I'm saying is, they need a *criminal psychologist*. They're the ones who assist law enforcement on capturing criminals."

"There's crossover, no?"

There was.

Nadine shook her head. "Besides. We have a criminal psychologist on staff already. They'll assign him."

"I heard them mention you."

"Who did?"

"Detective Wernli recommended you to the new Homicide cop, Detective Demko." Juliette squeezed her hands together in front of her heart and fluttered her eyes. "Total hunk, btw."

Nadine was still in denial mode.

"He won't want me. They need someone to do predictive work. That's not me." Nadine was still jabbering, talking too fast and too loud.

"But this is a chance to assist in a major case. Double homicide, a wild one."

"I… I just don't think that kind of work is for me."

Juliette's tone turned conciliatory. "I wanted to give you a heads-up is all. Know you hate surprises, so… that's it."

Nadine forced her gaze to meet Juliette's and saw nothing but concern.

"I appreciate that." With a nod of farewell, she headed down the steps and into the courtyard, hurrying toward the street.

"Want a lift?"

Nadine deployed her umbrella for protection from the rain and Juliette's shouted question.

"I'm fine." This she called back without turning.

She wasn't fine.

Nadine splashed through rapidly forming puddles. Juliette could be wrong about the profiler request. Nadine was newest on staff. They wouldn't trust her with something this important. Plus, she was certain they would assign their criminal psychologist to this one.

Nadine hurried from the courthouse through the downpour, sloshing through the swelling puddles in the crosswalk that soaked her shoes. She arrived at the lobby of her building, two blocks away, panting with exertion and alarm. Safely inside the innocuous three-story cinder-block office complex, she let the tremors come. Years and years of therapy had made her into a functioning adult. But she wasn't equipped for this.

It was several minutes before she took the elevator to the third floor and the Forensic Psychology Services office, where she worked.

Inside, their new assistant called a greeting from behind the high receptionist counter. The young woman gave her a timid doe-eyed blink and shy smile. This was Tina Ruz's first job out of college, and she was fresh and innocent as a baby bunny. Nadine felt sorry for her because she recognized what the world did to helpless creatures.

"Dr. Crean wants to see you," said Tina.

"Now?"

"That's what she said."

The sense of dread returned, but Nadine merely nodded and hustled to her office to drop off her things and set her umbrella open to dry.

On the job here as a forensic psychologist for only three months, Nadine was anxious to make an impression. She wanted to do well here, but her self-protective instincts outweighed ambition. Always. And right now, her instincts were buzzing like a hornet's nest.

As she headed from her office down the corridor to the corner office of Dr. Margery Crean, she prayed this had nothing to do with the death investigation she'd discussed with Juliette. Her boss might wish to speak to her about anything, and not necessarily the recent slayings. She ignored the distant shrill of a siren in her mind, but her sweating palms were less easily overlooked.

Why did her thoughts go immediately to assignment to an active investigation? There were worse things.

As she walked through the outer office, she wondered again if she should have disclosed her past to her employer. If she'd told them, would they have hired her?

Keeping secrets was as exhausting as keeping everyone at a distance. But experience had shown her that being alone was preferable to being ostracized.

Nadine paused in the outer office, and resting a hand flat on her chest, she closed her eyes and breathed deeply. The self-calming exercise took only a moment. Afterward, she glanced down at herself. Yes, she was wearing a navy-blue suit, white blouse and low practical heels on small narrow feet. She checked the simple gold hoops in her ears and ran her hand over her hair pulled back at her nape. She straightened her shoulders, knowing that the panicky little girl within was invisible to all but herself.

Nadine walked with calm assurance toward Crean's office. She looked the part of the professional she tried to be and, if necessary, she could utilize very effective masking techniques.

Before she studied psychology, she had become a social chameleon. She didn't stand out. She blended in groups. Mimicked reactions. Copied expressions. Nothing too special. Nothing too odd. Hiding among normal people, like her mother had done for so long. The good ones, the successful ones, always did.

Crean's door was open, and as Nadine raised her hand to knock, the director of clinical services waved her in.

"Close the door," she said, glancing back to the computer monitor as Nadine complied. Crean's office phone blinked. "Excuse me." She lifted the handset.

Nadine admired Crean but didn't trust her, or anyone really. All Nadine's therapists said she saw every authority figure as a potential threat. A habit formed in childhood. She raised a hand to her cheek, certain she could still feel the sting that followed each slap.

Nadine dropped her hand and lifted her chin, forcing a placid expression, eyes on her boss. Likely, Crean knew as many tricks as she did, or she might be exactly what she seemed. She found that unlikely because no one was.

And figuring people out was Nadine's A game.

All she could ascertain pointed to a woman who was scary ordinary. But nobody went into this field because they were whole and happy. Two kinds of individuals settled into the profession of psychology, the broken and the ones who like to drive a pin through a living fly to watch it wiggle.

Which was Crean?

Her director was married to an outwardly normal guy who owned a landscaping business and bred dogs. They had one daughter away at college. Children didn't mean anything. Her mom had two kids. Reproduction was easy. Mothering was harder.

Crean played golf. She canoed. She was a member of the library board, and she volunteered at the no-kill shelter. Zero social media presence, at least with her professional name, except LinkedIn, which didn't count. Normal home, normal kid, normal life. Didn't add up.

Nadine settled in one of two chairs that faced the desk. Crean's brown eyes flicked to hers, still talking to someone about schedules. Her gaze danced away, giving Nadine a chance to take a good look at her supervisor.

Dr. Margery Crean was in her early forties, with intelligent brown eyes that centered a face that had fought many battles. Her fine, chin-length blonde hair brushed the collar of her crisp white blouse. Wispy bangs hid some of the deep lines in her forehead, changing the focus to her broad nose.

As Crean spoke on the phone, Nadine glanced at the shelves of books behind her, noting many familiar psychology texts. A single bookend was a cast plaster of an old hag draped in a cloak, clutching a pair of shears—the type used on sheep—on her lap. On the other side of the neat row of textbooks and diagnostic manuals sat a green ceramic canister holding several pairs of scissors with brightly colored handles. Nadine narrowed her eyes on the seemingly benign display.

On the adjoining wall, blinds designed to block the harsh eastern sunlight covered the window. Beside this was a framed print of a painting of two Roman lovers resting on marble steps while Cupid draped them in a garland of flowers. It pointed to Crean being a romantic, until you looked at the green-veiled woman in the image, holding wicked-looking shears above the pair.

Nadine had asked about the print. Crean told her the original was on display at the Ringling Museum of Art, and Nadine had later found the painting hanging in the modern wing. She learned that the shrouded figure was Atropos, oldest of the three Fates, and the one responsible for choosing each mortal's manner of death. While her sisters spun and measured the length of a human-life thread, she severed it.

Nadine glanced at the canister of scissors again, their presence taking a more sinister turn.

As she studied the painting, she tried to determine which of the entwined life-threads Atropos was about to sever. The blade of the shears looked familiar, like the carpet knife belonging to her mother.

She flicked her attention back to Crean. She respected her boss and her work with convicted felons. Crean was an expert on serial killers, published prodigiously, and Nadine had read every article of Crean's she could get her hands on.

Crean's academic knowledge of serial killers impressed, but it didn't compare to Nadine's personal knowledge.

*

At her mother's shout, Nadine spun around on the vinyl kitchen chair, the cracked spot scraping against her leg. Her mother stood in the trailer, completely naked. Water dripped from her wet hair, the droplets tinged pink.

"Dee-Dee! Get the trash to the curb."

Nadine hesitated, math homework forgotten, the gnawed pencil still gripped in her fingers. She rubbed the surface, feeling the indentures from her teeth marks. She had turned eight a week ago, but still hated going outside at night. There were big dogs and coyotes and the light above the trailer door didn't work, so it was dark and creepy. Nadine bit her lower lip, hunching.

"Do you hear me, girl! Now!"

She scrambled off her chair and gripped the seatback, her fingers sticky from the jelly crackers her brother, Arlo, had given her for supper.

"What are you yelling about?" Arlo appeared from the hallway, followed by the scent of the pot he'd been smoking. Six years her senior

and already in eighth grade, he was a good student, when he could be bothered to go to school.

He caught sight of their mother and pulled up short.

"Jesus, Ma. Put some clothes on."

"In a minute." She turned to Nadine. "Go on."

"Go where?" her brother asked.

When Nadine looked to Arlo, her mother lost it.

"What are you lookin' at him fer? Trash is your job. Not his."

"I'm scared of the dark."

Her mother threw her head back and laughed. She was in one of her happy-time moods. Nadine watched her breasts jiggle. Arlo stormed back down the hall.

When she stopped laughing and lifted an open hand toward her only daughter, Nadine scuttled past her and out into the carport, running a few steps and then turning back. The door slammed shut behind her, removing the square of light.

Nadine trembled. Something scuttled under the trailer. A stray cat? She hoped so, because the raccoons and possums had big teeth.

She inched toward the trash cans, guided by the light from Arlo's window. There beside the can was a dark garbage bag, exactly like last week. She lifted it and it thumped against her legs. The content was squishy and warm. There was a bad smell, too. She turned her head as she opened the lid. Piles of trash filled the bin. The stench made her eyes water. Why did her mother keep throwing away her clothes?

Why was the water on her face pink?

The beam of a flashlight illuminated the carport. The beam came from Arlo's window and it lit her path all the way back to the door. When she turned the latch, she saw her mother now stood at the sink wearing a sports bra and shorts.

"You have a look inside that bag?" she said, cigarette clenched between her lips.

Nadine shook her head. She was never looking in those bags.

*

"Nadine?" Crean was now off the phone.

Nadine gave herself a mental shake, pushing back her memories. In time, she'd learned exactly what had made those bags squishy, the blood-soaked clothing of Arleen and her latest victims. Even back then, she'd suspected, but been too terrified to look. She'd learned the contents of the final bag years later at her mother's trial. Trash day and murder day were so often the same that Nadine still shook when she saw a garbage truck.

"Thank you for stopping in."

She forced a smile, wondering if Crean saw the resemblance between her and one specific woman among her research subjects now on death row.

Nadine tried for a chipper tone. "What's up?"

Did Crean note the similarity in their hazel-green eyes? Did she know that Nadine was the daughter of a killer?

CHAPTER TWO

Worst nightmare

Crean tented her fingers before her and pinned Nadine with a speculative gaze. "Our police department has asked me to supply a profiler."

The frown came before she could stop it. Micro-twitches, the body's autonomic response that was too quick to control, but not too fast to draw notice by an expert observer. Nadine blinked and forced her brows up into an expression of surprise.

"A profiler?" Alarm bells sounded in her head, cymbals to accompany the percussive rhythm of her heartbeat.

"For the death investigation on the bay. I'm sure you saw the news," she said. "It's a double homicide."

Nadine's mother's first victims were Gail DeNato and Charlie Rogers, a double homicide. They were found on Deadman's Bend on the St. Johns River in Central Florida. She recalled the poster of the victims and the two inset images. She had not been meant to see this exhibit in court, but she had, and remembered the inset of rope connecting the corpses. She'd later asked Mr. Robins, the district attorney, why they were tied together, but he wouldn't tell her.

Her brow grew damp. Was the cold traveling over her skin due to the air-conditioning or fear?

"Nadine?" Crean's voice held a note of alarm.

"Isn't it early for a profiler?"

"Police have requested one."

Nadine wondered if the tremors attacking her body were visible to her boss.

"Would you like a recommendation?" she asked, hopeful that she might still get out of this.

"I don't need one. You are my first choice."

Immediately Nadine began devising a polite refusal.

"I have no experience profiling."

"Then it will be good experience. Could lead to new opportunities."

"Maybe." She frowned at the weak reply.

Nadine didn't mind criminals. She did mind the dead. Dead people were dangerous. Murder victims were the most dangerous of all. They would haunt her, adding to the specters she already carried. Each life her mother took condemned her, apparitions of blame, constant reminders of the cost of her silence.

Nadine might look like the rest of them—ordinary. But ordinary differed from normal. Appearances of normality did not always indicate a person was so, and Nadine had learned to mask atypical behaviors long ago. Her greatest fear was that what made her different was that, deep down, she and Arleen were the same. Panic over becoming like her mother kept her in a constant state of self-evaluation for any hint of a monster living within herself.

"You'll have help with your current workload. I'm already reassigning some of your cases."

Before you even spoke to me. The fear crashed in like a collapsing wave.

Trapped.

Nadine was the worst possible choice for this position, and she couldn't tell Crean why. Not if she wanted to keep her secrets.

A person doesn't go hiding who she is, and what she might become, for more than a decade, only to pop out of the weeds and yell, "Surprise! I have all the predilections of a serial killer."

Now here she was, assigned to a double-homicide investigation. To become someone who works with the dead to find monsters. But she saw monsters in everyone, including herself. Especially herself.

Crean let the pause stretch between them.

"I have the least experience of anyone in our office."

"You have all you need," she assured.

"Our criminal psychologist would be a smarter choice," said Nadine.

"Yes, true, if we had one, but we don't." Crean rose from her seat, signaling the end of the discussion.

"What about Gilmore Ross?"

She sighed. "He's resigned. He said he needed a change. Took a job in Lauderdale as a professor in the psychology department there."

Nadine felt the trap spring shut and glanced toward the exit.

"You'll be working with Detective Demko. He's lead on this."

Nadine turned back. "I don't know Demko."

"You will soon. He's also new."

Why give such an important case to a new psychologist and a new detective? Her suspicions rose. Inexperienced employees made mistakes and convenient scapegoats.

Did someone in power want them to fail?

"So, he just got his gold shield?" she asked, clarifying what Crean meant by "new."

"No. He's a new hire. He's worked some tough cases in Miami-Dade. That place has built an empire. Have you been there?"

Nadine shook her head.

"One of the best-funded departments in the country. Murder investigation experts. We are lucky to have him."

"Then I doubt I would have very much to offer."

"He is not a psychologist. He's asked for one. You will be taking Gilmore's spot until such time as I tell you otherwise."

Nadine started to shake her head and then realized this was not a discussion, but a directive. She'd lost.

Her jaw muscles relaxed, and she wiped the sweat from her upper lip. Crean gave her a once-over.

"You can do this, Nadine."

That was what worried her.

She smelled blood and her stomach heaved. Phantosmia, an olfactory hallucination, the stink of those garbage bags conjured by stress. Even at eight, she had recognized the difference between the scent of mud from a swamp and blood from a body. But she couldn't grasp how to process it.

Denial, her psychologist said. The fear that acknowledging the possibility of what was happening would place her in jeopardy, destroy her family and leave her motherless. Turned out that it did all three.

Cover-up was how she thought of it, despite the courts holding her blameless.

I wish I could do the same.

As a profiler, she would be great. But hunting a killer was hunting people, the job she'd avoided all her life because it was what her mother had said she was born for. Taking this assignment put her one step closer to her demons.

Giving a drunk a drink.

Crean stepped around her desk and motioned toward the door. Now Nadine's skin prickled with anticipation.

This is how it begins.

Rationalizing. Telling herself that she had no choice, when deep down hunting killers hiding in plain sight was exactly what she'd always wanted to do—if she were only brave enough. But the prospect scared her, brushing so close to what she most feared.

Nadine rose. "I'll do my best."

"I know you will." Crean smiled, satisfied at her win. "I'll alert SPD and send out a memo on your new role in the department."

A quicksilver stab of worry cut through her. An internal announcement of her change in position would put her in the public eye. Some clever, industrious reporter would work it out.

"I've told Detective Demko that you'll be an asset. He'd like to meet with you at police headquarters this afternoon at one."

Crean glanced from her to her door. Nadine hurried away.

At her office, she paused, head down, breathing hard. She'd spent her whole life striving to be different from her mother. But was she different enough?

Nadine returned to her office and tucked in behind her desk with her phone, pulling up a search browser.

She focused now on filling in the blanks in her mother's crimes, if only to eliminate the niggling suspicion that this double homicide shared certain commonalities with Arleen's victims. Nadine would sleep better knowing her worries were baseless. An online search on her phone quickly exposed how little she knew about her mother's crimes and victims.

Arleen Howler was convicted in 2007 for the murder of four couples. Nadine knew that all the victims shared the distinction of being involved in adultery and all but one had been married.

Back then, Dr. Nadine Finch had been Nadine Howler and, at fifteen, the star witness in her mother's murder trial.

Her memories of that time were vivid but incomplete. The lawyers and police had kept things from her. Before the trial, she'd been evaluated by a criminal psychologist, her first experience with that profession. Without that encounter, the therapy that followed and her aunt's willingness to adopt Nadine, she feared where she might now be.

She knew that the victims had been stabbed. The article said that Arleen had dumped all but one in the St. Johns River or a nearby lake. Most couples were recovered in the water, nude, with their wrists tied together with clothesline, which the prosecution proved Arleen had purchased. But they did not find the blade she used, nor the clothing or the wedding rings of her victims.

But Nadine remembered the knife because her mother had used it to fit a remnant of beige carpet in the trailer where they all lived during much of her early childhood.

Seeing all the women together on one screen, she was struck by the physical similarities. All the female victims were slim with shoulder-length dark hair and brown eyes. The men, however, did not follow any obvious physical type.

Her mother killed Gail DeNato and Charlie Rogers in 1994, discovered afterwards to be Arleen's supervisor and the head of sales at the carpet warehouse where Arleen worked as an installer when Nadine had been two. That was the year after her father had walked out on them, the trigger, the article claimed, to Howler's first murders.

Rogers had been incapacitated with several cuts to his legs before Arleen had opened the major blood vessels at his arms and legs. DeNato showed defensive wounds on her hands and suffered numerous gashes before her throat was cut.

Nadine read on.

The next couple had been murdered six years later. This was the only pair murdered at separate times and places. Lacey Louder had been first, kicked repeatedly until her ribs cracked and her trachea crushed. Then Arleen had sliced her with a knife. Like Gail DeNato, Louder had been repeatedly slashed with a blade.

Nadine would never forget this death because it had been her eighth birthday. Arleen had come home late, striding into the trailer in wet underwear carrying a boxed cake so warm the frosted flowers had melted off the top. To this day, those innocuous cake boxes with the clear-plastic tops made Nadine's stomach clench.

The article reported that sheriffs recovered Louder's nude body two days after her disappearance and her husband's tearful pleas for her safe return. Her death was not immediately connected to the earlier double homicide, and her husband had been falsely convicted for her murder. Even when a forest ranger, Drew Henderson, had been found butchered in his vehicle with a length of cord on his wrist, matching the one tied to Louder, the connection was not made to Louder or the earlier unsolved homicides. Only after Arleen's confession was Louder's husband released from prison, his sentence overturned.

The night of the discovery of Lacey Louder, Nadine had watched the news with Arleen, who had commented that home-wreckers got what they deserved.

Four years later, her older brother, Arlo, had moved out, and Nadine lived in a trailer with her mother and the latest man her mother had invited to move in with them. When he left, Arleen blamed her daughter.

"No man wants to be reminded that someone got there before him. Can't get any of them to stick with a sulking kid moping around." Maybe she had been right because none of them stayed, and despite Nadine's wishing and even praying, her father never came for her.

This particular man had worked with Arleen at the marina in Deland. When he split, Arleen got mean. Nadine, then twelve, stayed at school long after class, hanging out at the basketball court where Arlo played and smoked weed.

The article said that Arleen captured her next victims, Michelle Dents and Parker Irwin, in 2004. Michelle Dents, the mother of three boys, ran the small marina, owned by her brother, where Arleen had been employed. The male victim, Irwin, was a mechanic who fixed the engines of the houseboats. Nadine had met them both. He was always in the restaurant at lunch where Michelle often worked as hostess. They were both nice to her. Michelle gave her the small boxes of crayons meant for the little kids who ate there, and Parker once bought her some fries.

Her mother, whose job it was to clean the houseboats, told her later that she didn't like cleaning the bedding after those two had screwed. She'd taken them on a Friday after work and kept them until Saturday night or Sunday morning. The article said she had tortured both, keeping Dents alive several hours after Irwin's death. Then the bodies had been bound, wrist to wrist, and dumped in Lake Monroe. Arleen had returned the houseboat and cleaned the interior as always, removing evidence of the crime before disposing of their bloody clothing.

What Nadine recalled was that her mother had come home late on Sunday, used the garden hose to wash herself and shoved her wet clothing in a large black garbage bag with whatever else was in there. Nadine had watched from inside the trailer, terrified. When ordered to throw that bag away, Nadine had done as she'd been told—suspicious, but refusing to look in the bag.

Nadine had waited for the police to come and arrest her mother, frightened and hopeful. But they never came. If they even questioned Arleen, Nadine didn't see them. Did they think a woman couldn't do such a thing?

They were wrong.

Nadine scrolled down the page and was confronted with a photo of Sandra Shank, unchanged by the years. Her mother's last female victim was Nadine's math classmate, three years her senior, who liked to howl like a dog as Nadine passed. Back then, Nadine had been underweight, poorly dressed, often dirty and usually hungry because of her mother's neglect. An easy target at school.

But when Sandra went missing at the same time as her mother, Nadine refused to keep silent. After all, Sandra had come to Arleen's attention because of her, so this was partly Nadine's fault.

The upperclassman's disappearance that Friday, coinciding with her mother's, tripped some switch in Nadine's brain. Her fear of foster care, beaten into her by her mother, could not kill her determination that Arleen was a monster and that only she could stop her mother.

Nadine had been too late to save either Sandra Shank or Stephen White, the older man Sandra had been involved with, and she lived with that guilt. If she had told that first night, instead of waiting until Monday morning, could they have saved them?

The newspapers covered her mother's trial and revealed that Nadine's grandfather had also been a convicted killer, who murdered *his* boss with a forklift, and had died in prison serving his sentence; and that her great-grandfather had killed a man in a bar fight—and Nadine's life had changed from bad to worse. Nadine's photo had been on the national news and in all the newspapers. She was the famous daughter of the infamous killer. The girl who had turned her own mother in to the police.

The guilt was the worst part. She'd been haunted by not reporting Arleen sooner and saving her mother's final victims, while plagued with the guilt of turning in her own mother in the first place.

Nadine survived, took her aunt's surname and gradually disappeared into anonymity. Arleen had gotten the death sentence. Nadine thought her mother should have gotten eight.

She closed the search browser and tucked away her phone. Now armed with information about her mother's victims, Nadine was anxious to know more about the two victims recovered in the bay.

*

Nadine pulled up to police headquarters with her lunch knocking about in her stomach as if engaged in a tennis match. She realized there was one other way out of this assignment. She could quit her job, ghost her colleagues and vanish. Disappearing seemed a better option than waiting for the newspapers to connect Sarasota's new profiler to a serial killer's kid.

But who was better qualified to hunt a killer seemingly just like her mother?

Since her mom's arrest, she had worked to distance herself from the little girl whose image was televised on all news networks and on the broadsheets of every major newspaper.

Sometimes she wished she didn't have to hide. But she preferred it to being hunted by reporters again. Worse still, revealing who she was now would take necessary resources and attention away from this case. She wasn't having that. Focus must stay on the victims and catching this killer.

Nadine prayed that the similarities she noted in the manner of death in this double homicide did not signal the emergence of a copycat. It was too early to leap to this conclusion, but the seed of worry was firmly set.

Meanwhile, her focus was on her meeting with the overqualified detective from Miami-Dade and learning why he'd opted out of a top police force in the country for Sarasota. If he was so smart, why was he here?

After earning their gold shield, law enforcement professionals rarely moved. Had he screwed up over there on the Atlantic side?

Nadine left the lot and hurried through the stifling muggy heat that was their normal summer climate. She passed through security in the lobby and spoke to an officer at registration who told her that the detective would escort her back to Homicide.

After a few minutes, a tall man with an athletic build came down the corridor in her direction. On his belt winked a gold detective's shield clipped beside the holstered service weapon. He was dressed in business casual, with a blazer, khakis and necktie, and a wrinkled shirt. The detective had a confident air and powerful stride. His strength both drew and repelled her. Being with someone stronger was dangerous. So, why was she moving toward him?

He came to a halt before her and brushed his sandy-colored hair from his wide forehead, revealing a tanned face and deep blue eyes. He offered a smile and nod as he extended his hand.

"Dr. Finch? I'm Detective Clint Demko. Thanks for stopping by."

She hesitated only a moment before taking his hand. His was broad and dry, hers clammy and wet. She got that immediate zing. His brows lifted. She drew her hand back, breaking the contact that they held a little too long. She would be working with this man, which made him off limits. Even without that obstacle, the prospect of a relationship that invariably would include sharing intimate secrets about her past made her stomach knot. There was too much horror and too much risk.

His expression turned speculative and Nadine took a step back, widening the distance between them, ignoring the longing ache in her heart.

"Let's head to my desk," he said.

She followed him through an inner corridor to the elevators and rode beside him in the small compartment, smelling the enticing spice of his cologne while she stared at the floor.

Nadine couldn't resist a sideways glance. Demko's physique appealed on all counts. His legs were muscular and his chest and shoulders broad. He needed a haircut and a shave. His jaw was square and there was a bump at the bridge of his nose. His mirrored sunglasses sat looped in the front pocket of his sports coat. Yeah, he was the complete package, which meant his flaws were internal. He sensed her attention and cast her a glance and a winning smile. She swung her eyes forward.

The door drew open at their floor and he motioned her out. His eyes met hers, and she noted the dark smudges beneath his.

The elevator began to close, and he stopped the doors with an extended arm. She brushed past him, then waited as he led the way. At his desk, he offered the chair reserved for witnesses and suspects. She'd sat in a similar one at age fourteen.

The steel seemed to conduct coldness and desperation. She told herself not to shift but could not control the long swallow as he settled in his seat. Her mouth was too dry.

Nadine glanced toward Demko, to find him staring at her with an appraising glance. She swallowed again.

One of her superpowers was failing her because this detective made it clear, from his unwavering stare, that he did see her. She forced a tight smile.

"Do you have contact information for me? I'd like to reach you outside of the office."

In a moment, she had her card out and scribbled her cell phone number on the front. "Here you are."

He accepted the card, glancing down.

"Your card is wrong. Should say 'Criminal Psychologist.'"

"Well, that change just happened two hours ago and the department printer was at lunch."

His mouth turned up at the corners and he made a sound that might have been a show of appreciation.

"I see. So…" He glanced down again. "Forensic psychologist. I thought you guys had a criminal psychologist."

"Who just took a teaching job in Fort Lauderdale. They have assigned me in his place." Had he not requested her?

"Well, Wernli says good things."

She had worked with Detective Wernli more than once and wondered how she could repay him the "favor" of his recommendation.

The detective lifted his mobile phone and her card, typing something. Nadine's phone dinged, showing a text.

"That's me. Now you have my cell number." Demko brushed back a lock of hair. "What have you been working on recently?"

"I've been here since mid-April conducting clinical work. Mostly psych evals on suspects, some competency and court hearings and a few depositions. Also evaluations of inmates."

His smile faded. Hers broadened.

"I have zero experience in active criminal investigations, and I have never created a profile. What I do is paperwork. Occasionally I'm asked to sit in on an interview or interrogation." Nadine left out her knack as a walking lie detector. "That is the total of my involvement with law enforcement."

If you didn't count the Homicide detectives coming to her school to speak to her about her own mother, or the interviews that followed.

Did she know? Did she suspect?

Yes, on both counts.

Nadine mentally shook herself. This guy was a Homicide detective, proficient at interrogations. He'd find the smell of deception irresistible. She forced herself to maintain eye contact, knowing that he was likely aware this was a technique used by liars.

Nadine's smile felt unnatural. "Until today, all my work has been with suspects in custody or witnesses who still have a pulse."

His smile was back. Instead of disqualifying her, her answers seemed to strike him as funny. That made her scowl.

"What have you heard about the double homicide?" he asked.

"Not much. The medical examiner mentioned them."

"Is that common for you, speaking to the MEs?"

"She's a friend." Or as close to one as Nadine allowed herself. She hoped her affinity for Juliette wasn't because of the ME's relationship with the dead. That idea gave her pause and her stomach knots escalated to a sharp pain.

"I see. Well, we have identified both victims. Families have been notified." He blew out a breath and his shoulders sagged. His gaze sank to the desktop.

He was lead, but was he the sort to reassign the most objectionable duties? Or had he handled that dreadful task himself?

"By you?" she asked, taking a guess.

"Yeah. Rough. She had a little boy, about the age of my son."

Son? Nadine glanced to his ring finger. No wedding band. Was he married?

Demko continued. "And his wife is pregnant."

Nadine's eyes widened and she looked toward the ceiling. The details about the families of this young couple, where they worked and when they met, made her realize then that she didn't know as much about her mother's victims as she first thought. And she needed to go back and learn all the things that had been kept from a fourteen-year-old girl.

Demko turned to his computer, accessing a file. A moment later, images of bloated bodies in clear green water flashed past.

"Male vic is David Lowe, employed at DiGeronimo Market on Beneva, in the meat department."

A headshot of the victim, alive and smiling, sat to the left of the bruised ghastly photo taken on a stretcher.

"Lowe was thirty-four, married. His wife is expecting their first child in November."

His hand hovered on the mouse a moment and then flicked to the next. This was a professional headshot of a smiling dark-headed woman wearing a familiar sage-green uniform that Nadine recognized from the grocery store chain DiGeronimo's.

"This is Debi Poletti, twenty-nine, married mother of one. She also worked at DiGeronimo's as a cashier."

The next several photos flashed by. These were all from the crime scene and Poletti looked nothing like the living woman. Long dark hair draped a bruised shoulder. A close-up of ligature marks at her swollen wrist. A gaping neck wound and deep lacerations across her stomach. Finally there was a close-up of something. Cuts on her skin. Nadine leaned closer.

"The unsub carved this in Poletti's buttock. Looks like a hashtag, or number sign."

Unsub, Nadine had learned long ago was short for unknown subject, which their perpetrator, unfortunately, was.

Nadine peered at the image of flesh carved with a sharp object.

The marks seemed a random pattern of seven roughly horizontal lines with various angular slants to the right and left. An X pattern? she wondered, turning the photo. It was also possible that these cuts were arbitrary.

She narrowed her eyes, wondering. The wounds were in fatty tissue and placed like a brand.

He talked, and she took notes, as the photos changed to those of the suspected crime scene on the Intracoastal Waterway on Lido's barrier island. A sodden abandoned blanket lay rumpled and sand-covered on the beach between the scrubby vegetation and the shore. Twisted garments rested nearby on the sand.

"How far is it from the barrier island to the bayside park where the bodies were discovered?" asked Nadine.

"South Lido Park? A little over two nautical miles."

"Is that the same as regular miles?" she asked.

"A little more. Anyway, a morning kayaker spotted this and called us. The blanket appeared to be soaked in blood. Initial tests indicate human blood and the types match each victim's. Still awaiting lab results to confirm a match for each."

The next photos had the familiar yellow numbered markers.

"Recovered a bikini bathing suit top, orange. Swim trunks and a T-shirt, men's sandals. And this."

"Is that a soda can?" she asked.

"Tangerine seltzer," he said, and flicked to the close-up of a dented orange can. The next shot showed all the items laid out on a tabletop or floor.

"We had a rainstorm last night. Washed the beach and soaked everything."

"Any physical evidence from the perpetrator?"

"Unknown."

She'd been to the park at the south end of Lido Beach. The walk on the white sand along the Intracoastal was easy at low tide, but getting from the lot and under those huge pines was a challenge. The tiny pinecones were like burs and hell on bare feet.

"Where are her shoes?" asked Nadine.

He smiled, seeming to appreciate her line of thinking. "None recovered."

"Hmm." Had they walked in together? "Vehicles?"

"His car was in the lot. Hers was parked at the lot off Taft."

"Boat launch," Nadine said. "Public access to the water."

"Yeah."

"So, where's her watercraft?"

"Unknown. It's possible to walk to the south end from there."

"On hot sidewalks, without shoes?" she asked.

He made a sound of acknowledgment in his throat. "Or our unsub could have a shoe fetish."

Her mother had collected all her victims' clothing and discarded them along with hers.

"I'm not sure what you need to make your profile. Every psychologist I've worked with wants different information. So, I'll add you to my investigation. You can access my notes, sketches, photos of the crime scene and recovery site, evidence reports and autopsy photos when we get them. I'll be adding notes on the victims' timelines and interviews with the families today. Pick and choose what you like."

"That's fine. Thanks."

"No problem." He clicked away, granting her access.

"You think this is a jealous husband?"

"That's the obvious suspect. I've spoken to Poletti's husband. He was home with his son. No one to confirm. Waiting on phone records. Might be able to pinpoint his location."

He'd have to be stupid to bring his cell phone to a murder. But people did.

"I'd like you to see the bodies before autopsy. Photos only give you so much."

She said nothing, already dreading this. It occurred to her as curious that, though her mother relished taking life, Nadine had never seen a dead body.

He flipped to another crime scene photo, a body in the water and then a close-up, a hand with a mark around the ring finger.

"That's odd," she said, leaning in. "Is that a cut?"

"Skinned. Peeled away the flesh all the way around."

"Weird," she said.

"They washed up on the bayside, between the tiki bar and the botanic gardens. How they made it past all those anchor lines in the marina without snagging, I'll never know."

"Snagging?"

"Yeah. Didn't I tell you? They were tied together, wrist to wrist, with rope. Here." He clicked to the shot of the bodies in the water that showed a bright red rope clearly visible on one of the victims' wrists.

She sat back, blinking at the image.

*

Nadine chewed on a strand of hair as she took the stand. Her mother glared at her from the long table to her left, seated between two men in rumpled suits. The air-conditioning pinged and whistled, the only sound as she settled in her seat before the jurors. Behind the rail, they stared at her with the fascination usually reserved for animals born with two heads.

Mr. Robins, the district attorney who had prepped her for this day, approached, his posture confident and his smile kind.

On the easel beside the court reporter was a poster board, like they used for the science fair. Only, the photo of a naked man and woman was on this. A dead naked man and woman. The slices gaped on his legs, showing yellow fat and grayish muscle. There was an inset photo showing both victims in the water. A white cord connected them, his wrist to hers. Another revealed a series of small gashes on something, a thigh?

She gaped, her breathing sputtering as she tried to draw air past her closing throat.

The youngest of the attorneys noted the direction of her stare and hurried to the board, turning the placard around, so Nadine could no longer see the image. But despite that, Nadine still sometimes saw those images when she closed her eyes.

Her gaze flashed to her mother whose smug smile and glittering eyes showed what seemed like pride.

"Nadine," said the attorney before her. "Nadine?"

*

"Nadine? May I call you that? Or do you prefer Dr. Finch?"

She shook her head, clearing away the fog of memories. Detective Demko had moved his chair so he faced her and was giving her the once-over.

"Want some water or something?"

Had she gone pale? She couldn't tell except that her fingertips were numb, and his expression flashed concern.

That rope. Oh, no, the rope.

"Nadine?"

"I'm all right." She wasn't.

Could this be happening? The similarities were there. It wasn't her imagination. The couple. The slashing lacerations. The water. Now the rope.

"You don't look all right." He kept those blue eyes pinned on her, searching for clues. "Is it the crime scene images?" He closed the photograph file, and the victim vanished.

Nadine grasped the excuse.

"Maybe," she said.

He dragged a hand over his head. "I forget that sometimes. Sorry. I'm a little punch-drunk. Thirty-six hours on two death investigations. Just finished processing an apparent suicide and was called to the bay."

"You've been up for two days?"

"A day and a half."

Nadine tried to imagine how her brain would function after being awake that long. She now understood the stubble on his face, the rumpled appearance and the weariness that hung on him. Adrenaline could carry a person only so far.

"Sick bastard. We have to get him."

She met his eyes and saw a cold glint of determination. The hairs on her neck lifted, and she was grateful not to be his target. This man was a different sort of hunter. A hunter of hunters.

Demko had caught the scent of evil. He would not stop. All she could do was run or get on board.

Running seemed wiser. But if this was a copycat, wasn't she best suited for the hunt?

Nadine needed to get to her computer. She rose. "I'll let you get back to work."

"Great. Thanks for helping us out, Dr. Finch."

CHAPTER THREE

Louder than words

"Mr. Lancer, did you kill your wife?"

Morton Lancer started, and there was a long pause. Finally he laughed. The laugh was inappropriate, given the circumstances of his wife's recent death. Nadine marked it for what it was, a masking technique of an inexperienced liar.

"Are you serious? Detective, I did not kill Emily."

"I have to ask. You understand," said Homicide detective Brendan Wernli.

The detective had requested Nadine, so she'd come straight from the office on Thursday morning to the police department to sit in on the interview but was impatient to return to her initial profile.

Wernli was a veteran investigator with a solid solve rate and the man who had recommended Nadine as profiler for the double homicide. He was approaching the end of his career and had the gray hairs to prove it. His skin was smooth and dark, and his eyes a golden brown. He seemed the picture of concern, which was a mask for Lancer's sake. Beneath this facade was a shark smelling blood in the water.

The deceased's husband sat back, instinctively moving away from Wernli as the veneer of grief slipped. Was it occurring to him that he might be in trouble here?

"It was a suicide," said Lancer.

"Yes. Just a formality. Have it on record." Which was a lie, because telling the truth to murder suspects was optional.

"I see."

The interview rooms in police headquarters were claustrophobic by design. There was space only for a small table with rounded corners and the three uncomfortable gray mesh guest chairs that sat on drab brown carpeting. The air smelled of sweat and growing desperation. White walls were empty except for a surveillance camera perched high in one corner and a blank whiteboard. The only color in the room was the bright blue recycling container, which held Morton Lancer's first two water bottles. Soon he'd need a bathroom break, which he wouldn't get.

Nadine sat still in the interview room as Lancer kept his attention on the detective, who was the apparent threat. It was another error in judgment.

In her previous position, she spent most of her time with evaluations of suspects prior to their trial to gauge mental condition and with convicted criminals in conjunction to their parole applications. But she most enjoyed assisting in interrogations of criminal suspects because she was good at ferreting out signs of deception and because the role of observer seems safe.

"Did your wife leave you anything of value or mention any important papers before her death?" asked the detective, his voice mild and nonthreatening. He maintained an expression of sympathy while physically crowding the man in the hot seat.

The pause in Lancer's response was short but obvious to Nadine.

"'Important papers'?" asked Lancer, repeating the question. Liars used this technique to give themselves time to think. Think time was vital.

"Yes, insurance policies, mortgage, a will or instructions on how to proceed after her death."

"There were no instructions. I didn't know what she was planning."

"Or where she bought the rope?"

Mr. Lancer again repeated Wernli's words. "'Where she bought the rope?'"

Mention of the rope found twisted about his wife's neck might have caused all sorts of visceral reactions in a grieving husband, but not this wide-eyed stare.

"No. I have absolutely no idea."

Nadine wrote *absolutely* on her pad. Emphasis. Another clue that the speaker was being deceptive. She suspected that Lancer did know; at least that was what his body language relayed to her.

He sat straight in the chair while attempting an earnest expression as both his feet pointed to the exit. Meanwhile, his fingertips, invisible to the detective, tapped restlessly upon his knee.

He wore a smile that never reached his eyes, reinforcing her belief that Mr. Lancer, a puffy-faced retired communications manager, had murdered his wife.

Lancer moved his seat so that his back was literally against the wall. The detective leaned forward, further crowding Lancer's personal space.

"And what were you doing thirty minutes prior to discovering your wife's body in the bathroom?"

Lancer lowered his voice. "Listen, Detective, I've told you this already."

But not in this order. Nadine nodded in approval and then stemmed her telling body language. Detective Wernli was now having poor Mort repeat his story in reverse. Suspects rarely practiced their alibi this way. They memorized the tale in sequential order. Mort's eye contact was good, and that made Nadine trust him even less. It was a trick liars used to make themselves appear sincere.

"If you will bear with me," said the detective, looking down, flipping through his notes.

Mort's smile dropped and his gaze shot to the door. His leg now bounced with nervous energy.

"I'm sure you want to help us clear all this up."

"Sure. Of course. To be honest, she did seem more moody than usual."

Nadine narrowed her eyes as Mr. Lancer employed another distancing technique. The qualifying language, "to be honest," indicated that whatever followed would be false. He was separating himself from the lie by the assurance that he was about to tell the truth. Worse still, he was adding a new detail.

Lancer should have said he was at work and left it there. Instead, he provided many particulars, including the fact that his wife had not answered his text messages.

That was, presumably, because he had already strangled her and hung her like a damp towel from the shower curtain rod in the main bathroom.

While Wernli kept his head down, flipping through his notes, Lancer's lips curled in anger, the real emotion leaking through the mask of a distraught husband.

Nadine had seen enough and stood, stepping out into the hall. Detective Wernli didn't follow her. Had he not noted her departure? She waited for several minutes before Wernli joined her in the corridor. "How d'you get out here?"

"Teleportation. I learned it watching *X-Men*."

Wernli chuckled. "Well, don't show that trick to Mr. Lancer. Okay? I'm sure he'd like to disappear about now."

"No doubt."

The detective motioned her down the hall. They moved away from the door and paused, facing each other.

"You have an opinion, Dr. Finch?" he asked.

"Yes, he's flashing signs of deception."

Wernli nodded.

"Lots of body language. Micro-twitches and restless drumming of his fingers. His feet pointing toward the way out."

"And he put the water bottle between him and me. A barrier," added Wernli.

"Yes, I saw that."

"You think he killed her?"

"Unsure. But I know he isn't being honest with you, and while killing her would give him an excellent reason to lie, he could be protecting someone else."

Wernli's expression showed he didn't buy this explanation.

"Listen, I have to run. Competency hearing at ten."

"That the one that butchered the prostitute?" he asked.

Nadine nodded.

"What's your take?"

"He won't qualify for diminished capacity or as unfit to stand trial."

"Good. By the way, I heard you're the profiler for the double homicide."

A flash of cold lifted the hairs on her arms and her heart began drumming like a marching band.

"Yes," she said, repressing the shudder as her worst nightmares aroused. Bloated bodies. Ruined lives. "And I heard you recommended me."

He grinned. "Guilty."

If he expected her to thank him, he'd have a long wait.

"I told Demko about how much you've helped me since you've been here. Glad you got the nod."

She was happy someone was, because she felt nauseous every time she thought of this assignment.

Wernli thanked her for coming in and she hurried away, her mind racing with her footsteps.

*

After leaving Detective Wernli and his prime suspect behind at police headquarters, she took an early lunch, swinging by Selby Library to do some digging into her past. The research specialist pointed her in the direction of fifteen-year-old newspaper articles.

It was terrifying and surreal to see herself as a fourteen-year-old, all gaunt cheeks and big eyes.

She made several copies, scribbled notes and hurried back to the office, where she organized data and read the copies she'd made. She now had a list of Arleen's known homicides. Of course they'd been known to her ever since she'd given evidence against her mother, and even before that. But now the list was in front of her, in black and white. She was confronting information she'd had inside her for years and filling in the blanks.

When she was a girl, and her mother had made that first bizarre entrance into the trailer on Nadine's eighth birthday, Nadine knew Arleen had done something bad. What that something was took years to work out. But here they were, Nadine's formless fears, horrifying suspicions and final realization. Her mother had killed people. Four couples, eight human lives.

She also confirmed three gruesome similarities. First, her mother and this murderer dumped their victims in natural bodies of water in Florida. Second, all victims were involved in infidelity. And third, all but one pair had been tied together, and that pair, murdered at separate times and places, had both had a length of rope tied to their wrists. Arleen used clotheslines. This killer used red nylon rope.

Coincidence or copycat?

Further reading revealed no mention of odd cuts or marks left on any of her mother's victims, just stab wounds and lacerations intended to disable and kill.

Maybe Nadine was overreacting?

She navigated to her mother's Wikipedia page on her phone. Of all the gruesome dark websites out there, nothing could strike chills into Nadine like this page. As a teen, she had checked it obsessively, in a state of disbelief that her own mother had this kind of infamy.

As a student of psychology, she'd spent years absorbed in self-evaluation and therapy to deal with her tragic childhood. But the underlying terror, the fear that she never spoke aloud to anyone, was this: what if her mother had passed to her only daughter the same murderous tendencies?

Reading the page, Nadine was reminded that Arleen had incapacitated the males first. It also said that she kept her victims for longer periods as her crimes progressed, to spend more time torturing her female victims. The first two women, at least, were still alive when she threw them in the water. Which meant that her female victims were aware of what was happening as they were dumped in the murky, alligator-infested river to drown.

Nadine sat back, staring at the photo of her mother on arrest, and shivered because the image somehow captured exactly what Arleen Howler was capable of.

*

After her second Thursday happy hour with Juliette, Nadine headed home to her rental.

She lived in an area called Laurel Park, near the artists' community of Towles Court. The building boom had transformed this area into a highly desirable combination of chic vintage homes, eclectic cottages and sleek contemporary builds. All sat so near downtown that the shadows of the bayfront high-rise condominiums stretched over them at sunset.

Her place was a restored one-bedroom, one-bath cottage perched on concrete blocks on a quiet street overgrown with tropical vegetation. It was as close to Key West as you could get and still walk to the Sarasota courthouse.

She had fallen in love with the property, which was above her price range, and signed a two-year lease. Once she paid off this car, there would be more room in the budget. Until then, she could manage.

Alone at last with her incognito browser window, she navigated to the State of Florida's website, located the department of law enforcement, and slapped down twenty-five digital bucks for the criminal history of Arleen Howler.

*

The next morning at the office, she scanned her email, discovering the promised access to Demko's files. He'd been busy, adding notes until after 3 a.m., according to the time stamp.

Nadine wondered if he'd slept as little as she.

She expected a call from Demko on the autopsy, but the morning dragged on and no call arrived. As a distraction, she took a trip over to personnel to sign the forms to get her 401(k) and city's 6 percent match. As of her next paycheck, she'd be putting 5 percent away for the future. Nadine still had her doubts that she had a future, but she liked to picture herself somewhere ahead in time. It was preferable to looking backward.

She planned to grab the forms from an assistant. But the head of personnel was in the main reception area and ushered her into his office.

Gary Osterlund had thin brows, receding hair and eyes that sloped down at the corners. His mustache hid some of his narrow upper lip.

There she paused as he circled behind an L-shaped desk. Papers and files, Post-its and folders, covered much of the surface. Beneath the closed upper cupboards, several binders sat. Two framed images were wedged between the large printer and a silver rowing trophy. One held the school photo of a girl, perhaps eight, who looked familiar. Beside that, a framed image of the same girl, with a dark-headed boy, leaned. She wondered if they were his kids.

"You're a rower," she commented.

Rowing had become very big in the city since they'd finished the artificial lake and won the bid to host the world rowing championships.

"I was. Now I'm a volunteer at the regattas and races at Benderson Park."

"That's fun." She didn't like water, boats or getting too much sun, so it really seemed the opposite of fun, but she continued to smile.

"I hear you've had a position shift," said Osterlund.

Taken off guard, Nadine felt her face flush. "Yes."

How had he heard so quickly?

"Got the press release this morning. News travels fast," he said.

"Did the release include a photo?"

"Yes. Good likeness. Haven't you seen it?"

"Not yet. No."

This only increased her concern and her heart rate. The last thing she needed was for someone seeing her photo to recognize that Nadine Finch was Nadine Howler, the daughter of the state's most successful female serial killer.

Nadine glanced about, searching for a way to change the subject as her heartbeat pulsed at her temples.

The only things hanging on the wall were framed diplomas, service awards and photos of many Little League teams. The chaos of his desk did not match the uniformity of his public displays.

"Do you coach?" she asked, lifting a finger toward the grinning lineup of kids in colorful uniforms, redirecting his attention and their conversation.

"Every year. They also put me in charge of rosters, which is a nightmare." He motioned to the empty guest seats and settled behind his desk.

"Do your kids play?" She nodded toward the photos.

"Oh." He followed the direction of her gaze. "No, unfortunately."

The silence ticked with the second hand of the wall clock. Nadine held her rigid smile.

"But back to the retirement options. It's too good a deal not to take full advantage," he said, referring to the city's match.

He passed her the necessary forms, along with a list of holding companies.

"Bring these on back when you've filled them out. Call me if you have any questions."

She collected the forms.

"Seems a long way off."

"But anything worth doing requires planning. Planning is so important."

*

En route back to her office, Demko phoned. Nadine connected the call through the car's Bluetooth system.

"I'm driving. What's up?"

"Autopsy's at two. Can you make it?"

"I'll clear my afternoon."

"Be there early. I want you to see them before they cut."

Nadine shivered. Why did he say "cut" instead of "begin"?

"Blood work is back. Lido Beach is the crime scene," he said.

"I read that in your notes this morning."

"Maybe we could drive over to the barrier island afterward. You can have a look."

The pause stretched as she tore a piece of her thumbnail away with her teeth.

"Nadine?"

"Yes. Okay," she said, her words sharper than she'd intended.

She returned to the office and reviewed Demko's notes on the crime scene, eating at her desk, and heading over to the ME's office at the appointed time. The office manager checked her in, studying her identification. Then gave her instructions.

"Observation window only. You stay off the autopsy floor."

That was good news, as far as she was concerned. Seeing this kind of thing gave Nadine nightmares. Not right away, but they popped up after marinating in her brain with all the other horrors she couldn't forget.

Who was she kidding? She couldn't do this. She performed an about-face.

"Nadine!"

Juliette stepped out of an office, dressed in surgical scrubs and a cap, and slipping into a plastic gown. There was a plastic visor over her cap, tipped up to reveal her smiling face.

"You came! Clint told me you're his profiler! Congrats!" She tied her apron strings at the waist. "He's already here. Come on. Let me get you some protective gear."

She seemed so cheerful, as if she wasn't about to spend her afternoon cutting open human remains.

Nadine fell into stride with her as they headed into a changing room, complete with shower and toilets and private stalls. Juliette began selecting surgical scrubs, booties and an apron.

"I can't go on the autopsy floor," said Nadine, parroting the words of the office manager.

"Who told you that? You're part of the investigation. You can even touch the bodies if you like, with gloves."

If she liked? Who would like to touch dead bodies?

The answer came like a kick in the gut. Her mother liked it.

Nadine accepted the PPE.

"Were you the one who collected them from the bayfront?"

Juliette hummed an affirmative.

Meanwhile, Nadine pulled on the apron and fumbled with the ties as her heart pounded in her throat. Her emotions were all tangled up at seeing similarities in this case to her mother's.

Nadine tugged on the booties, which were ridiculously large, and the apron swam on her.

Juliette shoved the sleeves up for her. "Oh, sorry. We don't have extra smalls."

Nadine gulped.

"First autopsy?"

Nadine nodded.

Juliette patted her on the arm. "You'll be great."

The ME's confidence came from not knowing her well. Nadine believed it would be best for both of them to keep it that way.

Juliette paused at the door. "But if you are going to be sick or faint, step back and away from the body, okay?"

She nodded to this and trailed Juliette along the corridor and through the first set of double doors.

Demko stepped from the observation office to the left, also dressed in PPE. On his head sat a blue ball cap emblazoned with SPD. He wore black latex gloves. Protective glasses covered his eyes. He cast her a smile.

"Dr. Finch, you made it."

Juliette gave her another pat. "You two stand across from me. If you want the bodies moved, just ask. I'll be doing a superficial exam first."

She headed through the final set of doors, leaving Nadine with the detective.

He passed her a pair of gloves.

"I'm not touching anything," Nadine whispered.

Demko opened the wide door for her. Stepping into the room, she saw the autopsy area had four stainless-steel tables, beneath bright lights. Each table resembled the ones seen in commercial kitchens, except for the headrest, the lip that circled the perimeter, and the hole and drain beneath.

A garden hose and sprayer attached to a huge deep sink and a freezer with double doors filled much of the wall before them. The first two of four tables were empty. The tools of a surgeon sat beside the third. Nadine's attention turned to the body, the woman, as they stepped farther into the autopsy room. They stopped opposite Juliette, facing the female victim, with their backs to the male. Air vents hummed and Nadine was surprised that the smell was not overpowering. But her nose wrinkled at the caustic odor of ammonia and decay.

She swayed and Demko gripped her arm. He leaned in and whispered encouragement. Now she was thinking of his warm breath on her neck. A tingling awareness replaced the sensation of horror. She glanced up at him, noting the confidence reflected in his eyes.

"Seeing photos of victims isn't the same as seeing the victims. It's rough, I know, but the information you'll gain is invaluable. Autopsies are an important part of a homicide investigation."

She nodded, believing him. She didn't know what she would perceive, but anything that helped them solve this case was worth overcoming her apprehension.

"You can do this," he said.

Juliette had taken a position opposite them. The body lay between them, a grim offering to forensic science.

The deceased was only a year older than Nadine was now, fit, with long black hair. She was also naked. A thick mat of hair was plastered to her cheek and neck. Her arms lay neatly at her side and her legs were pressed together, making her look like a model for an autopsy textbook. Her eyes were not closed but peered at them through slitted lids, the cornea gone milky over the dark irises. Black eyeliner smeared her lower lids. The red lip stain and gray skin gave her a vampiric appearance.

Nadine scanned downward past the horrific gash in her neck to the perfect orbs of her breasts and fixed on her greenish bloated stomach. The wound there gaped, and intestines bulged. The swollen abdomen indicated that decomposition had begun. Farther down, a nest of sculpted black hair curled at her crotch. Death was so humiliating.

"My assistant washed her. You can see the wounds at the neck and lower abdomen. She was in the water for several hours. It speeds the decomposition significantly."

"Trace evidence?" asked Demko.

"I collected what I could. Honestly, I don't have much."

"Why is the wound so ragged? Did the unsub use a jagged object?" he asked.

Juliette shook her head. "No, that's predation. Fish got after her. Also the sand abraded the skin on her back. When the bloating occurred, the bodies left the bottom and were floating for hours, likely not on the surface or they would have been spotted sooner." Juliette lifted the woman's left hand. "This, however, is not predation. The skin was deliberately stripped from around the ring finger, making a bloody band, of sorts."

Nadine glanced at the hand. Turquoise acrylic nails tipped long slim fingers. Juliette extended the digit intended to wear a wedding ring. A thin line of flesh, circling the base of the finger, had been removed. She'd never seen anything like that before.

"They were both married," Nadine said to Demko.

"Yes. We've established that."

"Where are their wedding bands?"

He gave her a sharp look and his brow descended.

"I don't know."

Juliette chimed in. "None recovered. But see here?" She indicated the indenture above the denuded flesh. "She did wear a wide band and an engagement ring. It's left a mark."

Nadine looked away from the body. The thing before her looked less like a human being than a wax model in some house of horrors.

Demko gripped her elbow, lending silent support. She leaned against him, ashamed and relieved at his aid.

"The larynx and jugular were both severed," said Juliette.

Just like Gail DeNato. The woman sold carpets at a wholesale place in Ocala. They were murdered in 1994, two years after Nadine was born. DeNato had also been found tied to Charlie Rogers, with whom she worked. The similarities made her queasy.

Demko stared at her. "Could you show Nadine the cuts on her backside?"

Nadine mentally shook herself, trying to remain in the moment instead of looking back. She wanted to get out of this room.

Just a few more minutes, she told herself. *He thinks you can do this. You* have *to do this.*

Juliette used two hands to roll the body toward her, giving Nadine and Demko a view of the woman's back. Nadine realized the ME was stronger than she looked.

The abrasions had taken the skin off Poletti's shoulder blades. Nadine felt the bile rise in her throat and glanced to Demko. He pointed and Nadine peered.

Juliette spoke as she nodded toward the cuts.

"Superficial bruising around this wound on her left buttocks means the victim was still alive when cut. Seven separate cuts more or less horizontal. These are not deep. Except for the cut on her stomach, the other injuries targeted tendons and major arteries."

"To incapacitate and kill," said Demko.

"But not these and not the long cut across her abdomen. What was the reason to do this?" asked Juliette.

"Inflict pain. I think the killer wanted to hurt her, punish her," said Nadine.

They both stared at her.

"For what?" asked Juliette.

"Sleeping with a married man."

"They were both married," said Demko.

"But only the woman was tortured."

Nadine studied the marks, trying to glean their meaning. When she straightened, Juliette rolled the body back.

"David Lowe," said Juliette as they moved to the male.

Of course the first thing Nadine looked at was his genitalia. His scrotum was purple and swollen. She did not ask if that was normal, because she now had her eyes shut as Juliette recited the injuries.

"He showed defensive wounds to his arms. Artery severed at the juncture of leg and hip. Gastrocnemius tendons and biceps femoris tendon severed."

"Came at him from behind," said Demko.

"Yes. Then the arm wounds and finally the femoral artery and this again," said Juliette.

Nadine peeked and saw Juliette lifting the left hand to display a similar ring of denuded skin around the base of his finger.

"Nadine?" Demko's voice held concern. "You okay?"

She wasn't, but she nodded, hand still pressed to her mouth as she remembered the knife used in her mother's job as a carpet installer and later used on DeNato and Rogers. What had this killer used to fillet the skin from the muscle?

"Any thoughts?" asked the detective.

Nadine dropped her hand from her mouth and swallowed, then turned to stare at the red receptacle marked BIOHAZARD as she spoke, wondering if it would be better to throw up there or the sink. But the feeling passed as she gathered her thoughts and reminded herself why she was there in the first place.

"I'd say that the killer was using these victims as a target for displaced anger. The perpetrator didn't just stop the targets from breathing but cut major arteries before tying them together and dumping them naked in the Gulf. Treatment of the bodies shows a lack of regard and absence of personal connection to the victims."

"A stranger," said Demko.

"No. I don't think so. The killer likely knew them, because this does not appear to be a crime of opportunity. The cutting on the hands where the wedding band should be. Seems a way to focus on breaking their vows. That would mean the perpetrator knew they were cheating."

"Targeted."

"Likely. Look for a history of violence to strangers. Early victims might be someone or something more helpless, like a child or an animal. And you might find a current arrest record for theft and sexual assault."

"Any personal relationship?" he asked.

"Unlikely. I believe the unsub knew *of* them. But is the relationship personal? No."

"It's usually the significant other," he added. "But I called you because this looks like something else."

Was he thinking serial killer? She was but did not want to voice that opinion yet. This was different and the same. Very much the same as Gail and Charlie, her mother's superiors, made inferior by Arleen's knife.

Her mom's killing streak ran for twelve years, and would have continued indefinitely, if she had not taken Nadine's classmate.

Right after Nadine had told her mom that Sandra was terrorizing her, the high school senior went missing.

*

Nadine spotted them waiting by her locker and hunched, drawing her notebooks tighter to her chest. Sandra and two of her clique spotted her approach. Upperclassmen's lockers were across the building, so she knew they were there for her.

Nadine slowed and then lifted her chin. There were security cameras in every hall. They wouldn't do anything here. And the names, well, they hurt, but they didn't draw blood.

"There she is. The scarecrow!" chirped Sandra.

Her groupies laughed.

"Phew." Sandra fanned her hand before her face. "I can smell her from here. You stink, Howler."

The other two lifted their chins and howled on cue. They liked this joke, howling at Howler and calling her a mangy dog.

They blocked her locker. Nadine stood, head down, heart pounding. Finally Sandra sidestepped. Nadine quickly opened her locker and deposited her books, retrieving her backpack, leaving most of the homework she needed behind. She'd do it tomorrow before school in the library.

One of the others snatched her bag and walked off.

"Hey!" she said.

They all continued away with her property, growling and barking at her. Nadine closed her locker and followed. Stupid, because when they opened the door to the sidewalk that ran behind the school, they were in a security camera's blind spot. They stopped between the double doors and threw her bag out. The nylon scraped on the concrete, skidding to a halt and disgorging notebooks through the open zipper.

One of the two pushed her against the door and she staggered, losing her balance. Sandra snatched her phone from a rear pocket, throwing it out the open door and onto the concrete. Nadine gasped as the case flew off on the first bounce.

A tiny whimper escaped her. They'd broken her phone. She'd have to tell her mother. Now terror of a different sort filled her.

"Fetch, bitch!" shouted Sandra.

Nadine did, collecting the pieces of her phone, the bag and contents before returning the way she had come. A mistake, she realized as she saw the satisfaction glittering in their wolfish eyes. The pack closed in.

Coyotes surrounding a smaller dog.

Sandra pushed her so hard, Nadine's head struck the tile, making her ears ring. Then Sandra slapped her across the face.

Rage boiled in Nadine and she stood, fists clenched, as she took a menacing step. Sandra retreated to the pack, eyes widening, surprised that the little shrimp they'd tortured for months had finally been pushed too far.

Nadine read the fear and it scared her more than all three of these seniors. Fear of that rage inside her and what she might do if she unleashed that part of her.

Nadine dropped her head again. Sandra laughed and shoved her back to the ground.

"Teacher," said the lookout. The girls left her.

Nadine gathered her things and took the back door, walking around the school to find the buses pulling out.

She called her mother from the office, head down, hair cascading into her face to cover her throbbing lip. Arleen screamed at her but came to pick her up forty-five minutes later.

Inside the rusting Plymouth, her mother grasped her chin and studied her split lip. "What happened to you?"

And then Nadine did something she'd regret for the rest of her life. She told her mother everything.

A week later, Sandra was absent from school.

*

Demko steered her into a hard-plastic chair. Nadine glanced up at him in confusion. Then she looked about. She was in the hallway outside the autopsy room and near the changing area.

She didn't even remember leaving.

"Did I faint?" she asked.

"No. But your eyes were rolling back."

She hunched forward, cradling her head in her hands.

"How're you feeling?"

"Dizzy."

"Okay. That's enough for today. You want me to drive you back?"

She shook her head and moaned, embarrassment making her face hot.

"I'm fine."

He hovered. "Don't drive if you're dizzy."

She glared at him. "I won't."

"If I have questions, can I call?" he asked.

"Of course," she said. Should she tell him about the similarities she was noting? She could be wrong. But not telling him might give this killer an advantage.

She hesitated, afraid of sounding crazy. She needed more than that rope to connect these crimes to Arleen. What about those marks on the woman and the skin cut from the ring fingers? Her mother had done nothing like that.

But what if she had?

She needed to do some more digging.

"Call me if you have any additional thoughts."

He grinned and swept a strand of hair off her cheek. The dizziness vanished and a different kind of heat swept through her.

He used one crooked finger to lift her chin, staring down at her.

"Your color is better." His finger dropped away. "I'd better get back."

Nadine nodded and watched him go, wondering if he was having second thoughts about asking for her. The notion riled. She wanted to help catch this killer, but the similarities to her mother's crimes made her worry about objectivity. Could she even separate them in her mind?

Her past meant she was either uniquely qualified to handle this profile, or the worst possible choice.

He paused to look back and cast her another dazzling smile. They should register that smile as a lethal weapon, she thought as he vanished through the doors.

Nadine rose like an old woman and hobbled to the changing room. She left a few minutes later, feeling more herself. The emotion lasted until she reached the parking lot.

She was nearly back to her car when a terrible possibility formed in her mind.

What if…

If this was a copycat killer, did he or she know Nadine worked here as a profiler for this case? What if the killer was not only mimicking her mother's crimes, but toying with her? What if their perp had concocted those two murders to expose her? Or worse, just to watch her slowly lose her mind. Was their perp watching her right now?

It was possible. There were websites that highlighted the children of serial killers. Some children of killers did television interviews and authored books about their experiences. Others, like her, tried for a normal life by changing their names and disappearing. Nadine's photo, as a teenager, was still up on several websites. She'd changed her last name, so finding her might be challenging, but not impossible.

The parking lot now seemed too public.

Nadine glanced around. Two men loomed in the doorway of the adjoining building, smoking, watching her. Vehicles filled the parking area, the sun's angle making each a dark mirror of the storm clouds sweeping in from the west. Joggers and bicyclists passed on the sidewalk. It struck her that any one of them could be the killer, hiding in plain sight. Nadine turned in a circle, seeing menace from all sides, falling to pieces at the entrance to the medical examiner's office.

A man approached, meeting her gaze.

CHAPTER FOUR

One swallow doesn't make a summer

Nadine didn't remember rushing past the man heading toward her or bolting to her car, just the sound of the beep as the locks released and the door slammed behind her. She re-engaged the locks, panting now. Then she stamped her foot on the brake and pressed the ignition button. Hot air blasted her, gradually cooling as the air conditioner hummed, awakening the vents, driving off the heat and humidity, but not the panic. The man who had met her gaze had simply walked past without taking any notice of her. He was not a threat at all. The real menace was her fear. She needed to get control.

Nadine ground her teeth together and glared through the windshield as the buzzing in her ears diminished with her slowing heartbeat. If any part of her mother lived in her, then she was stronger than this. It was time to draw on that courage and use it to find this killer.

If she was right about this perp, she was somehow already involved. She was both the hunter and the hunted. This killer was playing with her, and that made this unsub a personal threat. One thing she knew. Threatening a Howler was a terrible idea. If anything, she was now more motivated to catch their perp.

It was narcissistic to believe these murders centered on her. Completely paranoid. Yet, she could not dismiss the possibility.

This killer already had her in his sights.

But their unsub might have underestimated her. She glanced about now with the predatory stare of a hawk, knowing she had one huge advantage over the victims. She didn't have to slip into the mind of a killer. She was the great-granddaughter of a killer. The granddaughter of a killer. And the daughter of a serial killer. She had survived among them and was well equipped to hunt them.

*

Later, on Friday afternoon, the autopsy photos from both murder victims were in Nadine's in-box. Juliette Hartfield's preliminary autopsy reports were there, too, and they also included photos. Lots of photos.

The sight was enough to bring on another panic attack. But having returned to the office after her meltdown in her car outside the District 12 ME's office, she held it together. Outwardly she reflected calm as she read each document. Diving into this rabbit hole was easier than she expected. That alone was troubling.

The sharp rap on her open door made her startle in her seat. Dr. Margery Crean stood in her office. Her body posture was rigid, and her strained expression set off alarm bells.

"Got a minute?" she asked.

Nadine braced her hands on her knees. "Yes. Everything okay?"

Crean stepped in and closed the door.

"The local television news is outside police headquarters. They have a source inside the department confirming that the two on the bay were homicides."

Nadine recalled the reporters crowding her as court officers escorted her to and from her mother's trial. Her fingers dug into her knees. Once this story broke, there would be no avoiding them.

"We do not want to scare away visitors, because our city's tax base depends on tourism. If you are asked, remember cause of death is still undetermined."

Nadine raised her brows. Was this sort of concealment routine? "I understand."

Crean remained where she was. "How goes the profile?"

"Slow."

"I suggest you review the information available on the FBI's website but don't reach out to the Bureau's Behavioral Analysis Unit. This is a local matter."

Nadine frowned "The FBI is expert at profiling."

"Not my call."

Nadine tried again. "Dr. Crean, wouldn't you be the more qualified one to create this profile on this sort of suspect?"

"Two bodies killed at the same time is hardly enough to make that leap."

"Then why am I working on a profile?"

"Because of the viciousness of the attack and the possibility that this might be a disturbed individual." Crean stared in silence, her expression giving away nothing. "This is an opportunity, Nadine. *Your* opportunity. You have all the ability you need to support the police in this investigation."

Why was she doing this? Was Crean avoiding a powder keg or striving to give her new hire a boost? Nadine sensed a trap. She maintained a placid expression as suspicions swirled.

"Profilers sometimes come to the attention of the killers they pursue," Nadine said. "It can get personal."

"More likely, he or she would be inclined to toy with the press or police. We can hope. Engagement with us in any form would help."

"You've met killers, Dr. Crean. You don't want them toying with you. Their games are dark and hideous."

"All true. And all the more reason to catch this person quickly." She raised her hand, signaling both an end to the discussion and a farewell. Then she turned, opened the door and glided toward her corner office.

Nadine returned to the photos, the picturesque view of palm trees and bobbing boats on mooring lines spoiled by the two bloated bodies in the foreground.

She studied Demko's notes. Debi Poletti owned a paddleboard, now missing. She often paddled on the bay and through the mangrove tunnels, according to her husband. Both victims' spouses had solid alibis for the night of the murders. Demko had discovered no obvious enemies or rivals, but had learned that the two had been engaged in an affair for over a year. Most of their coworkers were aware of their liaison. Some had even covered for one or the other at work. Debi Poletti wore a wedding ring and engagement ring, both missing. Trophy hunting? David, who worked with machinery for preparing meat, did not wear a wedding ring.

Her first draft of the profile assignment contained inferences from the attack approach that this was a confident killer, experienced enough to dare to attack two victims simultaneously with only a knife. Initial attack on the male showed a desire to incapacitate, but not kill. Demko's description of the male, David, likely being in an upright position, kneeling, during the first strike to his legs and then on his seat for the cut to his femoral artery, backed this up. Absence of water in David's lungs meant he was dead when he entered the water. How much of the attack on Debi had he witnessed?

The female victim's defensive wounds meant she saw her killer and made an attempt to escape. But the killer did not find her a threat. Her attacker made a frontal assault, incapacitated the victim, then cut flesh from her finger and carved the strange hash marks into her flank before making the final strike.

She put forth that this was likely a male or a powerful female somewhere between thirty and forty-five, with multiple prior victims, beginning with smaller, less dangerous targets. The attacks were premeditated, the victims selected and surveilled for some period before the attacks. From the bloody wedding rings carved in each victim, she theorized that the killer sought to punish or expose their infidelity. She reported that the carving on the woman's flank had some obvious, as yet unknown, meaning, or was a message from the killer to either the world or the victim.

Both victims were taken by surprise, which meant the killer was capable of planning, stalking, incapacitating and disposing of the bodies quickly and without notice.

She believed the color of the rope was significant. Red. The color of blood, lust and passion.

She speculated this was an organized killer who blended with his or her surroundings. They were looking for someone who lived and worked in the area, with some higher education, who was employed in a white-collar job, was not in a relationship and lived alone in a single-family home. This perpetrator would have few close friends but might be involved in community organizations, as was the case with John Wayne Gacy, or their church, as was the case with the BTK Strangler. Serials often used community groups to lend an air of normality. Their unsub was strong, fit, neither overweight nor skinny. Neat and tidy. Methodical. With some anatomical knowledge. Pathologically self-centered. Meticulous in planning. Their unsub had avoided detection, though likely initially covered in blood, and thus had probably driven a vehicle, likely their own, to and from the murder site.

After the attack, the disposal of the bodies included simply letting them float away. She speculated that the perpetrator likely bathed in the same waters. With the bodies removed from the scene, choosing to leave the blankets and garments as evidence,

reinforced her belief of the unsub's confidence at escaping apprehension for these crimes.

The Intracoastal Waterway's moving water and changing tides
gave the perp time to put distance between them and the victims,
while showing disregard for the deceased. To the killer, this pair
merited no respect. To the unsub, they were not people. Once
finished with them, they were trash, disposable as an empty water
bottle.

She scanned her profile and then sent a link to the preliminary
report to Demko and Crean, more worried than ever. This was
a smart, experienced and vicious killer whose confidence would
only grow.

Nadine knew that if this were a serial killer, their cooling-off
period could be as little as a few days. Her mother had gone years
between kills. However, if she were right, this was only the first
of four acts.

Had the killer already targeted the next couple? She needed
more to connect these crimes to her mother's homicides than a
hunch, paranoia and a length of rope. And she knew where to get
it. It was time to visit her big brother.

*

Saturday morning, travel mug of coffee in hand, Nadine drove
north to Lawtey Correctional, as she did once a month, to visit
an inmate. Her brother had not legally changed his name, like
her, and remained Arlo Howler.

After clearing security, she waited in the visitors' area, a dreary
concrete room between a glass observation office and a catwalk
where armed guards watched from above, like perching eagles.

Arlo strode in. His incarceration had not dampened his
swagger. She smiled and stood beside the fixed table and bolted-
down stools that she had chosen.

She knew he was here for good reason after attacking his girlfriend. The charge had been reduced in a plea deal to sexual assault, largely due to the girlfriend's refusal to testify, but Nadine knew it was battery and rape. Since he was her brother, she couldn't help but love Arlo, but in her heart, she thought the parole board was right to deny his early release.

"There she is. The new forensic psychiatrist."

He always got her title wrong. She smiled and kissed his cheek. That got the guards on the catwalk shouting about physical contact as they separated and took a seat.

"How goes the new job?" asked Arlo.

"It's good."

"Listen, sis. I appreciate the money you send. It makes life possible in here."

She swallowed the lump in her throat. "You're welcome."

"I was wondering, now that you got a new job, do you think you could send a little extra? It's been the same amount for years and things cost more."

She thought of her student loans, car payment and the apartment that blew her budget.

"Sure. I can do that."

"Great. So, what's up?"

Arlo had been eight when Arleen had killed Charlie Rogers and Gail DeNato, while she had been only two. He'd have specifics about the cases and about their mother that she couldn't. He might know the triggers to her mother's murders, how she selected her victims or any number of details not found in any record. And if she was right, and this killer was imitating her mother's murders, this sort of information could help her create her profile.

"I got a new assignment. I need your opinion."

"Yeah? Does it involve mopping floors? Because I'm a whiz at that."

"It doesn't, unfortunately." She smiled. Her brother looked too thin and extremely pale. His brown hair was limp and needed a trim. Seemed he hadn't shaved this week, either. But the mischief in his eyes was still there.

"Do you know if anything happened to Mom right before she killed that first couple, Rogers and DeNato?"

"In '94?"

"Yeah."

"Like what?"

"Something traumatic. A breakup, a death in the family."

He shook his head. "Nothing like that. She got fired, though. I remember, because I had to walk home. Four miles, and when I got there, the place was empty, dark."

"How do you know she was fired?"

"She told me the next day. She came home drunk with some guy. That wasn't unusual. But she'd always picked me up. The next morning, he was gone, and she said that bitch in the showroom had it in for her. Said she needed to get work, or they'd take our car."

Was her mother's trigger losing her job? "What's this about, Dee-Dee?"

She knew two things: Arlo was dangerous but had protected her more than once during their childhood. Plus, she trusted him completely. That was why she was going to reveal case details that were confidential.

"You can't share what I'm going to tell you."

"Okay."

"I mean it. Not with anyone."

"Yeah. I heard you. What's going on?"

"We had a double homicide in the city." She told him they had two victims in the water, one male, one female.

"That's odd," he said.

"I saw the bodies."

He glanced about, leaned in, whispering. "How?"

"The autopsy."

He held his hand to his chest and exhaled. "Thank God."

"Arlo, I'm assigned as a profiler."

"You mean like on TV?"

"Yeah, I suppose. Listen." She told him about the carving on the ring fingers and the one on the woman's backside. "You know if Mom did anything like that?"

"Mom's in prison."

"Yes, I got the memo. I'm afraid of a copycat."

"Oh, God!" Arlo wiped his hand over his mouth and then blew out a breath. "No. I never heard about that."

"You went to her trial."

"Some of it. I was working, so I went when I could." Arlo looked sickened and that was unusual. He had a high tolerance for gore, unfortunately.

"But she used a rope?" she asked.

"Yeah. She definitely tied her couples together with two deviations. The second couple was killed at separate times and places, but she still put a rope on each of them and cut the end. Then, on the last couple, she hadn't quite finished with them, so no rope."

She sat back. Worried. Perhaps she was overreacting. The rope connecting them might have been used just to drag them to the water.

"You think that losing her job was her trigger?"

Arlo held his fist before his mouth and then spoke again. "I'm sure it was part of it, but she hated that woman. Really loathed her. Called her a 'skank' and a 'homewrecker' because she was doing the guy she worked with. The one in the warehouse. So, tell me about the bodies."

She got that prickle of warning again. The sparkle in Arlo's eyes made her hesitate. She wasn't certain if he was interested in order to help her or for reasons of his own. She changed the subject and chatted with Arlo about her job and his application to join a program to train service dogs. She thought that would be good for him.

Nadine left the prison with a better picture of her mother's mental state before the first couple's murder. Unfortunately, nothing she'd heard had convinced her there wasn't some link between those crimes and this new death investigation.

When she got to her car, she wondered again about telling Demko about the commonalities she was noting between this homicide investigation and her mother's homicides. But then she recalled the unanswered questions regarding his hasty and unexpected departure from the Miami-Dade police force. She needed to do more digging before she trusted him with this.

Before leaving the lot, she made a call to a classmate from graduate school who worked in Miami-Dade County and got his voicemail. She left a message specific enough that he would know what she was after, just to save time and give him the opportunity to ignore her call if he didn't feel like speaking to her about why Detective Clint Demko made such a suspicious job change.

Getting to be a homicide cop was hard. And it was a position of honor and respect in all police forces. To gain that post, he would have had to work his way up through other departments, receive specialized training and have made more than a few important arrests. Why throw that all away and start over at a smaller, less active department?

It didn't make sense.

CHAPTER FIVE

Recon couple two

Places remote enough for clandestine lovers make excellent spots for murder.

The secluded preserve doesn't even have a security camera. This spot adds another city and different county to the tangle of jurisdictions. I'm not sure if Arleen did this intentionally, but it certainly worked in her favor. Many hands might make light work, but too many cooks spoil the investigation.

I park behind my choice's car and watch her gather her beach bag and chair. She strolls to the nature trail as I lift the kayak and carry it to the launch, twenty feet away, then return for my paddle and pack.

Emulating Arleen's work is more difficult than I imagined. My usual targets are runaways. But hers double the risk. That alone merits my homage. And she demands respect. She wants to draw Nadine in as much as I do.

I'm sure that her daughter noted the similarities and the differences between my work and her mother's. Nadine was young then. How much does she remember and how much was kept from her? I'm thinking plenty. But she is a bright girl. She'll catch on.

Were they too different?

Arleen stabbed Gail DeNato in the neck, while I slit Debi's throat. And I never hit David Lowe in the head before I cut. Worst of all, I forgot to take their clothing. It was wrong.

I've spoiled them. I ball my fists in fury at the realization and at my mistakes, and hurl my pack to the shoreline. For several minutes, I fume. Then I collect my gear and launch the kayak.

Today is just a scouting mission. I've chosen my next pair and will witness them betray their vows for fleeting gratification. My gratification will follow.

I glide along the shore past a place where the nature trail opens to the water and spot her again, setting up her chair on white sand. The wide-brimmed hat doesn't hide her long dark hair, secured in a practical braid. She settles in her seat with irrational confidence, as if she is safe here.

A white egret glides in, landing in the shallow waters of the inlet. Hope retrieves her digital camera from the tote.

I sweep past her before heading bow-first into the tangle of arching mangrove roots. The narrow gap beneath them gives views of the water and the motorboat making a course straight for her. The motor slows and idles as the single man turns the craft and backs in. He deploys the anchor and moves to the stern. She is already on her feet, meeting him in the shallow water as he helps her aboard. The pair disappears and I don't think the rocking is due only to the gentle waves lapping the hull.

What a lovely private place for a rendezvous.

CHAPTER SIX

Fuel to the fire

On Monday morning, Nadine arrived early to find Crean waiting at Tina's reception counter and puffing like a power lifter preparing for a difficult weight. She held a newspaper in Nadine's face. Beside the political headline was this:

Police Hire Profiler for Recent Double Homicide.

"The newspaper has confirmed that the Bayfront Park deaths are homicides and that we've provided a profiler."

Panic gripped her.

"Call this reporter and tell him you have no comment." She extended a Post-it.

Nadine took it. "I will."

Crean spun and stomped away as Nadine diverted to the coffeemaker behind Tina's desk, calling the number as her coffee brewed. The reporter was very persistent, so Nadine hung up on her. Then she spent the morning reviewing her profile, including that this unsub likely experienced a violent family resulting in prior court contact and included a history of truancy, suspension or expulsion from school. She read over her notes and closed the document and sent the update to Demko as an attachment.

By midmorning, she'd heard from the office assistant that two men were in custody. Both had confessed to the double homicide. Nadine's hopes dropped when she reached Demko by phone to learn that neither detainee got the cause of death right.

"They just parroted the news story. Thought the victims were shot." His sigh came through loud and clear. "But the press got one detail right. They were murdered. It's official. We have a leak."

Nadine's disappointment cut deep.

"Listen, I gotta go," he said.

Demko phoned back after she returned to her desk with a deli sandwich and chips. He had a nice voice. Stressed, but nice.

"You got anything else for us?" he asked.

"I added a preliminary report to the file share."

"Give me the highlights."

"This killer experienced or witnessed violence at home. Likely had some court contact or arrest as a juvenile. The MO shows the killer is organized, confident and premeditative, choosing specific targets. Surveillance is likely involved. In other words, this unsub is targeting victims because they match some characteristic or criteria."

"Infidelity?"

"It's on my short list."

"So, following the vics?" he asked.

"Likely more than once. Learning their habits before choosing a time and place. Preparing entrance and exit and bringing necessary equipment."

"Agreed. I've asked for patrols in known hangouts."

"A good idea."

"What else?" he asked.

"Killer uses a blitz-style attack."

"He sure the hell does."

Nadine gave an audible snort at this and continued. "Look for individuals picked up with psychiatric disorders."

"In addition to earlier crimes and possible sexual assault or theft you mentioned at the autopsy?"

He got points for listening, she thought.

"Yes."

"You think our killer has a record?"

"Possible. A third of these sorts of killers have been diagnosed with a mental disorder. Many have prior contact with social workers resulting from truancy or school suspensions."

"But not necessarily arrested," he added. "And medical records are closed."

"It's a starting place." It was all she could offer.

"White male, right?"

An image of her mother flashed in her mind.

"I wouldn't say that. Not even necessarily male. Likely, but not definitely."

"But most serials don't kill outside their race," he said. "Right?"

"They can. They have, on rare occasions."

He paused, and she waited for him to process this change to his perception.

"What do you make for motive?" he asked. "This a jilted lover or someone who can't get off with a woman?"

"I don't know. Sex. Displaced anger. Past breakups?"

Nadine wondered again if revealing the connection to her mother's cases would help solve this case or be leaked and give the killer an advantage.

For all she knew, Demko might be the leak.

Bottom line: too many unknowns. She didn't trust him.

And there was no hurry. Time was on her side. There had been six years between her mother's first murders and the next couple, when Nadine had been eight years old.

"Anything else?" he asked.

"Experience with a blade, knowledge of the area, owns a vehicle, active in the community with few personal friends," she said.

"Well, if you're right, we have a proficient hunter in a public space, who killed and dumped the vics. Then walked away."

"Or swam or… I don't know." She did know. "Paddled?"

According to her research, her mother had used her vehicle and the family's battered aluminum canoe to get to and from her kill sites. Nadine recalled playing in that canoe, dragging the craft from beneath the trailer, imagining adventures. She recalled the sour smell, wondering if it was mildew, as she'd assumed, or something darker.

"Hadn't thought of that," said Demko.

"We agree these murders seem premeditated. So, I'd look for similar crimes elsewhere. Less decisive attacks. This could mean not fatal stabbings or brutalizing animals."

There would be some. She was certain. Whether there would be a record was another question.

"They could be anywhere in the country. He or she might have a route that includes southwest Florida. The trick is to find the first. That one might be personal or have been committed in home territory." She was on a roll, but that should have been a warning. "If we find that first murder and are very lucky, the killer could have known the victim, while these recent ones are more likely to fit some criteria established early on."

"I'll look in the databases for stabbings," said Demko.

"Dumped in water," she added, realizing belatedly that her mother's victims would pop up on that search.

Her mother's bodies were all recovered in water. No wait. Not all. There had been the forest ranger and, also, the last pair, the ones Arleen never had time to dump… because of her.

*

On the last period of Friday, Nadine walked into math, the sole high school freshman in the mixed group of sophomores taking Algebra 1 for the first time and juniors and seniors, repeating. It was the one class she shared with Sandra and her groupies. Nadine glanced about the room, immediately noted Sandra's absence, and sighed in relief, delighted. Possibly Sandra's little clique might let her be. But then she realized the only empty seat was behind Madison and Emily, two of Sandra's favorites.

The girls ignored her as she slipped behind the desk. Instead, they took advantage of the distraction caused by the substitute's ineffective attempts to get one of the boys back in his seat to continue talking. Nadine overheard the pair.

"Weird. She's not answering my texts," said Madison, glancing at her phone.

Olivia, who sat in the row ahead of Madison, spun in her seat to join the discussion.

"Her mother called me," said Olivia. "Sandra didn't come home last night."

Olivia was third in the pecking order, but the one with the best car.

"With him? Did they run away together?" asked Emily.

Nadine narrowed her eyes. Who was the "him" that they mentioned?

"I dunno. She said they might," said Madison.

"Did you call him?" asked Olivia.

Both Madison and Emily glared.

"No!" said Emily.

At the same time, Madison said, "That's not how it works."

Emily deferred, and Madison continued.

"He calls us, not the other way around," said Madison.

Sandra was involved with someone. They all were. Was this how three kids from the West Ocala neighborhood afforded new phones and great clothes?

"But what if she's not with him?" said Olivia.

The implication struck her. Nadine's gasp brought one of them around. Madison fixed her with a contemptuous glare.

"What are you lookin' at, bitch?"

Nadine shook her head and lowered her eyes.

"She heard," said Olivia.

Madison aimed a purple pencil at Nadine's nose. "You say anything, and I'll break more than your phone."

Nadine did not ask permission to leave the room. She collided with the door frame on the way out and dashed through the halls, ending up in the locker room, huddled on a toilet, rocking like an insane person.

She did it. Nadine knew it. Her mother did this. All the way home on the bus, she thought of what she'd say when she confronted her mother. But Arleen never came home. So, she called Arlo. Now twenty, he had moved out and was living with a girl who worked with him at a fast-food joint.

He picked up on the third ring. She could tell from the sounds in the background that he was at work on the grill.

"S'up, Dee-Dee?"

She told him about the girls at school, her phone and telling their mom, ending with Sandra's disappearance.

"This is bad, Dee-Dee."

"I know! What do we do?"

"If it's her and you tell, the state will take you, Dee. Just like she said."

"You could take me."

The pause stretched. "Yeah. Uh, maybe."

She started crying. "I'm calling the police."

But she didn't. Instead, she sat up all night, waiting for her mother. When Arleen finally returned on Sunday night, she had another sticky bag of garbage for her daughter.

This time, instead of doing as she was told, Nadine tucked that bag away under the trailer.

*

Nadine's classmate from grad school returned her call that afternoon.

"How's the new job over there?" Mitch asked.

She lied and said it was wonderful. She remembered to ask about his new wife, apologizing again for missing their wedding. It had conflicted with Arlo's parole hearing and she'd made the choice. Turned out her support didn't matter. They'd denied his request for the second time.

"Listen, about that detective. Wow. There's a lot. He got tangled up in an evidence-tampering investigation here. Suspended for a while, then reinstated. One of the other cops in his department got fired. I couldn't get a straight story on why he wasn't. One guy told me he made a deal, the other said they didn't have enough to charge him. One of the gals in records told me that she heard he'd flipped on the guy they fired. Broke the blue wall to save his own skin. If that's true, he's lucky to have any job. But it's a mess. They had to drop charges on eight pending cases. The district attorney's office is fuming over all the motions for mistrials on previous convictions. Kind of a career ender, especially if he was also tampering."

"He wasn't charged?"

"Nope. Got a recommendation, apparently, but was that to get rid of him? And off he goes to your department. I'd keep a close eye on him. Maybe they just pushed our garbage in your direction."

"Wow."

"You can say that again. Watch your back, shrimp."

She'd never liked his chosen nickname for her but thanked him.

"Sure. Let me know if you need anything else. Hey, come see us if you get over to this coast. All right?"

"Will do. Thanks, Mitch."

Her mind reeled. Was Demko a dirty cop?

He seemed so competent and she'd seen no indications of dishonesty. She'd liked him. More than liked him, she had felt a distinct attraction. This was so bad.

"I can't trust any evidence he…" Oh, God, he could blow this case. If he was implicated in tampering, it didn't matter if they caught the guy. The case would be challenged.

Tina popped her head in the open door. "You asked me to remind you in time to get to the courthouse."

"Courthouse?"

"Bench trial."

"Oh, shoot!" Nadine scrambled to get her things and hurried out, taking her car instead of walking the two blocks. Travel time was the same, but the car had AC.

Nadine was one of three expert witnesses called to testify before a judge in her first bench trial.

She reported that the defendant, who had fired at a lineman working in a bucket truck, was delusional at the time of the offense, believing he was under attack by alien invaders.

She was off the stand and out of the courtroom in less than thirty minutes. The entire experience would have been a positive one if the court officer she'd just recently been discussing with Juliette, Nathan Dun, hadn't been lurking in the back of the court as she left the stand. As she reached the center aisle, he dropped his hand from his fly, and she winced. Had he been touching himself?

She slipped past him, but he followed her out.

Dun was small, with sparse light brown hair that was evacuating the crown of his head. His most distinctive feature was his bulging brown eyes and the perpetual dark circles beneath them. His gaze ran over her and he licked his upper lip, touching off a shudder that she failed to suppress.

"Hi, Nadine. You were great in there."

Nadine swallowed and forced a smile at her one-man fan club.

"Thanks." She turned to go.

"Wait. I wondered…"

Nadine paused, facing him. He shifted from side to side, arms limp and his broad forehead shining with sweat. His nervous demeanor only increased her concern.

"There's a free concert at the Van Wezel on Friday. It's jazz this month. Would you like to go… with me, I mean?"

Nadine gaped a minute, looking at those frog eyes with both repulsion and pity. She dropped her gaze and, unfortunately, spotted his erection.

"Oh, I'm sorry, Nathan. I don't date people from work."

"It doesn't have to be a date. We can go as friends."

She held a smile, not wanting to hurt him, but not wanting to encourage him, either. The guy had issues. "Well, no, again."

He looked away and her attention shifted toward the elevators as she considered making a break for it, when the creepy part happened. He lifted his thin brows and stared with those bulging brown eyes.

"You should reconsider, seeing how we have so much in common."

Nadine didn't like his smile. It was mean and his eyes were hard. Her skin stippled. What was he talking about?

"Is that right?" she asked. Nadine's voice no longer held empathy. She knew a threat when she heard one, even without understanding what he was implying. "I'll see you around, Nathan."

"You will," he said.

Nadine glared and turned to go. He didn't call her back. All the way out of the courthouse, her mind spun unlikely links between herself and the creepy court officer. Back at her office and on her computer, she discovered exactly what they had in common.

CHAPTER SEVEN

In plain sight

Nadine scanned the article. In 2007, Arthur Dun woke early in his Jacksonville, Florida, home and bludgeoned to death both his wife and the young daughter sleeping beside her. Then Arthur drove to the savings and loan that held his delinquent mortgage and chatted with the teller before shooting her in the face at point-blank range. He then murdered five additional victims and fled ahead of police. After an intensive four-hour manhunt, Dun chose death by cop to capture. He was survived by two sons from a previous marriage, Anthony and Nathan Dun, both nineteen.

Blood pulsed behind her eyes as the rage threatened to take her. But thoughts of becoming like her mother froze her fury. Nadine feared she might never have a normal life. But she wouldn't do anything that would land her in prison.

That didn't mean she'd let Nathan bully her. So the following morning, she was waiting for him outside of the courtroom.

"Nadine. What a pleasant surprise. You're not on the docket to testify today, are you?"

"No. I'm here to see you."

"Really?" He grinned. "Change your mind?"

"I don't date men who threaten me. So, you don't speak to me again, or I file a complaint with personnel."

"Seems the daughter of Arleen Howler could do better than that."

"I could."

His eyes went wider than usual. She was certain that her expression mirrored her mother's at her most volatile. There was something about crazy-dangerous that was instantly recognizable by the deeper parts of the brain. Dun stepped back, the smirk gone.

"We done?" she asked.

He nodded.

"Good."

*

That Wednesday morning, she saw Nathan Dun outside the courthouse. He glared at her, his mouth tight and his face flushed. But he didn't approach or try to speak to her. Message delivered, she supposed.

Was there a hierarchy to murder? Did serial killer trump spree killer? She wasn't sure. All she knew was that she would do almost anything to avoid the isolation, guilt and shame that she'd experienced as a teenager after her mother's heinous crimes became national news.

If that meant keeping to herself, she could do that. Lonely was preferable to blackballed. Unfortunately, there was no guarantee Dun would keep what he knew to himself.

On the walk back from the courthouse, her aunt phoned.

Donna was her father's only sibling. After her mother's arrest, Aunt Donna had taken custody of Nadine. Donna had been a single law student at the time. She had graduated soon after, and now worked as a real estate attorney for a firm in Orlando. She had married a financial planner, Stewart Finch, and had two wonderful kids, aged thirteen and eleven.

Nadine lifted the phone, cleared her throat, and forced herself to sound happy.

"Hi, Aunt Donna!"

"I just read about the double homicide. Are you all right?"

"I'm the city's new profiler."

"Oh, no," she said. "Is that wise?"

"Who better?" said Nadine, refusing to break down. Her aunt had been there when they'd led her mother away in handcuffs. She'd taken Nadine in. The last thing she wanted was to cause her aunt more trouble.

"Come home. You are always welcome. I came home for a bit after graduate school. No shame in it."

Nadine stopped walking and squeezed her eyes shut. Her aunt was such a blessing in her life.

"Thanks, Auntie. It's okay. I can handle this." Could she? "How are Lisa and Laura?"

"At camp, thank goodness. Laura is a junior counselor this year."

"Give them my love, and to you, too. I have to run."

"Call me if you need *anything*!"

"Will do. Love you." Nadine disconnected and pressed the phone to her heart, realizing how lucky she was. The normality, the help getting into college, all of it had kept her from a dark, hopeless place.

Talking to Donna helped bolster her and she needed that right now. Had to summon her courage for the battle ahead and her focus on stopping this killer.

*

On Wednesday afternoon Nadine took a pause from reading research studies by the FBI's Behavioral Analysis Unit to head over to the county administration offices on Ringling. The receptionist was not at her desk, but Gary Osterlund stepped out to greet her.

"Dr. Finch!" He gave her the double handshake, sandwiching her hand between his. His smile seemed genuine as he motioned her in. "Come in. Come in."

She followed him to his office, where his computer's screensaver flashed photos of one kids' baseball team after another. Kneeling kids, in colorful uniforms, beamed out at her. Atop the upper cabinets, a series of multicolored ball caps rested, their brims poking out over the doors. Each held the letter *C*, for coach, she assumed.

Piles of paper and stacks of files still littered his desk. Beside his keyboard sat his cell phone and a mug that read: KEEP CALM AND LET HR HANDLE IT.

Where were the framed photos of his kids? She spotted them now on the windowsill on the far side of the room.

"What brings you in today?" he asked.

Nadine stopped her exploration of the room and lowered her bag to the floor, folding into a seat to find the completed paperwork.

"I filled out the forms," she said, holding out the application.

He took the seat beside her instead of sitting behind his desk. Nadine pivoted toward him as he accepted the application.

"You could have dropped this in the mail."

She could have, but she had been considering a complaint against Nathan Dun—something she was now reassessing.

Osterlund cocked his head, a curious expression on his face.

"Is there something else?"

How could she lodge a complaint without revealing what they had in common?

She stood, casting him a wide smile. "No, nothing."

Dun had been right. The daughter of Arleen Howler could do better than a complaint with personnel. But she prayed she would not need to.

*

Demko showed up in her office doorway at noon on Thursday, occupying the space, casual about the deadly weapon and shiny gold shield, both clipped to his belt. Over one shoulder was the frayed black nylon strap of his computer bag. His smile was generous. It made her wish she could share more than case files with him. Then she imagined telling him about her mother, and all thoughts of sharing died.

She admitted she was attracted, but all signs pointed to a bad end. The truth didn't completely crush the longing and she stood to offer her hand. Demko stepped forward, taking her hand, seemingly as eager as she was to have the excuse to touch again.

He smelled wonderful. She allowed herself one long look at him and his sculptured mouth. His blue eyes turned progressively darker as they reached their outer limits. She'd never seen eyes that color before and meeting them gave her a shiver of excitement. Nadine forced herself to remember all the questions raised by her conversation with Mitch and broke eye contact.

When he released her, her skin tingled all the way to her elbow. She motioned him to a seat. He lifted the guest chair with one hand and repositioned it, so they sat, side by side, facing her computer monitor.

"I've got some things to show you." He drew out his laptop. One of the grips of the bag was torn, as if someone had sawed through it with a butter knife.

Demko wore a crisp wrinkle-free button-up, with a striped necktie. The cotton sleeves hugged the muscles of his arms. She caught the scent of sandalwood and leaned forward, closing her eyes for a moment as she took in the enticing fragrance.

He entered his password on his laptop and then peered at her. Their eyes met and held again. Her breath stopped.

"What?" he asked.

"Your eyes are a beautiful blue."

Color flooded his cheeks. He glanced back at the laptop, clearly embarrassed by the compliment. She found this to be adorable and all thoughts of why pursuing a relationship with a detective, who worked in her department, might be connected to evidence tampering and who was hunting a serial killer, momentarily disappeared from her brain.

"Thanks," he said. "A gift from my mother."

She imagined his mother sitting on the bleachers at sporting events and driving him to his friends' houses. He probably called her once a week, while she used her brother to supply news of her mom to distance herself from direct contact.

"Are you and your mom close?"

His smile seemed genuine. "Yes. She basically raised me and my little sister. My dad was always working." His expression tightened. His fingers glided through his short hair and settled on his neck. It was a gesture that told her that he was uncomfortable talking about this subject and needed to self-protect. "Yeah. So, we both have Mom's blue eyes."

The urge to ask him a follow-up question was tempting, but he was already shutting down. So, she dropped her gaze and landed on his shoes. Beyond his pressed hem, one leather toe showed numerous tiny punctures and there was a chunk missing from the sole.

"What happened there?" She pointed.

He chuckled. "Molly happened."

"Molly?"

His smile was back, broad and inviting.

"Yeah. She has teeth like a piranha and seems to prefer my shoes to the chewy toys I get her. Teething, the vet said. She also shredded my gym bag. But she's so cute. Here, look." Out came his phone and photos of a wrinkly puppy with a huge head and pink belly. A video of her rooting around in her crate and shaking a helpless blanket followed. Then several more as her age turned from weeks to months. Mostly, Nadine saw the pure joy on the face of Demko in every single selfie he had taken of him and the pup.

"Boxer?" she asked.

"Yup." Finally he closed the photo app. "That's my girl."

Suddenly she wanted a puppy.

"Aren't you away a lot?" She recalled the thirty-some hours he'd spent processing the scene of one of the body dumps.

"I have a neighbor, a retired preschool teacher, who can take her out when I can't get home. Plus, Molly is in doggy daycare. I go there at lunch whenever possible to spend time with her."

His lunch date was a boxer. That made her smile.

"Doggy daycare?"

"Yeah. It's a thing. Obedience school, too, on Saturdays. Missed it last week, but she was there this weekend."

While Nadine was in a federal correctional facility.

"Well, Molly is adorable."

"She's three months old already."

Trying to put puppies and blue eyes out of her mind for the next hour, she studied Demko's work. He had teased out specific details on both recent homicides and put them in a spreadsheet. From here, she could see victimology, including age, gender and occupation of both victims.

"We have a general time of death within a five-hour window. The storm tells us the blanket was on that beach on Lido at ten p.m. We have a tide expert who said the bodies couldn't have gone into the Intracoastal at Lido or they would have ended up in the Sarasota Bay, north of the bridge. I say, the blood matches and nobody moved that blanket. We've canvassed the parks on Lido. No witnesses so far."

"Physical evidence or DNA?" she asked.

"Seltzer can, blanket and clothing are all with the techs. Hopefully, they find something the perp left behind. The ME has taken samples. Also, no evidence either victim was raped before or after death. Any idea why the unsub didn't kill Lowe immediately?" he asked.

"Perhaps the killer wants an audience."

He gave her a look of horror and quickly reined that in. "Have him watch as he killed her? That could be it."

"The lacerations to the male were dealt to subdue, but the initial cuts to the female were different. The woman was the real target," said Nadine. "I think this perp likes the mess and the water provides easy cleanup. Also, use of a knife can be symbolic of sexual penetration."

"Hmm. And this killer shows proficiency in its use. What do you make of that?" he asked.

"Experience. Military training is a possibility. Research suggests that a third of serial killers had some. Perhaps an outdoorsman, hunter comes to mind. His male victim was a butcher. That's also a profession that knows knives."

Demko jotted something down on a pad.

Here would be a good time to mention that she saw a similarity between these murders and the ones committed by her mother over a decade ago. Or even to ask him about his departure from Miami.

But that little voice of caution piped up. Was there a way to find out more about Miami without asking him? She thought about bringing her concerns to Crean and rejected the idea.

Had he planted evidence? If he did that in this case, their killer could walk.

She decided to keep both her mother's crimes and her doubts to herself for now. After all, she had time, because if it truly was a copycat of her mother, they would disappear for years.

"No attempt to hide the crime scene. The perp could have tossed all this in the water and the Intracoastal would have washed it clean."

"But the unsub wanted us to find it. Part of the thrill," she said.

"Maybe. I'm also struggling to decide if the killer saved any clothing, like her bathing suit bottoms, for instance. And her rings are missing."

"And is that to prevent detection by removing evidence or part of some stylistic ritual?"

"Trophy hunting," he added.

"Some such killers keep trophies. If he left physical evidence on those bottoms, he'd be wise to pocket them. Taking them is a way to destroy evidence. And use of the water and possible removal of garments make me suspect this is more about evading capture than trophy hunting."

According to her mother's prosecutors, her mother cut away the clothing to remove any traces of her left on their garments and then collected them, kept them and disposed of them in her household trash.

Why her own trash?

Nadine motioned to his database. "This is good work. I'd add that this person has moved in and out of the murder site without detection, so they likely blend in with their surroundings."

"Nothing out of the ordinary."

"Exactly."

Now that's a topic she knew something about. Just like her mom, who displayed perfectly normal behaviors when it was advantageous to her, Nadine had mastered the art of blending in. "Faking good" made spotting psychopaths exceedingly difficult.

Overlooked and underestimated, she thought and grimaced.

"Any luck on finding similar murders in other areas?" She twisted her index finger as she waited for the answer.

"Yes. I went back ten years. A few registered on both knife wounds and recovered in bodies of water. Some cases were partially recovered remains in which the cause of death was undetermined due to animal activity." He glanced up from the laptop. "Gators."

Nadine made a sound of disapproval in her throat.

"None with this sort of slicing wound. But here they are."

He opened his laptop and they studied the cold cases. She found nothing similar enough to make an obvious match.

"Hmm. Discouraging." Nadine had hoped he'd find Arleen's crimes on his own, removing her dilemma, but his search stretched back only ten years. "Any thoughts of bringing in the FBI?"

"Both the chief and the mayor agree, for once. They want our department to handle our own cases."

"But the Feds have more experience."

"Maybe. Maybe not," he said. "Do you know how many killers they have studied who disposed of a body without transport and by concealing it in water?"

Nadine shook her head.

"None. Zero. There aren't any or there aren't any in custody."

They had one such offender in custody, but no one from the Bureau had ever spoken to Arleen. And like this couple, Arleen had stripped away all clothing from her victims who were found naked and roped together at the wrist.

"According to the mayor, the city is already experiencing a ten percent decline in hotel bookings." Demko rolled his eyes at this. "The mayor does not want us splashed across the national news up in the northeast. Bad enough that we are the lead up in Tampa."

"They will pick up the story, eventually. I'm frankly shocked they haven't already."

"School shooting and the twisters in Texas have kept us off the national news."

It was hard to be grateful for children who murdered their classmates or for natural disasters that took everything from the poorest of their citizens.

"We haven't released the identities of the victims. But when we do, reporters will learn the two were involved, and this will blow up. Salacious stories sell papers."

"And ruin families," she added.

"We need a suspect in custody before then."

Odd that he didn't say the perp. Was he willing to pin this on someone to make his case? Had he done so before?

"Hard to do with so little evidence."

"We are doubling patrols of all public parks with access to the bay and have eyes on potential body dumps. Maybe we get lucky."

"Here's hoping."

Demko stored his laptop, then settled the strap across his chest. She again noticed the flopping, frayed handle and smiled.

"I'm heading over to see Molly. Want to come?"

She paused. Had he just asked her out?

"I didn't bring a lunch today," she said.

"We'll grab something on the way back. My treat."

Yes. He'd just asked her out. She grinned like a fool, then remembered the tampering issue and looked away.

"Detective, are you married?"

"Oh, no. Not anymore. Divorced."

"I'm sorry." She wasn't. Now her face was hot.

"So, how about it? Would you like to meet her?"

"Sounds fun."

"Great."

"One more question... I am very attached to my footwear. Will these be in any imminent danger during this visit?"

She showed off one designer suede loafer with the bit-style embellishment. When she glanced up, Demko was staring at her legs.

"I'll protect you and your shoes," he said, but his gaze was hungry.

Nadine had three long beats to say no. Instead, she nodded her acceptance, hoping she wouldn't regret this.

He drove them to the daycare building on 17th.

Molly and the other puppies were completely adorable. Who knew getting slathered with dog saliva could be so precious? Nadine was tempted to go there every day for lunch because the visit left her so happy. The emotion was so unfamiliar that she thought she might be coming down with something.

They grabbed some takeout on the return trip, and he had her back in the lobby only a few minutes late.

He stood grinning at her and she got that zing again. His gaze dropped to her mouth and she knew it was coming. Could have stopped it.

Didn't.

He aimed for her cheek, his mouth warm as his lips brushed her skin, touching off a shiver of awareness. He lingered, his breath fanning her ear and sending desire spiraling through her body. He leaned away, meeting her gaze, and cast her a seductive smile that offered her more.

She lifted her hands and pressed them to his chest, to return the kiss on the cheek, and contacted the Kevlar vest. Reality returned.

Nadine stepped back.

"Should I apologize?" he asked.

She frowned. "I'm not sorry."

"Me neither."

She didn't regret it but realized she might. All that Mitch had said flooded back. It was one thing to work with a guy you didn't wholly trust. Quite another to let him kiss her, even just on the cheek. She wasn't going any further until she got some answers.

"Clint?" She tried on his first name. It felt strange. Her heart was beating so fast it hurt. But she wasn't turning back.

He lost his smile first, sensing something, perhaps correctly reading the misgivings in her expression.

"What is it?"

"Why did you leave Miami?"

CHAPTER EIGHT

Birds of a feather

Nadine witnessed a complete shifting of his expression from open to closed as he shut down. His features hardened. He looked intimidating as hell. It took all she had to hold his gaze and not shift under his scrutiny.

The silence stretched as he assessed her, likely deciding what tack to take.

"How did you hear?"

She wasn't supplying him with anything that would help him formulate a reply by gauging how much she knew.

"It's a simple question."

"Not so simple." He rubbed his hand over the back of his neck, then let it fall to his side. "Okay. I discovered one of my men planting a knife in a suspect's vehicle. We had a strong suspect but just couldn't bring a case. He made a mistake, an irredeemable one. I confronted him and he denied it. I brought the incident to my lieutenant. The other detective blamed me, said I planted it. Internal Affairs took over. I told them what I had seen. He was suspended and later dismissed."

"They believed you."

"I was telling the truth."

Was he? Or was he just a very convincing liar?

"I don't know how much you know about cops, but I broke the code."

"'Snitches get stitches,'" she said, quoting her mother.

"Something like that. It seemed best to move on."

"You turned in a friend."

"Yes."

"Because he violated the law?"

"Why else?"

"Well, there are two reasons I can think of. Either you're a man with a strong moral compass, or you're a man willing to turn over a colleague to save his own neck."

He didn't even twitch, just met the accusation in her eyes.

"You're the psychologist. I'll leave that judgment up to you."

*

"Sorry," Nadine said in that high-singing way women reserved for apologies. Juliette waited alone at a table in the bar for their standing date for Thursday happy hour. A glance showed that Juliette's designer-drink glass was empty. One piece of bruschetta lay on the oily plate before the vacant chair because Nadine was late.

"I only ordered this." Juliette waved a hand over the nearly empty dish. "Feel like more appetizers or a meal? I need something to soak up the alcohol."

"Either. I'm starving."

She pushed the remaining toast toward her and Nadine accepted it gratefully.

"Thanks."

"Ten minutes left in the happy hour menu. Want some pork sliders? They're half price."

"Sounds great."

Their server returned to check in and they ordered the sliders and a second round before the cutoff.

Nadine's waiting wine was tepid and the glass sweating. She took a sip.

A bartender delivered their second round for Nadine and something colorful for Juliette. Nadine stared at the martini glass swirling with ice chips and garnished with a bamboo spear holding three melon balls.

"What's that?"

"Cantaloupe Cooler. It's a martini with fresh melon, cantaloupe vodka and cucumber."

"Yikes. How is it?"

She leaned forward, conspiratorial. "So good!"

They laughed. Juliette made her feel almost normal. Was the ME better at working with the dead than the rest of them? Perhaps seeing the unpredictability of life daily on the autopsy table gave her the capacity to enjoy each moment. But Nadine preferred puppies.

They clinked glasses. The Cuban pork sliders arrived, and the aroma of spicy barbecue sauce made Nadine's mouth water.

Juliette adjusted her three sliders on the narrow plate, peeking beneath the buns at the coleslaw topping the pulled pork. "I found a new fishing spot."

Juliette had thus far been unsuccessful in tempting Nadine out to join her fishing in a kayak, or on her morning jogs.

"It's up in Bradenton. Robinson Preserve." Juliette raised her voice to be heard over the thumping music. "Great spot with views of the sunset over a little island."

"Sounds peaceful." Nadine lifted one of the sliders, crunching through the cold coleslaw and the soft tangy pork.

Juliette finished her first slider. "Oh, and I almost forgot. I heard something about that new detective."

Her attention shifted from the sliders to Juliette. "Me too."

"Really?"

"Yeah. You first," said Nadine.

"He moved here to take care of his brother."

That was both admirable and troubling.

"Going blind."

Nadine lowered her sweating glass of Pinot Grigio. "Demko?"

"His older brother. Danny Demko. He's only in his early forties. He and his younger sister have had to move him from his house into an assisted-living place."

"That should take a weekend. It doesn't require quitting your job."

"Well, that's what I heard."

The detail about his brother was sad. But as a story, it stunk of excuses.

Juliette lifted her next slider, took a bite and paused for a second before continuing. "Anyway, he's definitely recently divorced. I'm still trying to find out why. Ten years on the force, started in Property Theft, worked Narcotics, promoted, and six with his gold shield, so I figure he's between thirty and thirty-five. Lives in a house off Bee Ridge Road. Sometimes he bikes to work."

"Dangerous," Nadine said. Bike riding in a city was always dangerous, but when you took into consideration the age of many of the snowbird drivers, it bordered on suicide.

"I'll bet he got on the wrong side of a superior," Juliette said, and picked up her last slider.

"Maybe."

"What did you hear?" asked Juliette.

Nadine resisted the urge to spill all the dirt she had on Demko, unwilling to spoil his reputation. She, more than most people, understood the importance of reinventing yourself.

"I heard he wanted a fresh start."

Didn't they all deserve one of those?

Juliette lifted her glass. "Here's to that! Anyway, he's cute as hell." She clinked Nadine's wine goblet.

Nadine forced herself not to shift under Juliette's steady stare.

"Do you like him, Juliette?"

"Me?" She sounded incredulous. "No! I thought *you* did."

"I haven't thought about him that way." That was a lie. Should she tell Juliette that he'd kissed her cheek? About the energy between them?

Telling Juliette something personal changed their relationship, might lead to deeper revelations. Nadine's skin prickled a warning.

Beyond being easy on the eye, Demko had a great body, killer blue eyes and the voice of a radio DJ. Plus, he made her shiver all over with just a touch. Add to that, he was a man who caught murderers and locked them up. She wasn't sure if that part was arousing or if the fascination was the sort that a moth holds for an electric light.

"Well, he's thinking of *you* that way. He can't keep his eyes off you."

"Stop it."

"No. He's smitten."

"That's a great word, 'smitten.'"

The ME finished her appetizer, then turned to her second martini. Nadine hoped she wasn't driving.

Juliette glanced around for their server. "Where is she?"

Was she going for three drinks?

"You want to get a table?" Nadine asked, deciding to ease them out of the bar.

"Another round."

The remaining melon ball floated in Juliette's drink like a dead body.

"I let him take me to lunch," Nadine admitted.

"Really?" Juliette was agog. "How'd that go?"

"We went to see his boxer puppy at doggy daycare. Who knew being slobbered on and having your shoes chewed could be so uplifting?"

Juliette laughed at that. Then her gaze turned serious. "How goes the homicide investigations?"

"Moving along. No suspects. Spouses have solid alibis. Seems like a stranger."

"A serial killer."

"Early for that moniker," said Nadine.

"You're not worried about a repeat?"

She was. The only thing that allowed her a moment's peace was knowing there were six years between her mother's first and second couples in the series.

"Always a worry."

"Well, I know you guys will catch him."

That optimism again. It was so pure. Nadine could almost believe that Juliette was a kindergarten teacher, surrounded by innocence and potential all day, instead of up to her elbows in the gore associated with death, violence and tragedy.

"I'm sorry about the autopsy. Glad Demko noticed and got you out."

Nadine flushed, her pulse relaying the shame to her cheeks and neck.

"Was that your first one?" asked Juliette.

Admitting that seemed preferable to revealing the recollections seeing those bodies caused. She pondered sharing something about her past and then took a long swallow of her wine.

Think time was important, especially for liars. You had to keep track of what you had said.

"It's complicated. I had some stuff happen when I was a kid. It's why I went into this field."

Juliette's thin brows lifted, making her look like a puppy that didn't quite understand her master.

"I wondered about that," she said.

"I'll tell you about it sometime." That was the alcohol talking, because Nadine doubted she would ever tell anyone. Ever.

Juliette gave her a long stare over the rim of her Cantaloupe Cooler.

"You aren't alone. I'm a good listener. If you want to talk about anything… beyond work."

Nadine laid a hand on Juliette's forearm. She was not a hugger. That much might be obvious. But this woman was so normal and such a godsend. Nadine had only ever intended that Juliette be an acquaintance, someone to talk work with. Now she wished she could open up to her. Tell her everything. But that would crush any chance at keeping even a casual friendship.

Wouldn't it? She was so tempted to take a chance.

"Thanks, Juliette. I appreciate that."

Nadine drew back and lifted her empty wineglass and gave Juliette's a clink.

The restaurant had emptied as the after-work crowd departed following the early birds. The soundtrack switched to a mellow jazz. When the season wasn't in full swing, even Thursdays could be quiet.

The high table they had was private, tucked behind the bar and against the wall. Juliette set her empty plate aside. The wine and food combined in Nadine's bloodstream, bringing a quiet indolence.

"Oh, and to add to my wonderful week, Nathan Dun asked me out."

Juliette barely managed not to spit the melon ball in her cheek across the table. She used her hand to cover her mouth, and once she got hold of herself, she said, "I saw that coming."

"Did you? I should have. But I've never encouraged him. And what is he, forty?"

"I don't think he's that old. It's the hairline, makes him look older. Did you let him down easy?"

"Not really. He got nasty, so I told him not to bother me again."

"Ouch."

Nadine debated telling her what she'd uncovered about Dun's family history but stopped herself, as it was too like her own. The odd coincidence of that unsettled her again. The wine and food now turned heavy and foreign in her stomach.

"I feel sorry for him," said Juliette.

"Then *you* go out with him."

"No, I'm not ready for all that. Boyfriends tend to lead to husbands and kids."

"Not for you? That's fine. Not everyone wants a family." She didn't. Time for someone in her genetic tree to take an ax to it. Or better still, burn it down.

"Well, it's more than that." Juliette fiddled with her empty martini glass and glanced about for the server once more. "I think I'd better switch to seltzer."

"Good idea," said Nadine.

Juliette finally met her gaze. Her eyes were brimming with tears. Nadine braced for whatever bombshell was about to drop.

"I'm adopted."

The psychologist inside her brain clicked into action. That was not a reason to be wary of matrimony. Having abusive parents would be, or divorced parents, but not adoption.

"I see," Nadine said in what she hoped was a friendly, open tone.

"Listen, if I tell you something, can you keep it to yourself?"

Nadine's immediate thought was *I wish you wouldn't.* Instead, she said, "Sure."

Juliette pressed her lips together, as if making up her mind on whether or not to say something.

Nadine tried to look safe, which was one of her fallback expressions. Her eyes shifted to the exit and back to Juliette as she resisted the urge to leave. The socially appropriate thing was to listen, but a warning buzzer was sounding in her head.

Across the table, Juliette nodded, reaching a decision. "My birth mother is Lola Gillerman."

Juliette paused as if that name should mean something to Nadine. Was that a celebrity or something?

"Actress?" she guessed.

Juliette exhaled and squeezed her eyes shut. Nadine had guessed wrong. Whoever Gillerman was, Juliette was having difficulty getting it out. Time slowed as terrible possibilities filled Nadine's mind.

"I'm sorry. I don't recognize the name."

Juliette looked around, checking that their conversation would remain private before leaning in.

"Right," said Juliette. "You're not from the Panhandle. Still, it was national news. So… my birth mother… she already had three children before me, all six and under. Her boyfriend told her that he didn't want kids and broke up with her. I guess she was desperate to keep him."

Nadine braced for a human tragedy. Was this the woman who drove her children into a lake and told police that some carjacker took her car with the kids in the backseat?

She could not swallow past the overwhelming horror.

Juliette continued. "They were all in the car, the backseat. She turned around and shot them, all three. My older brother, twice in the chest. My sisters in the stomach and neck. Then she drove them to the hospital emergency room."

This revelation struck like a hammer to a bell, vibrating through her in waves. Nadine thumped back in her seat, bracing her hands on the table.

Juliette's mother was a murderer. She had killed her own children. Nadine's nostrils flared as she tried to catch her breath.

"She told police that some random guy shot them and that she sped to the ER to try to save her babies. But witnesses testified that they saw her driving below the speed limit. Taking her time while the kids all bled to death. My brother was alive when they got to the hospital. He didn't make it through the night. My sisters were both DOA."

Nadine could not disguise her horror. "Juliette, I'm so sorry."

"Yeah, well, as you can guess, my mother's story didn't hold up. Besides the witnesses, the bullet angles were all wrong. She was convicted of three murders."

"Terrible."

"Yup. She didn't know she was already pregnant again, with me, until after her arrest. I was born in prison during the trial and seized—that's what they call it, 'seized,' like I'm contraband. I didn't know any of this until high school."

"Have you ever contacted her?"

"My mother? No way. She murdered my family."

Why did it take her until this moment to draw the correlation? Nadine had been so caught up in Juliette's story that she had forgotten her own. Was this what they had in common? Was this why she was drawn to Juliette?

Her next thought was even worse. The possibility of two daughters of convicted murderers sitting at the same table, working for the same county, was remote. Add to that Nathan Dun's employment here and the chances dropped again. Now they were working a case on a serial killer who seemed to be imitating her mother's murders. The panic grabbed her and squeezed the air from her lungs. She glanced around the bar, sure she was being watched.

Juliette's eyes brimmed with tears once more as she continued, oblivious to Nadine's rising panic.

"My mom murdered my brother and sisters because they'd become an inconvenience. The only reason I'm alive is that she couldn't kill me without killing herself. But she would have, eventually. I'm certain. Anyway, I don't talk about this. People I've told in the past, well, they get weird."

Why hadn't Nadine anticipated that a medical examiner might have a personal tragedy that led her to that profession?

"Anyway, I thought, wondered… I mean, you deal with survivors of brutal crimes as part of your job, you're trained for it. If anyone could understand, it'd be you."

Nadine didn't answer, just stared at her, her mouth hanging open.

"That's terrible, Juliette. I'm so sorry."

Her brain was trying to tell her something past the shock.

If this was not coincidence, then what? A second possibility dawned, dropping like a 747 out of the sky. Juliette had been in Sarasota only a month. She might have tracked her down, followed Nadine here. This woman might be the one messing with her.

Suspicions burned like acid contacting bare skin. What was happening?

"Juliette, I'm sorry. I… My stomach is upset."

"You're sick?"

Nadine nodded, certain she had gone pale and likely looked ill. She needed time and distance to sort this out, see if her suspicions were just her narcissistic tendencies making Juliette's tragedy about her or if there was something here.

"Did I say something wrong?" Juliette now looked befuddled.

"No. Not at all. My stomach is acting up."

Nadine wobbled as she collected her purse. She didn't know what to believe, so she followed her instincts.

"You're going?" asked Juliette. Her mood was evolving from confusion to offense.

Nadine began tossing out excuses like beads at a Mardi Gras parade.

"I may be coming down with something. I don't want to get you sick."

"Do you want me to drive you home?"

"No. I can drive. I'm sorry to spoil our happy hour. I'll see you tomorrow." Belatedly she recalled the bill and drew a twenty out of her wallet and pressed it to the table beside her plate. She shouldn't have looked at Juliette but did. She was crying.

"Nadine. What the hell?"

Clearly, Juliette was not buying her excuses. But Nadine hustled away, moving at a fast clip between the tables. She didn't stop until she was home with the door locked and the dead bolt engaged.

CHAPTER NINE

Small world

On Friday morning, Nadine had just opened Demko's updated report on the victims' timeline. They hadn't spoken since yesterday when he'd kissed her cheek and she'd challenged him. Had she done it to sabotage their relationship before it ever started? Her therapist told her she cut people out if they got too close. But really, wasn't that wiser than letting them abandon her?

Like her father had done to her? Damn it, the therapist was right.

Her phone rang at the same moment a knock jolted her attention from the screen to the doorway.

"How's the profile coming along?" asked Crean.

"Fair." She ignored the call, sending it to voicemail.

Crean folded her arms and gave Nadine a critical stare. "You look tired."

"Do I?"

She nodded and drew out her phone. "Did I show you the new litter?"

Her supervisor stepped into her office turning her phone toward Nadine. The screen showed nine wiggling, whining balls of fluff, with brown bodies and black snouts. Some pups had white stripes down the center of their adorable faces, many had white paws, and all had black button noses and wrinkly foreheads.

"Aww! Puppies," she said, wishing she could pick one up and press it to her face.

"My husband raises them. These are three weeks old."

"What breed?"

"Boxers."

Boxers. That was the breed that Demko owned.

"I can hold one for you. If you like. They'll be ready at eight weeks."

This time her smile was genuine. "Maybe. Anyone else around here adopt one?"

"Yes, in fact. Clint Demko had the pick of the last litter, two patrolmen got others, and one of the assistants over in personnel wanted the runt. My husband is a very responsible breeder. The new kennels are cleaner than my house and he certifies all the puppies."

"Hmm. Let me think about it."

"Don't think too long. They go quick."

Crean left her to her work.

Nadine turned to her voicemail, and the one missed call. It was from Nathan Dun, who said that he'd spoken to Juliette and mentioned how she had treated him.

"Funny thing," he said. "I saw you leaving your building yesterday with Detective Demko. Interesting that you'll have lunch with him, but not with me. Would you like to talk about that? Call me."

Was he watching her? Her coffee rolled over in her stomach, turning sour as old milk.

Her instinct was to erase the message. But something told her not to. If she decided to lodge a complaint with personnel, she would need that recording as evidence.

Nathan Dun didn't look dangerous. But neither had Jeffrey Dahmer.

Think, Dee-Dee.

She could go see Crean and explain what had happened, or call Demko again, or she could visit Osterlund and file a complaint. She shelved that last idea. She wanted to call Juliette. But she'd abandoned her when Juliette needed her. That was either the wisest or cruelest thing she had ever done. She wished she knew which.

The hollow ache of isolation yawned. How could she protect herself if she reached out?

She held the phone a moment longer and then lowered it to the cradle. She'd keep the message, avoid Dun, and stay alert. For now, that would have to do.

As lunchtime approached, Nadine rejected the impulse to phone Juliette. There was something too coincidental about them working in the same county. The fluke raised all her internal alarms.

She wondered if their easy relationship resulted from Juliette's optimistic personality, or because they were cut from the same genetically damaged cloth.

Should she tell Demko that Juliette had kayaked in Lido? No, because it was a coincidence. Hundreds of people kayaked all over the place here.

Nadine's earlier web search revealed that Juliette's birth mother, Lola Gillerman, was serving consecutive sentences for the three murders of her own children, in the same maximum-security facility as her mother. Same prison, different wing. Gillerman wasn't on death row and might be released after another twenty-five years. Meanwhile, Nadine's mom sought to avoid the death penalty by dangling the lure of identifying additional victims to authorities. According to Arlo, her attorney's offer of Arleen's cooperation in the resolution of an unspecified number of unsolved cases, in exchange for a reduction of Arleen's sentence to life without parole, was still under consideration.

Nadine tried to refocus on her workload. She ate alone at her desk, then struggled through the day, thankful at 5 p.m. to switch off her desktop and leave the office.

Once at home, she scrolled to the Wiki page on her mom and the second pair in the series of her crimes. They found Louder and Henderson days apart, and the cases were not immediately connected. They were the only couple not killed together. Lacey died first and was discovered floating on a turn in the St. Johns River. They recovered Forest Ranger Henderson in his patrol jeep on Cows Bluff Road. They were not killed on the same day or the same place. How did they connect them?

Nadine compared the photos of Gail DeNato, her mother's first female victim, to Debi Poletti, the young woman recently murdered. Then Charlie Rogers, Gail's partner, to David Lowe, Debi's lover. The women were similar in appearance. The men were not. Like all her mother's female victims, Debi had medium-length brown hair and the same dark eyes. This killer seemed also to be targeting the women. Taking special pains to make them suffer most.

Nadine knew two things in that moment. First, that she would go visit her mother and, second, she would regret that decision.

After another web search, Nadine learned the procedure for visiting at Lowell Correctional Institution and that procedure scared the hell out of her. First, she had to fill out an application, and, the worst part, she must include all her personal contact information so the officials could return the form to her home address.

The corrections facility homepage directed her to request a form for visitation from the inmate.

Which brought Nadine to another problem. How inclined would her mother be to assist the daughter who had turned her in and testified against her?

Late in the evening, Nadine wrote her mother a short, clinical letter requesting an application for visitation.

*

On Saturday morning, she drove north and secured a postal box in Tampa. The larger city was over an hour up the coast, which was not far enough, but at least her mother would not learn where she lived from a Sarasota cancelation stamp.

After checking that her key worked to open her new box, she returned to the counter, holding the letter addressed to her mother. The older man behind the counter smiled.

"Key work all right?"

"Yes. Perfectly."

"That's fine." He extended his hand for the stamped envelope. "You like me to mail that for you?"

*

Over the next week, Demko's attentions diverted to two homicides, with a suspect in only one in custody. He and Detective Wernli began building a case against a convicted felon for the murder of her longtime boyfriend and simultaneously worked a homicide investigation of a man found in his vehicle with a fatal gunshot wound. On Wednesday, this last death investigation led to the arrest of two fourteen-year-old males. Nadine's work evaluating these two suspects, and assessing a mentally disturbed woman prior to her sentencing for arson, occupied much of her time.

Demko called on Thursday, frustrated at having no leads in connection with the double homicide on the bay. She shared his frustration but preferred that to discovering her suspicions of a copycat might have some basis in fact.

Demko dropped in on Friday to let her know they'd cleared both Poletti and Lowe's spouses of the crimes. They went over his timeline for the victims' whereabouts the day of their deaths. He still had no suspects and that clearly aggravated him. Add to that, he was getting heat from both his supervisors and the local news, which had discovered that the couple had been found nude. The salacious detail fueled speculation. Nadine knew that reporters were pressing for the release of the death certificates and cause of death.

On the first Sunday in August, Nadine found her mother's reply waiting in the rental box, along with three additional letters. The tsunami of mail had begun. Nadine planned to cancel the postal box as soon as she got approval for visitation.

She didn't regret writing, yet, because she was anxious to help solve the double homicide and that meant investigating her copycat theory.

Her hands trembled as she opened the first envelope. Inside was a letter and the application for visitation. She set aside the message and filled out the form right there on the counter of the postal place and mailed it. Now all she had to do was wait anywhere between two to six weeks for approval to land in her home mailbox to discover if she was cleared to visit her death row inmate.

Nadine feared that once Arleen recognized that her daughter needed something from her, she would lead Nadine on for as long as possible to get as much as she could in return. The trouble was, Nadine couldn't anticipate what her mother would want. It worried her.

But if she could learn why her mother picked each victim and how she subdued couples, including men who were bigger and stronger, Nadine might gain insight into how this new killer operated. This was assuming that Arleen would tell her the truth. This was a huge leap, as her mother lied about most everything.

Nadine vowed to keep her guard up and be ready.

As if anyone ever could be.

Which was more terrifying, trying to get herself into the mind of a serial killer or visiting her serial killer mother on death row?

Nadine returned to the letters, unfolding the opened one, when she noticed the young guy behind the counter watching her. No doubt he was curious about the customer who received nothing but correspondence from Lowell Correctional.

"If it's a pen pal, it's not worth the thrill," he said. "You should drop him. Those guys are in there for a reason."

"It's my mom."

He paused at this and lifted his phone. She got a bad feeling that he was going for his camera, so she left the box wide open and hurried out of the shop.

It was 8:45 a.m. and she still had another hour's drive home.

She had spotted a breakfast place down the road, the kind that made their own bread and where guests lingered at tables. Nadine headed there and a few minutes later she sat in a quiet booth with her bagel and coffee. The other customers seemed to be mainly retirees planted at their booths and one mom hurrying her teenagers, who were dressed in sports uniforms.

Beside Nadine, the purse of letters sat like a coiled snake. Would it be better to read all the letters before seeing her mom or walk in without all that crazy swirling around in her mind?

The clinical psychologist inside her knew that there would be much to learn from her mother's writing. The daughter of the killer didn't want to open herself up to more pain.

Nadine deferred, focusing on her breakfast. The meal sat in her stomach with the hard knot of dread.

"Fine," she said, and opened her bag to retrieve the envelopes arranging them by postal mark.

After sorting, she began with the first letter, which opened with *My Dearest Baby Girl.*

The letter bubbled with manic delight at her request to visit. Her long hope that they would reconnect. Nadine wondered if her mother had ever spared her a thought until writing this. As a rule, narcissists didn't consider the needs of others, unless it was for exploitation to meet their own.

Unlike their interactions in real life, Arleen did not call her stupid or ask her if she was stupid. Instead, her questions were designed to reveal as much about her daughter as possible.

Where did she live? Was she married? Kids? Arleen asked if she was a grandmother. How many children? What were their names and ages? The exchange drove home to Nadine that Arlo had done as she asked and avoided sharing details about her with their mother.

Arleen asked for photos, which she would never get, and told her all the things she might long to hear. She thought of Nadine each day and prayed over her before bed. She wanted them to be good friends and was now ready to be the mother she couldn't be on the outside. Without the distractions, presumably of killing people, she had focused on self-improvement. She was a new woman.

If only.

Nadine set the letter facedown and picked up the next.

"More coffee?"

Nadine startled, both hands going up involuntarily.

"I am so sorry," said the man beside her table. He held a carafe and wore a neat button-up shirt, apron and an anxious expression. "Deep in thought, right?"

He refilled her cup.

"Would you like some half-and-half?" He reached in the pocket of his apron for the plastic containers.

"I'll get it from the station."

"Sure. Sorry to startle you."

He cleared her plate, and Nadine returned to the letters. The second one began with *Dear Dee-Dee.* In this, Arleen had lost some of her exuberance. There was a clear concern that her daughter might be changing her mind about visiting.

She should. She really should. But Nadine could not let this new monster escape, and would do all in her power to help Demko catch this unsub. Something connected this killer and her mother. She hoped that she was not that connection. It was narcissistic to think so, but she had learned from the best.

In the third letter, Arleen, as Nadine now called her, reminded her that she was cleared to visit, though she had yet to receive that clearance. She reminded her to bring fifty dollars in small bills for use in the vending machines. She reminded her to bring photos of her family and home.

Nadine knew why she asked. From such images, she could make a fair guess at the amount of money her daughter made, based on the furnishings she saw. Information she could twist and use to get to Nadine.

How many times had Arleen told Nadine that, if anything happened to her, Nadine would end up in an orphanage? That she was too stupid and ugly for anyone to want to adopt? The fear of that future had kept Nadine mute for years.

Nadine glanced back to the letter. Did she remember her eighth birthday, when Arleen had brought her a yellow cake with pink icing, and how the bakery had written *D-D*, instead of *Dee-Dee*, on the top? Wasn't that funny?

Nadine remembered that cake and the birthday because it was on a Sunday night. Arleen had come into the kitchen dressed in only a bloody bra and panties, holding a box from the grocery store bakery. The next day, the family of Lacey Louder made a plea to the public. The twenty-four-year-old mother of three had gone missing. They later found her body floating in the St. Johns River. The following week, the papers reported the brutal slaying of a forest ranger in his jeep. Leave it to Arleen to get her to remember not just one of her murders, but two, by reminding her of her eighth birthday.

Nadine slapped down the letter. She hadn't even seen Arleen yet, and already her mom had made her return to her childhood.

She balled her fists on either side of her coffee as she struggled to slow her breathing.

Damn her and damn whoever was doing this. She didn't want to remember that kid who had picked up that bag on her eighth birthday, seen the blood, smelled the urine and said nothing.

Nadine stuffed the letters in her tote. Sometimes she thought she'd survived her upbringing. Other times she feared she never would.

Her mother wasn't going to help her, and any information she gained would come at a cost.

Then she remembered a person who might know more about this case than even her mother. She sat back at the realization. Was there a way to get case details without paying a visit to death row?

CHAPTER TEN

Two birds with one stone

Nadine looked up the district attorney's office. Not hers, but the one that had handled her mother's case. The lead prosecutor had been a man named Bradley Robins. But she found no employee listing under that name. After a phone conversation, she discovered that Bradley Robins had retired. They declined to furnish his home number.

Regardless of the roadblock, she needed to find a way to get Robins's contact information. The details he might remember could change everything for her current case.

Meanwhile, Juliette did not text about their weekly happy hour date, and Nadine had not contacted the ME since her own rude departure last week. Guilt nipped as she left work early and found permission in her home mailbox to visit the correctional facility. She was certain this turnaround time broke a governmental record.

On Friday, she had no messages from either Demko or Juliette all day. She called Juliette but got no answer. At home, she read all the rules and directions on the prison website in preparation for her visit.

The following morning, Nadine rose exhausted by the night-mares, which had returned after a long absence. Garbage trucks, plastic bags filled with something that was still moving and now new terrors, including metal detectors, pat downs and vicious drug-sniffing canines.

Her weariness did not stop her. She was determined to do everything in her power to help Demko find this unsub, who, she was more certain by the hour, was copying her mother's crimes.

She drove up to Lowell, Florida.

At the prison, Nadine learned that the inmate's uniforms were pale blue with a white stripe down each leg, making the convicts look like surgeons attending a formal affair. Nadine waited for her mother to pass through the prisoners' entrance, her heart drumming. She wiped her sweaty palms on her skirt for the second time as another unfamiliar face appeared. Her skin prickled and an invisible band constricted her breathing. Her mother was unpredictable, dangerous and possibly held answers that she needed. But there would be a price to pay.

Finally her mother stepped through the entrance. Arleen Howler looked older and thinner, but Nadine was not fooled by appearances. Her mother was still deadly.

"There's my girl," Arleen said upon recognizing her, establishing both a familial bond and a dominant position in the same instant.

They didn't allow physical contact, which suited Nadine fine. Hugging her mother was nearly as repellant as taking out one of Arleen's trash bags.

Two guards, both large and female, stood in proximity. Nadine noted that other inmates did not receive this special attention.

Nadine shifted as Arleen swept her with an assessing gaze.

"Well, look at you." Arleen's fist went to her hip. "Don't look like a scarecrow now, do ya?" Her mother referred to the name her classmates had used to bully her. "Nice clothes. Expensive. You're still too thin, though."

Nadine regretted her choice of designer shoes, soft charcoal-colored A-line skirt and the fitted white blouse. The outfit had seemed subdued, but to her mother, it looked like money. She hadn't said a word and already made her first mistake.

"What's the matter? Cat got your tongue?"

"Hello, Arleen." The words, her first to her mother in more than a decade, were stiff and her voice hoarse. She cleared her throat.

"They strip-search you?" asked her mother.

"No." Was that a thing for every visitor? she wondered. "Just a metal detector and a pat down afterward."

Arleen took in this information. Nadine recognized too late that she had made her second mistake, feeding her mother details she intended to exploit.

"Then they have dogs to check for cell phones," said Nadine.

"And drugs."

"Right," she said, lifting a finger at the point her mother had made. "I have to go through that again if I use the restroom."

"'Restroom'!" The word struck her mother as hilarious and the cackle she emitted chilled Nadine's blood.

They stood in the visitors' area inside the prison. Around them, other inmates greeted their guests. Gradually the incarcerated and their family members settled on the stools anchored to the rectangular tables. The configuration reminded Nadine of her old high school cafeteria. The similarities between this institution and that one was not lost on her. But here, the vending machines were full of junk food instead of water and healthy snacks.

Before the soda machine, Nadine watched a young inmate greeting an older woman and a shy toddler, who clutched a tattered yellow blanket. Arleen noted the direction of her gaze but not the subject of her attention.

"Did you bring the money?"

Nadine reached into the pocket of her skirt. It held the three items permitted for visitors to the correctional facility: one car key, her identification and fifty dollars in small bills. After a moment of fishing, she extracted the money from the rest and held it between them.

Arleen snatched the cash and spun, hurrying toward the vending machines, leaving her daughter to follow. Nadine reminded herself that the letters and the endearments were all a means to an end, a way for her mother to meet her needs. They had nothing to do with her daughter. If Nadine wanted her needs met, she'd have to meet them herself.

Her mother straightened out a five in preparation for insertion into the bill reader, and Nadine recognized she had already lost control of the situation.

She reached the soft-drink machine and plucked back her money out of Arleen's hand. Arleen turned on her, bloodshot eyes blazing. But she restrained herself. Her face flushed from the effort.

"I was just getting us something. What do you want? Anything you like."

Arleen was generous with her daughter's money and the prison's machines. Nadine's mouth twitched but never lifted to a smile.

"What I want is information. I'll buy it from you for this."

"Sure. I'll tell you anything."

Nadine snorted and turned to the machine. "What would you like?"

Arleen made her selection and Nadine pressed the buttons. The plastic bottles rolled out, one after the other.

"What else?"

Her mother picked two kinds of salty chips and three types of chocolates. Nadine gathered them all in her arms, like a squirrel, then returned to her table. Only when Arleen took her seat across from her did she pass over one soda.

"What about the rest?" Arleen asked, holding her smile and her temper. Her greedy eyes fixed on the hoard.

"After a bit."

The struggle was closer to the surface now. Nadine suspected her mother would like to call her "stupid, worthless, a mistake." Make demands. Issue ultimatums. But that might drive her daughter and the chocolate away.

A burly guard moved from one table to the next, pausing at the end of the row closest to them. Nadine felt his stare and met it, narrowing her eyes on him. He looked away.

When she looked back, her mother's smile was genuine. Her voice was low, and there was approval in it. "Now there's my girl."

The folded bills and change grew damp in Nadine's sweating palm. The room stunk of unwashed bodies and mildew.

She lined up the offerings of food and placed the money beside them. "I want to know about the murders."

Arleen rolled her eyes and pushed off the cafeteria table, keeping one hand firmly on the soda bottle.

"I don't talk about them."

Nadine made a show of gathering the chocolate and standing.

Her mother lifted her free hand in surrender. "Okay! Geesh. What're you doing, writing a book or something? *My Mother, the Monster?*"

"Why I need to know isn't important."

"You married, Dee-Dee? Because if you are, then you understand about men. What they're like. They sure have no use for a woman with kids."

Her mind tripped back to Demko. He hadn't called this week or stopped by, just a few texts, all business. That was good. Right?

Yesterday she'd called to ask how he was and immediately wished she could delete the message. He hadn't called back.

But somehow it made her feel sad and lonely. She knew she was sending mixed signals. She wanted to connect and also feared doing so.

"I'm not here to talk about my life."

"Oh, right." Arleen opened her soda and took a swig. "You hear from Arlo?"

"No," she lied. She didn't want Arleen using Arlo to get to her. He had enough trouble without that.

"He writes me about once a week," said Arleen. "You heard about his parole?"

Nadine shrugged, noncommittal.

"He got denied, again. Four more years on his sentence. You could help him out when they spring him."

"I plan on it."

Arleen took another drink. Nadine watched her guzzle the liquid. Her mother lowered the bottle and made a sound of satisfaction.

"How about those chips?"

"Did you hunt for your victims in a territory or did you target couples?"

Arleen stared at her with dark eyes, her mouth pulling down at the corners.

"Long time ago. I don't recall."

Nadine tore open the chip bag and Arleen folded.

"I'd pick them first. Follow them and watch where they did it."

The chips slid across the smooth surface of the table.

"Then I'd wait."

Arleen's vocabulary often led people to underestimate her and they did so at their peril.

Her mother, the spider, she thought.

"Did you always attack the man first?"

Arleen finished opening the snack bag and peered inside, selecting a large chip, and lifting the golden oval to admire.

"Yeah."

"Why?"

"I wasn't there to get my lights turned out. 'Course I hit them first."

"You killed them *in* the water?"

"Yes and no. Nearby. I liked it best when he was watching when I cut her." She closed her eyes and sucked in a breath, her shoulders rising as she savored the memory. Then the cold eyes met hers. She was smiling now. "I'd drag them in, usually as they were bleeding. Once, I used a Taser."

She had, on her third victim, Nadine knew. Lacey Louder. The working girl sleeping with a forest ranger, one of Lacey's regulars.

"If you're in water, it's easy to clean up. Wash off the blood. Two birds with one stone."

"Where was the knife?"

"In my hand or my shorts with the rope. It was small. You seen it. The carpet knife. Had blue paint on the handle from when we painted Arlo's room."

Nadine had seen it in her mother's tool kit in the carport. The curved blade was not small.

"Your clothing was bloody. I saw them."

"So, you did look in the bags. I hoped you might."

Was it Arleen's wish to pique Nadine's interest? She'd succeeded in engaging her curiosity and then her revulsion. One week after her eighth birthday, a new bag of garbage waited. Smaller, because it contained only Arleen's clothing, since she had killed the ranger in his jeep.

"I testified that I did in court. Don't you remember?"

"I didn't listen. Blah, blah, blah. Too much talk. Should have listened to that part, though."

Was that thrilling for her mother, knowing her daughter had looked inside? Did she think the sight of the blood would arouse or repel Nadine? Either thought sickened her.

"And you deposited the bodies right there?"

"'Deposited'? No. I cut him and watched him thrash. Then I'd work on her, while he drank his own blood. Sometimes I'd give him a little shove, see him lose his footing, fall in the mud and wallow, like a pig. But one of 'em grabbed me, and I had to stab him in the stomach to get him to let go. So, after that, I cut and stepped back to enjoy."

"Didn't they call for help?"

"Sometimes."

"Did anyone come?"

She smiled and slowly shook her head. "Nope."

"Did you have a type?"

"What do you mean? Like what sort of people did I pick?"

Nadine nodded. Arleen worked on her chips awhile before answering.

"That's easy. I took homewreckers and the miserable scumbags who left their wives and kids at home while they fucked around."

"Did you target him or her first?"

"Both. I worked with most of 'em. The carpet store. The marina. That whore lived in the trailer park. Got to stay home all day, while I was out cleaning swimming pools. Ranger Rick was always dropping by in his work vehicle, along with others. She told me that he was gonna leave his wife for her. The skank. I hate homewreckers."

Why didn't Nadine know that Lacey Louder lived in their development?

Arleen continued talking. "And you know how I found the last pair. Don't ya?"

Nadine did know. Shank was a classmate. White was Arlo's dealer. Arleen knew them both. But how did she know they were sleeping together?

"Did you follow them?"

"'Course I followed them. It ain't difficult, Dee-Dee. All you have to do is go where people fuck. Then you sort out the fumbling teens and the professionals. The married ones usually come in separate cars. Nice ones. They pick out-of-the-way places to be alone. That works for me. Quiet. Remote. All perfect for killing.

And you know they're cheating, because if they weren't, they'd be home in their own damn beds instead of rolling around in the back room or the backseat. Sinners!"

Murder was a sin, too, but Nadine kept that to herself.

"Those bitches. Just like that bitch that stole my husband. Soon as I had kids, he started cheating. Men are men. So, I blame the women. If you take what's mine, you pay the price."

Nadine leaned in. "What was the other woman's name?"

"What do I care?" She smiled then, a look of satisfaction that gave Nadine a chill.

"Dad moved in with her?"

"Run off with her, more like. Left us flat. No child support. Zip! And I wasn't the only one he owed money. He ever turns up, he owes me a buttload of cash. Men are animals."

Nadine thought of Demko and felt a shock of realization. Was this the real reason she had not told him of the similarities she'd seen? Because she didn't trust not only him, but any man, with the possible exception of Arlo? Her mother had been feeding her an anti-man rant for as long as she could remember. Suddenly Nadine felt cold right down to her soul.

That tore it. Arleen was not silencing her any longer.

She was telling Demko everything she'd noted on the similarities between the double homicide and her mother's crimes at the first opportunity. She would not let her mother's poison prevent her from doing everything she could to help him solve these murders.

"You know how many men I slept with when you kids were little? How many made me promises? Then I'd mention you kids, and they'd turn into magicians. Poof!" She used both hands in an exploding motion. "They'd disappear. Men want us for one thing, and it ain't to have kids."

Nadine rubbed away the chill that lifted the hairs on her arms.

"It's your job to survive, Dee-Dee. That's what nature intended. Get what you need when you can. You gotta defend them from trespassers. Be tougher than they are, and you are, Dee-Dee. Trust me on that. You are."

This was the kind of toughness that Nadine had tried to crush. It was that part of her that asked questions like, *"How much can I get away with?"* and told her, *"Laws were for losers."* It was her mother's voice, the voice of true evil, whispering in her ear.

Nadine continued with her questions, trying to learn all she could about Arleen's method of targeting her victims and probing to see if there were any obvious triggers prior to each kill. The why and who were as important as the where and when. Understanding those could help her make connections between Arleen's homicides and this new killer or they could eliminate Nadine's copycat theory.

Arleen had the chip bag up to her lips and poured the remains into her mouth.

"Why the long gaps between the murders?"

"Busy with work, men and you kids, mostly."

That didn't quite fit. She'd been busy with all that when she'd killed each one of her victims.

"You killed eight people."

"They convicted me for eight. Put them out of their damned misery. Save their wives the cost of divorcing their ass. One of them widows even got insurance money. You know that?" She drummed her greasy fingers on the tabletop. "Did them a favor."

The implication hung between them. Were there more than eight? Nadine resisted the diversion.

Arleen smiled. "How about a chocolate bar?"

The ease with which she went from speaking about murder to asking for sweets turned Nadine's stomach.

Nadine pressed her lips together, aware her mother's attorneys were working on a plea deal involving additional murders. Nadine needed to know. Not for the case, but for herself.

"Arleen, are you saying that you killed more than eight people?"

She snorted and rolled her eyes. "You think I woke up twenty-five years ago and picked up a knife? That what you think?"

This was a secret dread for Nadine. She always wondered, and even allowed herself to speculate on occasion.

"Who was the first?"

Arleen gave her an enigmatic smile, but no answer.

"Did you always use a knife?"

She turned her hand over and motioned with her fingers, demanding food as payment.

Nadine dropped a chocolate bar into her mother's palm. Arleen took her time peeling the wrapper. She sniffed the chocolate. Her eyes closed.

Nadine took the instant to glance toward the door, wishing she could leave, knowing she couldn't. Not yet. When Nadine looked back, Arleen's stare pinned her.

"Tough, isn't it? Gets claustrophobic. This here, today, is the closest I've been to free air in fourteen years. Now my own daughter treats me like some caged monkey. You ought to be ashamed. What do you do out there that gives you the right to judge what I done?"

Nadine was ashamed every day, but not of this. Of her.

She redirected. "The others?"

Arleen ignored her daughter and gnawed on the chocolate bar. Her teeth were stained yellow like the teeth of a rodent. Nadine didn't succeed in hiding her revulsion.

This was getting her nowhere. If there was a trigger, Arleen hadn't revealed it. And the only obvious common thread between the victims was that they had fallen under Arleen's notice and she had learned of their affairs.

She looked again toward the exit and considered walking away. Then her mother could fill that post office box with unopened letters, and she could get clear of her again.

"I had others. A few. They never did connect them to me, and they can stay cold cases, for all I care. They aren't going to come speak to me, they can go to hell."

Nadine faced her mother. Had Arleen noted her inattention? Perhaps rightly assumed Nadine considered leaving—and so she had told this final secret to keep her interested?

"Couples?"

"Most. Not all. Burned one in his bed. Used what was left of the whiskey and his matches. Soaked his shirt, dropped a lit match. He woke the fuck up then. Ran around screaming like a human torch."

"When was this?"

"Let's see. It was hot. And it was between when I worked at the carpet place and when I dumped that whore at River Forest Park."

Nadine sucked in a breath. No one had ever attributed this death to her mother.

"Did they determine it was arson?"

"It wasn't arson. The inspector said he burned himself up. Not even a cold case. Accidental." Arleen chuckled and reached for one of the remaining chocolate bars. "What about you, Dee-Dee? You ever think about it? What it feels like?"

"No."

"Thought maybe your interest was personal. You killed yet?"

Yet. As if the killing were only a question of *when* and not *if.*

"I'm here to talk about you. Not me. You," said Nadine.

"My favorite subject." Arleen laughed, the sound hoarse and grating, like a rasp on dry wood.

"Do you know the arson victim's name?"

"'Victim'?" She snorted. "Ha."

"Name?"

"Clem or Mel, I think. He lived at the trailer park there. Don't you remember? No, you weren't even in kindergarten yet, and

I was working at that carpet-cleaning outfit until I got caught stealing. You know that cocksucker left that money out there as a test. That's entrapment. Bastard."

The name popped into Nadine's head. "Milo Strickland?"

"Yeah!"

"Did you tell anyone, a detective or therapist, about any of the other people you killed?"

"'People'? He was a mean old drunk who screamed at Arlo. I did his family a favor. The state too. They were going to put him in a home. The whole neighborhood should thank me. Not a person there was sorry to see him go. Did them all a favor."

"You mention that arson to anyone else?"

"I said no, didn't I? You deaf? Quit now, you're like a broken record."

Nadine quit. Arleen finished the next snack: salty vinegar-flavored chips. Her mother had said no, and maybe that was the truth.

And maybe not.

Nadine returned to the reason for her visit. If she could refute her suspicions, she could put the notion of a copycat to bed. And if she confirmed the parallels, she'd need to tell Demko.

If they could catch this killer, everything could go back to the way it was. Then she could cancel that damned post office box and drive south.

"Did you do anything to the women? Leave any marks, for instance."

Arleen's eyes glistened. "Like what?"

"Cuts or gashes. Something you did to each one of them?"

Arleen sat back and folded her arms. Her smile broadened. She sucked air between her upper teeth as she regarded Nadine.

"Don't recall."

"Arleen. Of course you do."

"You're like them now. Aren't you? Want to know what I done. Why I done it. Why you want to know all of a sudden?"

Nadine hesitated. She was not telling Arleen of her suspicions or of the current double homicide. So, what plausible reason could she offer?

"I'm trying to understand you."

Arleen's laugh echoed her skepticism. "Right. Then why not ask about the others? The ones no one ever pinned on me."

Nadine blanched. *What others?*

Nadine tried to retain her focus and redirected. "I'd like to talk about the couple murders."

"Well, I don't."

They faced off, Arleen blocking and Nadine looking for any cracks in her mother's defenses. "What are you, a cop? You wearing a wire, Dee-Dee?"

She should be. "No wire."

"How about you get me another soda and some more of those chips?"

Nadine's legs wobbled as she made the trip to and from the vending machines. On her return, she handed off one bag of chips and another soda.

"You know they'll strip-search us as soon as we get through that door. Make sure you didn't pass us anything. But you could give me that twenty. I might get it through."

What would twenty dollars buy in here?

"That's illegal."

"Shit," her mother said, and sat back with her chips.

"The marks?" Nadine asked.

She snorted. "You know I killed one by accident. First man I ever killed. Just went over to talk. He owed me money. Wouldn't pay up. Kept sayin' he was out of work. Meanwhile, he was dealing. All cash business and giving us nothing."

Arleen was leading her off track. But Nadine could not resist the bait.

"Name?"

Arleen pressed her lips tight. Should she push her or move on? Nadine judged her mother's expression and decided she needed to find the name another way.

"What happened?"

"He told me to go fuck myself and I stabbed him in the stomach. Then in the neck. Bled all over everything. We were outside on his driveway, fighting, like always. Afterward, I used a hose to clean up the blood. It rained, too. That helped."

"His body?"

"Buried it. Not too far from that hooker that landed at Hontoon Island State Park. But far enough. They listed him as missing. He owed folks. Not just me, but the wrong sort."

Nadine thought her mom fell into the category of "wrong sort."

"Police figured he skipped town. They're still looking for him." Arleen's smile was wicked and self-satisfied. "Good luck with that."

"Did you use your car?"

She shook her head. "His. Stuffed him in one of those big tubs where he kept his camping gear. Then I hosed down the outside and put him in his truck."

"Wasn't he too heavy to lift?"

"He was. But I was stronger then and I had help."

"Someone helped you move a dead body?" That was a big ask. "Who?"

"Guy."

"Guy? Your brother?"

"No, I called some stranger named Guy. Of course my brother. We drove out there and buried him. Used his shovel. Was gone all night. Covered with bug bites and dirt. When I brought his truck back to his place, we swam in his pool. Then we left."

"Didn't they question you?"

"Sure. But not for more than a week. I was cutting lawns then. Scratches and dirty fingernails wasn't anything to bother about. And he wasn't dead. He was missing. And he owed me money, too. I told them they better find him, because I had kids to feed. They never bothered me again."

"What about Guy?"

"What about him?"

"Was he questioned?"

"I don't think so."

Arleen chugged a third of her soda, then lowered it to the table. "Easier to let the water take them. So, I did that from then on. But it's nice to know *that* one is just where I left him."

Nadine sat in uneasy silence as her mother smiled.

Finally Arleen snapped her attention back on her daughter.

"I learned two things that night. It's safer if you don't know the guy, and it takes a long time to bury a body."

Nadine believed her mother had learned something else that night. Her mother enjoyed killing. This was not what she'd come here for. She led Arleen back to the first couple murder. "This was before the two from the carpet place, DeNato and Rogers?"

Arleen snorted and lifted her drink.

"So, you dropped Gail DeNato, Charlie Rogers and Lacey Louder in the water. But not Drew Henderson."

"Geesh, Dee-Dee, you got them all memorized? All right, put this in your book, it's a kick to watch him realize what I done. See that light come on in his brain when he understands two things—he's bleeding, and I'm going to kill his bitch before his eyes. But it's quick. Too quick. And sometimes the water would take them, and I couldn't see it happen."

The pause stretched as Arleen sipped at her soda, waiting.

"See what happen?"

"The moment they see that I did this to them. That I killed them, and they can't stop me. The rush… there is nothing in this world like that moment. So, I started thinking, what if I took them somewhere more private? I could make that moment last."

"You're talking about torture."

Arleen rolled her eyes. "These women are scum, Dee-Dee. They don't see us at all, except to spit on us. Think they're so much better. Mean bitches and homewreckers. I done the world a favor. Believe me."

Nadine sat in numb silence at her mother's outburst, not sure if she had gleaned anything useful or if she had just added to her own anxiety. Was this all tied back to that other woman? The one who ran away with her father? But Arleen had said she didn't just wake up twenty years ago and start killing. Had she started with an easier target?

A child? *Please, not a child.*

"That first one was a bitch, too." Arleen shook her head.

Nadine perked up. First kills were often personal and there would be much to learn from her mother's initial murder.

"How old were you the first time?" Nadine asked.

"Young. And it was easy. Never looked back."

"How young?"

That smile again and the lips pinched firmly shut. Arleen shook her head and released a sigh as if completely content.

"That one is only for me."

"Was it one of the couples? The ones you were convicted for?"

"Nope."

"You said the one you buried was the first."

"I said the first man."

Nadine blinked. She knew her mother's attorneys were offering a confession in exchange for a reduced sentence. She knew the offer was to close more than one case. Was this unknown person, the first woman, the first victim, one of those on the table? Was the man whom her brother helped her move the other?

A worse possibility struck. How many more?

Nadine changed course.

"And the last two?"

The last two were her classmate Sandra Shank and Sandra's pimp and dealer, Stephen White, the final victims. It was a long list. First was Charles Rogers and Gail DeNato, coworkers at the carpet store where Arleen worked for more than two years; next, Lacey Louder, the single mother who lived in their development, and then her regular customer, Ranger Drew Henderson. Next came Michelle Dents and Parker Irwin, her mother's boss at the marina on the St. Johns River and the mechanic she regularly slept with in the houseboats Arleen was then ordered to clean. Four couples and now Nadine had learned of an unknown man and an unknown woman. Were there others?

All she knew for sure was that Sandra Shank and Stephen White had been Arleen's last, because of her daughter.

Arleen leaned in. "You curious about what I did to her, your classmate? They wouldn't let you hear it in court. But maybe you read about it since, or do you remember me being gone? Took 'em together at his place. Had them for days. Left him for the ants, staked out behind the barn near the manure pile."

"The what?"

"I worked in the stables at that place up in Ocala. Remember? Took care of horses and took care of that cunt from your school," she said. "I kept her in a cage, the little bitch. Teach her not to mess with my family. Not so tough then, I can tell you. Had her for days before I remembered that we had a hay delivery coming Tuesday. Might have had her a month or more, if not for that damn hay." She smiled at the fond memory of torturing a seventeen-year-old girl.

The pair had been found dead by police several hours after Nadine reported her mother in connection with Sandra's disappearance.

This was her fault. Nadine had told her mother what happened, about the taunts at school and the broken phone. She had unleashed this monster of rage on Sandra Shank.

"Didn't the owners hear her?"

"Owners were up north for the season. You remember? Just me and the caretaker, and he drank. Plus, he was deaf. He never came out to the stables. Had the run of the place. Me and the horses that they didn't bother taking back up to Virginia with them." Arleen glared at her daughter, narrowing her eyes. "Are you crying?"

Nadine lifted a hand to her cheek and found it wet.

"Shit, Dee-Dee. Don't ask me stuff and blubber about it. You have to be tougher than this." She shook her head, gazing off across the room before swinging her attention back to Nadine. "For a minute there, I thought you understood. Thought you were like me. Maybe you already killed one and you wanted to hear from me that it was okay or maybe how to keep from getting caught. But you aren't tough enough for this."

"Tough enough to murder an innocent girl?"

"'Innocent'? That's a laugh. And you know exactly what she was. Tell me your life didn't get better with her gone? Them others never dared bother you again. Did they?"

They hadn't. School had gotten better until her mother's arrest. Then it was far worse.

"And if that's all you think this is, then you'll never know."

"I'm not a killer."

"But you could be. You're like me, Dee-Dee. You've got my blood and you are out there. You can continue what I started."

Her mother reached across the table and captured both of Nadine's wrists.

"No physical contact!" The shout came from one of the guards.

Arleen released her hold. Her hands went to her lap. Nadine's wrists tingled as if scorched. When Arleen spoke again, her voice was hypnotic.

"You got a killer instinct. All of us got it. Born with it. And you are good at getting what you want." She motioned to Nadine's ammunition, the remaining single candy packet and the empty wrappers. "But if you don't let yourself be who you are, if you go around scared all the time, pushing down your natural instincts, you'll never know how it is. What it's like to do what we do."

"I don't want to know."

"Sure you do. You're curious. Everyone is. That's why all the girls in here want to talk to me."

Before and during the trial, Arleen insisted she was innocent. Nadine found it interesting that her mother now owned her crimes. Was that because being a serial killer gave her a certain gravitas in here?

"You should tell someone about the other murders. The ones you were never convicted of."

"Screw that. I don't need you to write my story, Dee-Dee, if that's what you're doing."

As if Nadine wanted to pin her title and reputation to that.

"Did you tell anyone about the man you buried? The one who owed you money?"

"Tell who? Check the records. I ain't had no visitors. You all abandoned me when I got locked up." She chugged her second soda and slapped the container hard on the tabletop. "I tried to get the FBI down here. Heard they were interviewing people like me. Doing some big research project. But I never did see them. You know why? Because they don't include *women* in their studies. I've written them. That's how I know. It's despicable." She threw up her hands, raising her voice. "Fucking men!" She slapped her hand on the table, making the empty bottle topple. The crack brought a guard in their direction. Arleen did not notice or, perhaps, did not care. "How fucked up is that? We're half the population. It's like the damned medical studies. They study men's heart attacks by the million. Then a woman walks into the emergency room telling them that she's sick and they tell her to go home and take a nap. Guess why? We ain't in the damn studies!" She pointed at the closest male guard. "Sexism. That's what it is."

And like Pavlov's dog, the guard made his approach. Her mother seemed oblivious, now on a tear.

"Lower your voice, Arleen."

She didn't.

"Fuck him!" She waved a dismissive hand at the corrections officer, who now stood at their table, arms folded.

"Settle down, Howler," he said.

Her mother drummed her fingers on the table as she spoke to the guard. "It's bullshit. Not including us. I killed more than that guy in California and more than the guy up in Green River. Way more than that cannibal guy."

All the examples she used were old. It seemed Arleen had made a study of the killers caught before her incarceration.

"But they're *all* famous. You know why? Two reasons. First, they all got a cock." She stared at the guard's groin. "Second, they all got cool names."

"Up," said the guard.

"I can't do nothing about the cock. But I can give myself a name. *Night Slasher!*" She turned to Nadine. "What do you think, Dee-Dee?"

Another guard arrived. Arleen laughed as they pulled her to her feet. She'd worked herself up into a rage. Nadine sat frozen as they dragged her mother away. Arleen went with them, shouting obscenities about men.

After the door closed behind them, the room was so quiet, Nadine could still hear Arleen shouting. She stared at the remaining unopened package of chocolate and the empty soda bottles, now on their sides. All the folded money was gone.

She stood, the stares of every inmate and their guests on her as she walked from the gathering area. It was not until she cleared security that she began to shake. Nadine cleared the last security check and sat on the curb of the hot sidewalk, head in her hands.

Instead of details on the couple murders, she had added two bodies to her mother's grim list of homicides. A man she had buried and someone, a woman or girl, whom Arleen had killed when she was young. How young?

Every single thing about this interaction had been horrible. Nadine felt as if Arleen had sucked away her life force, leaving her with the crushing weight of obligation to solve these murders as well. But she'd need help and that thought terrified her.

Had she learned anything useful? Yes. Arleen had worked with or lived near all female victims. And she had targeted them, just as Nadine feared this new killer was doing.

Nadine pushed herself up, brushing away the bits of gravel that clung to her palm. When she reached the parking lot, the stench of mildew and unwashed bodies still lingered in her nostrils.

She paused to breathe fresh air and spotted someone just ahead of her who looked familiar.

She squinted in the bright sunshine. The man leaving Lowell Correctional before her was Detective Clint Demko.

CHAPTER ELEVEN

Skin in the game

Nadine called to Clint across the prison lot a moment before some part of her brain re-engaged.

"Detective Demko?"

He turned and she suppressed the urge to hide, because seeing him here meant that he would also see her. She wanted to know why he was here but didn't want him to have the same information. It was too late to retreat. Demko had already spotted her and looked taken aback. She had caught him off guard, judging from the expression of bewilderment and his fists pressed to his hips. Curse his sunglasses for hiding his eyes. His brows lifted and his mouth hardened. He wasn't happy to see her.

"Nadine? This is a surprise." His smile seemed tight at the corners.

"Yes. It is."

"We could have ridden up together," he said.

Up until this minute, she had been ready to tell him all she knew. Now she paused.

Why was he here?

"I'm sorry I didn't return your call. I dumped my phone in a swimming pool at a home invasion yesterday and had to get a new one. I just got your message this morning."

"I see."

"What brings you up here?" he asked.

"Psych evaluation." Partly true, as she did evaluate her mother. "You?"

"Parole hearing."

"Ah," she said, nodding. They didn't do parole hearings on Saturday, and it was very doubtful that she would do a psych evaluation on the weekend, either. They were both lying, and even as she accepted his bullshit excuse, she recognized that he was doing the same. Neither of them called the other out. Both wanted to keep their secrets more than they wanted answers.

But Nadine planned to dig further into Detective Demko's past to see who among the inmates he might know.

Why hadn't she seen him in the visitors' area? Could she have missed him in her preoccupation with Arleen? Had she noticed anyone? Just vaguely. Why didn't he see her, then? She had walked right up to the vending machines, past most of the families and prisoners.

Had he been somewhere else inside the prison?

"You this way?" He motioned in the direction opposite Nadine's vehicle.

"Over there." She pointed.

"Oh. Everything okay with you?"

"Yes. Fine." She did not like this new awkwardness between them.

"My cell number is the same, despite the new phone."

"That's good. I have it."

She noted that he was rocking from toe to heel and back again, eager to be gone.

She glanced toward her car, which seemed miles away.

"So, I'll see you at work?" he asked.

Would he? "Oh, yes. Of course." Nadine nodded, though they had made no plans to meet, and after seeing him here, she was not anxious to see him again. Not until she got some answers. A cold spike of dread tore through her as she recognized he would also be searching for answers, and he was a professional at that job.

Had he been here to visit her mother? Did he see her with Arleen and change his mind?

He looked expectantly at her and she realized she had missed something.

"What was that?" she asked.

"I wondered if you're free tomorrow. I know Molly would love to see you again."

He'd been in her office last week, but that seemed a lifetime ago.

"I'd like that." What in the wide world was she doing?

"Great. We'll pick you up at eleven for brunch. We'll have to go somewhere with an outside table, since dogs can't go inside."

"Where do you have in mind?" she asked.

"The French café on Main is good, or there's that gastropub on Lemon."

Nadine could walk home from either. "Let's try the French place. Their bakery is amazing. I'll meet you there." *Because I'm not getting into your car.* She knew it might be an overreaction. But she didn't wholly trust him.

She imagined a police report for her homicide. *She seemed to have known her attacker.*

Not this girl. Nadine didn't think Demko was a killer, but he was flashing signs of deception. And she wanted to know why he was really visiting this prison.

"Oh, all right," he said. "I'll reserve us a table. Eleven okay?"

She nodded.

"See you tomorrow."

Nadine held her smile as he took both her hands, then leaned in to kiss her cheek, trying and failing to staunch the longing in her heart and the heat ignited by his touch. He moved back and away, taking four steps before turning to wave. She waved back. Then he headed off toward his vehicle.

Had she just accepted another date? What was wrong with her?

*

She had a three-hour drive to consider why Demko was up at Lowell. None of her reasons were good ones and all pointed to him being a liar. Takes one to know one, she thought grimly.

Was this just more crazy? At the Fruitville exit off I-75, Nadine pulled into a drive-through for dinner and drew out her phone. No calls from Demko.

When the car behind her blasted its horn, she tucked away her phone and placed her order.

A little less than an hour later, her tires crunched over the crushed shells lining her driveway. Inside the door to her cottage rental, she paused, hand still on the door latch, as she glanced at the main room. All the dinette chairs were stacked, one upon the other, in the center of the glass surface. The narrow coffee table balanced on the couch arm like a teeter-totter. The television was on. None of this was as she had left it this morning.

Every hair on Nadine's body stood up.

Someone had been in her house.

Was someone still in there? She dropped her takeout meal and backed up, hand still clutching the latch as the other gripped her keys.

Nadine's vision blurred and for a moment she was afraid she would pass out. Was it one person or more than one? Images of the Manson Family darted like an arrow through her brain. She shuttered, freezing cold in the ninety-degree heat.

Help.

She needed to call help. Looking about, she saw no one. Nadine fumbled in her purse with sweat-slick hands as her vision faded at the periphery. Where was her phone?

Was she going into shock?

Nadine's knee hit the planking and the pain jarred her attention back to the open door. Why was she looking for her phone, when there might be someone watching her?

Run away, whispered her survival instinct.

Nadine stared into the yawning maw that had been her portal to safety. Someone had invaded her personal space, violating her without ever laying a hand on her.

Her breath now came in trembling pants, but she was breathing. She could see. The fear was morphing into fury.

Who would do this? Who would dare?

She squatted and searched her purse, finally gripping her phone. She held it in two hands, as if it were some holy chalice. Her lifeline, a chance to bring help, if she could muster her voice back from the small desperate hole where it now hid.

What is my passcode?

Nadine blanked out that information, and it took precious seconds to remember to use her fingerprint to unlock her device.

Once in the phone app, she somehow successfully dialed 911. When the dispatcher asked, "What's your emergency?" she gasped and sputtered.

"Hello? This is emergency dispatch. Please state your emergency."

"I need help. I... Break-in."

"Yes, ma'am. You are reporting a break-in. Is that correct?"

"Yes."

"Are you alone? Is there anyone there?"

"I don't know. I don't know if they're still here."

"Yes. I understand. Please move to a safe location or somewhere where you can lock the door. I'm sending a unit to you. I'll stay on the line until they arrive."

"Thank you. I could... I'm... I could lock myself in my car."

"Yes, ma'am. Do that. Let me know when you are in your car."

Nadine fumbled with the keys, setting off the panic alarm, before finally releasing the door lock.

Once inside, she used the remote to lock all doors. The air was already stuffy inside. She started the engine, turning up the air conditioner.

"I'm in the car." Nadine hardly recognized her own voice.

"Where is the car located, ma'am?"

"My driveway beside my house."

"Please tell me the make and model of your vehicle."

The dispatcher asked Nadine more questions. Exact location of her house. What made her believe there was a break-in? Were there any pets inside the home? Was Nadine employed? And then Nadine realized the woman was keeping her talking and breathing until help arrived. She was grateful.

Sirens screamed, growing louder.

"I hear them!"

"That's great. I'll just hold on here until you see an officer. I informed them that you were in the car. Wait for them there. Do not go out to meet them."

Two units rolled up. In a matter of minutes, they had her out and away from her Lexus and in the street, out of sight of her cottage. Both of the first responders waited with her until a third unit arrived, followed by a familiar undercover police vehicle. She recognized the driver.

Detective Clint Demko stepped into the street. Of course he would have heard the dispatch call and officers responding to her address. Apprehension tingled, blending with relief at his appearance. He adjusted his belt, which shared his service weapon and prominently displayed shield. Then, spotting her, he headed in her direction.

Demko took hold of Nadine's arm and led her back to his vehicle. There, he faced her, gripping her by both arms, perhaps because he noted that she was unsteady on her feet.

He spoke over her to the officers. "Go check the house."

They approached her front door with guns drawn. She watched from the street as they entered. It was a fearsome sight. She waited as the minutes ticked past and her heart raced. Who could have done this?

"You're all right," said Demko, still holding her forearms, supporting her.

She was so grateful for his presence. But Nadine's teeth were chattering, and she couldn't even tell him so.

One of her neighbors pulled out of her driveway and drew parallel to them. She rolled down her window.

"What's going on?" she asked.

"Break-in," said Demko, stepping to Nadine's right side, firmly holding on to her upper arm now with a steady grip.

"Oh, my God, that's awful! They take anything?"

"Ma'am. Move your vehicle. This is an active crime scene."

Crime scene. My home?

Nadine's neighbor blanched and rolled on, craning her neck for one last look. Nadine narrowed her eyes. She'd been through this before. Gawkers. Friends who pretended concern so they could get all those titillating details. It wouldn't take long for the neighborhood watch to be buzzing, walking in pairs, shining their flashlights into the backyard and her business. She blew out a breath, fuming now.

She glared at the cottage as if it were suddenly the enemy.

The property sat on an alley of a road surrounded by so much vegetation that she couldn't see the neighbors on either side. The fence that ran from the driveway to the backyard was only three feet tall, making it charming, decorative, but oh-so-accessible.

At the front entrance, a narrow wooden deck ran the length of the cottage and faced the drive of crushed shells. There were steps at each end. On the street side property, a gravel path navigated the three-foot gap to the unlockable gate. The backyard was small, with dense foliage and a view of the neighbor's project, a vintage airstream trailer. Someone in that trailer would have an excellent view of her place. The fence had a rear gate, unlocked, that led from the road right to her backyard.

She looked at her rental with new eyes. Yes, the exterior was still an appealing tropical blue and the front door was a funky yellow, with a vintage porthole window. But the window looked into her dining and living rooms and didn't have a curtain.

What had she been thinking renting this cottage?

She was torn between leaving her place forever and staying, precisely because someone wanted to frighten her away.

Unless the message was something else, something darker. But that was just her weird instincts again.

The officers exited her home and circled the property in opposite directions. Demko waited until they reappeared. She noticed then that he had his free hand on the grip of his service weapon.

"Clear," said the taller of the officers.

Demko drew her toward the house, stopping beside his vehicle.

"What happened?" Demko asked.

And she was babbling again, telling him about the dining room chairs, jabbering about the coffee table on the couch arm, that she never left the TV on and…

"… it was on, and the volume was turned up, and the kitchen cabinet doors were all open, and…" She could hear herself talking, but it sounded as if she stood some distance away. Her fingertips tingled and her cheeks burned.

Demko opened the back door to his vehicle and pressed her to the seat.

"Okay. Sounds like there was someone in there. It also seems like they're trying to scare you."

"Well, they're succeeding." She cradled her head in her hands, wiping hot beads of moisture from her forehead. Her skin was slick with sweat and fear. She could taste it, metallic and salty.

The officers returned. Demko stepped to the front of his car to meet them. She watched the four of them converse. He glanced back in her direction as one of the men motioned toward the house.

Detective Demko returned to explain the situation.

"Someone has been in your home. Moved things. The back slider is off the track. You don't have an additional lock on the sliders?"

She shook her head.

"An alarm system?"

"It's a rental. I have whatever was already in there."

"Listen, Nadine, I'm calling in the crime techs."

She knew crime techs processed major crime scenes. Not home invasions. There was neither time nor money for that.

"Why?"

"Might be connected to our current investigation. The public knows you are our profiler. If we get lucky, we get physical evidence."

"I understand," she said.

"I want to walk you through your place and then we need you out while they are processing. Would you like me to call someone to be with you? Is there somewhere you'd like to go?"

"How long will this take?"

"That depends. A few hours, minimum, and they're going to leave a mess. Black powder from fingerprinting, for starters. I have the name of a cleaning service. They do a good job afterward."

"Do they work on Saturdays?"

"They work anytime there's a crime scene."

Demko leveled her with his gaze. "I need to warn you…"

That was never good coming from a detective.

"What?" Nadine's mind went to various terrifying possibilities. A corpse in there? A noose hanging from her shower curtain? They'd thrown an injured animal into her tub. She wrapped her arms around her middle and rocked forward and back. Nadine's imagination was more terrible than reality.

CHAPTER TWELVE

The cat out of the bag

"The intruder placed an object on your bed," said Detective Demko.

Nadine found herself too afraid to ask the obvious question as he guided her into the cottage, where they toured the kitchen. Every cabinet drawer and cupboard was wide open.

"Take a look inside but don't touch anything. Check if anything is missing," he said.

She did as he asked.

"Hard to tell. Nothing seems missing."

She wasn't certain.

In the living room, Nadine pointed out the obvious, dinette chairs stacked, and coffee table perched on the couch's arm.

They crossed the living room past the sliding door, still off its track. Nadine glanced into her bedroom. The dresser drawers were open. The contents looked untouched, but someone had been here in her personal space, standing where she stood, looking at her intimate clothing. The sense of fear and violation struck like a slap.

Nadine shivered. Was the air-conditioning especially aggressive, or was this a stress reaction? She extended her hand, glancing down. Yes, her hands were still trembling, and her fingers were still icy.

"Ready?" he asked.

The door blocked her view of the bed. This, of course, was worse than showing her the disturbing thing because her mind immediately leapt to dead bodies, dismembered bodies, and body parts. Nadine entered first.

Something large and dark lay on the coverlet. They stopped at the foot of the bed.

"Any idea what to make of this?" asked Demko.

She stared at the black trash bag, carefully tied, and resting against her pillow. She didn't realize she was retreating until she collided with the dresser, sending the objects on it toppling.

"Nadine? What is it?"

Nadine pressed her hand to her mouth and squeezed her eyes shut. She knew what it was.

He took hold of her shoulders and gave a little shake.

"What's in there?" he asked.

She kept her eyes closed and head lowered. "I don't know."

That was true. She didn't know, but she did know what used to be in those black half-filled garbage bags. The bloody clothing belonging to Arleen and her victims. The bait she thought would rouse her daughter's killer instinct.

Nadine began to sob.

"Okay." He took her out of the room, stopping in the kitchen. "Settle down."

She tried. The effort to rein in her tears took several minutes. He handed her a paper towel to mop her eyes.

"What do you think might be in there?"

She shook her head. "Something terrible."

He glanced back the way they had come.

"All right," said Demko, "There's one more thing."

Nadine didn't think she could take one more thing.

"Ready?"

She wasn't.

He offered his hand and led her through the house to her bathroom. There, scrawled on her mirror in red lipstick, was *Legacy*.

She gasped. "What is that?"

"Does it mean anything to you?"

The only legacy she had was with murderers. She tore her eyes from the smeared writing, turning to Demko. "Get me out of here."

"Sure. Come on."

"Where are we going?"

"I need to get your statement. You all right to drive?"

If she said no, she wouldn't have her car, and that vehicle was her last safe space.

"I'm fine."

They drove in separate cars to the station, less than a mile from her house. A few minutes later, he sat with her as a detective from Home Invasions filled in the blanks in her statement. She told him truthfully that she didn't *know* what the writing on her mirror might mean, because suspicions were not fact. The report took over an hour and it was closing in on eight at night when they finally finished.

She didn't come up with many more details. Demko used his notes to remind her of several things that she had already forgotten. Honestly, it would be better if she could forget the entire thing.

With business done, Demko asked if she'd like to swing by his house.

"I need to let Molly out. She's been inside since my dog sitter left her at two."

She had no family to turn to, except her aunt, and she wasn't dumping this in Donna's lap. The closest thing she had to a friend was Juliette Hartfield. The thought of landing on Juliette's doorstep, after the way she'd treated her, did not appeal.

"Sure. I'd love to see Molly." Of course the danger of getting into a car with a strange man rose in her mind again. "I'll follow you."

"We could go in my unit."

"I'll follow you," she repeated.

He stared at her for several moments, trying to interpret, she assumed, what was meant by her refusal to ride with him. Finally he gave a nod and told her the address. She plugged it into her phone's navigation app, happy to avoid returning to her rental and the crime investigation team, crime photographers and police officers securing the scene.

She didn't want to leave her place, but it no longer felt safe. Her mind summoned an image of a black garbage bag nestled against her bed pillows. She shuddered.

Nadine reached her vehicle and followed him south to a development between Webber and Bee Ridge Road. He pulled in before a nice cinder-block ranch-style home wedged between larger residences as she parked on the street. His garage door and mailbox were both a matching cornflower-blue. The rest of his home was sand-colored. His lawn sported one small palm tree and a sprawling bougainvillea that overwhelmed the picture window with colorful pink blooms.

Nadine pulled behind him in the driveway and waited as he unlocked the front door. From inside came the near-hysterical bark of his dog.

"You own this?" she asked.

"Rental. It's a lot like the place we had outside Miami."

Nadine recognized that he said "the place *we* had."

He swung the door open. Molly bounded out, leaping and wagging with her exuberance, to greet her master. She spotted Nadine almost immediately, rushed to her, licking and leaping, before returning to Demko to sprawl before him on the step. Molly spent several minutes darting between the two of them and then dashed off to the yard, squatting to relieve herself. Demko peeked inside the door.

"Left her a little too long. Let me clean this up."

Nadine waited on the doorstep as he retrieved paper towels and mopped up the mess. Molly now explored the front yard, nose to the ground, wagging as she moved under the bushes and back out again. Demko returned with a pink leash and called for Molly. She was all wiggles and dancing on enormous feet as he clipped the leash to her collar.

"Okay to take a short walk?"

"I'd like that."

Molly had some training on a leash. She started at Demko's left side, but forgot her position often, tangling the line about them. At the end of the street, a small trail led along a drainage canal. They stepped through the fence at twilight.

To the west, the sky was orange. Demko took a knee and told Molly to sit. She did so instantly, tail thumping on the ground as he released her. He retrieved a tennis ball from his pocket and Molly howled and leapt, joy in motion.

Demko threw the ball an impressive distance down the berm beside the canal. The boxer raced off to chase her prize as Nadine strolled slowly along beside the detective. She pretended that the August heat was not overwhelming, even as her clothing grew damp. The dog seemed impervious to humidity and retrieved the ball, giving it a quick gnaw before dropping it at Demko's feet. Fetch was another skill already mastered by Miss Molly.

By the time they returned to his home, Nadine had almost forgotten where she had been earlier that day, and the reason for her visit now. The combination of the man and the dog beguiled and distracted her in the best possible way.

She hesitated only a moment before agreeing to come into his home. Demko left Nadine in the living room as he headed for the kitchen to retrieve drinks. Molly trotted along beside him and she heard Molly drinking from a bowl. Nadine glanced around.

He had chosen brown overstuffed leather furniture. The coffee table was solid dark wood with one corner gnawed by something. She suspected this was the work of his teething boxer puppy. She fingered the splintered corner and smiled.

The wall-mounted television was enormous and flanked by a high-end speaker system. Coffee-table books indicated he liked boating, kayaking and guns. A motorcycle helmet sat on the buffet beside a paddleboard, leaning against the wall beneath the dining room window. Her mind gave her a perfect picture of the man and dog paddling on the bay.

Demko returned with two bottles of water and they sat on the sofa. Molly followed to sit beside Demko, panting heavily from her exertions. Demko told her to go find her chewy, which she did, returning with a large knotted length of thick rope. Then she dropped to the rug to gnaw on the knot.

"Teething," said Demko. "The vet said that having a lot of toys would help her, but as you can see…" He lifted his pant leg and revealed a frayed sock.

Nadine asked Demko a few questions that bordered on personal but mainly were framed to pass the time. Yes, he did own a motorcycle. Yes, he did enjoy paddling with Molly, especially through the mangroves.

They finished their drinks and Demko suggested dinner. It was after nine in the evening and dark. She wondered if the techs were finished. The idea of returning to her mess of a house held no appeal.

"Sounds great."

"One car or two?" he asked.

She did not know if it was weariness, hunger or trust, but she answered, "One."

Twenty minutes later, she sat across from Demko at the Greek restaurant on Main an hour before closing. The place was crowded, but the weekend had arrived. Their food appeared, and Nadine ate the entire Greek salad and all of her spinach pie. Sometime between when the waitress cleared their plates and returned with the baklava, she grew melancholy as the possibility of a hotel room loomed in her future. Hotel rooms were lonely places.

Demko's phone sent out an alert signal. He retrieved his cell and glanced at the screen. "The crime techs have finished at your place."

"What does that mean?"

"It means that you can go home if you want to. Or I can call the cleaning crew. Be a real mess otherwise, but a few more hours for the crew to get that powder off the surfaces."

"Thank you." She wasn't just thanking him for dinner. She was thanking him for everything.

"So, call the cleaners?"

"Yes."

Demko pulled up the number and made the call.

The waitress returned with the bill and Demko snatched it so fast that she had no chance at retrieval.

She waited while he scribbled the tip and his signature; then they walked together toward his car and returned to his place. Molly was her excuse to linger. They took the gangly-legged pup on a shorter walk around the neighborhood.

Back at his home, he invited her in for a nightcap.

"Does anyone actually do nightcaps anymore?" she asked, already in his entryway.

Molly, freed from the leash, tore off into the living room. Nadine heard the squeak of the toy the dog captured. Demko paused to remove his shield and unclip the holster from his belt. He placed both in his satchel on the high table in the entranceway.

"I don't want you to head home. I'd feel better if you stayed here."

That stopped Nadine. Their eyes met and she tried to gauge his intentions.

He quickly told her that he had three bedrooms.

"One is a home office, but the other is all set up for guests, with two twin beds. My son uses that room when he visits. He's seven. My ex didn't want to move him away from his friends and his school. It's a great neighborhood." There was no difficulty in interpreting his expression. Demko didn't like being so far from his son.

"Oh, I see." She didn't see, and she had so many more questions, including why he divorced, when he saw his son, how often he drove to Miami, did she divorce him because of the evidence tampering, and did he still love his wife?

"Would you rather go back to your place?" he asked.

Nadine's stomach tightened at the thought. She had delayed facing this all evening.

Nadine shook her head. "I don't. But I could stay in a hotel."

"Of course. But my guest bedroom's all set up with clean sheets. I have fresh towels. And I make great pancakes."

She hesitated.

"I don't think you should be alone tonight."

Nadine had had a terrible day all around. She had not even had time to process her visit and her mother's crazy exit between two guards.

Demko had lied about his reason for his visit to the prison. She was certain of that. Her concern over that dishonesty pushed against her wish to know him better. After all, she'd lied, too.

She probably should go to a hotel. But she didn't move toward the door. Instead, she stepped forward into his living room.

Nadine lived alone and did not let others in. It kept her safe. It kept her isolated and afraid. She was sick of it.

Wasn't it past time to build relationships? She could do this. But what she said was "I'm not sure."

Nadine found her stomach quivering with a new emotion that could only be anticipation. She stood before him, her fingers laced and busy twisting back and forth.

"Tell you what," he said. "Let me show you the guest room and guest bath. Then we can come back here and have a drink."

He proceeded with her down the hall.

The guest bedroom had "boy" written all over it. Posters of unfamiliar animated warriors filled the space, presumably from some video game.

The curtains matched the bedspread and pillowcases. All had a pattern of gaping sharks. A large stuffed shark basked on one bed and a red stuffed octopus coiled on the other.

"My boy loves the ocean. And he's fascinated with sharks."

"Sharks and dinosaurs. Seems to grab all children at a certain age."

They toured the bathroom next. It was, thankfully, not adorned with sharks, and spotless.

"You have a very nice home."

They headed back to the living room, and Demko went to retrieve the promised drinks. She followed him to the kitchen, thinking it a safer spot to chat.

Nadine sat on a high stool at the counter as Demko opened a bottle of white wine and poured Chardonnay for her. Then he retrieved a beer from his nearly empty fridge, which he poured into a pub-style glass.

He leaned against the surface as they talked. Conversation was easier than she had hoped. She was comfortable with him in a way that did not make sense for the brief time they had known each other. It gave her hope. Hope that she could be normal.

Her mood dampened when she remembered again that he had probably lied about why he was visiting the federal prison.

She lifted her glass, knowing that she had many questions about Detective Clint Demko.

Relationships took time and everyone had secrets. What she wanted was to find someone with ordinary, boring, benign secrets. Her gaze flicked to his handsome face.

This man made her feel safe, but was that because she thought him equal to the task of protecting her or because he was dangerous?

She didn't know. But she was staying, at least until she had some answers.

"Anything new on the case?" she asked.

He drew in a long breath, eyes cast to the ceiling.

"I closed the crime scene. I've interviewed coworkers and family and got not one single lead. Nothing from the labs yet on items found on Lido's South Park. They are slow as a summer's day, and I don't have the budget for a faster turnaround. Photographs are all uploaded, and we've released the bodies." He wiped his mouth with a broad hand. "Timeline is tricky because of the tides, have to leave some of it as best guess. Man, I hate that."

Death investigations were complicated at the best of times.

"Is the press pressuring you?"

"No. I'm getting heat from my lieutenant, who gets it from the chief and the mayor. When the press learned it's a homicide, they want a suspect in custody. Bodies on the beach are bad for business."

"That should be on a bumper sticker," she said.

He cast her a warm smile. "Would you like more wine?"

Nadine lifted her glass in response.

He poured her more than a generous glass and she had nearly finished the last already. Then he lifted those bewitching eyes. He leaned in. She knew it was coming and knew how much she wanted to feel his mouth on hers. She didn't stop him. His lips were firm and warm. He cradled the back of her head and deepened the kiss. Her body quickened to his touch, unconcerned, it seemed, for the inconsistencies that troubled her mind. He tasted of hops and citrus. She closed her eyes as she savored the thrilling glide of his tongue on hers and struggled with the need to touch bare skin.

She pictured him naked and wondered if she was willing to ignore the warning signs just to have him.

Yes, definitely.

He drew back. His hair was tousled from where her fingers raked through.

"Wow."

She smiled.

"Would you like to sit in the living room?"

She would like to sit on his lap. His couch was out there, that big soft supple brown leather. And just down the hall, she imagined, he had a king-sized bed.

Sometimes you realized you were about to make a mistake and you did it, anyway.

Demko offered his hand and led the way. They settled side by side and the cushion sagged under his weight, tipping her toward him. She lifted her glass to keep from spilling.

"Oops," she said, falling against him, but miraculously not spilling a drop.

His body was firm and warm. She pushed herself upright and sipped her wine. Demko set his beer on a coaster and waited. She made him, keeping the glass up and gazing at him over the rim. Finally she offered him her drink and he placed it on the table. He slipped an arm around her waist and pressed her into the backrest. In his arms, she came alive, the need building with each caress.

When they surfaced for air, Nadine was certain that they had something here. Was it simple chemistry? But how much could they share beyond need if she didn't really know him at all, and if she wouldn't let him know her?

Perhaps attraction was a start. In time, the rest might follow.

She told herself not to overthink. This was good. A beginning. She was making a connection here. That was something.

He tugged at his shirt, lifting the Kevlar vest off his shoulders momentarily, and making a face. How hot and uncomfortable did it have to be wearing that all day?

"I'll be right back," he said, standing.

Molly followed him as he headed toward his bedroom and Nadine considered doing the same. She also considered leaving but disregarded both options and instead took another sip of wine.

Nadine glanced around the big empty living room. He had electronics, but no artwork on the walls. There were no knick-knacks, no color. His world was as bleak and lonely as hers. He was here, in this strange place, without his son.

Molly returned first. She had something in her mouth. Too small for a shoe.

"Come here, Molly," she cooed, and set aside her wine.

Molly did and then lowered her head and shoulders to the carpet dropping her prize. A brown wallet, already showing a puncture in the leather and a damp slobber stain.

Nadine made a grab for the billfold, but Molly was quicker, snatching it up. Nadine got a hold of the flopping half and pulled. Molly tugged, enjoying the game.

"Drop it," she said, and, much to her surprise, the dog did, but cards and cash spilled from the main opening. Molly made another grab for her prize.

"No, Molly! Where's your squeaky?"

The dog bounded off as Nadine scrambled to gather the contents and place them on the table. She laid out the money first and the condom. Lubricated. How nice.

It wasn't the sort of wallet that had spots for photos. But his son's picture was there, bent on the corner. It was a school photo with a background of the colorful fall foliage you just didn't see in Florida, ever. His boy had his father's stunning blue eyes and someone else's dark brown hair. It was too early to see if he would have his father's square chin or the interesting bump at the bridge of his nose. She slid the photo back into place and noticed the folded sheet of paper on the floor. It was a newspaper article, clipped, discolored, and worn on the fold lines, now open like a tent. The headline popped out at her.

Valerie Nix Sentenced to Life for Ordering Husband's Murder.

Nadine carefully picked it up and scanned the article, which detailed the conviction of a murderous mother-and-son duo. Her breathing rate sped as she read about Valerie Nix, convicted of masterminding a plan to collect 2.4 million dollars in insurance money by the murder of her podiatrist husband. Her eldest son, from a former marriage, carried out the hit. Connor Nesbitt, age twenty-four. He entered his stepfather's medical offices via an unlocked rear entrance, wearing a latex Halloween mask and carrying a loaded shotgun. Patients in the waiting room heard Dr. Nix say, "Connor? Is that you?" followed by a shotgun blast.

Paramedics pronounced Dr. Alan Nix dead at the scene. His stepson, Connor, was arrested the same day. His mother denied knowledge of the plot but was later taken into custody as her story began to unravel. The article mentioned that the murdered podiatrist and his wife had two other children, Caleb Nix and Caroline Nix, ages nine and seven at the time of the writing of this article.

Was this a case Demko had solved?

She flicked her gaze to the top of the page. There, someone had written the date of the paper in blue ink. It read: *3/19/1999.*

Nadine stared at the article as if she had found a suicide note. Then she pounded the newsprint with her fist.

"No!" The denial was there, but it didn't stick.

The fuzzy warmth, generated from both the company and the wine, drained away in the harsh slap from reality.

Why did he carry this? She did the math, subtracting her best guess at his age from the date written on the top and realized the younger son would be somewhere in his early thirties now. She swallowed back the sour taste in her mouth as possibilities rose in her mind, snakes in the garden.

Could Clint Demko be Caleb Nix? Even as she thought this, she took the next logical step. If true, the reason for the detective's visit to federal prison was clear. The maximum-security facility held women, convicted felons, some on death row. The article said that police arrested Valerie Nix. And she had three children in 1999.

Nadine had her phone out and was searching the web for Caleb Nix.

"Please, oh please…" What was she even asking for? She didn't know, but she hoped that she was wrong.

Up popped several relevant results. She scrolled and chose a link to an article written seven months after the one in Demko's wallet.

Then she scanned, listening for his return.

Caleb and Caroline Nix, the children of Dr. Alan and Valerie Nix, were in court today.

There was a photo of a woman, identified as the siblings' aunt, Melissa Demko of Miami, Florida, leading the children from the Jacksonville courthouse.

The murdered husband's sister, she supposed.

Nadine studied the photo. The boy had light hair and stared right at the camera. He had one hand on his younger sister's shoulder, guiding her along. The boy's face, younger, rounder and softer, was unmistakably Detective Demko at about age ten.

She tucked away her phone.

She needed to think. She shouldn't jump to conclusions about their current case. Demko might be a victim here.

Except he had access to law enforcement databases, to her property and to her.

Was he the one messing with her?

It would be easy to discover about her mother. Easy to learn her address, her work history, perhaps the documents that changed her legal name from Nadine Howler to Nadine Finch.

Simple to break into her place after she drove away.

And his response time to her home invasion bordered on an Olympic record. Unless he already knew.

Had he raided her home just to get her here? Or worse, in order to get physical evidence from her?

Evidence tampering—she remembered what she'd heard and what he'd told her. Nadine's gaze flicked to the wineglass beside the damp wallet, the one that had her prints all over it.

He had told her that he wasn't responsible for planting that knife in that suspect's car, but, really, she had only his word. The case had stalled. If he were a dirty cop, how far would he go to apprehend a suspect and restore his reputation?

Had he pinned the evidence tampering on a colleague? Was he about to pin these murders on her?

It was possible.

He'd moved here just before this case and gotten assigned to lead investigator.

Her mind made another leap. What if he were the killer, setting up a case he could solve? Ready to frame an innocent to be the hero.

Had he done this?

Nadine shivered at the thought.

She, Juliette and Clint all had mothers convicted of murder. She headed to the foyer, fumbling with the door locks as she heard the tap of footsteps. Too late to run.

She turned, spotting Demko's satchel. In a moment, she gripped his pistol.

Nadine slipped off the safety, pointing the weapon down and to her side.

Demko stepped into the living room, his sports coat gone. He wore a different shirt. Nadine was certain he had removed his body armor.

Bad timing, she thought, gripping his pistol.

CHAPTER THIRTEEN

Speak of the devil

"Caleb? Caleb Nix?" Nadine asked.

Demko lifted a hand in Nadine's direction. "I can explain."

"Great. Do that."

His gaze swept from the article on the table to Nadine's hand gripping his gun.

"Nadine, put down the gun."

She shook her head.

"Are you Caleb Nix?"

"Yes."

"Who's Melissa Demko?"

"My father's older sister."

"Why did you come here?" she asked.

"Put the gun down and we can talk about it."

She didn't.

Molly brought Nadine her toy, dropping it at her feet, silently asking her to take it, but Nadine kept her attention on the threat. The foyer was small, but if she stepped back, she could retrieve her purse and get him to unlock the door.

"Who is Valerie Nix?"

"My mother. Nadine, enough. Put down the weapon."

"Oh, no. You do not get to tell me what to do. You weren't up at Lowell Correctional for a parole hearing, were you?"

"I was visiting her."

"She murdered your father."

"No, she didn't murder him. My half brother, Connor, did that."

"But she had the plan. She talked him into it, didn't she?"

"Dee-Dee! Get the trash to the curb, now!"

"You're just like me, Dee-Dee."

Was she? The opportunity stared her in the face. Such a handsome face.

"It's you. Isn't it?"

"It's me, what? Nadine, whatever you think this is, we can talk about it. Just put down the weapon."

"You're the one who moved my furniture. Did you plant evidence in my house?"

"Nadine, I didn't."

She pointed with her left hand at the article on the table as Molly sat on Nadine's foot.

"Don't pretend. Both you and Juliette. Are you doing this together?"

"Juliette? Hartfield?" He shook his head, the perfect image of befuddlement.

His shoulders rose and fell as his hands hung limp at his sides. He did not look like a sociopath or psychopath with narcissistic tendencies. He just looked… confused.

"Just tell me the truth!" she shouted.

"I am telling you the truth, Nadine. Whatever you think I did. I did not frame anyone."

That was his second noncontracted denial and, according to her psychology training, an indicator he lied.

"Do you know my birth name?"

He blinked. "What? Your birth name?"

He had repeated the question, using another technique of liars, giving him time to think. But was it also a technique used by a confused man facing a threat?

Either way, for the moment, she could not trust this man.

"Why didn't you tell me?" she asked.

"Tell you? About my mother? It's not the kind of thing you talk about on a first date." His voice turned sarcastic. "I'm a Pisces who likes motorcycles and long walks, and, oh, yeah, my mother's serving life in prison for murder. Co-conspirator with my half brother. We're not close, he and I."

Co-conspirator. *She* had been that. Just like Connor. She had known what her mother was doing, taken out the evidence and destroyed it well after she had figured what was in those bags. But she'd been a minor. So, no charges. Still, she knew the truth.

Back then, fear and guilt filled her. How could she keep silent? What would happen if her mom went to jail? The battle between self-preservation and protecting others had kept her mute. She was afraid of her mother and she had been afraid *for* her mother.

"I'm going to step back. Unlock the door so I can go."

"Fine," he said, mouth tight and eyes alert.

She inched away and he moved forward. When Nadine adjusted her grip on Demko's pistol, Molly abandoned her toy and leapt before her.

"No, Molly," she said, glancing at the jubilant boxer that confused the gun for a new toy.

In her momentary distraction, Demko took her wrist in a punishing grip. When had she removed her finger from the trigger?

The gun clattered to the tile floor and Molly dropped her nose to the ground to sniff the unfamiliar object. The canine folded, the weapon between her front feet, as she made a yodeling howl. Her stub of a tail wagged, inviting one of them to engage in this new game and recapture the strange thing.

"Molly, get your squeaky," said Demko as he dragged Nadine against him, her back to his chest.

His dog dashed to the kitchen. Demko snatched up his weapon. He held Nadine by the wrist and aimed a finger at her.

"Stay here."

He marched back through the room, pistol in hand. Molly followed, head up, squeaking her toy in her jaws. Nadine snatched her keys from her pocket and headed toward the front door.

She fumbled with the door locks, releasing both, but the door would not open. Molly returned, squeaking her plastic ducky once, before dropping it at Nadine's feet. Nadine burst into tears as the enormity of everything hit her. What did she really think? That Demko could be a killer? No, she didn't really believe that. She'd let her panic overwhelm her faith in this man. Why had she immediately believed the worst?

But she knew. Her mother. Arleen's duplicity had made Nadine unnaturally suspicious. But he wasn't Arleen. Demko was a good man and an excellent detective and she'd ruined everything.

He found her there, sobbing, squatting beside Molly. She pressed her forehead to Molly's warm neck, clutching his dog with one hand and the doorknob with the other. The detective guided Nadine to her feet and she let him help her to his couch. There he wrapped her in his arms.

"It will be all right," he whispered into her hair.

The pup nudged her with her nose. Her duck toy now rested on Nadine's knee. She placed a hand on the dog's head and stroked the velvet softness of one ear.

"Good dog, Molly." Her voice croaked. She sniffed and sagged back against Demko. "I'm sorry."

"Hell of a first date," he said.

She pinched her eyes shut, squeezing out more tears.

"Doggy daycare was our first date."

He released her and gave her a look of pain that nearly broke her heart. She realized then that he'd been through this before, in Miami, when he lived under the taint of both evidence tampering and reporting one of his own. When their eyes met, she felt his weariness and sorrow ripping into her.

"Whatever you think I did, I would never hurt you."

"I saw that article and thought you could have broken in. You were tied to that evidence tampering."

"I turned in the guy who tampered with evidence."

"As part of a deal?"

"What? No!"

"I might need you to prove that."

"Okay. I think we need to hit the pause button. Are you accusing me of a crime?"

She swallowed. "No."

"Great. Just so you know, drawing a weapon on a police officer is a felony."

"Are you pressing charges?"

"I'm just trying to understand what happened here."

Yet, he didn't yell, name-call, threaten or hit. He just sat there, his expression of hurt and puzzlement tugging down the corners of his mouth.

"I'm not anxious to file a report that says I was held at gunpoint with my own weapon."

That would be embarrassing.

"Where is your gun?" she asked.

He made a sound, a humorless laugh.

"Like I'd tell you." He dragged a hand over his mouth. "Nearly pissed myself when I saw you had the safety off." He pointed toward the bedroom. "It's locked up. Should have done that when we came in. Usually, I get changed and lock it up at night."

"I couldn't shoot you."

"You sure had me fooled."

"Why couldn't I get the door unlocked?" she asked.

"Landlord has a duplicate set of keys. So I added a slide bolt at the top."

She turned and spotted the lock high on the door, above eye level, and groaned. Then she turned back to him.

"You know about my mother?" she asked.

He was silent for a moment. "Is that who you were visiting today?"

"You knew?"

"Suspected. No competency evaluations on Saturdays, right?"

"Or parole hearings."

He snorted. "Busted."

"You really don't know who my mother is?"

He shook his head.

"You are Caleb Nix?"

He nodded. "I was. Took that family name after our aunt adopted us, my sister and me. They're gone now. My cousin Danny lives here in town. He's a cellist."

"Going blind," she said.

He gaped at her.

"Juliette did some nosing around."

"And the evidence tampering?" he asked.

"Okay, I was also nosing around."

"The police ought to recruit you both." He moved away from her now and she straightened, turning so she could face him. "Any other questions?"

She shook her head.

He wiped a hand over his mouth and stood. "You want a drink?"

"Sure."

He headed to the kitchen. She expected him to return with a glass of wine, but instead he carried a high-end whiskey and two glasses, each holding two cubes of ice. He set them on the table and poured the amber liquid. Demko offered her a glass and then clinked his against hers before taking a swallow.

She lifted her tumbler and took a tiny sip. The liquid burned all the way down her throat. The heat came next.

Demko settled one cushion away on the sofa and draped himself along one wide armrest, idly spinning the cubes in his drink.

"So, who is your mom?"

When she told him, he asked the question she would expect from a detective.

"Did you know at the time?"

Nadine nodded. "I figured it out."

Then she told him about the garbage bags smeared with blood and her mom's prolonged disappearances and late-night returns. About her guilt at not calling the police sooner.

"The trash bag on your bed. Now I understand."

She drew a breath and kept going, anxious now to get it all out. When she'd finished, he'd looked at her exactly the way she had been looking at him when she held him at gunpoint.

Clint Demko was the picture of indecision.

Finally he sat on the coffee table, facing Nadine. "I'm not sure the homicides and the break-in are related. And although I can see a similarity between this case and your mother's homicides, that rope between our victims could have been there for a number of reasons."

"Name one," she said.

"Made it easier to drag them to the water. Use it as a tow behind a boat and then drop them."

"It's a copycat."

If she were right, this unsub was just getting started. Now her truth was out there, she had to do everything in her power to convince Demko and to stop this killer.

"Double homicide and a rope. Is that enough to connect them?" he asked.

"And a couple. Having an affair. Killed together with a knife and dropped in water."

He lifted his eyebrows. "Okay. Maybe. But what about the signature cuts on the ring finger and the marks gouged into the female? Did your mom do that?"

"I don't know. I was up at Lowell to ask my mother, but she refused to answer that question."

"What did you ask?"

"If she'd marked all the women with common sorts of cuts or gashes."

"And her answer?"

"She accused me of being a narc. Asked if I was wearing a wire."

"Listen, if there's a connection, we have to find it. The case is stalled. No leads, no witnesses, and little physical evidence."

"And two bodies," she said.

"Yes." His expression was grim. "Can you think of anyone else who would know?"

"The district attorney who prosecuted the case. But he's retired and they wouldn't give me his contact info."

"Who wouldn't?"

"The district attorney's office in Ocala."

He stared at the ceiling now, processing. She had another swallow of the whiskey and sputtered as her throat closed. Nadine's stomach burned at the arrival of the 80 proof and she set the tumbler aside.

His gaze flicked back to hers. Those eyes, she thought, they were the same blue as the Hope diamond and just as hard.

"Let's try again."

Demko made a single call to the police department in Ocala and had the home number of the DA in five minutes.

He used the magic words "ongoing investigation" and his title. Then he asked about the lead detective on the Arleen Howler case.

She waited as he listened, thanked whoever was on the other end of the call and hung up. Once off the phone, he passed her the number.

"Lives in Winter Haven now."

"Maybe we should drive up and see him."

"'We,' huh?" He lifted a brow.

She smiled. "Are you going to contact the detective who handled her case?"

"Can't. He's deceased. Heart disease. All they have are his case notes."

Nadine recalled the man as unsmiling, stern and intimidating. When she was a teen, he'd frightened her, so she could not explain the stirring of loss she now experienced.

Demko raised his glass, gulping the remains. She watched his Adam's apple bob and wondered if it was the alcohol, the man or the stress that made her so aware of his physical presence.

Then a terrible thought struck her. What if it were the topic of conversation Nadine found arousing?

Her stomach clenched.

"You all right?" he asked.

Had her color changed with her mood?

"You're kidding. Right?"

"Some water?" he asked.

"Sure."

Molly, sleeping at his feet, lifted her head and watched as he stood. He headed for the kitchen. When he returned with the bottle, she closed her eyes. He removed the cap and handed Nadine the water.

She took tiny sips. Her stomach accepted them, averting the crisis.

"Why did you think I was working with Hartfield to set you up?" he asked.

She told him what Juliette had confided to her ten days earlier.

"Her mother is Lola Gillerman?"

Nadine nodded, struggling to contain the tears.

"Have you been in contact with Juliette since she told you?"

Nadine shook her head.

She was so tired, perhaps a little drunk, but it was a struggle to keep her eyes open.

Demko retrieved his laptop and began his search of police databases. She answered the questions he needed to get started, sitting next to him as he tapped away on the keyboard. The arrest record for Lola Gillerman appeared, followed by her mother's image, first young and then a more current one, with Arleen wearing the baby-blue prison uniform.

"All in Lowell Correctional," he muttered.

Next flashed an image of Nadine and one of her brother, Arlo, leaving court.

Demko dove down the rabbit hole, pulling up Arlo's conviction record from a law enforcement database. He glanced at her as she sagged against the armrest.

"Your brother is also serving time?"

She yawned and nodded. "Assault."

"Sexual assault. Plea deal. Recently denied parole."

Nadine yawned again. "He's like her. If they let him out, I worry about what he'll do."

"You mean for a living?"

She shook her head. "I'm afraid he could become like Arleen."

"Because of the sexual assault."

"It's associated with serials. A commonality. And it was rape, not assault, and would have been murder, but he was interrupted. He lost his mind. And if that happened once, it could happen again."

But he used to read to me at bedtime. Her eyes were impossible to keep open.

Molly lay against the couch, her legs sprawling under the coffee table. Her soft snores lulled Nadine to sleep. She awakened to a dark room, with vague memories of being helped down the hallway.

She woke in daylight with something wet touching her face. She opened one eye and found the lanky boxer pup beside her bed, tail wagging as Molly booped her again with the cold wet nose. Nadine stroked the canine's head and neck as she glanced about, finding herself in the guest bedroom. She lay under the bedspread and clutched the stuffed shark under one arm. Her phone sat on a charger on the bedside table. Except for her sandals, her clothing was all still on.

Sunshine streamed through the venetian blinds and the phone's clock read six minutes after eight on a sunny Sunday morning. She stretched and wondered if it was too early to call the DA. She needed to discover if any of her mother's victims had suffered any mutilation similar to their current cases.

Nadine retrieved her phone and the scrap of paper with the district attorney's number and made the call.

"Hello, Mr. Robins? This is Nadine Howler."

*

On Sunday afternoon, Nadine drove Demko up to Winter Haven for their appointment to visit retired district attorney Bradley Robins at his home.

The man she recalled from court hardly resembled this paunchy graying senior. But his handshake was firm and his eyes bright. He admitted them into the modern ranch situated on one of the fifty lakes in this Central Florida community. A peek out the back showed a boat lift and water views.

"My, my, Nadine Howler. I'm not sure I'd recognize you."

When she was a teenager, he'd spent time priming her for her court appearances, helping her prepare for the sort of questions the defense might ask. She'd been a minor and only in court when she took the stand, though the trial lasted many days.

"This is Sarasota Homicide detective Clint Demko. We are working together on the double-homicide case I mentioned."

The men leaned in and shook hands.

"Thank you for seeing us, sir," said Demko as they broke apart.

Nadine accepted a bottle of water from Robins's wife, a trim woman dressed in activewear and holding garden gloves, which explained the spectacular flowers growing in front of the property.

Robins then ushered them into his study, and Nadine perched beside Demko on the sleeper before a wide coffee table. The shelves were lined with books on law, awards and certificates in gilded frames and a bass fishing trophy. A folded American flag sat inside a triangular case on a middle shelf.

"I wondered what happened to you. Criminal psychology, huh? Terrific."

"Forensic," Nadine said.

"Potato, pa-tah-to," he said.

She managed the small talk and then steered the conversation to details about her mother's case, admitting that she knew just what was reported by the newspapers and furnished by the State of Florida's database.

"You were only in court four days," Robins recalled, sitting forward in his reading chair. "Important days. But we tried to shield you from the worst of it."

Nadine had destroyed her mother's alibi and provided the physical evidence, in that black bag, tying Arleen to her final victims.

"I've read everything I could, but I wonder if you might have details not in the papers."

"Oh, well, we left a great deal out of the papers."

"Why?" asked Nadine.

"At first, to weed out the kooks and disturbed who make false confessions for the notoriety. Detectives kept some case details private so that when they caught the guy, they'd know from the confession it was their man. Or, in this case, woman."

"But at the trial?" asked Demko.

"The lead detective always believed that Arleen had help with these crimes. Specifically moving some of the bodies. He convinced me to withhold a few unique facts on the possibility that they might need them if they ever discovered a co-conspirator."

"Did you believe she had one?"

Robins shook his head. "Not convinced. But I didn't need the details to make my case. We had her clothing soaked in the victims' blood. So, we compromised."

He returned to his filing cabinet and pulled out three pocket folders and stacked them on the table.

"Transcripts," he said.

"Do you think I could make copies of these?"

"Public record," he said. "There's an office center in town. We could go together after we chat."

"That would be very helpful."

"So, a double homicide. What similarities have you seen?"

Demko took that one. "Vics are male and female. Both engaged in an affair. Killed with a blade, then dumped in water." He finished by telling him about the rope.

"Then I guess you'd best copy the binders as well." He stood and went to the closet in the office, withdrawing a file box.

"What's this?" she asked.

"Police reports. Photos of the crime scenes and body dumps. Autopsy photos."

"I thought you said that was in these." She motioned to the thick folders.

"That's transcripts and evidence. These are the photos and information not submitted in court, and everything I could get from the police. As I said, some images we kept back, out of public record."

Demko nodded.

"Always thought I'd write a book. But it turns out I'm only good at writing legal briefs. Real crime is a whole different animal." He turned to her. "I have copies of everything. I'd expect no one alive knows these crimes better. Besides your mother."

"Can you contact any of the detectives from the case?" asked Demko.

Robins shook his head. "The lead has passed."

"I heard. I'm sorry," said Demko.

"So was I," said Nadine.

"All of us were. I'm not in touch with any of the others." He turned back to Nadine. "Do you ever visit her? Your mom?"

"I have, yes, once."

"Be careful. She's dark, all the way through."

"Could you tell us about commonalities among the victims?" asked Demko.

"Boy, could I." Robins's eyes lit up and the edge returned to his features. She could see him now, the hard-hitting cross-examiner who destroyed the defense's case.

Nadine and Demko listened as Robins talked, flipping from photo to photo. She stopped him at a close-up of a victim's left hand, pointing at the missing strip of flesh.

"What's this?"

"That's Michelle Dent's left hand. Worked in the office at a marina in Deland. Sister to the owner, I think." He glanced from the photo to Nadine. "But this was interesting. All but your mother's last female victim had the same thing. A strip of skin cut from the left ring finger."

Nadine's skin stippled and she forced herself to sit still. She glanced at Demko. His face had gone grave.

"She was carving a ring in their hands. Admitted as much in interrogation. Make them remember their promises, she said. You knew that all her victims were married?"

She thought of her classmate. "Well, not all. There was Sandra Shank."

"Right. The one not given the blood ring. So, all but one married. But Shank was definitely sleeping with married men."

Perhaps this was more about punishing unfaithful men, regardless of whom they chose. Punishing men and torturing women.

"And all the men were killed while committing adultery. She was kind of a vigilante, you know. We theorized this was because your father cheated on her and then abandoned your family."

Nadine's heart banged around in her chest so hard that she thought she might have internal bruising. She met Demko's intent stare.

"If our killer made this mark," she said, "we have a serious problem because the only ones who should know about this are the investigating detectives, crime techs who took this photograph, the people in this room and my mother."

CHAPTER FOURTEEN

Couple two part one

She arrives early, standing knee-deep in the calm waters of the inlet, holding her hand up to her face as a visor while she searches for him. He's not coming, I've seen to that by punching a hole in the fiberglass hull of his boat.

She wears a ball cap, with her long dark hair thrust through the gap to cascade down her back. I can see the slim column of her neck and the inviting slope of her tanned shoulders. The delicate fabric of her top flutters transparent over bare skin and bikini top. Small nylon shorts hug her long muscular thighs. Her tiny wafer sandals sit forgotten on the narrow scrap of beach. Here, past the mouth of the river, the isolated bay nestles in a circlet of green mangroves broken only by the calm azure waters of the cove and the thin lip of fine white sand.

Now she's humming as she lifts the camera in her hands, zooming in on her target as I zoom in on mine. She hears me approach in my rubber boots and turns as I tase her in the back.

She emits a high-pitched scream as her body convulses, muscles spasming, and collapses. I keep the trigger down, prolonging her tremors, as several baitfish go belly up all around her. The electricity and the water are a bad combination. I release the button and wonder if the water is still electrified as another, larger fish rolls to the surface.

This is Arleen's progression. Her early kills were quick, too quick to savor. As she advanced, capturing her prey and spending more time became her way. This increases the risk, but also the thrill and the pleasure. For Arleen, this series took fourteen years. But I am measuring in days, and instead of enjoying my success, I am already anticipating the ones to come.

Better to stop and smell the roses, or, in this case, the acrid odor of urine staining her shorts. I stand in ankle-deep water as I worry the Taser has killed her and press my ear to the soft mound of her breast.

Bruising doesn't happen after death. Damage will, broken bones and so forth. But for bruising to occur, you need bleeding, and for that, you need a beating heart.

I hold my breath and listen. And… there it is, faint but audible. A heartbeat.

Relieved, I kick her repeatedly in the ribs and stomach. It's important that she bruises like Lacey. She rouses enough to struggle. I retrieve the carpet knife from my pocket, letting her see the blade. The widening of those dark eyes gives me a tingle, power chased with joy.

I'm not certain Arleen did this exactly, but she told me she watched their faces as they died. I like that part, too.

The blade slips into the abdominal cavity. Once, twice, and I lose count. She's making too much noise now, so I punch the steel between the ribs on one side and then the other. You can't scream if your lungs collapse and the cavities are full of blood. Pink froth comes from her mouth as I drag her to shore to finish.

I twist her leg and she rolls like a chunk of wood. Then I cut away her clothing and slice the mark on her ass. A moment later, I've removed her rings and stripped the skin from around her finger, spinning the knife in soft flesh to make a blood band. Then I loop the rope about her limp wrist and cinch it tight. A final cut severs the cord. I slice her throat, stepping back to watch as her blood spills into the clear water.

A night heron swoops in and lands on the lacework of mangrove branches. The arrival of the nocturnal bird warns me that other boaters will soon appear.

Standing in the shallows of the estuary inside the preserve, I stare out at the rippling water of the Manatee River while gripping the body by one lifeless leg. She's just meat now.

I glance back at her. She has gone luminous and pale in the morning light and I can see the slim athletic build crisscrossed by my marks. Then I see the punctures.

Wrong. All wrong.

I yank her off the sand. The body drifts in the easy current, then sinks into the water.

No air in her lungs, so she can't float. I should have thought of that. Arleen didn't stab Lacey. But I had. How many times?

Too many. Damn it. I've ruined another one. I lift her heavy camera, hurling it after her and miss.

I stow her rings and garments, washing away the blood in the warm inlet waters, then step onto the mangroves' tangled roots, never letting my feet touch the sand. My kayak carries me past the place where the body sank. But the knowledge gives me no spark of joy because my mistakes steal all my satisfaction at this kill.

CHAPTER FIFTEEN

The apple and the tree

She no longer had to sell Demko on the idea of a copycat. Their visit with the district attorney had done that.

They returned to Sarasota and collected Molly, arriving at his place with the two identical copies of all Robins's transcripts, court documents and the investigating Homicide detective's reports, now in their new binders. She went straight to work while he ordered dinner. When it arrived, forty minutes later, she didn't even notice the bell until Molly started barking. After the meal and a short walk for Molly, they both settled into reading the case material.

From their conversation with former DA Bradley Robins, they learned that her mother's male victims had either the skin sliced all the way around their ring fingers or a circular gash, cut to the bone. All of her female victims, but one, had the same mark, plus what Robins described as a semihorizontal slashing pattern on their backsides. The detectives could not determine its meaning, and Arleen had refused to explain.

"More coffee?" he said.

Demko had caught her dozing at his dining room table, the binder before her still open.

"No, I just need to stretch out."

She glanced at her phone and realized it was past midnight. Then she settled on his comfortable couch with the binder she had been reading. The next she knew, she roused to a dark room, to find Demko sitting beside her on the coffee table, attempting to take the binder she held on her chest like a sleeping baby.

"What time is it?" she said.

"After one."

"Did you read all those transcripts?" she asked.

"I started with the detectives' report, the DA's notes and the evidence he provided to the courts."

So he'd seen the photos of all of her mother's victims.

She squeezed her eyes shut as the familiar shame of association swept through her.

"I didn't finish the transcripts. But I will."

She pushed herself upright, swinging her legs to the floor. Then she scrubbed her face with both hands, trying to force away the drowsiness.

"You think your mother really went years between murders?"

"I did. But since visiting her, I've changed my mind."

"Why?" he asked.

"I was trying to learn why she made those marks, but she led me off course, hinted that there were more, in addition to the couples. She mentioned two specifically."

How many more? Nadine realized she might never know.

She repeated what she knew about her mother's attorney's trying to negotiate a plea deal for Arleen's confession to additional unsolved murders. She relayed what Arleen had said about the arson death, an unknown woman and about killing a guy after an argument over money. "She also said her brother had helped her move that one and bury him near where Lacey Louder was found in Hontoon Island State Park."

"When?"

"She wouldn't say."

"What's your uncle's name?"

"Guy Owen."

"You know his whereabouts?"

"I haven't seen him since I was a kid."

"Is it possible he knows about the marks?"

She thought about the times she remembered her uncle living with them. He and her mother had been close, no doubt. Close enough to move a body. Had he helped her with more than one?

"Yes. It's possible. Demko, do you think he could be her co-conspirator?"

"Hmm. Maybe. I'll try and find him. You know his date of birth?"

She shook her head.

"Anything happen in 2002 that you recall? Any new men?"

"Why 2002?"

"I've found a few missing persons reports that popped up in Ocala Forest that year."

In fall 2002, Nadine had turned ten. She remembered her mother had been working cleaning swimming pools and her uncle had visited around Easter. He'd stayed through the end of the school year. She and Arlo called him "Uncle Tinsel" because he had a silver front tooth. But he hadn't been around for Arlo's birthday in August. A guy she worked with moved in around September, but that didn't last long.

"My uncle was there in the spring. And she had a breakup with a guy around Thanksgiving."

Another bleak holiday, she remembered. Arlo had taken her to a fast-food joint, as Arleen had been working.

"Name?"

"I don't know."

"After that? What about in 2004?"

"Well, that was the year she killed Dents and Irwin. You think there were other murders around then?"

"Maybe."

Nadine thought back. "She lost her job as a pool cleaner. Started working at the marina in Deland for Dents. We had to move."

"And men?"

"I don't know. There were a lot of them. Maybe a new one around then. Let me think." Nadine remembered a stranger in the kitchen when she stepped into the room for breakfast.

*

"This your girl?" asked the shirtless hairy man standing before the open refrigerator in their kitchen. He was huge and even his shoulders were furry. He wore only sagging blue boxers. His cheeks were dark with stubble and his hair was long and fixed in a single braid.

Nadine pulled up short. It was the first day of school and her mom had promised to drive her.

"What?" Arleen appeared wearing her underwear and an overlarge T-shirt. Her hair was mussed, and she had a red mark on her neck.

Nadine wished Arlo were here. But he'd moved in with his girlfriend and she hardly ever saw him. When he was here, she didn't mind the men in the house. But now she felt scared all the time.

"That's Dee-Dee." Her mother glared at her. "Well, come in and say hello. This here is Bo."

"Hey, little lady." He turned to Arleen. "Ain't she a peach."

"Yeah, and if you're thinking of takin' a bite, I'll cut your dick off."

He laughed at that, but as her mother pushed past him to retrieve the milk, the man's gaze traveled over Nadine in a way that made every hair on her body lift in fear.

Nadine backed out of the room.

Her mother's voice followed. "Hey. Where you going?"

Nadine had left the house with her backpack, no lunch and no breakfast.

Her feet pounded on the sandy path that led out of the trailer park. Pounding, pounding.

*

"Okay. That's enough for now." Demko relieved Nadine of the binder, thumped it on the coffee table and stretched.

Nadine blinked, giving herself a mental shake.

"You all right?" he asked.

His expression changed from concern to something more intimate as he took her hand. Her smile faltered as her heart rate accelerated. He did that to her with just a simple touch.

"Want to have a swim?" he asked.

"It's dark."

"Best time. The stars are all out."

"And the bugs."

"It's a caged pool. Water is eighty-eight degrees."

That did sound lovely.

"I don't have a suit."

"Even better."

She placed a hand on her hip, trying and failing to ignore the surge of sexual energy his words stirred.

"You do remember that I tried to shoot you."

He laughed and rose to his feet. "That was yesterday. Besides, I like dangerous women."

That comment made her flush and it took some restraint not to step into his arms.

Dangerous women. Like his mother? That thought spoiled the urge to reach for him.

"Sounds fun."

She followed him to the master, where he opened the drapes to the sliders, revealing the covered pool deck. The water glowed pale blue from a single submerged light. He rolled open the glass door. Warm air crept into the room with the hum of insects and the trill of tree frogs.

He tugged off his T-shirt and stepped out of his slacks, dropping both on the floor. His chest was bare, and he wore only loose boxers.

She stripped down to her lace bra and underwear.

He offered his hand. "There's a step down."

Demko flipped off the pool light. They crossed the deck, hand in hand. Molly followed them out. The stairs at the shallow end led them into warm water. Nadine glided to the opposite side of the pool and then rolled to her back staring up at the heavens. Through the screening, she could see Orion and the Big Dipper.

"So beautiful." She drifted into the shallow end. He moved in beside her, holding her suspended in the water, and walked them in a slow circle. She rolled to her feet, coming up in his arms.

"I'd be in here every night." She laced her hands behind his powerful neck.

"I usually am. It's a great stress reducer."

Molly danced along the pool deck, watching them.

"She doesn't swim?" asked Nadine.

"She will but doesn't like it."

"Good. I have you all to myself."

He swept her wet hair back over her shoulders.

"I love your hair."

"Really? It's just an ordinary brown."

"It's like silk."

She smiled and he leaned in. She lifted on her toes, pressing her breasts to the solid wall of muscle, and kissed him. His mouth opened and his tongue brushed her lips. Their tongues danced as they bobbed in warm water.

The tingling excitement flared as she pressed her stomach to his hips and felt his arousal. The animal growl in his throat made her shiver. His hands ran the length of her back, slowly drawing off the straps of her bra. He trailed kisses down her neck and back up to her earlobe, which he tugged between his teeth, sending a delicious shot of heat straight to her core.

Then he set her on the top step and stripped her out of her bra. Warm hands pressed her needy flesh and she thought nothing had ever felt so good, until he took her nipple in his mouth and flicked the beading tip with his tongue.

Something cold and wet touched her back.

She yipped and jumped, twisting to see what was behind her.

Molly stared at them both, with tongue lolling and her brows pulled up in curiosity.

Nadine laughed. Demko scowled.

"Thanks a lot," he said to Molly.

"She's jealous!" Nadine giggled.

"Where were we?" he said.

Nadine stood and retrieved her bra, now floating nearby.

"I'm heading back inside to that comfortable bed."

"Would you like company?"

"You, yes. Molly, no."

He followed her back inside, and Molly remained outdoors for the next hour.

Nadine had known it would be good between them. How good was still a shock. When she finally rolled to her back, replete and thoroughly satisfied, Clint groaned. He'd asked permission, used protection and then blown her mind, twice.

She admired his endurance. When her breathing slowed, she planned to tell him so.

"Now you've tried to kill me twice," he said, and chuckled. Then he gathered her close.

She fell asleep with her head beside his on a single pillow, her hand on his chest and a leg splayed across one muscular thigh.

She was vaguely aware of him rising to use the bathroom and retrieve his dog.

When he came back, she snuggled into his arms.

"Why did you divorce?" she asked.

He stiffened, clearly taken off guard again. Then he sighed.

"My wife was fed up with me, my distractions, absences. I missed I don't know how many family dinners, most of my son's football games and all the school awards ceremonies. He won a writing contest. Missed that, too. She started calling me Detective MIA. She told me that if she was going to live alone, she might as well be single. Then I got suspended during the internal investigation. That was the last straw for her. The whole thing blew up and she asked for a divorce."

"I see." She stroked his bare chest, listening to the steady thump of his heartbeat. "Do you still love her?"

He made a rumbling noise, the vibrations rippling through her cheek, now on his bare chest.

"Not for a long time. I stayed for him. The divorce, lawyers and court appearances killed what little we had left."

"I'm sorry," she said.

"I'm sorry for my son. But not about ending our marriage." He toyed with a strand of her hair. "Besides, if not for that, I'd have never met you."

She smiled and nestled closer as he rhythmically brushed her shoulder with the tips of his fingers. Her eyes closed and she slipped into sleep again, rousing several hours later to the sound of Demko speaking to Molly and the dog's toenails clicking on the tiles as they headed for the kitchen.

A glance at her phone told her she needed to get up if she was to have time to get home and change before driving to the office.

She gathered her clothing and carried them into his bathroom. After a pit stop, she dressed, tugging at her damp bra and panties. Back in the bedroom, she discovered Demko sitting on the rumpled bed dressed in his boxers and a tight white undershirt that revealed his strong, muscular arms.

Demko smiled and stepped forward to greet her, dropping a kiss on her that curled her toes. He drew back, meeting her gaze.

"Good morning," he said.

"Yes. It is."

He glanced behind her. She felt the change in his body as he tensed, going from relaxed to alert, his attention on the window.

"Something is happening," he said.

Nadine turned. "What?"

"I hear activity on the street."

The violent knocking at the front door jarred them both.

"What the hell?" said Demko, already heading into his walk-in closet.

The doorbell chimed from the other side of the house in sequence with the app on Demko's phone. He returned wearing jeans and dragging on a navy-blue Police Athletic League T-shirt. She'd never seen him in jeans and thought he should wear nothing else from now on because his ass was spectacular.

"I'm about to arrest somebody," he muttered, glancing at his phone, which gave him a view of whoever intruded. Molly followed her master as the two headed toward the front door. Nadine retrieved her sandals. Molly had shredded the back strap of the left one with her sharp teeth. She carried them with her as she hurried after Demko.

Out in the foyer, Demko stood with the door half opened before a crowd of people.

"There she is," shouted a woman in a fuchsia dress. She thrust a microphone past Demko into his house. "Dr. Finch, is your mother helping you profile? Does Sarasota have a serial killer?"

CHAPTER SIXTEEN

Two more minutes of fame

Clint Demko was the picture of calm at his front door as he told the reporters to get off his lawn. Meanwhile, Nadine cowered in the dining room as they shouted questions.

"Detective Demko, how long have you and Dr. Finch been together?"

"Detective? Did you know about her mother, Arleen Howler?"

From the window, Nadine peered out between the blinds at the news vans lined up, with satellite dish antennas deployed. The news crews blocked the drive and both of their vehicles.

How will we get out of here?

Nadine was too numb to cry. Every terrible hidden part of her horrific past was now out there. Front-page news and the lead on the evening reports. Everyone around her would soon discover, if they hadn't already, that her mother was a monster.

She'd lived this before, suffered the curious looks, suspicion and pity, interrogations by police and covert surveillance by neighbors. Nadine had had her dirty laundry aired out and she hated it.

Now, after more than a decade, and after she had gotten an education, job, home and a few friends, she found herself right back where she started, holding a bloody trash bag outside their double-wide trailer.

Just like that, she was Nadine Howler again. How long before they discovered who Detective Demko was?

Demko threw the dead bolt. A moment later, the knocking and ringing resumed.

Nadine peeked out through the blinds again. Likely, they were already broadcasting. Belatedly she realized that she must be visible, because some of the reporters hurried toward her, negotiating the narrow gap between the window and his bougainvillea bush. She heard their shouts through the glass.

"Dr. Finch, could you answer a few questions?"

"Dr. Finch, how long have you known a serial killer was preying on Sarasota's citizens?"

"Nadine, did your mother give you any words of advice?"

"Nadine!" Demko's voice was harsh. "Step back."

He motioned from the hallway and she followed him and Molly to the bedroom.

Now both his cell phone and the doorbell rang. He glanced at his screen. "Shit. I have to take this."

Demko headed into the bathroom as she retreated to the guest bathroom to clean up before heading to the kitchen, ignoring the noise from the door. Molly followed her there and looked hopeful as Nadine made coffee.

Down the hall, she heard the shower flick on and then off again in record time, followed by the buzz of an electric razor.

"You want your breakfast, darling?" she asked Molly. "I don't know what you eat."

Nadine changed the water in Molly's bowl and opened the refrigerator, finding half a loaf of high-fiber bread and giving Molly a slice, then made toast.

The doorbell punctuated more pounding on the door. Molly continued to growl and give an occasional "woof."

Demko returned, fully dressed, his hair now wet.

"Coffee?" he asked.

It was hard to concentrate with the reporters hammering like woodpeckers.

"Can you do anything about that?" she asked.

"My guys are en route. They'll push them back to the street and make sure my car isn't blocked. They'll get video of us leaving, but no audio."

Nadine buttered her toast with more care than necessary, enjoying the scraping sound of the blade on the charred outer layer. Meanwhile, Demko fixed Molly's breakfast and two mugs of black coffee.

She offered the toast and he took it, passing her one of the mugs.

This gave her an odd sense of normalcy amid chaos. As if they were having a quiet breakfast in a space capsule as it hurdled, nose cone aflame, through Earth's atmosphere.

"You going home or to the office?"

"Will the press be at my house?"

"I would assume so." He lifted the mug, taking another swallow. "You can take your car, or I can get one of my guys to drive your car over to your lot later on."

"That sounds good." But then they'd get images of them leaving together. Was that preferable to separate cars? Who was she kidding? It made no difference.

"The story, plus the evidence from Robins, and the brass can't deny the possibility that we have a serial killer. Maybe we can get the FBI in here."

"I thought you said you can handle it."

"Yeah. I said that. I said that exactly. I just got this job. So, when the chief of police, my new boss, tells me I can handle it, I handle it. But I knew this one was different. That's why I asked for you."

"Hmm." She waited, but he said no more. "Juliette told me they won't let her enter the cause of death on the autopsy report until she gets the tox screening back, which can take weeks."

"Deniability," he said.

"Tourist season."

They lifted their coffee mugs in a mock salute and drank in unison. The knocking stopped at last.

"Clint," she said, trying out his first name and finding it felt odd. "About last night."

"It was wonderful."

"I don't do that often."

"Then I'm a lucky man. Lucky you didn't shoot me, lucky you brought me to that DA and lucky you like to swim, along with other things." His grin was delicious and made her tingle all over.

"Was it a mistake?"

"Not in my book," he said, and kissed her on the temple. Then he refilled his coffee and hers.

They sipped in silence a moment. He glanced at her sandals, now resting on an empty stool.

"Molly?" he asked, fingering the ragged strap.

"Yup."

He sighed and drained his mug.

"How did you hear about this job?" she asked.

His mouth went grim. "Why?"

"Seems an unlikely coincidence. My hire and yours and Juliette's. Don't you think?"

"Yeah. I do." He snorted. "I met someone at a conference. She mentioned an opening."

"Dr. Crean?"

Demko nodded.

"She's done work in the prison system, interviewed and tested hundreds of serial killers. She would know your mother and possibly you."

"Did she interview your mother?"

"I don't know. But Crean couldn't have hired Dr. Hartfield. She's a county employee."

He set aside his empty coffee and glanced at the entrance, aware of the disconcerting silence.

When he spoke again, it seemed he spoke to the door. "Crean was on my interview committee."

"But why would she want this?"

"What about Osterlund?" said Demko.

Nadine took a minute to place the name. "The head of personnel? What about him?"

"He is responsible for countywide hiring. He makes the final decision," he said.

"But does he? The chief of police would have the real final decision for your job, and Crean is in charge of the Criminal and Forensic Psychology staff. Pathology? I'm not sure. Is that director of operations for the county?"

"Crean serves as criminal psychologist for some of District 12. I know she covers DeSoto," Demko said.

"But Crean doesn't do the hiring there."

"Neither does Osterlund."

"Think there are more of us?" she asked.

"Maybe. You have any other new hires?"

Nadine thought back to Tina, their shy office assistant.

"Receptionist. Tina Ruz."

"You think she has someone to visit at Lowell?"

"I don't know. But she's a new hire. So, maybe."

"Let's have a look."

Demko used his laptop to search the database for Tina Ruz for wants and warrants. He used the known associates and then leaned in, like a hound catching the scent.

"Bingo."

"What?" asked Nadine, leaning over Demko's laptop to see what he had found.

"Christianna Jacinda Ruz. Known associate in federal prison," he said, pointing.

That prickling at her neck returned. Juliette and Demko both had incarcerated parents. Now she could add Tina to that list. She took a stab.

"Mother or her father?" *Not her mother*, she thought. *Please, not her mother.*

"Her mom is a convicted felon. Yvette Jewel Ruz."

"All four of us have mothers in prison." She squinted at the name, which looked familiar.

Demko stopped reading from the computer screen and gave her a serious look. "We're being played."

"What do we do about that?"

"For now, I'd like to keep it to ourselves," he said.

"Rethink that. The press will figure this out and when they do..." She used her hands to simulate the explosion that would follow.

"Maybe. We need to get out in front of it. But you understand, whoever did this is living inside our house and powerful enough to hire or at least influence the hiring choices of our city and possibly our county government."

That could be the mayor, the chief of police, a city councilor. Nadine's mind reeled with possibilities. She pushed aside her coffee, knowing that a third cup would give her a stomachache and make her as jittery as a cat locked in a dog shelter.

"I haven't been here long enough to know who to trust," he said. "So for now, I don't trust anyone."

He glanced back to the screen and Yvette Ruz's photo. Yvette was an older, more haggard version of Nadine's office assistant. But unlike Tina, Yvette's eyes were cold, dead and angry.

"Why do I know her?" she asked.

"Because it was a terrible case that got as much news coverage as we will."

His phone vibrated across the counter. The lock screen said that the caller was the chief of police.

"You going to get that?"

"I'm in the shower," he said, and scrolled through the record for Yvette Ruz.

"She helped plan an elderly woman's kidnapping in Fort Lauderdale, her neighbor. The widow made the mistake of telling Yvette that she didn't know what to do with the four hundred thousand dollars left to her by her husband."

It was coming back to Nadine, along with a rising sense of dread. "This isn't the case where they buried an old woman?"

He nodded. "Alive."

Nadine remembered now. Six or seven years ago, she thought, but time was funny when you weren't serving a sentence. You lost track.

"She and a co-conspirator dug a grave *before* they captured her neighbor, then they beat and tortured the seventy-year-old woman to retrieve her personal information."

"Pin numbers," she said, recalling.

"Social Security numbers, bank account locations, everything they needed to go on a spending spree and hit up the ATMs. Then—"

"They buried her."

It was no worse than what her mother had done. Was it? No, but it was still terrible.

She recalled Tina's big doe eyes and her nervousness as she tried to please. All her insecurities and hesitancy took on new meaning.

This was what people would soon do to her, re-evaluating, applying the fresh information to what they already knew about her. Judging. Distancing. Looking at her like something familiar and benign turned dangerous. She had become a recalled crib discovered to cause the deaths of multiple toddlers.

And Tina made the third person in her circle who had a convicted murderer as a parent. She now considered someone else.

"What about Nathan Dun?"

"Who's he?"

"A court officer. He asked me out."

"Not illegal."

"But he knows about me. He told me we had a lot in common."

Demko began a new search.

"I did that already," she said, pointing at his computer. "His father killed his wife and his young daughter, then drove to the bank that held his home mortgage and shot and killed six people."

"Spree killer," he snarled as he continued working his database. "Says here that Arthur Dun left two surviving children, Anthony and Nathan Dun." He continued scrolling. "Anthony has a record, time served for sexual assault. Nathan pops only for a single car accident. Driver error. No charges." He searched known associates and she sat cradling her empty coffee cup.

Molly had given up trying to extract anything else from her empty bowl and retrieved a knotted rope. She sat under Demko's feet, half under his stool as she gnawed away.

"No known associates with a criminal record." He sat back and pushed the laptop away. "I'll have a chat with him, anyway."

Someone had brought them all together in some sick form of a fishbowl and, lo and behold, a serial killer emerged to turn up the heat.

"What should we do?" she asked, afraid again.

"Listen, in light of what you believe is possible concerning our hiring, I'd ask you not to share the similarities between these crimes and your mother's murders with anyone. Not yet. The media will be doing that soon enough. Right now, it gives us an advantage because the killer can't be sure what we know."

"All right," she said. "Are you still going to tell the chief?"

"Yes. Because we need the Feds."

"Who has access to my profile?" she asked.

"You and me."

"That's it?"

Jenna Kernan

"Yes. That's it, for now. It's my investigation."

"Good." But she felt uneasy. Why was that?

"I'm going to take you to the station to speak to Truman. He's the detective handling your break-in. Don't tell him the connection to the garbage bag. Okay?"

She nodded, swallowing the lump in her throat.

CHAPTER SEVENTEEN

The drawing board

Crean was waiting for her when she reached work. One look told her that her boss was pissed.

"My office, Dr. Finch."

Her supervisor stormed past reception. Nadine followed, shuffling in her torn sandal.

"I got a call from the mayor's office this morning about my new hire and Detective Demko making the news."

"Yes. That was unfortunate. I'd had a break-in."

"I'm aware. A hotel would have been a better option."

Nadine remained silent, waiting for the rest.

"Nadine, I don't blame you for not wanting to go back to your apartment after the break-in. But you could be fired for violating our county policy. So I would highly recommend that you do not schedule any more sleepovers with Detective Demko."

Her face flamed. This was none of Crean's business, but good advice, nonetheless.

"I understand."

"Do you? Because I had to defend you. We have no suspects in this case and you appear to be spending your time sleeping with the lead detective. Your behavior reflects on all of us."

"I understand," said Nadine again and hoisted her bag, glancing toward the door but waiting for Crean to release her.

Instead she folded her arms and lowered her chin. Nadine braced for a longer reprimand.

"Do you not believe you should have told me that your mother is Arleen Howler?"

Nadine tried to determine if her boss's outrage and anger was real or artifice.

"I'm not required to tell you anything about my family."

Crean huffed like a bear. "I'll need a statement from you for the media."

Nadine made no promises.

"You can go."

She did, and remained in her office all morning, having lunch at her desk.

In the afternoon, Tina delivered a package. Inside was a pair of sandals, very like the ones Molly had gnawed, and in the correct size.

The note read:

Miss Molly is sorry for the damage and Clint is sorry for not protecting your footwear as promised.

Before leaving for the day, she got an email with attachment from the Miami Police Department, requested by Clint Demko. A copy of the findings of an internal investigation. Everything in the attachment backed up what he had told her. He'd reported tampering. His colleague had then pointed the finger at Demko. The investigation recommended no charges on Detective Clint Demko and that he returned to duty. She lifted the phone to call him and then replaced the handset to the cradle.

*

The first call from Demko since they'd made the front page came on Wednesday night, around 8 p.m. She left the sofa in the junior suite of the business hotel, where she'd stayed since Monday, and retrieved her phone from the charger.

"Hey there," he said.

"Hi. I got the internal investigation report and the replacement sandals. Thank you."

"The what? Oh, yeah. Good." He sounded distracted. "Listen, just got a call from the Manatee Sheriff's Office. They've got a body up there might be connected."

"A body? It's too soon. Way, way too soon," she said.

Six years between the first and second couple, not a matter of weeks. Oh, God. Had this killer accelerated the timeline?

"Maybe not. Victim is a white female, Jane Doe for now, found floating in the Manatee River."

"How long?" She heard the starting pistol sound in her mind, the race to find this victim's lover before the killer.

"Unknown. Sheriff's got the body beside his boat. No second body. Yet, at least."

"There wouldn't be. My mother's second couple had been killed separately. Only the rope and their affair connected them."

"That's right."

Accelerated timeline. Why hadn't she considered that? Perhaps because to ignore that possibility gave her the luxury of time. But if this was their unsub, that was over.

"It might be a boat propeller, but he called because he thought I'd better see for myself."

"Where are you?" she asked.

"En route to the scene. I'll be there in twenty."

"Call after you've seen the body."

"Yup," he said, and disconnected.

Nadine flipped through her duplicate of one of Bradley Robins's binders, searching for the photo of Arleen's only female victim found alone, Lacey Louder. She floated in brown water, tangled in tall grasses that lined the riverbank in Hontoon Island State Park. The file provided a close-up of her wrist and the rope with its end severed. The DA had added notes, questioning the meaning of the slashes on Lacey's rump.

Nadine put her forehead in her hands and counted her breaths. Hyperventilating would not help her or the man who was connected to the victim up in Manatee.

Maybe it was a simple drowning. *Please let it be a simple drowning.*

But he'd said "boat propeller." She grimaced.

If this were a copycat, the next body would be a man who was possibly still alive. Someone like the ranger, Drew Henderson, who would be found stabbed in his jeep. Police would testify that the rope on his wrist would be an exact match to the one on Lacey Louder.

In the transcript provided by Bradley, she read that her mother told detectives under interrogation that, after targeting the couple, she grew impatient waiting for them to be together and killed them separately. Was there already another victim out there?

Nadine's thoughts flashed to Hontoon Island State Park and the fishing trip she had taken with her mom and brother when she was twelve. Arlo, then eighteen, had told her that they'd found a body in the water here. Much later, she discovered why her mother thought this park was a perfect spot for family outings. Arleen got a thrill from returning to the site of Louder's death.

Nadine wrapped her arms about herself as she wondered, had her dad known what his wife was up to? Was that why he left?

Much of what she knew about Dennis Howler came from her aunt Donna, who remembered her brother mostly from the time before he took up with Arleen. Dennis was born into a family of musicians, played trumpet and had a full ride to college, but then he got mixed up with both drugs and her mother. He lost his band scholarship, dropped out and they'd been married before Arlo arrived. Then he'd joined the army to support his wife and newborn son, or get away from them, as Arleen contended.

After her father left, Nadine's mother brought home a string of men. None stayed for long and, according to Arleen, that was her kids' fault, too.

"No guy wants to raise another man's brats."

Nadine closed the binder.

"Enough for now," she said, and headed to her room's kitchenette to brew some tea because she'd drunk all the coffee. Chamomile or English breakfast. She growled and picked the black tea.

Demko called three hours later, at eleven-thirty, rousing Nadine from a doze.

"Okay, I'm here. Sheriff brought me out in one of their boats. About one hundred fifty yards from shore." His voice muffled as he asked someone something and then returned to her. "Near the Desoto Memorial. I can see the lights on the cross. We're bringing her in."

"Is the ME up there?"

"Yes. On shore, waiting. It's also District 12, so I've requested Dr. Hartfield. Have you spoken to her yet?"

"No. I've been… no. Not yet."

"I know we discussed keeping it between us for now, to avoid leaks, but I've been thinking she should know about the four of us. Especially since the media might get ahold of it."

"Yes."

"Want me to do it?" he asked.

"No. I'll tell her. I need to apologize, anyway. I'll call her."

"Fine."

"Is there anything to link this death and the double homicide?" Nadine squeezed her eyes shut and prayed.

"Definitely multiple lacerations. Hands are bagged, so… wait a minute."

Bagging the hands of murder victims was standard procedure, a way to preserve evidence, though the water might have removed or destroyed anything useful.

Another side conversation ensued. "Sheriff said he saw a cut on the ring finger and there is a red rope, nylon, diamond pattern on her wrist. Short, maybe a foot or so."

"The rope was cut?"

"He says so."

"Clint, you need to find out if this victim was having an affair. Whoever it is will be the second victim."

"I hear you, but no ID on her yet."

"You have to find him, now!"

"Yes. Working on it."

"What does she look like?"

"Caucasian. Dark hair. Slim build."

"The wounds?"

"Hold on."

She did.

"Sent you a photo. Looks like multiple stab wounds."

Her phone dinged and she opened the text, staring at the image of numerous punctures in a naked abdomen. She wrinkled her nose. Her stomach pitched and she wondered again if she was strong enough to do this.

She spoke into the phone. "They looked like stab wounds. That's wrong, Clint."

Nadine's mother had broken Lacey Louder's ribs, struck her repeatedly in the chest and neck until her trachea collapsed.

"She used a knife only to slice Louder's throat, carve the ring and carved marks into her backside."

Was this unrelated? But the rope…

"We're coming in. Call you back."

*

He didn't. Not for four hours. Her phone rang, rousing Nadine from the small sofa in the junior suite. Her neck ached from the awkward position. She rolled and the binder slipped from her lap and thudded on the floor.

Demko continued the conversation where he'd left off.

"Yeah. Beyond multiple stab wounds in the abdominal cavity and two to the torso, right and left. Hartfield says those injuries likely collapsed her lungs, thinks that beyond the soft tissue damage and internal bleeding, there might be cracked ribs and a possible ruptured spleen. Marks on her torso indicate her killer used a Taser on her."

"The Taser is right."

Nadine had learned at her mother's trial that this was a new toy that Arleen first used on Louder.

Demko continued his description of the victim. "She was repeatedly kicked in the midsection."

"That matches," said Nadine.

"There are tread marks on her skin, contusions from the footwear worn by the perpetrator. I'm running the prints through SICAR."

"Through what?"

"Oh, sorry. Shoeprint Image Capture and Retrieval. It's a national database of footwear prints."

"No kidding?"

"Looks like boots to me," he said. "From the extent of the internal bleeding, broken bones and contusions, I'd say she suffered the attack for several minutes.

"Also, on the nylon rope. It's the same. Red, with a black-and-yellow diamond pattern. Unfortunately, they sell it at every home improvement center in the country."

"Her left hand?"

"Same marks on the ring finger and gashes on her backside."

Her heart now pounded at her temples and in her throat. This was the same. Their killer.

"Any identification on the victim?"

"Like the others, she was recovered naked. No water in her lungs this time," he said.

"So dead before she went under."

"Possibly. Or the punctures in her chest cavity made it impossible to draw a breath."

Nadine knew she'd fixate on that later, wondering at the pain of needing air but being unable to bring it to her oxygen-starved body.

Her mom wanted the women to suffer, punishing them for their infidelity.

"Hold on, Sheriff wants to talk to me."

She waited, retrieving the binder from the floor and thumping it on the coffee table.

"He said there are no abandoned vehicles in the lot."

"What lot?"

"It's… hold on." She heard him shouting to someone. Then he resumed his answer in a calm voice. "Robinson Preserve. It's a city park up here. Tidal marsh, mangroves… mosquitoes. Man, I hate outdoor crime scenes!"

Robinson Preserve. That was the park Juliette had once mentioned. She kayaked up there. Nadine wondered at the coincidence as suspicions niggled.

She suddenly wished it were another ME on scene. Juliette was in a unique position to remove evidence or simply fail to report it.

"Clint? Juliette told me she kayaks at that preserve. And Lido," she added.

This was met with silence.

"It's a coincidence. Right?"

"Lots of people use city parks."

Yes. Of course they did.

"But they don't all have a mother like ours."

She gritted her teeth, unwilling to condemn Juliette on something so circumstantial and yet unable to shake the worry.

"Okay," said Demko.

She wasn't sure if he was speaking to her.

"Is it three in the morning?" he asked.

"Yes."

"I'm sorry, Nadine. I'll call you tomorrow."

"Find the man she's sleeping with, Clint. He's in danger. Find him."

CHAPTER EIGHTEEN

Couple three

I have found the perfect pair. They work in the same restaurant and, at first, I thought they were married. Of course they are, just not to each other. They are so obvious, can't keep their hands to themselves. I've been eating all my meals there and saw him push her up against the wall through the look-through into the kitchen. Nick knows how to put a smile on Carla's face.

I'd like to get right to it, but first I have to finish with Hope's side gig. Why she ever got divorced, I'll never know. Clearly, that old flame never died.

He's next, but his schedule is unpredictable. I missed him again today. I need to find him without leaving a digital footprint, which is turning out to be harder than I expected.

As for Carla and Nick, they leave work in separate cars and park at Phillippi Estate Park. He likes to fish, or that's what he likely tells his wife, because I've never seen him use the fishing pole he totes around. Carla just tells her husband she's covering for another girl. I've heard her on the phone.

"Hey, honey, Tammi is a no-show again. I'm on until eight. I know. They should fire her. Anyway, we could use the tips."

I've got a tip for him, drop in at the restaurant and see if she's where she says she is, because, news flash, she isn't.

I follow them to the lot and wait as they park, side by side. She slips into his SUV via the rear. He follows her. The backseat is already stowed, giving them a nice flat, carpeted area. In a moment, the vehicle bounces on its shocks. He should get those checked.

I decide on an evening stroll and wander past the grand estate now on the National Registry of Historic Places, searching for cameras. I reach the fishing dock, thinking I am alone, but, no, I spy a likely candidate to invite to my place. But if she takes offense, she might remember me, and I don't want to be connected to this place. The last thing I need is a sketch artist drawing my face.

So, I let her go, wishing her a great weekend. This is a test of my endurance and my restraint. I pass easily.

She smiles.

I'm smiling also, but for different reasons.

CHAPTER NINETEEN

The devil you know

On Friday, Nadine both called and texted Juliette but received no reply. If she wanted to apologize, it seemed she needed to do so in person.

The Bradenton Police had still not identified the Jane Doe recovered from Robinson Preserve, though they'd asked the public's help. Nadine grew more desperate and phoned Demko to see if there was anything they could do to find the man she was certain their killer had already targeted.

Demko was in contact with the sheriffs but told her that he couldn't find a possible partner until they had an ID.

"No abandoned vehicle?" she asked.

"None."

"Well, how'd she get out there? Boat?"

"We don't know. Uber. Paddleboard. She could have come in from the Gulf or the Manatee River."

"Clint, if she was having an affair—"

"I know. I know. We're trying."

"The tip line?"

"Nothing useful."

"Dental records?" Was she actually telling him how to do his job?

"No national database. You have to know who it is to check those."

She groaned.

"I'll call you the minute we have anything."

"Why doesn't her family know she's missing?"

"Great question," he said. "I'll call when we make an ID."

"Will…" She hesitated and then pushed on. "Will I see you this weekend?"

The pause seemed endless.

*

On Saturday morning, she was sick of leaving messages for Juliette, sick of staring at her psychological profile, sick of waiting for Demko to call and sick of making no contribution to the case. So, instead of moving back into her cottage, as planned, she drove to Tampa and the post box she'd rented, pulling into the lot a little after noon.

Nadine found twenty-two letters in the Tampa mailbox. She tossed them into a reusable shopping bag, telling herself that she would read them later, but, really, possibly never.

Then she continued north to Lowell Correctional, hopeful she could finesse something useful from Arleen. She reached the visitors' parking area with only ninety minutes left in visiting hours.

She had developed a theory too dark to consider, and that was exactly why it clung. She needed to know the reason Arleen continued to bring the clothing of her victims home and disposed of them from there. It was an incredibly risky decision, and one that she was certain Arleen had not taken lightly. There was a reason and Nadine aimed to find out what it was.

She also wanted Arleen to tell her what she'd refused to tell the DA: why she made those ritualistic cuts on her victims and whether she had an accomplice.

The screening process was less upsetting this visit. She was becoming accustomed to the intake procedure. Routine was routine, even if it involved a pat down by an overweight matron wearing latex gloves.

Her mother relieved Nadine of the first twenty before they sat down.

"Didn't expect you so soon," said Arleen, and then turned toward the vending machines. Nadine waited for her mother to return with the food, none of which was for her daughter.

Arleen seemed to recognize this, only after sitting down.

"You can get this junk anytime you want."

Nadine conceded the point and moved to the reason for her visit as Arleen tore open the chips.

"Why did you make me take out those bags?" Nadine asked.

"What bags?"

"The ones covered with your victims' blood."

"Well, I couldn't do it. Then there would have been blood on the outside of the bags, too."

"I didn't put them in a second bag."

They faced off a moment. Nadine waited for Arleen to lose control, but her mother surprised her.

"Well, no difference now," she said.

"Why me? You could have done it then or any other time afterward. You could have asked Arlo or dumped them on the way home."

"In my underwear?"

"A woman who remembers to bring a knife and rope could have packed extra clothing."

Their eyes locked. Nadine ground her teeth and Arleen lifted her chin, taking a defiant pose.

"It wasn't some sick attempt to make me be like you. Was it?"

Arleen's smile was chilling.

"Was the ring around their finger symbolic of the wedding band, the vows they had forsaken?"

Arleen lowered the bag. "'Forsaken'? Shit, Dee-Dee. Hauling out the ten-dollar words."

"The cuts to the ring finger, why?"

"Make sure they didn't take off that ring again." She grinned. Bits of food clung to her teeth.

"What about the marks on the women's backsides?"

"What about them?"

"Why did you make them and what is their meaning?"

Arleen snorted and crumpled the bag in one strong fist.

"You hear from Arlo?" she asked, changing the subject without answering.

"We aren't in touch," Nadine lied.

"Well, he's working with dogs up there. Ones for the blind, and shit. Sounds really into it."

"Are you going to tell me about those marks?"

"Nope."

Nadine changed tack. If Arleen wouldn't say what those marks meant, she could at least ascertain if she was working with anyone on the outside.

"Are you in contact with anyone from the Gulf Coast?" Nadine did not want to mention the exact city where she worked.

Arleen scrunched up her face, amplifying the wrinkles. "Maybe. I get letters from lots of folks. Get 'em every day. Some come to see me here. Some just send crap. Pages and pages."

Nadine shifted on the hard-plastic stool. Was one of those correspondences from their unsub?

"Maybe I could see those letters."

"Don't keep 'em. I read 'em, some anyway, and toss 'em." The smile that curled her mother's lips said otherwise.

Nadine decided to see the warden about gaining access to her mother's correspondence.

Arleen waved a hand in disgust. "It's not just letters. They come in here or talk to me over the computer from their fancy offices, sitting in front of a wall of books. Oh, I'm so impressed. Make me look at smiley faces and ask how I'm feeling. Shit, how would you feel smelling bleach and cunt all day?"

Nadine blinked in astonishment at the vulgar language. It had been some time since she'd been exposed to Arleen's coarseness.

"I've been thinking about our last visit. All them questions and you taking an interest." She grinned, as if her daughter had finally made her proud.

Nadine couldn't suppress the shiver that slithered between her shoulder blades.

"You could write them down for me. Then I could tell you all about them."

And then Arleen could relive her fantasy at the same time she planted all those horrors in Nadine's mind. No, thank you. Nadine's longing for a relationship stopped at her mother.

"I'm not here to write your story."

Arleen glared and then tucked away the expression so fast that Nadine questioned whether she had seen it.

"I'm so glad to see you, Dee-Dee. I want you to keep coming up here a couple times a month. It's the best thing to happen in years, us getting back together again."

Was Nadine supposed to feel guilty that all she could think about was getting out of here and never coming back?

"I want to ask you about a woman who was here. Her name is Dr. Margery Crean. She visited as part of a research project?"

"Hell, experts line up round the block to talk to me. Research! Shit! You'd think I was the cure for cancer."

"She would have given you a brief survey," said Nadine.

"She the one had a test that they give to the male serial killers?"

"That's right. The Hare Psychopathy Checklist."

"Doctor, is it? Sure, I remember that one. Bottle blonde, big honker, stuck-up snot, she was. Pretending she wasn't all into it. But she was here, wasn't she?"

"Did you tell her about the cuts on the victims' ring fingers?"

"Nope."

"The marks on the women's buttocks?"

Arleen smiled and closed her eyes, as if reliving some fond memory.

"Arleen? Did you tell her?"

"I didn't tell that bottle blonde nothin'."

"You're certain?"

"Yeah. Just did her little survey. That's it." Arleen pressed a fist under her chin and rested her elbow on the table.

If she hadn't told, then a person associated with the investigation had leaked that detail.

"You must have told someone."

Arleen was all business now as she leaned across the cafeteria table.

"How you figure?"

Nadine considered telling her about the copycat and rejected the notion.

"How about I get you an ice-cream sandwich and you think of everyone you told about what you did to the victims' bodies?"

Arleen waved her hand dismissively. Nadine headed to the vending machines for a frozen snack, passing it to her mother on her return.

"Well? Did you tell anyone about the cuts on the victims' fingers?"

"How'd you find out about that, Dee-Dee? Didn't come up at trial. Not sure why, it was some of my best work. But I'm wondering, how you found out?"

Nadine looked her mother straight in the eye and lied again.

"Arlo told me," she said, confirming her mother's suspicion that she and her brother were in contact.

"Yeah, I figured."

Inside, she groaned. Arlo could have told any number of people. Had her brother helped their mother move the bodies?

"So. Who else knows?" asked Nadine.

"I might have mentioned it to some of the inmates and Guy, of course."

"What guy?"

"My kid brother, Guy."

"He's been to visit?"

She snorted. "I told him when it happened."

Nadine forced away the look of disgust, but not quickly enough. Her mother's eyes narrowed.

"Did he help you move the bodies of the couples?"

"I didn't need no help."

"But you told me he helped with one, the guy who owed you money."

"'Cause it rattled me. Didn't plan that one. For them others, I had things laid out."

"No one helped you?"

Arleen's temper flared. "You think I needed help? That I couldn't do that myself? Well, I don't need help from nobody!"

Nadine did not know if this was the truth, and she had no way to verify anything her mother said. The futility of this visit struck her hard, but she continued on, trying her best.

"Where does Uncle Guy live again?"

"Damned if I know."

Her mother sat back, arms folded, and flashed Nadine another chilling smile. The expression vanished instantly. Nadine recognized that look, had studied it in school. It even had a name—Duping Delight.

It was the satisfaction derived from deceiving someone. Arleen was pulling one over on her. She suspected that her mother knew exactly where to find Guy.

She made a mental note to ask Demko if he'd found any-thing on her uncle. Her own memories of him were vague and disturbing.

"What about your other victims. Did you also cut their fingers?"

Arleen narrowed her eyes. "I don't talk about them."

"You told me about them last time," she said.

"You're my daughter. I trust you."

"Even though I testified against you at your trial?"

Her mother gave her a long look as the corner of her mouth turned up in a sneer. "Everyone has a right to protect themselves, Dee-Dee. Don't you forget that. It's rule one."

Nadine rubbed her tired eyes. Seemed Arleen had spoken to everyone except the law enforcement professionals who could close a cold case. She'd told so many people it might be impossible to use this information to catch their killer.

"Anyone else?"

"Yeah. I told Constance, for sure, but they executed her in 2009, so she ain't talking, at least not to anyone who can hear her up here." Her mother laughed at her grim joke. Nadine did not join her, and Arleen cast her a disgruntled look.

"Any guards?"

"I don't talk to guards! 'Cept maybe to tell them to go fuck themselves."

Arleen peeled open her ice-cream sandwich and began licking the melting edges before taking several bites. Watching her eat, Nadine wondered, not for the first time, about Arleen's upbring-ing. She thought back to what she knew about Arleen's father.

Once in a drunken rage, Arleen had told them that she wasn't the best mother, but at least she hadn't raped them like her father had done to his kids. Nadine remembered asking Arlo later how a man raped another man. Arlo said it was possible.

Nadine's maternal grandfather, Lewis Owen, served eighteen years for the murder of his boss before dying in prison. Arleen said that her dad's conviction was the best thing that ever happened to them.

Both her mother's parents had been dysfunctional. She knew from Arlo that their maternal grandmother had been mentally ill, possibly schizophrenic, long before she went to a nursing home. She had visited her grandmother Idell there, but Nadine was too young to recall anything but the stink of the place and how scary the old people had seemed. Both her mother's parents were gone now, leaving Arleen with only the scars. Her sole living relatives were her kids and possibly her younger brother, Guy.

Arleen noticed Nadine watching her and extended the half-consumed treat.

She waved off the offer.

Arleen wolfed the last bite and then wadded up the sandwich wrapper, shooting it like a basketball toward the open garbage can and missed. Then she turned back to Nadine.

"What did you think about my idea?" she asked.

Nadine gave her mother a confused look.

"In my letters, about picking me a name, something catchy, like the Boston Strangler or BTK Strangler. If I got a name, I could get some attention. Hell, I killed more than that guy out in California. Just because I didn't eat any of them or hide under their beds and shit. That just made me smarter. You know there isn't one single book written about me? It's criminal."

Nadine thought that might be her cue to leave.

"You sound angry," she said, falling back on one of her go-to therapy techniques. Verbalize the emotion clients display. But Nadine didn't ask Arleen to explore that emotion because she didn't want to hear more on this topic.

"'Angry'?" Arleen blew a breath out between her teeth as color rose into her cheeks.

If Nadine were eight, this would be her signal to get lost or to stay and get slapped.

"Not even a news interview. *Twenty/Twenty. Dateline. Forty-Eight Hours.* They should be beating a path to my cell. It's bullshit. Men get all the jobs, all the media coverage."

"'Jobs'?" Nadine asked, picking out the one item on her mother's list that didn't quite fit.

"Yeah. You know how many chances a man gets? A hundred. No, a thousand. You know what they give me?" She held up a finger. Her jaw was sticking out and there was fury in her gaze. The blood vessels in her mother's eyes grew red.

"Fucking foremen, supervisors, assholes, all of them. I hope they all…" Her gaze cut to one of the guards who had moved to stand at their table. "Settle down, Lupe. I'm just talking."

"No shouting." The corrections officer pointed to her name badge. "And it's Officer Funez."

"I wasn't!" She thought better of whatever she was about to say and locked her jaw. Her chin remained up and out, a display of anger from the now-silent killer.

"Thank you, Officer Funez," Nadine said, and Funez cast her a look as if Nadine was something unwelcome that she had just discovered on the bottom of her shoe.

The corrections officer moved on.

"She's such a bitch," said Arleen. "You just know she'll be the one making me squat when I leave here."

Nadine grimaced at the mental image.

Arleen tore open a bag of nacho chips with more force than necessary and stuffed several in her mouth, crushing them between her molars as she watched the guard retreat. Finally she turned back to Nadine.

"Like I was saying, it's all about the name. One that scares the piss out of people. Without it, I'm nothin'. And I need someone to tell my story." She lifted her thin brows at her daughter. "You've got a college degree, right? Took English and shit. I know you can write, 'cause I read your master's thingy."

"Thesis?" Nadine's face contracted as her neck muscles tightened. Was that possible?

"Yeah! You could write a book for me."

Back to this again. Nadine stared across the table at her mother. The idea came half formed.

"You going to tell me about *all* the murders? Not just the ones you copped to?"

Arleen twisted her mouth up before answering. "Maybe."

Negotiations had begun.

These unsolved murders were her mother's only bargaining chips, her capital to avoid the state carrying out her sentence. They were also a vehicle to achieve fame and status. Unfortunately, one thwarted the other. For Nadine, they were a means to see if her copycat killer knew everything.

The cheese dust had turned her mother's fingertips orange. Arleen continued to root about in the bag, retrieving progressively smaller and smaller bits of nachos.

"I'll think about it." Nadine stood.

"What's your hurry?"

"Got a long drive."

Arleen set aside the empty package; interest piqued. "How long? Tampa, right? Got someone waiting for you?"

Nadine smiled and Arleen scowled. She was not giving her mother any details about her life. The fact that Arleen had read Nadine's thesis was horrifying enough to keep her up for hours.

She leaned forward, pressing her hands to the table. "Thanks for the chat."

When Nadine straightened, she left a twenty-dollar bill folded neatly beside the empty chip bag. Arleen swiped her hand over the money, making it disappear.

"See you next week, then," Arleen said.

Her mother waited for confirmation that Nadine did not give. She left Arleen with a wave and hurried into the late-afternoon sunshine. Huge white-domed clouds billowed thousands of feet into the blue sky. One had already formed an anvil head. Building thunderclouds, she knew.

She nearly made it home before the gray sheets of rain overwhelmed her wiper blades, forcing her to pull over. The cloudburst extended her drive from three hours to four. At the hotel, Nadine made a list of all the known contacts whom Arleen had told about the unreleased marks on the bodies and avoided the letters she had written. She found nothing on her uncle via her web search and hoped Demko had fared better.

At midnight, she tucked away her laptop, ceased checking her phone and went to bed. In the morning, she ate breakfast in the hotel dining area with her laptop for company, before continuing to read the court transcripts, trying to glean any useful information for her subject-based profile and for her geo-profile, a predictive map of the probable area of this offender's activities. But with only three data points, the map was less than useless. This included the kill site for the first couple. The point of discovery for their remains and the body dump for their latest female victim. So, Nadine made another, one that included all her mother's known victims. The software generated likely areas for activity and illustrated a region for unsubs' work and home. Nadine studied the results, surprised at the accuracy of this second profile.

Demko's call came late in the day on Sunday.

"We have an ID for the Manatee Jane Doe."

Nadine's mouth went dry. Were they already too late to save the other man?

"She's Hope Kerr," said Demko. "Resident of St. Pete, Florida. Disappeared sometime Sunday. Married for the second time. She's got one kid, a boy from the first marriage. I sat in on the interview with the husband up there. He came in voluntarily. He appears distraught. He also has a solid alibi. He was in Miami with his mother and sisters the weekend of his wife's murder. Cell phone records, receipts and ATM withdrawals confirm his location."

"Not a suspect?"

"No."

"Where is her boy?" she asked.

"Sleepaway camp. I checked."

Nadine found she could again breathe past the pain in her heart.

"Why didn't he report his wife missing?"

"He did, when he came back on Tuesday, to police in St. Petersburg, where he thought she was. But they asked him to wait seventy-two hours."

"Three days."

"Right."

"What about the affair? Is she sleeping with someone?"

"I'm getting her phone records. See if anything pops. But her husband says no. Adamant about it. Actually, he threatened to punch me in the nose."

"He wouldn't know."

"True, but from what her sister says, Hope was devoted to her husband and son. Worked as a wedding photographer, hobby was photographing wildlife. She says no other men in Hope's life."

"The ex have visitation rights?"

"I don't know. Why?"

She paused waiting for him to figure it out.

"Okay. I'll ask the sheriff to go speak to her ex."

"Any missing persons? Caucasian male in the right age range."

"Zippo."

Nadine pursed her lips. "It doesn't make sense. Why kill her, why carve the ring and initials, if she wasn't unfaithful?"

"We're checking into it."

"She's sleeping with someone. Release her name to the press with a warning. We have to find him right now or our unsub is going to kill him."

*

Whoever dug the hole in Tina Ruz's yard had done a great job. The receptionist showed Nadine a photo on her cell phone first thing on Monday morning. The pit looked just like a shallow grave. It sat outside her town house window, directly below the balcony.

"One of the cops talked to my landlord. They're not renewing my lease. Already got the notice." She sighed, resigned as any child who had lived in the shadow of an infamous parent.

"They think you dug it?" asked Nadine.

Tina lowered her gaze and fiddled with her paper clip holder. "Not exactly."

"Listen, Tina, I know about your mom."

Tina's eyes rounded. "How?"

"Demko. We did a background check. It showed on known associates."

Tina nodded, but no longer met her gaze, and her cheeks flushed.

"You stay at your place last night?" asked Nadine.

"No way. Hotel on the North Trail. All the ones out by I-75 were booked up. World Rowing championships," said Tina absently. "So it's weird, right? You and me?"

"Yeah. You could say that."

"So the murder up in Bradenton is related to your case," said Tina. "Saw the news story. Reporter said police are asking for help finding some guy she's with. They interviewed the husband. He's both grieving and pissed. Said he's suing the police."

"Get in line," said Nadine.

"I guess."

She hoped that if Hope Kerr had been unfaithful, today's news coverage would help them locate her partner.

"I heard you had a break-in a few days ago," said Tina.

"Yeah. Disturbing. Similar to what happened to you. The person left me a reminder of my mother's crimes."

Tina put a hand to her throat. "Inside?"

"Afraid so."

Tina blanched.

"I wasn't there and I've been in a hotel since."

"Should I, like, leave?"

"I don't know, Tina. But I don't feel safe at home now."

"I could stay at the hotel, I guess. Or with a friend."

"Might be wise."

Detective Demko arrived in their offices and their conversation paused. He was unshaven and his clothing looked as if he'd worn them to run a 10K.

"Got a minute, Nadine?" asked Demko.

Nadine glanced to the clock. "Yes. Of course. But I've got to head to a competency hearing in a few minutes."

"Have to wait. The FBI wants to see you."

"FBI? What?"

"Yeah. I convinced the brass to bring them in. I've briefed them on what we have so far."

"Maybe they can find him," she said, thinking of the next victim in the series.

"Does she need a lawyer?" asked Tina.

Nadine glanced at Tina, shocked that she hadn't thought of that, and also at the discovery that her assistant had her back.

"What? No," said Demko. "They want her help with the case."

"Are they taking over?" Nadine half hoped they would but was also reluctant to step aside. Deep within herself, Nadine still felt she needed to be involved in this case.

"Joint investigation. Or so they say. They requested the help of Dr. Crean and they've requested you."

Crean seemed an obvious choice.

"Why me?"

"You have unique insights."

"Translation, my mother is a serial killer."

"And they liked your profile," he said.

"Patronizing."

"And they floated the possibility that this unidentified suspect may be imitating your mother's crimes as a way of targeting you."

Tina gasped.

"'Targeting'?" The ringing in her ears returned. Her mouth went dry as she stared at Demko. That prospect was exactly what she feared and what she had tried to pass off as her own narcissism.

"That's the word they used. Your recent break-in has them rattled. Me too, actually." He placed his fists at his waist, waiting. "Do you need anything before we go, laptop, purse?"

"Go where?"

"They're setting up a field office in town."

"That was fast."

He didn't reply, just waited, her escort or jailer, she wasn't sure.

It was clear they were going, whether or not she agreed. She and Tina shared identical blank stares. Their office assistant was more like Nadine than she had realized. They both had the same dead-eyed look. PTSD for the children of killers, a club that no one wanted to join.

"Come on," urged Demko.

She retreated to her office and he followed. There she gathered her things, then trailed him out.

"Does Crean know about the FBI?" she asked.

"I told her. FBI had already been in touch."

"How'd she take it?"

"Not sure. She's hard to read."

"I'll say."

They left the offices together.

"You get any sleep since I saw you last?" she asked.

"I sleep better with you there."

His words both warmed and troubled her. Relationships were complicated under any circumstance, and she and he carried extra baggage.

Inside the elevator, he gave her a kiss that lasted until the compartment doors swept open. They stepped out in unison, like two trotter horses, in matched stride, professionals again, and she felt uncomfortable at sneaking around.

"You get a warning from your boss?" he asked.

She nodded. "You?"

He grimaced and inclined his head. "Yeah. Seems the least of our worries."

She paused and looked out the windows that circled the lobby.

"Are the reporters still there?"

"A few."

Nadine made a face.

She'd effectively avoided the reporters until she arrived at work. They got plenty of footage of her leaving her car and hustling to the entrance to her building. Reaching the office felt like standing on "home free" in a game of hide-and-seek. But she wasn't home, and she wasn't free. Neither one was in her future until she caught this killer so he couldn't hurt anyone else.

"I visited my mother this weekend."

"Really?"

"She mentioned my uncle again. I can't find anything on him. Did you?"

"Zip. Maybe the Feds will have better luck."

"I think we should get my mother's correspondence from the prison." And she knew she needed to read the letters her mother had written, a task she dreaded.

"Why?"

"I'm afraid that she and the killer are in contact."

"I'll tell the Feds. They'll have an easier time with that one."

"Did you give them the material from Robins?" she asked.

"They have it."

Should that make her relieved or unsettled?

"I have to tell you something," he said.

All her internal alarms sounded.

"I found a Halloween mask on my pool deck this morning."

Whatever she had expected, this wasn't it. Nadine's brow knit. "A what?"

"A mask. Or I should say *the* mask. Fucking clown."

Nadine had her head cocked like Molly when she didn't comprehend the command.

"I don't understand the significance."

Demko sighed. "Connor wore a mask when he broke into my dad's medical offices and shot my father in the chest."

"Oh!" It all clicked. "*The* mask." Nadine's eyes widened. "You found the same sort of mask that your brother wore that day."

"Yes," he said.

"Did you report it?"

"Hell yes. Crime techs couldn't lift a single print and it's a goddamn latex mask. No fibers or hair samples."

"You think it's our guy?"

"Last Saturday, you had a break-in. Yesterday Tina Ruz found an open grave in her backyard. Now I find this mask this morning in what amounts to my backyard."

"We need to warn Juliette!"

"Already on it. We have surveillance set up watching her place."

"And you warned her?"

"I did. Personally. We were both at the scene in Robinson Preserve, so…" He seemed to be waiting for her reaction.

Her relief came in a long exhalation. "Thank you."

He glanced about the empty lobby and then back to her. "I thought you were going to speak to her."

Nadine shook her head. "I've tried. Left another message. She's not taking my calls."

He nodded and made a humming sound of consideration, but no comment.

"Where was it, the mask?"

"Propped up on a chair on the lanai, facing the sliders to the pool."

"The story is out there," she said. "Anyone could have done this."

"Someone put a black plastic garbage bag on your bed before any of this got out."

"You think it's our perp?"

"That is what the guy from the FBI Critical Incident Response Group thinks."

"That's bad."

The reassurance that she wasn't losing her mind came with the knowledge that someone dangerous and disturbed was targeting each of them.

"This unsub brought us here and has left us each something to remind us of our parents' crimes," said Demko.

"Why involve us all? Why bring together the children of convicted killers and then begin this series of kills?"

"Unsure," said Demko. "You have a theory?"

She shook her head.

"You asked me to find if Hope Kerr was sleeping with anyone. I haven't turned up a single indication of an affair. But I did track down her ex-husband. Turns out he's on our force."

"Was he sleeping with her?"

"He says he wasn't."

"You believe him?" she asked.

"Let's say I'm still digging, but nothing to prove otherwise."

"Did you warn him?"

"I sure did."

"You believe he understood the seriousness of this?"

"Nadine, he's a police officer. He knows how to look out for himself. He understood that I believe Hope was targeted because of infidelity and that her partner, whoever that might be, is a second target."

"Did he have any suggestions on who she was sleeping with?"

"No. He didn't. Oh, you also asked me to alert you of any missing persons. We now have two."

"Two?" Nadine's stomach dropped as the emotional roller coaster launched again.

"Let me finish. They don't match the profiles, but I wanted you to know. We have one female, a teenager, and I know your mother's last victim was seventeen."

Images of Sandra filled her mind.

Fetch, bitch!

"The other is only two years of age."

She gasped and slapped her hand across her mouth. *A child!* He was speaking again, but his voice seemed far away.

"… toddler who might be with a family member, and the teen has a new boyfriend and the parents object."

Nadine wobbled and he caught her by the elbow, steadying her. Her equilibrium was wacked. She was dizzy from spinning, but she had not moved. The vertigo receded.

A teenage girl. A teenage girl, just like Sandra. No. Too early. This wasn't right. The killer wouldn't change the series.

"They don't fit. The toddler doesn't fit. That's not her." She said this more for herself than for him. She needed to hear that again, out loud. "Not her."

"Not her? Who?" he asked.

"My mother wouldn't kill children. She's a monster, but she wouldn't…"

Nadine thought of Sandra Shank. Her classmate. Seventeen years old. A beauty full of potential, veiling a thin line of cruelty. She'd met her match in Arleen. If Nadine had remained mute, would she have killed the entire clique?

"But you didn't find who Lacey was sleeping with?"

"It's not Lacey. It's Hope. This isn't your mom, Nadine."

She nodded in a frantic sort-of bob. "I know that."

"Do you?" His hold on her elbow was tight enough to get her attention.

He drew her to a lobby bench that flanked a window. That alone made her anxious, but she was back in the here and now, trying to focus. Everything was happening too fast.

Was she having a nervous breakdown? No. There was no time. She had to concentrate, or she'd get away with it again.

"The FBI should speak to my mother."

"They are. Or have."

Nadine let her head drop back and stared up at the ceiling. Of course they were. Her mother had the FBI interviewing her. She'd be in heaven.

*

"Dee-Dee, trash night," Arleen's voice was musical.

The sound sent a chill up Nadine's spine. She groaned. She was twelve now and preferred being alone. Her mother's absences troubled her, but with Arlo gone, it was better by herself, because her mother's drinking and erratic mood swings kept Nadine mostly locked in her room when Arleen was about.

She left her room and found her mother in the kitchen, naked, using the nylon brush and dish soap to scrub her nails.

"Stick that other bag inside the white one," her mother said, working up a pinkish lather.

Nadine collected the kitchen trash and headed out. It was still daylight and the black plastic trash bag sat on top of the outside bin.

She glanced back at the trailer, hesitating. Then she tore open the bag and dragged out a large pair of jeans wrapped around a familiar T-shirt and an unfamiliar bra, all sodden with blood.

A small mewling sound came from her throat as she lifted the lid. Nadine dropped in both bags, praying that someone would see the blood and stop her.

*

Demko took her hand. "You still with me?"

Her gaze snapped back into focus and she nodded. "I'll tell them everything I know," said Nadine. "I'll give them my profiles and the binders."

"They've already contacted the DA. They have everything on the case, or they will very soon. Just one more thing." He sat beside her, taking her hand as he considered his words.

"What?" she finally asked, letting the anxiety leak into her voice.

"I have information about the contents of the bag found on your bed."

CHAPTER TWENTY

Wag the dog

The shiver took Nadine, and she began to tremble. He waited, watching. Had all the color left her face? Her hands and feet were freezing.

"Tell me," she whispered.

"It was women's clothing. Shirt. Denim skirt. Panties, stockings, shoes and a bra. All cut with a knife and covered in blood."

He kept her from toppling off the bench as he continued.

"The blood was bovine."

"Bovine? Cow blood?"

"That's right."

Nadine sagged. "Oh, thank God."

"The bad news is that the clothing appears to be new and they recovered no hair or fiber evidence."

"And no prints on the plastic bag. Like your mask."

"Yes. Someone is leaving us reminders of our mother's crimes. Or in my case, my half brother's."

He distanced his mother from responsibility for his father's murder yet again. The courts had determined that his half brother had acted on her orders. But Demko continued to give his mother a pass. She didn't like it.

But today was not the day for that.

*

The FBI had set up its own field office in a storefront off Main Street and Links Avenue in what was once a restaurant. They had papered all the windows and were feeding the press a regular diet to draw them from the police station and their residences, including Nadine's. The best part about their location was the walkover from the parking garage, which prevented the media from recording who came and went from their headquarters.

The Bureau had transformed the interior of the restaurant. Instead of an open space of tables and chairs, there were partitions and cubicles to rival any accounting firm in town. The Spanish tile floor remained, and the lighting was too ornate for an office, but the desks, computers and conference areas were all spot on.

Some stereotypes find basis in fact. But she was unprepared for the men who checked them in. They looked so much like the agents who had come to her high school to speak to her about Arleen's murders that she did a double take.

Each agent maintained their regulation haircut, looking as if they just left some elite military unit and had substituted a uniform for a suit. Dark colors pervaded, heedless of the subtropical climate. All had service weapons clipped to their belts, and FBI identification cards hung on lanyards around their thick necks. One of their reception committee escorted them into the interview room.

"Dr. Finch." Another man of identical height and haircut stepped forward. His face showed more age than the others, but his body appeared youthful and fit. "Thank you for coming in. I'm Special Agent Sean Torrin, out of the DC Field Office and lead investigator for this case. This is Special Agent Fukuda, also from DC. In addition, we're coordinating with agents out of the Tampa Field Office." He waved to the outer area and the men who had escorted her in.

She glanced from Torrin, whose fair coloring and features made her think he might have looked comfortable in a kilt, to Fukuda. His multiracial features blended in a handsome face, or he could have been handsome if he didn't look so grim. His short hair was light brown and his eyes a deep brown.

"Gentlemen." The calm in her voice was inexplicable and welcome. She felt focused and irrationally confident. Perhaps this was adrenaline. Whatever the cause, she was grateful.

They shook hands all around. Who would have guessed that suits came in so many selections of gray?

"Detective Demko, if you wouldn't mind waiting out there?"

His expression told Nadine that he minded, but he gave a curt nod. Then he looked to her. "Ask for me if you need me."

Nadine's smile held as she wondered again about calling a lawyer.

She paused at the door to the inner office. The interior more resembled an interrogation room than conference area. Torrin turned to face her.

"Am I here to help with your investigation, or is this something else?"

"Just an informal chat," said Torrin.

That was vague, and anytime the FBI wanted to speak to you, it was not informal.

"Am I under suspicion of a crime?"

Torrin's smile never wavered. "No, you are not."

"I was told you want my help with the recent homicides."

"That's true."

Only then did she follow Torrin and Fukuda into the interview room. The glass partitions did not rise to the height of the ceiling and she sat facing inward, so she could not see what Detective Demko might be doing. Pacing, she imagined. Fukuda and Torrin sat across from Nadine, shoulder to shoulder, placing her in the corner and blocking the exit.

The questions began as she would have, when approaching a new patient. They were general and all ones to which they already had the answers. Easier to compare her responses to the unknown, if the interviewer was familiar with how she answered the baseline. That impressed her.

There was a pause as Fukuda glanced at his notepad. The man had the body of a distance runner and looked capable of chasing down a cheetah.

"May I ask a question?" asked Nadine.

"Go ahead," said Fukuda.

"Is it true that you have two missing persons?"

Special Agent Torrin took that one. "No. We've located both the child and teen, safe and sound."

The stone in her heart lifted and she smiled.

"That's good news."

"We are interested in your copycat theory," said Fukuda.

This launched them into a prolonged interview on her recollections of her mother's crimes and then Arleen's involvement with men. They brought up names that she had nearly forgotten. Men whom she had met. Men who had left, and some that she never heard of before.

They mentioned women, neighbors and some who she remembered worked with her mom at different job sites.

Torrin fired off another name.

"Infinity Yanez?"

Nadine thought that sounded familiar but could not place it. "I don't know. I don't think so."

Torrin continued with another name, a male name.

She thought back, quiet in reflection before answering. "No. I don't recall him, either. I'm sorry. Who are these people?"

"Missing persons cases."

"Recent?"

"No. From the 1990s and 2000s."

Nadine's attention moved from Torrin to the table before her. Missing men and women, at least a dozen, and all had disappeared before her mother's capture. It was harder to breathe now.

"Could I have some water, please?"

Fukuda retrieved a small bottle of cold water from the mini-fridge in the corner and offered it.

The liquid helped, but not enough.

They moved from her recollections to recent events, focusing on the break-in. It became clear that they had suspicions she was the one who moved the furniture and added the bag of bloody clothing to her own bed.

"You see a therapist, yes?"

"Yes."

"And you have various prescriptions for anxiety and depression."

"Not all that uncommon."

"Have you ever considered harming yourself or others?"

Nadine knew how to answer this one with her eyes closed. "No, never."

"Would you be willing to take a polygraph to eliminate yourself as a suspect?"

"Am I a suspect?"

"Not really. It'll help with the media."

This reply was designed to appeal to her need to avoid the public spotlight and might be intended to entrap her for crimes she did not commit. Refusing would only make her look more guilty.

However, she was certain that a polygraph would show deceptive answers and behavior because it was part of her DNA to be deceptive. Since she had nothing to do with any of the string of murders in Sarasota or the break-in, she could answer honestly. Her involvement with her mother's crimes would not be so easily overlooked. *Aiding and abetting* was how she referred to her actions in her mind, regardless of the fact the prosecution maintained that, as a child, she couldn't have aided or abetted anyone. In the eyes of the law, she was another victim.

So, why do I feel responsible?

*

Nadine disobeyed her mother and tucked the garbage bag far under the trailer.

Her mother had not replaced Nadine's phone, and she kept her cell on her so Nadine had no way to call for help.

"Get to bed, Dee-Dee. It's a damned school night." Her mother waited in the doorway in her underwear as she climbed the stairs into the trailer.

Last night, the local news was full of pleas from Sandra's mother and father to find their daughter. Her disappearance was now linked to a man, Stephen White, thirty-three. Nadine remembered him.

Phone records connected the pair. White had priors for drug arrests and pandering. The police were treating this as an abduction, which Nadine suspected it was. But not by Stephen White.

She paused, determined to ask her mother what she'd done to Sandra.

"Well? Do I have to get the strap?"

Nadine rubbed the back of her thigh at the memory of the last beating she had taken. She headed to her room. Her mother had long ago placed bars on the rental's windows, to keep out thieves, even though the shabby trailer had nothing to offer.

It had been over two years since the last bag. That time, Nadine had finally gotten the nerve to look inside at the men's jeans and woman's beige bra, both soaked in blood and sliced. At twelve, she had known what would happen if she told, and what would keep happening if she didn't.

Now at fourteen, she lay on her bed, listening to the rain beating on the tin roof, and knew the police were never going to catch Arleen.

If this was ever going to stop, she was the one to do it.

*

On Monday morning, when she dragged the bin to the street, she left the bag behind. She spied a corner of the black plastic again on the way to the bus stop and thought she would throw up.

What was she doing? They'd come and take her. No one would want to adopt her, and her mother would be arrested.

Another thought struck her. Sandra might still be alive. Please let her still be alive.

Nadine marched toward the bus stop.

The garbage truck rumbled past her as she repressed the urge to run back and do what her mother had ordered her to do.

Throw out the trash.

*

"Dr. Finch?" said Special Agent Torrin.

Nadine snapped her attention back to the FBI agent, who eyed her cautiously; she considered again asking for a lawyer.

The agent seemed to expect this and told her that Detective Demko had already taken a polygraph. But law enforcement officers were not required to tell her the truth.

"I'd like to hear that from him," she said.

"We'll bring him right in," said Special Agent Torrin.

Nadine waited with Special Agent Fukuda, who stood silently at her periphery. It occurred to her during the wait that Detective Demko also did not have to be honest regarding the polygraph. It would come down to if she trusted him.

Nadine did not like this new position as crash dummy. Special Agent Torrin returned with Detective Demko. Both gave reassurances and they wheeled in the machine.

The polygraph took about forty-five minutes. It was painless and distracting to watch the needle dance as she made her answers. Afterward, the agents asked her to wait with Demko in the reception area. Nadine assumed this gave them time to analyze the results. She lied on several questions about her childhood, but on none regarding her current state of mind or lack of involvement with the murders.

"They don't want our help," she said. "They just want us eliminated as suspects."

Demko took hold of her hand. "That's the first step."

An FBI officer ushered them back into the interview room and they took their seats across from Torrin and Fukuda.

"Dr. Finch, your profile interests us, particularly your theory that the disfigurement of the ring finger was associated with infidelity." He sat forward. "That detail was not revealed at your mother's trial. How did you hear of it?"

"I reached out to the district attorney who prosecuted my mother."

"Bradley Robins."

"Yes."

"And you had no prior knowledge of this mutilation?"

"I did not."

"Yet you thought the recent double homicide was a copycat."

"There were other similarities," said Nadine.

"Such as?"

She listed them: the rope, the slashes on the female's buttock, the victims were engaged in an affair. The men were all dispatched first. The women shared physical characteristics, such as their height, build, eye and hair color, and most were found naked in a natural body of water. And there was a progression of holding and torturing the female victims for increasing lengths of time.

"I see. Well, we have our people speaking to Bradley Robins now. He's assured us that this detail and the marks on the women were not revealed during the trial and that he has not relayed that information to anyone but you and Detective Demko. But the person who killed the first victims in the most recent murders,

Debi Poletti and David Lowe, must have had firsthand information about the case or some association with your mother. How do you think the unsub learned of it?"

Had Nadine just stuck her head in a noose? She eyed Torrin, judging whether he was speculating or accusing.

"I don't know," she said, and stopped talking.

"We are impressed with the speed you made this association and reached out to Mr. Robins. It was between the double homicide and your visit to your mother. Is that correct?"

She shook her head. "After the initial murders and my first visit with my mother."

Nadine felt more like a suspect by the second. Her knee began to bounce, and she quelled the nervous motion.

Torrin continued to watch her.

"We have contacted the warden at Lowell, at Demko's suggestion, because you alerted him that there may be correspondence between your mother and the killer."

"It's a possibility."

"We think your connection could be useful," said Fukuda. "Would you be willing to pose a series of questions to her?"

"That depends on the questions."

"Fair enough," said Fukuda. "I will say that we tried to interview your mother, and she was less than cooperative."

"Because you excluded her from your study."

"I beg your pardon?" asked Torrin.

"The recent study published on your website by the National Center for the Analysis of Violent Crimes. That's part of the FBI's Critical Incident Response Group in Quantico. Right?"

Fukuda nodded. "That's correct."

"The study indicated that you did not include kills for hire, medical practitioners who committed serial murders or women." She couldn't believe that she was going here. But here she was. "You have a statistically significant population of female killers and failed to include them. It seems an obvious gap in your research."

"Point taken. Now back to the serial killer we are pursuing. Do you feel it's a woman?"

"I don't make predictions based on feelings. My mother's cases and these show a strong correlational relationship. It might, in fact, be some kind of tribute to her. Or..." Nadine's gaze drifted, and she closed her mouth, not ready to say this next part aloud.

"Or?" prompted Torrin.

Nadine glanced to Demko. He gave her knee a brief tap and she couldn't read the significance. Was this a warning or encouragement?

"Or," she continued, "it may be a call to action."

Torrin and Fukuda exchanged blank looks and then turned their vacant expressions on her.

"Explain," said Torrin.

"I've been considering why this is happening here and now. It occurs to me that I am the same age as my mother was when she committed many of these crimes. And having me here with Detective Demko and Tina Ruz and Dr. Juliette Hartfield is too strange to be coincidence."

"What do Hartfield, Ruz and Detective Demko have to do with this?" asked Fukuda.

Now she and Demko exchanged blank looks. *They don't know.*

"Someone hired us all. And all of us have mothers convicted of murder."

Torrin was on his feet and out the door in a matter of moments.

"You have a suspect?" asked Fukuda.

"No. But it would have to be someone in personnel or a supervisor, Dr. Crean, for example. Perhaps an influential person on the city council?"

"An office assistant responsible for collecting résumés," added Demko.

Fukuda had his hand across his mouth and his elbow on the table, thinking. Finally he dropped his hand.

"It's an interesting theory, considering Dr. Crean's obvious connection with serial killers."

"Female killers," she corrected.

"Well, we'll bring Crean in," said Fukuda.

Torrin returned. "We're collecting a list of all city employees involved in the hiring process."

"Great," said Fukuda. "Now, our own profiler is relatively certain that this is a male offender. Average intelligence. A social misfit who holds a job that involves physical labor, potentially also a fisherman, considering knowledge of the waterways and fishing spots, who likely owns both a truck and a motorboat. Married or recently divorced and whose wife is, or was, unfaithful. He is using others to punish someone who cheated on him."

Nadine snorted. "He give you a model on the boat?"

Fukuda glanced at his notes. "I don't think so."

Demko chuckled.

"You disagree?" asked Torrin, picking up on her sarcasm.

"It's very specific."

"And differs from yours," said Torrin. "A copycat who idolizes Arleen Howler."

"Yes," said Nadine. "Our unsub has formed some connection with my mother. I know she has correspondence from all sorts of people. The prison records for incoming mail is a start but don't ignore who visits, calls or emails her."

Torrin scribbled something else on his pad.

"The mutilation on the fingers, our profiler agrees this is a calling card. Can you explain why you think this maiming is indicative of infidelity?"

"The mutilation is always on the left ring finger. That's significant. My mother told me she intended this as a permanent wedding band. A reminder of the vow they broke."

Fukuda nodded. It seemed she and the profiler agreed on that one.

"What about the marks exclusively on the women? They are all on the fleshy part of the buttock, all approximately four inches long and each series include seven cuts, six roughly horizontal lines and one vertical one."

"I'm sure they have significance. But perhaps only to the killer."

"Our profiler believes this is a way to further humiliate the females. A defeminizing."

"No. That would involve cutting or removing the breasts or damaging the sex organs."

Fukuda dropped his head again to record something.

"The marks are similar to the ones left by your mother on her victims," said Torrin.

"Female victims only," she corrected.

"Would you be willing to ask her about the meaning?"

"I have. She wouldn't tell me."

"You have a theory?" he asked.

"Yes. My mother had a special hatred for women who slept with married men. Not all her female victims were married, but the men all were. Check back. She attacked the males to incapacitate and kill, often carved them a new wedding band postmortem. But she carved the married women's when they were still alive. She wanted them to suffer. It was the women she was after, her real targets. And all got that mark or brand. She called them 'mean bitches' and 'whores.' She said they were…" Nadine's thoughts whirled as she spoke, and the pieces snapped into place. She gasped as a flash of insight tore through her and she pinned her gaze on Demko.

"I know what they are. The marks on the women. I think… no, I know what they mean."

CHAPTER TWENTY-ONE

Out of the loop

"My mom called these women 'whores' and 'bitches' and… 'homewreckers'! The gashes, they're letters, initials. *H* and *W.*"

"Hold on," Demko said, and reached for his phone, pulling up a photo of Hope Kerr, the female victim found floating in the inlet off Robinson Preserve. He zoomed in on the marks. It seems so obvious now. The letters were sideways in the image but would have been vertical to someone carving them with a blade.

"Rotate it," she said.
Demko turned the image ninety degrees.

She glanced to Torrin, triumphant, and saw his eyes narrow on her. She sank back in her chair. This man was not impressed. He was suspicious.

Demko noticed the pall that had descended over the room.

"She's right," he offered.

Torrin's gaze flicked from him to her.

"Dr. Finch," said Fukuda. "You just stated that you asked your mother about the marks but were unable to obtain an explanation. But now, remarkably, you have deciphered their meaning?"

"Yes."

"I see. Also your profile conflicts with our profiler, who believes this offender is a social misfit."

"Not a misfit, a social chameleon."

Fukuda glanced to Torrin and shook his head. Torrin ignored him, turning back to Nadine.

"Our profiler states that the male is attacked and killed first. You say the male is attacked to incapacitate."

"Yes. I think this unsub likes him to watch." She held his gaze as he winced.

Fukuda read from his notes. "'A strong white-collar worker, educated, highly intelligent and living alone. Possibly working inside the city or county organization *and* has been in contact with your mother.'" Fukuda turned to Nadine. "Is that a fair summary?"

"Yes."

Fukuda and Torrin shared a long silent exchange. Finally Torrin turned back to Nadine.

"Dr. Finch, we'd like to make you an adjunct member of our team. A consultant."

That was the bait. The lure to gain her attention and flatter her before the real proposal, whatever that was. She braced for their request.

"Is that what you'd like?"

Torrin's brows rose, and he nodded, surprised, she assumed, at her ability to target threats. After surviving her teen years, this was child's play.

It occurred to her that most people would say something like "I'm honored" or pledge their intention to do all in their power to help, while she skipped that part and went right to her suspicions: expecting a trap.

"I'd like you to begin by identifying similarities between your mother's victims and the recent homicides. What we are after is a comparison, victim by victim. Could you do that?"

She'd already begun two geo-profiles, comparing her mother's couple murders to this current series.

"Yes." Her ears were hot—a sure sign something was wrong.

"Wonderful."

From Fukuda's expression, it was clear that he did not agree.

A minute ago, she was a suspect. The speed of the transition made her head spin.

"Special Agent Torrin, your next move should be to find out who Hope Kerr is sleeping with. Because that person is the next victim."

"You believe this crime matches that committed by your mother against Lacey Louder."

"Don't you?"

"There are substantive differences. Louder was working as a prostitute. Kerr is married, owns a business and there is no indication she was engaged in any extramarital affair."

Fukuda spoke. "Mr. Kerr has been eliminated as a suspect. Our profiler feels this was a crime of opportunity. Our unsub found her alone on a beach and took advantage, maiming her hand and adding the rope to make the crimes match the next in the series."

"It's not a crime of opportunity. She was targeted. Someone chose her for a reason. Her lover will have some position in public service, similar to the park ranger."

"Ranger Drew Henderson."

"Yes."

"Agree to disagree, then." Fukuda opened a folder, drew out a photo and laid it before Nadine. Her eyes went wide in recognition.

"Do you know this man?"

The photo was of Nathan Dun. It looked like an official photograph as he sat in his uniform, head cocked, beside an American flag.

"Yes, that is one of our court officers, Nathan Dun. Is he missing?"

"We observed him trespassing at your residence on Sunday night," said Torrin.

A shiver rippled over her skin and stabbed into her jaw. Nadine's nostrils flared as she tried to process this news. He'd been at her place when she'd been at the hotel.

The FBI now had her home under surveillance.

"You're watching my house?"

"Seemed a logical step," said Torrin.

"I'm not staying there," she said.

"Not common knowledge," said Fukuda. "A man entered your backyard through a neighbor's property. City officer saw him peering through your bedroom window early this morning. Sarasota Police approached, and he fled, dropping the bag he was carrying."

"So he's in custody?"

"No. Still at large. He had a crowbar and a trash bag on him. Description matched Nathan Dun."

Nadine sucked in a breath before speaking. "Do you think he's the one who broke into my house last Saturday?"

"We believe so," Torrin said.

"His father was a spree killer."

"Yes. We are aware."

"Dun is of average intelligence," said Fukuda. "His coworkers describe him as an oddball. He owns both a truck and a boat, and his marriage ended recently after he discovered his wife cheating."

In other words, Dun was a near-perfect match for the FBI profile.

"Here's the interesting part," said Torrin. "Four years ago, Nathan Dun was injured in an auto accident, suffering a debilitating back injury. He is currently collecting a disability benefit and resides in Miami-Dade County."

She blinked at Torrin a moment. "I don't understand."

"We sent agents to his house to speak to him. He's in custody."

"So you have him?"

"We have Nathan Dun. But the man working as one of your court officers is not Nathan. We believe that is Nathan's brother."

"An alias?"

"It's fraud and identity theft. Nathan was an accomplice in the ruse. The court officer's real name is Anthony Dun. He took his brother's name after his brother's accident."

"So he was collecting employment and unemployment?"

"Disability. They run cross-checks, but not often enough."

"Why did Anthony Dun do that?" she asked.

"Criminal record," Demko supplied.

"He's got a felony conviction for sexual assault, and, more recently, Anthony Dun was arrested for domestic violence and served four years. No way he could have gotten through the background check to be a court officer."

Nadine's skin crawled, and she stretched her mouth tight in disgust.

"He raped someone?"

"A coworker. He was seventeen, tried as an adult. Been out for three years. Anthony Dun ticks all the boxes and is our prime suspect."

"He asked me out," said Nadine. "I said no, and he left an odd message on my office voicemail."

"We need that," said Torrin.

"I'm sure my office assistant can retrieve it for you."

"Good."

"Do you know if Dun had any contact with my mother?"

Torrin looked to Fukuda.

"We'll check," said Fukuda.

She sat back in her chair, breathing through the wave of relief. If it could only be true, that this was the guy. Their guy. They could stop this. Catch Dun and save the others.

Then it hit her. Either their profiler was right, and it was Anthony Dun, or she was right, and they were targeting the wrong man.

If she believed in her profile, then Hope had an unidentified lover who might be murdered at any minute.

She hesitated. Who was she to contradict an expert? This was her first profile. She had zero experience at this and was monumentally underqualified.

She grasped Demko's hand and squeezed. Then she lifted her chin and spoke.

"It's not Dun."

*

After her disturbing interview with the Feds, Nadine had so many questions about the names the FBI had mentioned. Cold cases. She didn't know any of them. But one name sounded familiar. She wondered if her brother might know. She needed to reach Arlo and did not want to wait for the weekend. Then she remembered the prison chaplain. Arlo once said that in an emergency, the chaplain could get a message to him.

The web search provided the number, and she made the call on Tuesday at lunch, claiming a death in the family.

Arlo called back forty minutes later.

"Dee-Dee? Who died?"

"I needed an emergency to get you on the phone."

"Dee-Dee, I thought it was Mom!"

She wondered, not for the first time, what it would be like when, and if, her mother really got the needle; she shivered.

"Mom's fine."

She heard Arlo blow out a breath.

"So… what's up?"

The pause stretched as she tried to think where to start. The silence beat between them like a bleeding heart.

"I saw Mom Saturday."

"Again?" He sounded surprised, and why not? She hadn't communicated with her mother in years. A toxic relationship, her therapist called it.

Amen to that.

"How'd this one go?"

"Terrible. I asked her about her victims."

"Yikes." He gave a low whistle. "You didn't think she'd be helpful, I hope."

"Stupid of me."

"She always gets better than she gives," he said. "You be up this weekend?"

She didn't want to make promises. "If there's no… special assignments at work."

"Fair enough."

"She did say that she told you about the cuts she made on her victims' fingers."

Arlo made a sound of disgust. "A while ago. Yeah."

"Why didn't you tell me?"

"Dee-Dee, you were fourteen, heading for a new life with Dad's sister. You didn't need that."

"So you knew?"

"Heard in court that she sliced them up. But about the fingers? No, I didn't know. But she writes me. Sometimes about her victims. She mentioned the finger thing."

"Do you have those letters?"

"Shit, I can hardly stand to read them. I chuck 'em. Sorry."

"Did you tell anyone else about the way she mutilated her victims?"

"No. Guys here know I'm Arleen's kid. Hard enough as it is."

She believed him on both points.

"Can I ask you about Stephen White?" Nadine recalled she had met her mother's final victim only once and with Arlo.

"Oh, that dirtbag."

*

Arlo took her to her favorite fast-food place, but when she got there, she saw several of her classmates and asked Arlo to use the drive-through to avoid them. Arlo had picked up on it. After they ordered, he parked.

"Come on," he said, climbing out of the vehicle and then staring back at her.

"What about my milk shake?"

"Later."

She feared he would pick a fight or something. But he surprised her, heading over to a tall man dressed in a hoodie and jeans. He had a sleeve of tattoos reaching all the way to the top of one hand and he smoked. She wrinkled her nose at the stink. She'd seen this guy hanging around and talking with some of her other eighth grade classmates. Something about him gave her the creeps, so she'd kept her distance.

Arlo introduced her.

"Dee-Dee, this is Mr. White."

The man had taken hold of her chin in a grip that frightened Nadine and lifted her face, studying her features.

"She'll do."

Arlo knocked away White's hand and the two faced off, chest to chest. Nadine stepped behind her brother, clutching the tail of his shirt.

"She's my sister," Arlo said, his voice hostile. There was a threat there that Nadine had never heard, a menace, and it had lifted the hairs on her neck. "Wanted you to meet her in case you saw her around."

"Oh," White had said, stepping back. "Gotcha."

But Nadine didn't understand. Safely back in the car, she'd asked Arlo and he'd said White "ran girls." She still didn't understand. He'd also said that White was his dealer. Did "ran girls" mean "sell to them" or" use them as pot dealers"?

*

"Dee-Dee? You still there?"

"Yes. I'm here. Was White using girls from my school as escorts?"

"'Escorts'? No. They were whores. He took sixty percent."

"Is that why you introduced me?"

"You were growing up, Dee-Dee. And you're pretty. He'd have hit on you eventually, offered you stuff. Gifts, drugs. It's a slippery slope."

"I only just figured all that out."

"You were a kid."

"Thank you, Arlo. For all the times you protected me."

He cleared his throat again. Was he choking up, too?

Nadine thought of the woman he attacked, his then girlfriend, and the irony of her trusting a man who could do such a thing. Despite his crimes, she still loved her brother.

Nadine could hear other men speaking to their families on the bank of phones in the visitors' area.

The pause seemed endless; the only sound, his breathing.

She had one more question about the woman the FBI had mentioned, the one she thought she should recall.

"Arlo, what was the name of the lady that Dad left Mom for?"

"Infinity."

"Her last name?"

"Yanez. Infinity Yanez. What are you getting at, Dee?"

The cold grip of suspicion grabbed Nadine, making her gasp.

"Do you know what happened to her?" she asked.

"They ran away together. He had warrants out for failure to pay child support."

"What did Infinity look like?"

"I saw her once. Biked over there to talk to Dad. But I couldn't get up the nerve."

"Describe her, Arlo."

"Young. Hot. Short skirts. Skin was light, really light brown. Her hair was straight and black. Hung down to her waist. She wore a lot of makeup."

"Eyes?"

"Brown."

Meaning Infinity was a physical match to her mother's and their copycat's victims.

"Dee-Dee? What's happening?"

*

By Thursday, Nadine was sick of living out of a suitcase in a business hotel, tired of dumping all the voicemail left by reporters and fed up with being cut out of the loop by the Feds. Her new assignment as a consultant for the FBI meant she was no longer profiling for the city, but reported to work in her regular office. There she worked on her comparative profile requested by Torrin, with possible characteristics of their current unsub. She also continued work on her geographic profiles of her mother's and their unsub's series. The geo-profile would direct law enforcement to areas statistically most likely to be in the copycat killer's comfort zone.

Special Agent Torrin showed up that afternoon, seemingly to tell her they'd not located Anthony Dun. She waited for the real reason for his visit.

"I heard from the prison chaplain in Lawtey you had a family emergency?" He stared, stone-faced.

"Yes." She stopped talking.

"Your conversation with your brother was helpful?"

She pressed her lips together and nodded, ignoring the heat burning her face and neck.

"I'm glad to hear it. How's the comparative profile coming?" he asked.

Nadine met his stare. "I'll show you mine if you show me yours."

"Yes, all right," said Torrin. "But first, no more web searches on your mother's crimes on unsecured servers. That one from the coffee shop could have been hell for us."

Nadine's skin crawled as she realized she was under surveillance. She'd been at a coffee shop on Wednesday after work and she'd used their Wi-Fi server to access a Wiki page. Was she their real prime suspect? Was Anthony Dun really missing at all?

She didn't know.

"We're arranging an interview with your mother. We would like you to come along."

"Would you?" She met his gaze. "Yes, all right."

"Great. Also, your home security system arrived. Wouldn't want it stolen off your porch."

Nadine watched him go. Torrin's earlier insistence that she was not a suspect did not reassure her.

After work, she drove to the hotel and packed her things, moving back to her rental cottage. The reporters had given up and she had the place to herself. The home security system that she had ordered sat on her porch, just as Torrin had said.

The cleaning crew Demko suggested had done a good job and she found black powder only on the inside of one cabinet door. Still, the sight was disconcerting.

It was Thursday. She missed Juliette and their happy hour. She called, yet again, and got her voicemail but didn't leave a message.

The texts from Demko were longer, the conversation stretching over several messages. Though Hope Kerr's murder was not in his jurisdiction, he was still trying to find anyone connected with her, but so far found nothing to support Nadine's certainty that Kerr was involved outside of her marriage.

Despite being glad to be home, she felt anxious, no longer comfortable here. Maybe she should get a dog, as Crean had suggested.

Instead, she opened the box and took out the instructions on how to download the app to the new security system.

Demko called her before she turned in. Hearing his voice comforted, even when he was talking about the case. It seemed the FBI had not cut him from the herd, yet.

Before going to bed, she armed her security system for the first time. She glanced out into her dark backyard and then dropped the roller blind.

On Friday morning, she continued work on the comparison requested by the FBI, creating a geographic profile, adding in all the details about where her mother's victims were found and making inferences about where they might have been dumped based on recovery details, time of death and the way the river flowed. This type of profile would help illustrate her mother's comfort zone and the territory where she hunted, captured, held and dumped her victims. Once she had this first map fleshed out, she turned to their recent murders, adding the information to the program and allowing the predictive software to do its work.

Anthony Dun was a tempting suspect. He'd abused women. He insinuated himself here under false pretense. He'd been married and divorced, as their profiler predicted. But, according to Demko, the FBI had made no connection between her mother and Dun. Not even a web search.

If he was fascinated enough with Arleen Howler to copy her crimes, then he had to have studied her crimes. Where was the link?

She turned back to her profile. She was here to assist, and she was going to give that all she had, despite the fact that she spent more time leaving messages than answering them. It seemed her consulting involved using her to gain access to her mother and mentioning her in their press conference as a means to engage their killer.

Nadine accessed the software for geographic profiling, studying her two maps. She'd created several mock versions while in Quantico, but the map of her mother's series was the real deal. Unfortunately, the one for their copycat now had data from three victims.

After lunch, she checked her office voicemail. It was from Demko and very brief.

"Call me when you get this. It's important."

Her skin stippled. While she was in the process of calling back, her cell phone rang, and Demko's name popped up on the screen. She connected the call.

"Hey there! What's up?" she asked. *Please let it not be Kerr's lover.*

"Where are you?" he asked.

"My office."

"I'm up in Bradenton. Sheriff there thinks he found the murder site of our second female. It's a beach on the Manatee River in Robinson Preserve. We collected a beach chair and camera bag tossed up in the tall grass. It's got traces of blood. Initial test is a match for Hope Kerr."

Nadine's hand went to her throat as the implications came together in her mind.

"And there's something else... remember you told me that Dr. Hartfield had recently been kayaking in Manatee?" he asked.

Nadine scowled. "Yeah, up in that preserve. You said lots of folks do."

"Lab techs just phoned. Because of what you said about our unsub working on the inside, I asked them to run a print from the seltzer can we found at the initial crime scene from Lido Beach against our city employees."

Nadine's hand went around her throat. She knew what he would say before he even spoke, and it filled her with horror.

"It's a match for Juliette Hartfield."

Nadine reeled. How could this be happening? "Are you sure?"

"Certain. It's a match."

"She might have dropped it at the crime scene," said Nadine, but even as she spoke the words, she knew that no investigator would discard garbage at an active homicide scene.

"She wasn't at the crime scene. Only the body dump."

"What does that mean?"

"I'm trying to find out. I've got to bring her in for questioning."

"No!"

The implications leapt and twirled in her mind, maniacal monsters dancing around a campfire.

Nadine rose to her feet, backing up until she hit the window ledge, one hand pressed to her pounding heart.

No one knew human anatomy better than Juliette. She handled a blade as part of her work. Plus, she was the one gathering samples from the bodies of their victims, giving her the opportunity to manipulate evidence. She was constantly in that damned kayak and was the only woman that Nadine knew who enjoyed fishing.

Nadine had seen her tackle box. A murder kit disguised by fishing lures. Juliette had everything she needed to kill someone.

How long had Nadine been standing there with the phone in her hand?

Demko's voice seemed far away.

"Nadine, stay there. Do you hear me? Don't move. I'm sending a unit to your location."

CHAPTER TWENTY-TWO

Anyone's call

Demko ended the call and Nadine put her head on her desk as the implications of her part in this crashed in like a collapsing ceiling. He had run a search based on her suspicions. But there had to be an innocent explanation.

For the next hour, Nadine tried to clear her email in-box. She couldn't focus. What was taking so long?

She pictured Juliette at the police station getting fingerprinted.

"Nadine?"

She startled right out of her seat to find Crean standing in the doorway, arms folded and looking cross.

"Detective Demko just called. He told me they're picking up Juliette Hartfield for questioning."

"Did he?" Her voice was a squeak.

"They are having trouble locating her. So, he has arranged a patrol unit to escort you home."

"'Patrol unit'?" He'd told her that. Hadn't he? She seemed lost in a thick fog.

She gaped at Crean. This was a waking nightmare.

"You have a protective detail until they locate Hartfield, and this is settled."

"Is that necessary?"

Crean lifted one brow. "*I* don't think so. But *he's* the detective. Escort is downstairs now."

Nadine stood and retrieved her bag.

When she passed reception, Tina cast her a worried look and Nadine realized their office assistant had overheard the conversation.

Nadine ducked out into the hallway.

In the building's lower lobby, a young officer waited. He was fresh-faced and muscular and introduced himself as Officer Pender. He explained that he would follow her to her residence and then wait there for the detective.

Nadine hustled out to the adjoining parking lot and her white Lexus. The interior was stifling. She tossed her bag on the passenger side and folded the silver sun shield that stretched across the windshield. By the time she got under way, the patrol unit was right behind her.

At her rental, Nadine left her vehicle in the drive and her escort parked on the street.

The officer met her on her narrow porch. "Let me do a walk-through first. Wait here."

Nadine switched off the alarm with the fob and unlocked the door, then stepped aside as he headed into the place that once had been her sanctuary.

The patrolman reappeared a few moments later.

"It's all clear," said the young officer. "Cute place."

"Thanks." She used to think so. Now she recognized that she lived in a fishbowl. Would she ever again sit on the back porch and not wonder if someone was watching?

"Until Detective Demko gets here, I'll be parked right there." He pointed to the squad car. "Flash the lights if you need me."

"Thank you."

He gave Nadine a two-fingered salute and descended the steps from the porch to the driveway.

Nadine ducked inside, locked the front door and armed the system. If anyone opened a door or window, it would now trigger the alarm.

She dropped her bag and sank into a dinette chair, resting her elbows on the glass surface before burying her face in her hands. Above her, the ceiling fan spun, sending cool air whispering over the back of her neck.

This queasiness was so familiar, reminding her of sitting in the counselor's office back in high school, with the adults whispering outside the door.

*

Nadine's stomach twisted as she walked straight from the bus to the counselor's office. The secretary smiled.

"Well, Nadine. We haven't seen you in a while."

Nadine clutched her books before her like a stuffed toy.

"Are you here to see Mr. Pierson?"

She nodded, letting her hair fall over her face.

"He's not here right now. Do you have an appointment?"

"No," she whispered. What was she doing? Was she really going to tell?

"I can have him call you out of class when he has an opening."

Anxiety coiled around her ribs like a python. Her mother might see that bag of garbage under the house. She might get rid of it. Then it was only her word against her mother's.

Nadine remained where she was.

"Why don't you head to class. You don't want to be late."

"I need to see him right now!"

The secretary startled at Nadine's change of tone.

"Well, if it's that important, I'll have him paged." Her hand hovered over the receiver, as if paging him were a bluff.

Nadine stood her ground and the secretary finally picked up her phone. Then she motioned with her other hand.

"Go on in and have a seat."

Nadine headed into the counselor's office and sat. She needed to get someone to find Sandra before it was too late.

The sour taste in her mouth returned with the same seasick pitching.

"Snitches get stitches." *That's what her mother said.*

She didn't care. She was doing this.

Outside the counselor's office, she heard Mr. Pierson greet the secretary. Then the whispering began.

*

The western sunlight bounced off the glass surface of the table, bright as a flashlight in Nadine's face. She stood, stiff. How long had she been sitting?

It couldn't be Juliette. Impossible. But was it?

Juliette drank that damn flavored seltzer all the time. She'd kayaked at both Lido and Robinson Preserve. Circumstantial. But finding her fingerprint at a crime scene was not.

Demko thought the threat serious enough to give her a protective detail. That frightened her most of all.

Nadine headed for the front door. From the porthole window, she thought she caught movement along the thick greenery in her neighbor's yard. She peered out between cupped hands and saw nothing. But the sense of being watched was unmistakable. The hairs on her neck lifted and her cheeks tingled.

The police unit sat across the road, beyond the front entrance, just as it had been. The squad car blocked much of the narrow street.

Nadine waved. But the patrolman did not notice her.

Annoyed now, she released the door lock and stepped onto her porch. Her alarm chirped, reminding her the system was armed. She recovered the fob and hit the button before it set off the siren. Then she paused inside the door.

She flashed her outside light as Pender had directed. Then she waited. No movement came from Pender's car.

His head was tipped forward.

Was the guy asleep or on his phone?

"Well, hell."

Her approach started as a stomp, but as she crunched across the crushed shells in the drive, her sense of danger engaged. The sun had dipped behind the tall condos that lined the bay.

Something was wrong.

The dense cover of oaks gave the street the look of twilight. Low-hanging storm clouds swept in from the east. Gusts of wind tore through the leaves, shaking the branches and sending debris raining down on the patrol car. A limb, the size of her arm, thudded on the unit's hood. Inside, Pender didn't move.

Nadine stood in the street, facing the parked squad car. To reach Pender, she would need to walk beside the wall of palm fronds.

She crept to the front bumper. The wind blew dirt and sand into her eyes and mouth. She snorted, expelling the dust in her nose.

The temperature was dropping, alerting her that the rain was closing in. A glance toward the east showed the blue-gray streaks of rain streaming from the storm clouds, releasing torrents of water, moving in her direction.

The officer's windshield reflected the oak branches better than the driver, but she made Pender out as she inched forward.

Nadine gripped the door handle and swung it open.

The smell was unmistakable.

Garbage day.

Blood coated the dash and dripped from the ceiling. The officer's eyes were wide open, and his shirt was soaking wet. Beneath his strong chin, a black gash oozed thick dark blood. His hand slipped from his lap, revealing the red cordage tied about his wrist and neatly severed at a length of only a foot.

Nadine backed away, catching her heel on the curb and toppling to the ground. There, she scuttled, crablike, until she collided with the trunk of the oak.

She flipped to her hands and knees, screaming. Only her vocal cords had constricted, and the sound that came from her throat was a strangled roar.

Her phone… was in the house. She stumbled to the hood of the vehicle, using one hand to push herself erect. Before her, the narrow street stretched, and beyond glimmered the safety of her house.

Nadine froze in the drive.

She'd left the front door open.

She ran for the cottage, her breath frantic little pants. She pounded along the porch and across the threshold, stumbling through the entrance as the rain raced down the street behind her.

Where was the killer now? Where was her phone? She glanced to the dinette and, spotting it there, took one step in that direction.

Someone called her name. The voice came from inside her cottage.

"Nadine? What's wrong?"

Nadine stared at the woman standing in her living room just past the couch. For a moment, she thought it was her mother.

"Nadine?" She stepped forward, coming toward her, and Nadine recognized her now.

Juliette Hartfield was in her house.

CHAPTER TWENTY-THREE

Best-laid plans

Nadine didn't think as she leapt from the porch and dashed to the road.

"Nadine?" Juliette was after her again, pursuing her out into the torrent.

Nadine faced her, fists up, as Arlo had taught her, ready to strike.

Rain beat down on the street and surrounding rooftops at deafening volume. The rain fell in sheets, but the tree protected her from the worst of the downpour.

Juliette kept coming, gripping a knife.

The flash of silver from the blade was unmistakable. Had the storm washed away the blood?

Nadine lunged, punching her hard in the face, landing a solid blow to Juliette's eye socket before leaping away. Nadine's knuckles stung from the blow, but she kept her chin tucked and her fists raised.

Juliette dropped to her knees, her hands coming up.

Should I hit her again or kick her? No. Grab the knife and…
Do everyone a favor.

The knife fell from Juliette's hand, clattering to the concrete. Nadine glanced at the weapon and saw only a cell phone.

Nadine sucked in a breath as her gaze darted to Juliette's open empty hands, now pressed to her face.

The blade. A cell phone. The situation tipped on its head. Juliette hadn't threatened her. But Nadine had punched her in the eye.

Juliette dropped her hands. Already, her cheek was puffy and red.

"You hit me!"

"What are you doing here?" Nadine shouted, confusion and anger blending like the wind and rain.

"You texted me," Juliette said.

"I didn't."

Raindrops beat off the glass screen as Juliette reached for her phone.

The adrenaline and the fury at being confronted in her home still roared inside Nadine. Loud. So loud she couldn't think.

"See?" Juliette turned the screen, still on the ground, as she extended her arm.

Reading a text through the violent rain was impossible, because she'd have to step closer. She wouldn't.

"What does it say?"

Juliette turned the phone and read aloud. "'It's Nadine. Lost my phone. Using neighbor's. Come to my place, please! Right now! Emergency!'"

"I didn't lose my phone. I didn't write that." Nadine began shivering.

Juliette held her unoccupied hand to her injured face.

Nadine was shaking.

"You've ignored my texts for nearly a month. But now you come here when I call?"

"You said *emergency!*" said Juliette.

"You could have written it. Used another phone. You could have killed him."

"Killed who? Nadine, what are you talking about?"

"You were there. At Lido Beach. They know, Juliette."

"I don't understand."

Rain soaked Juliette's clothing. The pale blue cotton blouse was nearly transparent, and the slacks stuck to her legs. Her mascara ran down her cheeks with the water droplets. Juliette's perky hair was plastered to her skull. Nadine had never seen her hair without its characteristic spikes. Juliette looked younger, frightened, lost.

What am I doing?

Nadine lowered her fists. Juliette hesitated, then stood.

"They sent me home with a police escort," said Nadine.

"What? Why?"

Nadine didn't answer that.

"Did you see Detective Demko?"

"When?"

"Today. This afternoon."

"No. I was out on a call. Just got back from a multivehicle accident."

They stood in silence, two gunfighters on opposite ends of the thoroughfare.

Juliette's jaw was clacking now, and she hugged herself against the cold and the wet.

"The officer they sent to watch me is dead."

"Watch you what?" Confusion wrinkled Juliette's brow as she looked toward the police unit.

"He's dead. Murdered."

"What officer?" She glanced about. "Why is he watching you?"

"Go check him."

She did, giving Nadine a very wide berth as she sidestepped past and to the patrol car. Juliette bent at the waist, resting her empty palm on the roof of the squad car, adding her prints to Nadine's. It was a smart move... if she were the killer.

Nadine balled her hands to fists, ready to strike again if necessary.

Juliette straightened fast and stared back at Nadine, blinking in the downpour.

"Somebody slit his throat," she said, checking for a pulse. Then she drew back. "I'm calling the police."

"Yeah. Do that." Her mind was jumping around, trying to tell her something, but also flitting from thought to thought, erratic as the flight of a butterfly.

The rain let up. Nadine had left the patrolman's door open. Blood ran from the vehicle into the storm drain.

Doubts. They filled her like the rain flooding the street. Doubts that Juliette was the unsub.

Nadine watched her make the call and that thought, the one she couldn't quite grasp, finally popped up from her subconscious.

If Juliette was innocent, she might be looking in the wrong direction.

Nadine turned in a circle, glancing about at the familiar street that now seemed full of dangerous places to hide and watch. The thick fronds of the Arenga palm moved. Was that a face?

"Hey!"

Nadine dashed toward her neighbor's fence, tracking the movement in the waving greenery. From somewhere off to the east came the shrill shriek of sirens. At the fence, Nadine paused as the practical part of her brain re-engaged. If there were someone there, she'd like to know who it was, but chasing them through dense cover in the rain might be a terrible idea. No, it *was* a terrible idea.

Instead, she wobbled back to the street as her knees gave way. She sank to the curb.

The rain had moved away, and steam rose from the road, visible now in approaching headlights.

Where's Juliette?

"Juliette!"

"Behind the patrol car," she heard Juliette call.

"Why?"

There was a hissing sound, air escaping from between clenched teeth. "So that you don't hit me again."

"Did you see someone running away?"

"I didn't see anyone."

Vehicle doors opened as several police units arrived from two directions. Nadine turned to the hedgerow beside her house and saw the palm fronds moving again. Whoever had killed the officer outside her home could be long gone. Or they could be watching right now.

CHAPTER TWENTY-FOUR

Couple two part two

I heard it on the scanner, pick up and escort. I followed her to her home, tailing the patrol unit. And who do I find on assignment? My target, Howard Pender, the guy who just can't let go. Unbelievable good fortune.

What luck! I'd been unsuccessful at finding Pender alone and vulnerable. This is Nadine's street. It's right in the city but on such an out-of-the-way corner. And the vegetation. Truly amazing. A real tropical jungle.

Bringing them together on such short notice was difficult enough. Bringing them together as adversaries took real genius.

En route, I sent Juliette a text from a burner phone. Getting to Pender was ridiculously easy. I showed the cop my county ID, and he opened his squad car door to speak to me. He remembered when I called him in and seemed nervous.

Pender is so like the ranger killed in his truck. I'd never find a better chance than this. It took real daring, and the thrill is indescribable.

There he was, sitting right in front of Dee-Dee's cute little home, all alone. I loved that place, inside and out.

Officer Pender told me way too much about why he was there. Nervous, you know, that I understood he was on assignment.

I told him I was sorry for his recent loss.

Then I slit his throat with a fish fillet knife. He was still breathing when I stabbed him in the chest. Those Kevlar vests don't stop knives, and this blade makes deep yet narrow cuts. Unfortunately, the arterial spray got me.

I tied the rope as he gasped, sucking blood and air through the wound in his neck and into his lungs. He reached for his radio. It was easy to hold down his arm, and for a few lovely quiet moments, he was all mine.

I'm riding such a high.

After the kill, I watched Nadine from the side yard as she went out and Juliette walked in. Perfect timing, magnificent. But Nadine botched it. A complete whiff.

Way to spoil a perfect day. Soured my mood and just made me cross. I really thought she was stronger. It's not from a lack of lineage. That's for sure. Maybe she gets it from her father's side, that weakness.

My part is the push. Apply the right pressure to anything and it will eventually change shape or break. Nadine is tough but still pliant. She'll transform and I'll be here to witness that moment.

Doesn't she see the grand plan of God's design? I am her god now. As soon as she kills, she will be mine.

This girl is no innocent. I've read the court transcripts. She knew her mother was murdering people. She helped her clean up the evidence and did not say a word about it to anyone for years. She's like us. Why won't she accept that?

I was dripping with blood. But folks in that area all have garden hoses right on the sides of their houses. In a few minutes, I was a shirtless jogger caught in the rain. My only complaint was my socks. I hate jogging with wet socks.

CHAPTER TWENTY-FIVE

Perfect storm

The slam of a vehicle's door preceded Detective Clint Demko's appearance. He herded them into the cottage, not waiting for an invitation but marching them right into Nadine's home. In that moment, she had an inkling of what it must be like for her mother in prison, having no privacy and no control.

There she and Juliette waited until a female officer and FBI crime tech arrived and collected their wet clothing as evidence. They were questioned individually. Finally Juliette was escorted out, wearing SPD sweats, and with an ice pack pressed to her cheek.

That had been four hours ago, and at midnight, the crime scene techs still swarmed her yard and cottage, but she was swaying where she sat, struggling to keep her eyes open.

Some part of Nadine still wanted to blame Juliette for something that appeared not to be her fault. Why, when Nadine realized that Juliette held a phone and not a weapon, was her first reaction disappointment?

"You've got my blood, Dee-Dee, and you are out there. You can continue what I started."

Nadine's mind flicked back to Officer Pender. She no longer wondered if she was being paranoid. This death was on her doorstep. Someone was toying with her. But it wasn't Juliette. The ME seemed to be a pawn, perhaps a rook. But not a killer. Not *the* killer, despite the evidence linking her to a crime scene.

Pender had a rope on his wrist. She'd bet all 452 dollars she had in her checking account that the cut end of this rope was an exact match for the one found tied to Hope Kerr.

Had their unsub chosen unrelated people at random, or were they involved?

The living room was suddenly awash with lights. Shouts came from outside the cottage. Her front door's porthole window illuminated like a lighthouse beacon.

The shouting continued and the jumpy officer moved Nadine to the couch, away from the light streaming through the front and kitchen windows a moment before Demko returned.

"Television van just showed up reporting on Pender's homicide. Stay clear of the windows." Demko pointed to the patrolman. "Close the kitchen shade."

The floodlights flicked off. The young officer drew down the blind.

"Nadine, I'm suggesting you stay in a hotel again, tonight."

"Can I take my car?" she asked.

He shook his head. "Inside the perimeter. I'll drive you."

"Aren't you lead?"

"FBI. Handling the press and most every other damn thing."

"Ah."

"Pack a bag. I'll be back."

She headed to the bedroom and grabbed the roller suitcase. Her blind was raised, and she paused a moment, staring out at the blackness of her yard, and shivered.

Had the monster been out there? Their killer?

Demko returned as she zipped the suitcase closed.

He escorted her out and they headed away from her home, again. The lump in her throat grew.

"It's not Juliette."

"Why's that?"

"It just isn't. Couldn't someone have…" She stopped talking.

"Couldn't someone have what?" he asked.

She shook her head. What she had been about to say was *Couldn't someone have planted that can?* And right off, she knew what he'd think.

"You think I did that. The can? Right?" he asked, his tone accusing.

She shook her head, not looking at him.

"I mean, I was at the scene. I was front and center in an evidence-tampering indictment. Could be me."

"It's not."

"Because you don't want it to be me."

"Maybe."

He nodded. "You want me to call someone to drive you, or shall I?"

She thought that over and then cast her lot.

"Let's go," she said.

The closest was a boutique hotel on the North Trail. A patrol unit followed them. By the time she checked in, it was nearly two in the morning.

He joined her on the elevator and walked her to her room, paused in the hallway and asked her to check inside. It was empty, but she turned on all the lights.

Demko leaned on the doorjamb. She was not inviting him in. He studied her face and seemed to come to some decision, because he reached out and took her hand and pulled her forward, holding her tight. Tears trickled from her eyes as he cradled her. This was what she needed, the comfort and strength of his body.

Her shoulders shook as the tears fell. He made quiet shushing noises and whispered reassurances.

"It can't be Juliette."

"I agree," he said. "But if she didn't drop that can, and that evidence wasn't planted—"

"The killer planted it," she said.

"That's my theory."

Nadine pulled away. He had to go, had to get back to work, but she longed to keep him here with her.

She looked into his handsome face and read concern in those alluring deep blue eyes.

"I'm glad you're all right, Nadine."

They shared a smile. They were both safe. But the killer was still out there. Her smile faded.

"We have to stop him… or her."

He nodded, his expression turning hard at the mention of their unsub.

"We will."

"Thank you for taking care of me," she said.

He released her hand and then brushed the hair from her face. His thumb grazed Nadine's skin, the pad rough against her cheek. Now she was wide awake, and her skin tingled all the way down her arms to her fingertips.

He moved away, holding her gaze, but nothing else. "You'll have a patrolman stationed at the elevator all night. Tomorrow you'll need to come to the station to sign your statement. I'll see you then."

"Are you going back there?" she asked.

"I have to notify Pender's next of kin. Just waiting for records on that."

What a miserable, unenviable job that must be, telling a fallen officer's family that he'd been murdered on the job.

"I'm sorry," she said.

He rubbed his neck. "Yeah. Hate this part."

She stepped forward, pressing both hands to his chest, and lifted on her toes to kiss him. Their lips met. She tried to give him the comfort he had given her. The contact was gentle at first. But quickly blazed with heat. He retreated and scrubbed his mouth with his palm.

Something was wrong. She read that much in his expression.

"Nadine, I have to tell you something about Officer Pender."

She didn't need skills on reading body language to see that whatever he was about to convey would be terrible.

"Remember I told you that the ex-husband of the wedding photographer found dead in Robinson Preserve was on our force?"

Nadine braced, already knowing what he would say, as her ears buzzed as if she'd just left a heavy metal rock concert.

His words confirmed her assumption.

"It was Pender. He was married to Hope Kerr."

CHAPTER TWENTY-SIX

Better late than never

The migraine, which Nadine should have been expecting, arrived at four in the morning. She had packed her medication and took it before she started vomiting. It was a near miss. At six, she swallowed another pill and slept until ten.

Pender's ex-wife was Hope Kerr, the woman who had been pulled from the Manatee River. It now seemed apparent that the pair had been sleeping together. Demko had told her that Kerr's ex-husband was an officer on their force, but the patrolman had denied sleeping with his ex. Demko had turned up nothing to prove otherwise.

Why hadn't she put together last night that Pender was that officer?

Nadine wasn't exactly surprised that they could find no evidence of infidelity. Though divorced, Kerr and Pender had a son. That sort of connection never broke. The two communicated regularly about their son, visitation rights, school assignments, where the boy had left his cleats for soccer practice. They even attended some school functions and sporting events together. It would have been simple to meet for sex.

Why he denied the affair seemed obvious. Such a salacious story would eventually find its way into the news and hurt his son.

Demko had warned Officer Pender, but, still, their unsub had managed to murder an armed police officer. Had Pender recognized his killer? Perhaps trusted this person and had been put off his guard?

Now Demko was blaming himself for not doing more to protect Pender, despite his denials.

The man whom Nadine had asked Demko to find had been assigned to Nadine's protection. And the FBI profiler's theory, that Kerr was just a convenient target who stumbled into the killer's territory, was blown.

She retrieved her phone and checked her messages. She'd forgotten to switch off the privacy setting, which kept her cell on silent mode from midnight to six, so she'd missed Demko's texts. He'd also sent one photo: Officer Pender's left hand, which was not mutilated.

No time, or is it because he had not remarried? she asked herself.

Nadine headed to the shower and then dressed in golf shorts and a blouse covered with a pattern of small pink flamingos floating inside lime-colored inner tubes. In the hall, she found the promised police protection.

"Good morning, Dr. Finch," said the young female officer. "I'm to drive you to headquarters to review and sign your statement."

Nadine sat in the front of the squad car, just like the day she had been escorted from her high school. The interior smelled like Lysol spray and pine air freshener. This woman was not chatty.

At the station, another officer recorded her fingerprints, using a live scan technique. She rolled her fingers on a glass plate, as instructed, uncomfortable that her prints were now in the system. Would they be kept for only six months and then destroyed, like the ones taken for her background check, or were they now a permanent part of state and federal databases?

This was the kind of question a criminal would ask.

Her anxiety persisted and she kept rubbing the pads of her fingers, as if that would somehow erase those records. The point was, it wasn't under her control. That bothered her.

The FBI also bothered her because she really didn't know where she stood. Was she a consultant, suspect or bait?

The same guy who had taken her prints escorted Nadine from intake to homicide.

"Here we are," said the officer, motioning her in.

Across the nearly empty room, Detective Wernli waited. Nadine had worked with the veteran Homicide detective on several cases, most recently the staged suicide of Emily Lancer by her murderous husband, Morton. She respected Wernli, but she was disappointed not to find Demko.

Nadine gave a mechanical thank-you to her escort and headed toward the detective; she was still carrying her overnight bag and purse.

Wernli stood, revealing wrinkled slacks, and he had a bit of leaf debris stuck in his hair. The redness in his eyes pointed to a night on the job.

"Where's Demko?" she asked Wernli.

"Press conference. Asking for help on finding Officer Howard Pender's killer."

An image of the officer's bloody body and the car's interior flashed in her mind.

Howard Pender, she thought, *rest his soul.*

"If you'll have a seat," said Detective Wernli. "I'll review your statement and get your signature."

"Is Dr. Hartfield here?" she asked.

"Released."

*

Nadine left the station and drove to Juliette's home. She rang the bell and waited. Juliette's face appeared at the window. Should

Nadine wave, like an old friend dropping by for a visit, or throw herself, barking at the door, like the madwoman growing inside her? The last time they met, Nadine had punched her friend in the face.

She assessed the damage. The swelling had receded as color bloomed. Juliette's eye was mostly open, but the ring of purple went from her eyebrow to her nose. Her cheek looked puffy.

Nadine supposed she should blame Arlo for teaching her how to fight.

"Hi, Juliette. Could I come in for a minute?"

Juliette's expression was cautious, and her shoulders slowly rose and fell with the weight of her sigh. Then the dead bolt clicked. The metal slide of a chain lock followed, and she opened the door, inviting the devil inside.

Despite all their meetings for drinks and dinners, Nadine had never been in her home.

The first-floor garden-style apartment was as interesting as oatmeal from the outside. But the interior walls were a fresh mint green and the ceiling fans looked like woven mats. Juliette's dining room table was natural pine and topped with a huge live orchid covered with cascading violet blooms. More plants sat on the floor in the beams of sunlight. Nadine wouldn't expect a pathologist to have a green thumb. Juliette obviously did.

"I didn't do it," said Juliette. "None of them."

"I know it."

"Because I have a solid alibi or because you believe me?"

She hesitated. "Both."

"They found my print at the scene on Lido. A seltzer can."

"I heard."

"I was never there."

"Someone planted it."

Juliette nodded. "You were at the scene."

"I wasn't. After my stunt at the autopsy, I went back to the office. Never made it out there."

Juliette studied her in silence.

"This isn't my doing."

Her colleague was too polite not to invite her in and too trusting to order her out. She motioned toward the living room. More plants sat on the low half wall that separated the kitchen from the foyer. Her furniture was large, bright and overwhelmed the room.

"Hello!" The tiny voice came from the living area, sounding like Juliette's but shrunken.

A child?

One more step and Nadine had her answer. A sheet blanketed the floor. In the center sat a birdcage the size of a dishwasher with the door open. Atop the cage, a large white parrot stood on a wooden perch. The bird's crown of white and yellow feathers lifted as it rocked from side to side.

The parrot's speech was a song. "Hello. How you doin'? Hello! That's a good boy!"

Juliette motioned toward the bird. "This is Jack-Jack. I named him after the baby from *The Incredibles* because he is just as much trouble. He's a rescue. Sulfur-crested cockatoo."

"He's beautiful." Nadine moved closer and the bird lifted his snow-white wings, the underside a buttery yellow. It glided back and forth like a street performer.

"I'm not sure I'll keep him, but he was plucking his feathers, so I'm fostering him for a while."

Juliette lifted a finger. The cockatoo wrapped a black leathery foot about her extended digit and climbed up her arm to her shoulder. Jack-Jack had found his person, and Nadine would be shocked if he ever returned to the refuge.

The pause stretched as both Jack-Jack and Juliette regarded her with unblinking eyes.

"Ah, I wanted to apologize for how I treated you after you told me about your mom. And for not coming to you sooner to say so." She drew a breath and forged on. "And I'm so sorry for hitting you." The amount she had to apologize for was almost comical.

Juliette motioned to the dinette. "Have a seat."

Nadine took the chair she offered as her host placed Jack-Jack on the back of the opposite one and dropped a dish towel on the tile floor beneath him. Then she disappeared into the kitchen, returning to offer the bird a grape and Nadine a coaster and a bottle of cold beer. Finally Juliette sat between her and Jack-Jack, who seemed preoccupied with his grape.

"I should have told you about my mother," said Nadine.

"Arleen Howler. Saw it on the news."

"Yeah."

"Isn't that something? Both of us. Huh?" Juliette rubbed her index finger with her opposite thumb. "When did the crime techs finish?"

"I don't know." Nadine gave her a summary of the hours since the police separated them.

"They had me there all night. I only got home a few hours ago."

Juliette stared in silence and Nadine took a long swallow of the beer.

"I watched the police chief's press conference at nine," said Juliette. "Did you see it?"

"No."

"Reporters asked why the ME's office hadn't released the cause of deaths yet."

Jack-Jack had somehow eaten all the flesh from the grape and dropped the empty skin on the floor before wiping his beak on the back of the chair. Then the cockatoo lifted one foot and waved it toward Juliette. "Step up. Step-up-step-up-step-up."

Juliette placed two hands on the table and pushed herself to her feet. Then she took him back to his cage. The bird swung inside, using his beak, and then hung upside down by one leg, with the grace of a circus performer, as he whacked the small bell suspended from a length of rope.

"Weird how much he sounds like you," Nadine said.

"They're mimics. He also imitates my text message alert chime. Very convincing. Sometimes, after he pulls that little stunt and sees me checking my phone, I can hear him laughing."

Nadine narrowed her eyes on the bird, which now seemed too clever to be a proper pet. More like a toddler in a feather suit.

Juliette returned with a second bottle of beer, another coaster and a half-consumed bag of mini-pretzels and released the clip. She grabbed a handful and pushed the open end in Nadine's direction.

In the living room, Jack-Jack now sat on his perch, beak tucked under a wing. He kept one beady black eye on Nadine. Smart bird.

Juliette lifted her beer and took a swallow.

"So," Nadine said, restarting the conversation, "Officer Pender's ex-wife was Hope Kerr."

Beer and half-masticated pretzels spewed from Juliette's mouth and across the table. She was on her feet, holding her hand over her mouth, as she headed for the kitchen, returning with paper towels to clean up the mess.

"Holy shit!" Juliette finished her mopping and tossed the sodden paper towels in the trash. "I'm off the case. I won't be doing Pender's autopsy."

That was bad.

"Who, then?"

Juliette mentioned the other ME for District 12. "He'll also be reviewing all my earlier autopsies," she fumed.

"I'm sorry."

Juliette reached across the table, bridging the distance between them, and momentarily clasped Nadine's hand.

"Me too." She drew back. "I feel so sad for his son. Two homicides and the scandal. What will happen to him?"

Nadine shook her head. She didn't know. But she did know that a murderer's victims included more than the dead.

"This case must be so hard for you."

Every instinct told Nadine that this really was genuine understanding. Had she found a person who could look beyond where she came from? Someone who knew the truth and still accepted her?

Hope battled with the cynicism and the belief that she didn't deserve such a friend. She teared up.

"Nadine? You okay?"

"No. Not really. I've been so afraid to tell anyone."

Juliette nodded. "I know."

And she did. Nadine was certain that if anyone could understand, it was Juliette.

"I think whoever is behind this," said Nadine, "is working from inside our county."

"Did you tell that to the Feds?"

"Yes. They're looking into it."

"Hmm. Well, *I think* this killer was trying to get you to murder me," Juliette said. The calm in her voice was chilling.

Why had that thought not occurred to her?

"Oh, my God!"

"Exactly."

They sat in silence, each with their thoughts. Finally Nadine spoke.

"Who do you think set us up?" asked Nadine.

Juliette pressed her mouth into a sad, grim line. She toyed with the beer bottle.

"Demko told me that the text to my cell came from a burner phone, so no way to trace it."

"I think the FBI is using me as bait. Or I might be a suspect."

"You and me both." Juliette shook her head, disheartened.

"They're cutting me and Demko out of the investigation."

"Well, we can't let them, because if you think you're right, this copycat is playing with us. We have to stop it."

"'We'?"

"You and me. We're a team."

Perhaps she had no right, but she told Juliette how her profile conflicted with the FBI profiler's, that Dun was the FBI's prime suspect. And then she told her about the mothers of Dun, Ruz and Demko.

"Oh, God. How many of us are there?"

CHAPTER TWENTY-SEVEN

And your enemies closer

Nadine called the station on Sunday and was told that Demko was on another line, so she just headed over there, stopping at her favorite gourmet grocer on Osprey en route. She arrived at the city police station after eleven and found Demko at his desk, looking like a potted plant left on a fire escape unattended for months.

He glanced up at her arrival.

"Did they call you back in?" he asked.

"Yesterday. When did you eat last?"

He gave her a surprised look and then glanced at the grocery bag she carried. "Um, I had some cold pizza yesterday."

"Break room?" she asked.

He rose and motioned to the door. "That way."

Once seated at a small circular table in the dreary room, she withdrew three plastic containers of salad: macaroni, soba and German potato. She added napkins, disposable plates, iced tea in bottles and two deli sandwiches wrapped in white paper and taped shut with the label sticker.

"Roast beef or smoked turkey?"

"Roast beef," he said, and she handed him the sandwich.

She opened hers over the paper plate.

Demko poured out some chips onto the open butcher paper no longer surrounding his sandwich and offered to pour them for Nadine.

"Yes, thank you."

He shook out a generous portion.

She watched his sandwich disappear with astonishing speed. After offering her a helping of the macaroni salad, he ate the rest right out of the plastic container. Then he downed the iced tea and started on the potato salad. Watching this reminded Nadine of those food-eating contests. Finally he came up for air and placed a hand on his stomach.

"Wow. I was hungry."

"Yes. You were." She offered a smile.

He took her hand and brought it to his mouth, pressing a kiss to her palm and making her nerves ring like a singing bowl.

"Thank you for lunch and breakfast and last night's supper." He set her hand back beside her plate.

"My pleasure." She'd like to make this a more permanent responsibility, and that surprised her. The implications brought immediate fear and worry. Her smile slipped. "Do you often forget to eat?"

"Sometimes, when I'm investigating a homicide. Time is critical, and evidence collection—well, you only get one shot to get that right. But this case is worse than usual, because it's not just about catching the perp. It's about saving the ones to come."

"In the series."

"Yeah. And despite his denials, I didn't adequately protect Pender."

"You questioned him. Warned him."

He shook his head, rejecting her attempt to let him off the hook.

"You spoke to Pender's family?" she asked.

"Yeah. He listed his ex-wife, Hope, as emergency contact. But now it's just his older sister. Parents died a while ago. Hit by a drunk driver on I-75."

"Are you still processing the scene?"

"No. Finished. Were you okay last night? The hotel?"

"Yes. Thank you for the protective detail. I went to see Juliette this morning. She told me she was cleared of the homicide out on Lido."

"Solid alibi."

"Then I told her about the FBI's prime suspect."

He blew out a breath. "We haven't found Dun yet. Listen. We have another missing persons case."

She gasped, hand to her throat. "Why didn't you call me?"

He grimaced. "On my to-do list. I wanted to verify some commonalities to the case first."

"And?"

"Involved in an ongoing affair. And they vanished together. We recovered their vehicles. No use of credit cards or bank accounts since their disappearance, so I suspect they did not run off together."

"Who?"

"Carla Giffin and Nick Thrasher. Coworkers. Both married."

Nadine's lunch cascaded about in her belly like a ship in a storm.

"Both employed at the same restaurant. He's a part owner and cook. She's a waitress. I'm sure the FBI will be speaking to you about it. Add it to your profile."

"When?"

"Taken last night. Her husband called early this morning."

Nadine reached for the remains of her iced tea and took a gulp.

"You okay?" he asked.

She shook her head. "Not even slightly. The FBI is searching?"

"And investigating."

"Are you off the case?"

"No, Pender is still my case. These two are outside my jurisdiction. County."

"So, you can't investigate?"

"It's related to my case."

"She kept her third couple, Michelle Dents and Parker Irwin, for two days." She covered her mouth, thinking of the horror this pair might now be enduring and knowing they could still be alive. "Do they think Dun has them?"

"The FBI profiler says yes," said Demko.

She made a face.

"You disagree? Dun is unmarried. Works in the system, just as you said."

"He's divorced, which is different. And he couldn't have brought us all here, because he has no connection to or influence over hiring."

"That's true. You sure those two things are related?"

"Yes."

"Working with someone?"

She shook her head. "Unlikely."

"Their profiler thinks the pair will be in a park on the coast. They're searching down as far as North Port."

"Any luck?"

"Nothing yet."

"My mother held them on a houseboat in the marina where she worked, an unoccupied rental."

"They should already know that."

"The detective's case file said that she cleaned the insides so well that they had to use luminol to see any blood traces. She threw out the mattress from one of the cabins. Blamed it on the last rental."

"I didn't read that yet."

"You've been busy."

"So, this pair will not be killed out in the open, like Poletti and Lowe, found in the bay, or like Kerr and Pender, discovered at separate times and places."

Nadine shook her head. "No, the killer will want time with them inside. My mother kept her third couple in a houseboat Friday night and all-day Saturday. We should search similar places."

"Like where?"

"A shed, cabin, trailer, sailboat, houseboat, yacht…"

"Boats?" he said. "We've got hundreds in marinas and mooring fields just in the city alone." He reached for his phone. "I'll ask Sarasota Marine Patrol to begin a search."

"Good. And call Torrin. Tell him to check up as far north as Bradenton and only as far south as Venice."

While Demko made the call and spoke to Torrin, Nadine grabbed her bag and pulled out her laptop. She roused it from sleep and opened her comparison maps.

Demko ended one call and placed another. "I left a message for Torrin to call me. The marine patrol has been pulled for protection detail."

"Protection?"

"Governor's visiting."

"Terrific," she said with all the sarcasm she could muster.

"I'll call the chief. See if she can reallocate our guys."

She returned to her laptop and maps while he placed another call.

"I spoke to the chief. Convinced her to send our people out to search docked and moored vessels."

"That's great."

He tucked away his cell and peered at her screen. "What's that?"

"In addition to working on comparing our victims to my mother's kills, I've created two maps. This is my mother's crimes, a map of Ocala, and the red dots are the locations of my mother's kill sites and the green are where her victims were discovered. I'm trying to estimate where they were dropped by time of death."

He gazed at the map of the area she'd been working on for the last few weeks, alongside her offender profile work. The map of the Ocala region included many more data points than the one for this area.

"What are the dots?" he said, pointing.

"Each one is a data point. Capture sites, murder sites, body recovery sites."

"And these rings of color?" he asked.

The concentric circles looked most like a weather radar map, with amorphous rings of various colors. The red core acted, not as the center of the storm, but as the most likely area of activity.

"These are probability rings. The highest likelihood is here, at the center, and drops from there. This band, for instance"—she indicated the turquoise ring—"holds a sixty-seven percent chance of activity."

"Is this to prioritize suspects based on apprehension area?"

"Yes. It can be used for that. But also to place law enforcement inside the area of most likely activity."

He pointed at the screen. "Blue dots?"

"Capture sites. Some are approximations."

"So, Arleen began with capture, kill and dump together."

"All one spot." Nadine pointed at the map: a red, green and blue mark all together, indicating capture, kill and dump locations all in the same place. "Later, she captured, transported, killed and transported again. She held them for days."

"More risk."

"More fun," said Nadine.

He gave her a look that made her uncomfortable. This entire thing made her uncomfortable, but it was out there and so she was no longer hampered from making comparisons out of fear of being unmasked.

There was a certain freedom to that.

He set aside his phone and lifted the remains of the soba noodles as he focused on her laptop.

Nadine opened a second map. "Give me the location where Giffin and Thrasher were taken."

"Here." He pointed and gave her the address.

"This is our unsub victims on a map of Sarasota, Desoto and Manatee Counties." She added a mark to her document.

"Red marks for the murder sites?" he asked.

"Yes. The same." She pointed. "Blue, capture. Red, kill. Green, dump."

"I've never seen a map like this."

"It's a type of profiling," she said. "Geographic profiling. The FBI asked me to consult. Requested a comparison focusing on similarities between our victims to hers and an offender profile. A map seems a logical addition."

"Yeah. I agree."

"And I've expanded it. Trying to establish the boundaries where the unsub prefers to work and which ones they avoid. It helps define travel routes, range. For instance, it's clear that both perpetrators used a vehicle, at least to get to the locations of the body dumps. But my mother also used a canoe. She felt it left less evidence behind, like tire tracks and footprints."

"How did you make these?"

"Texas State software program. It's called the Rigel Software System, named after the star Rigel, the hunter. Determine the most probable area where the unsub lives."

"That's amazing."

"Knowing where to look helps with stranger violence crimes. Helps you weed out the tips."

"We have hundreds just on the Pender case. Fifty suspects, so far."

"I can imagine."

"What did Torrin think of this?" he asked.

"He hasn't asked to see my work. I suspect he doesn't care, just wants me inside the investigation. 'Keep your friends close—'"

"'And your enemies closer,'" said Demko, finishing the saying. "They are good at their jobs, impressive even. But they sure aren't forthcoming with the investigation progress." He leaned in, studying her work. "But he needs to see this."

Nadine pointed at the three dots, four dead.

"This is where they found Arleen's first two victims, together. Then this is the ranger, Henderson, found in his jeep on a dirt road in the Ocala National Forest." She moved her finger. "And this is where they recovered Lacey Louder. It's a state park on the St. Johns River."

"Okay."

"But this is where she held Dents and Irwin. Miles downriver. And here is where they found Sandra and White. Inland, away from the St. Johns, the other drops and kill zones. Really outside her territory."

"Why?"

"She changed jobs. This one had a private place with lots of outbuildings."

"We need to tell the FBI," Demko said.

"I tried. Everything I say is the opposite of what their profiler says. I don't even know what I'm doing."

"Yes. You do."

She did. She knew she had this right. Why didn't they?

Demko called again, and this time got through. Maybe the trick was to call twice in close succession. Nadine watched as he relayed Nadine's suggestions about the marinas. From him, the recommendation sounded more plausible. Before ending the call, he mentioned her geo profile.

"He says they have a geo profile already. But they'll add the marinas and mooring fields from North Port to Bradenton to their search area."

"How far is it from North Port to Bradenton?"

"I don't know. Fifty miles. Why?" he asked.

"It's twenty-two miles between Lido Beach in Sarasota and Robinson Preserve to the north. My mother's range stretched only twenty-five miles."

"Too far?"

"North Port is outside the probable geographic comfort zone. My mom lived in Ocala, she worked in Astor and hunted as far as Deland. Deland and Astor are only twenty miles apart."

Demko peered at her laptop and then lifted his gaze.

"What else is inside that zone?"

She studied the maps, side by side, on a split screen. There was something else here. Something she was missing.

She stared at her work.

"Torrin said they're focused on apprehending Anthony Dun."

"Dun didn't send Juliette to my house. And he didn't plant that seltzer can."

"I agree."

"Then who did?" she asked.

"My guess is the killer. Explains how it got there and fits your theory about an inside man who would have access to Juliette's trash."

"She's always drinking those things." Nadine took Demko's arm. "Clint, these missing people—Carla Giffin and Nick Thrasher from the restaurant—are still alive. If they won't find them, we need to."

He nodded. "Where do you suggest?"

She spent several minutes studying her map and then turned back to him. "Where's Molly?"

"At the pet sitters'. Why?"

"Want to take her for a walk"—she pointed to the yellow band encircling the central red on her map—"at Myakka River State Park?"

"I thought you said marinas," said Demko.

"FBI and our marine patrol have got those. And Myakka is a park inside the geographic comfort zone with outbuildings."

"All our homicides were on the coast."

"Not Pender's." She met his uncertain gaze. "And my mother used the state parks in Ocala Forest and remember—not all my mother's kill sites were on the St. Johns River."

"The last four."

She nodded. "Yes."

"Okay." He stood, gathering the trash from the table. "You think our next missing couple is there?"

"I'd like to cross it off the list." She had to do everything possible to find them, because each minute they were in the hands of this killer would be a horror.

Nadine rose and tucked her laptop and charger into her bag. Then tossed out the lunch containers.

"Ready?" she asked.

"You going to search the entire state park with a puppy?" he asked.

"Yes. I want you to look at the park's records. Cabin rentals. They are like the houseboat where my mother held Michelle Dent and Parker Irwin. She killed her boss from the marina, and the mechanic her boss was sleeping with, in a houseboat. She held them in private."

"RV rentals?"

"If they do that, yes."

"I've been out that way. They have RV sites, cabins, primitive campsites and a riding stable."

The thought of a stable made her go queasy.

"We can check the stable, too," she said.

Demko was aware that her mother had held her final victims, Sandra Shank and Stephen White, at the riding stable where Arleen worked. Why hadn't Nadine seen the Myakka stable on the map?

"Should we have backup?" she asked.

"Not to check the camping records. And the governor's visit and manhunt for Dun are pressing our limits. They'll have no available units."

"Super."

They headed out, collecting Molly, and driving from the city past the long stretch of barbwire fencing and cleared fields of yellow grass. The Florida Scrub cattle stood in groups under live oaks, tails swishing flies. After twenty miles, the landscape changed, giving way to flatwood pine and marshes of tall green reeds dotted with hammocks of palmetto palms. She knew they neared the park when they crossed the bridge. Here the huge live oak and palm trees grew tall along the banks of the gently flowing river.

Demko turned off first to the stables. There she waited with the boxer, presumably so as not to scare the horses, but, really, the idea of searching the property was too disturbing.

He was gone so long that she ended up waiting in the shade, where the visitors gathered for their trail rides.

Demko returned empty-handed, and they were off to the main park entrance, where the gate attendant directed them to the administration offices.

He scanned the lists of registered campers as Molly explored, to the extent allowed by her leash. The park had a small museum with taxidermy creatures that made the dog work her nose like a bloodhound.

"Nadine?" Demko said. Something in his voice brought her to full attention.

She looked at the name written on the registry beside his finger.

"Nathan Dun," she said. "He's here."

CHAPTER TWENTY-EIGHT

Sleeping dogs

Demko did not approach the cabin rented by Nathan Dun. Instead, he called Torrin, got his voicemail, and then called the county sheriff's offices and sent them to get ahold of the FBI. He and Nadine did a drive-by and were disappointed to see no vehicle at the assigned cabin. They finished the loop and returned to registration. With the north gate locked shut, this was the only way in or out of the park by vehicle. If Dun returned, Demko would be there.

"Everyone in the state got our BOLO," he said, referring to the broadcast issued to law enforcement. "Meanwhile, he's here. Restaurant, camp store, cabins. Didn't even need to be on the damn road."

Molly whined from the backseat, anxious to get out and explore. The cracked back window gave her only a tempting sniff of the wonders the old growth oak forest had to offer.

"Soon, girl," said Nadine, and petted Molly's neck.

"Right here the whole time."

Demko's phone rang from the cradle on the dash and Torrin's name appeared.

"Takes over my damned investigation *and* won't return my calls, but *now* he's phoning me." He glanced at Nadine and smiled as he let the phone ring again. "That's because of you."

She felt a momentary zip of pride as he took the call on speaker.

Thirty-one minutes later, the FBI arrived with the sheriff's and the highway patrol. Nadine and Molly waited near Demko's vehicle as the sheriff's office secured the perimeter, while they waited for FBI backup from Tampa. They were now in DeSoto County, well outside the city limits and Demko's jurisdiction.

As the afternoon rolled to evening, the crime techs van pulled in, but Demko did not return. She counted fourteen black SUVs. The FBI had arrived.

It didn't get cooler in the evenings, just darker and darker. Nothing was as black as a subtropical jungle at night. You couldn't see the stars past the tree canopy. Gloom pervaded beneath the old oaks even before dusk, so the sheriff's office had erected lights. Nadine saw them blazing from her location on the camping road.

They must have found something. But the absence of an ambulance made Nadine sick. While she waited, she alternated between walking Molly, getting her water, and sitting in the running car with the AC blasting. She drew out her laptop and opened her geo profile, then added the park's location, praying it was not a kill site. Nadine set the laptop on the dash. This spot didn't correlate to her mother's kill sites because, though it was well within the algorithms target territory of probability for this unsub, this location didn't match the data points on her mother's geographic map. For a match between the two, this couple's capture and kill should have been in an easterly direction, but this site was directly west toward the Gulf. It was the wrong direction. Or was it?

What was she missing?

She saw Fukuda emerge from the woods, heading toward her. She rolled down the window. Molly stuck her head out of the gap and tried to lick the agent's face. She was rewarded with a scratch behind both ears. Then he turned to her.

"What's happening?" she asked. "Did you find Dun?"

"No. We've got a potential crime scene. Blood from two different victims."

Her heart sank. *Oh, no.*

"How much blood?" She didn't want to know and braced at his grim expression.

"Too much."

Fukuda kept speaking and Nadine pressed her hand to her mouth and tried to focus on what he was saying instead of the screaming in her head.

"… waiting for blood type information on Giffin and Thrasher. But we are proceeding as if it's them."

"They're not there?" Was there a chance they were still alive, or had the unsub just moved them to the dump site?

"Techs say no one has been here for at least ten hours. It's just the blood. They've got drag marks, spatter and footprints. Maybe we get lucky and get a partial palm or fingerprint."

"I've been working on my geo profiles," she said.

"Yes. Demko mentioned it. But we have a specialist doing that already." He swatted at a bug.

"Did they pinpoint this spot?" She met his glare with one of her own. She was sick of being ignored.

"He's already told us that the perpetrator likely lives in the county of Sarasota."

"I'm not looking for the unsub's location. I'm looking for the *victims'* locations by comparing my mother's range and victims to this serial."

Fukuda's brows lifted. "Ah. That could be useful."

Could be? His attitude only underscored her suspicions that her real job was not to help solve this case. Too bad for them, she was aiming to do just that.

"We're organizing a search team to locate the pair," he said.

"They aren't here."

"How do you know that?"

"Well, Dun's car is gone. And all, but the ranger and last of my mother's victims, were found on the St. Johns River. If Giffin and Thrasher are missing, it's probable our suspect has dumped them."

"Where?"

"A waterway somewhere."

"You think they're dead?"

She did, and felt the disappointment gnawing at the marrow of her bones.

"My mother kept only her last victims for more than two days. If this killer is following the pattern, this couple is her third of four."

"You won't mind if we look for them?"

His tone and attitude fell on her like a slap.

Fukuda stared at her, blank-faced. "Special Agent Torrin is curious how you knew to look for Anthony Dun right here."

"I wasn't looking for Dun. I was looking for the missing couple using my comparison map."

"Is that so?"

Fukuda cast a glance at the map and Nadine wondered again if asking her to make this comparison was just a way to keep her busy and away from the real investigation. The thought nettled.

Funny that she, and not Molly, was now growling.

"Torrin will want to speak to you about your thought *process*," said Fukuda.

Nadine narrowed her eyes at his retreating form. The implication, or just the chip on her shoulder, was that she may have had some prior knowledge. Perhaps she was working with Anthony Dun, still at large.

She realized too late that her success in finding the kill site made her look like one of those people who throws a lit match into a can of rags soaked in gasoline and then yells "fire." The Hero Syndrome, misnamed, feeding her need for attention and adulation. Only what she craved was exactly the opposite of someone with Hero Syndrome.

Overlooked and underestimated. Her superpowers. Until now. Now the FBI saw her perfectly.

Nadine left the vehicle to storm and pace as Molly trotted along. After another ninety minutes, Molly rolled to her back and Nadine noticed several bug bites on her pink belly.

Finally, in frustration, she and Molly headed beneath the canopy of live oaks, the branches laden with clinging strands of sage-colored Spanish moss, along the beaten trail, through the undergrowth of fern and palmetto palm to the crime scene. She figured if they arrested her, at least they would transport her to somewhere with air-conditioning and a bed.

Detective Demko found her on the path before she reached the cabin. A mosquito landed on his forehead and he slapped it.

Molly became reanimated at his appearance, dancing about. He dropped to a knee and greeted his tired pup, cradling her head and accepting a lick on the cheek.

He straightened, facing her.

"Special Agent Torrin would like us to stop by tomorrow morning at their field headquarters at eight."

"All right. Would you like me to register for a campsite, or is someone planning on taking me home?"

She'd had nothing to eat since lunch and being a feast for the bugs made her cranky.

"That's right. We came out together, didn't we?"

Nadine did not dignify that question with a reply. She just stared back at him as Molly snapped at a mosquito.

"I'll ask one of the sheriffs to drive you home." Demko was glancing around. "Wait here."

She waited there.

Another thirty minutes ticked by before he returned.

"You ready?" he asked.

"Are you?" She motioned toward the lights that flooded the front of the cabin and the crime techs crawling about like large white insects.

"FBI has got it."

Nadine couldn't interpret whether he felt this was a good or bad thing. Her gifts for reading character and expression had shut off for the night. She could see only that he was also hot and tired.

He led the way back to his vehicle.

"Where are we going?" she asked.

"Hotel or my place."

"Hotel," she said, weary to her bones.

"What did you see in the cabin?"

He hesitated and she braced, watching him consider his words.

"They were held in the bedroom. Appears one was tied on the bed and the other to a chair facing the bed."

That would be the man, forced to watch, she thought.

"The punctures in the mattress and the blood indicate multiple stab wounds."

"Through the victim?"

He nodded. "From the amount of blood, my best guess is that he was killed in the chair. She was killed on the mattress." He raked both hands through his hair. "We missed them by ten hours!"

Nadine's fatigue and thirst and his comment struck her like lead. She'd failed to find them in time and began to cry.

He drew her in. "Hey, hey. It's all right."

"It's not."

He nodded, the whiskers of his cheek scratching her temple. "No. It's not."

Demko held her as she cried, further soaking his damp shirt. He smelled of bug spray and sweat. She nuzzled against him as he gently rocked back and forth. Their first slow dance.

"You and your map have any idea where they'll dump the bodies?"

She drew back. The worst was still out there, and so was the killer.

*

That night, she opted for the hotel, where she had clean clothing, her bathroom kit and no reporters. The following day, Demko arrived to take her to the FBI field office.

Despite getting little sleep over several days, Demko looked pressed and smelled amazing. He wore khaki-colored slacks and a white polo shirt, with the police logo embroidered in blue over his left breast. His gun, badge and phone were clipped to his belt. His more casual attire made her feel overdressed in her low heels and navy suit, striped blouse and knockoff designer gold pendant necklace.

He gave her an appreciative look and lingering kiss. Then said, "You look nice. Tired, but nice."

"Thanks. Any press out there?"

"Nope."

Once they were in the vehicle, she asked, "They find Dun or the other two?"

He shook his head.

"How's Molly?"

"Scratching her bug bites." He turned to her. "I'm sorry I left you two out there so long."

"We understand. Well, I do, anyway."

"Thank you for looking after her."

"She's a good dog." She stared out at the panhandler on the corner holding a cardboard sign that asked for money and reminded passersby that God was watching.

Was he?

"You think they're both dead? Thrasher and Giffin?"

His grim expression was answer enough. "Probably."

Her vision blurred, warning of tears, but she brushed them away, refusing to cry.

"Any more thoughts on a dump site?" he asked.

"Should be the coast, but my mom dumped Dents and Irwin in Lake Monroe, southeast of the river, so it could be a bay, inlet or lake. I was looking at all closest bodies of water to Myakka."

"The park has two lakes and a river."

"FBI will have looked there."

"Yeah."

"So what's southeast of Myakka?"

"Nothing. Farms and, well, Arcadia is there, and the Peace River goes right through town." His face was grim. "I'll share this with Torrin. Maybe catch the bastard dumping the bodies."

They parked in the second level of the garage and had the same escort into the FBI field office. They asked Demko to wait, ushering her into a conference room. Torrin and Fukuda met her there and introduced her to an unfamiliar man, an FBI psychologist.

The profiler? she wondered.

Torrin asked her numerous questions about why she'd directed Demko to check out Myakka River State Park. They went around and around as they pretended to need her to clarify but were actually asking her to repeat the same story in a variety of orders. It was a technique with which she was familiar. Trying to find inconsistencies. Finally, out of frustration, she asked, "Am I under investigation?"

"No," said Fukuda.

"Not at this time," said Torrin.

"Am I under arrest?"

"No," said Torrin.

"Then I think I am done 'helping.'" She used air quotes around the word "helping" and stood.

"Just a few more questions," said Torrin. "We could use your help."

Yeah, right, she thought, and resumed her seat.

Special Agent Torrin switched subjects, asking about her grandfather, whom she barely knew except through her mother's sporadic stories, publicly available court documents, arrest records and conviction reports. She had visited him in prison, but didn't remember any of that, had been too young. Nadine had read the newspaper article on his conviction that her mother kept. He had killed his supervisor by running him down with a forklift. The jury did not buy his story of mechanical failure and he served eighteen years, dying in prison.

Special Agent Fukuda took over to ask her about her father, who had left the family before she was born, and, finally and forever, when she was less than a year old.

She wondered what they knew about her father that she did not. A prickling warning rippled over her skin like an electric charge.

"He was an engineering student?" asked Fukuda.

"Yes. My aunt told me he dropped out of college when my mother got pregnant and they married against his family's wishes."

"That's Donna Finch, your father's younger sister?"

"Right. Anyway, after my mom's arrest, my aunt thought her brother might turn up. When he didn't, she adopted me."

"But not Arlo Howler, your brother."

"He was an adult then." Her throat was so dry. "Could I have some water?"

Fukuda offered her a bottle, and she drained half the contents.

"Tell me about your father," said Torrin.

"Why?"

"A theory I'm working."

"I need to get back to my profiles." Urgency tugged at her. She didn't have time for this now.

"Please. It's related. I promise."

She tried to conjure the man from the stories she had heard, the photographs she had seen.

"How is it related?"

"I'll explain. First, tell me about your dad."

"I don't remember him." Nadine glanced toward the door, anxious to leave. This topic made her sweat. "My aunt might better help you with questions about my father."

"We're in touch."

Of course they were. She pinched her eyes shut as she imagined an agent knocking on Aunt Donna's front door.

When she opened her eyes, Torrin was looking at his notes.

"Your father left the marriage in '92 and filed for divorce in August, granted January of the following year. Your aunt confirms he suffered from depression and abused drugs. Subsequent to the divorce, he was arrested for failure to pay child support. She covered his bond, but Howler missed his court appearance in March '93. An arrest warrant was issued, but they were unable to locate him. She says that she has not seen her brother since that time."

Much of that she did not know.

Nadine spun the half-empty water bottle in her hand, round and round, while her heel tapped a frenzy on the tile floor.

"Do you have any way to contact your father?"

"None."

Torrin scribbled something.

"Do you?" she asked.

"We are tracking him down now."

Nadine wasn't sure how she felt about that or about the possibility of him popping back into her life. Sleeping dogs, she thought, were best left to lie.

"I answered your questions. Now, what does this have to do with your current investigation?" she asked.

"We are working on a theory that your father's abandonment acted as a trigger for your mother."

She thought about that. "But DeNato and Rogers were not killed until two years after he left."

"True."

"Our profiler believes that the departure of other men from her life acted as a trigger."

Nadine thought back to the men who had come and gone as her mother played house. Had their leaving prompted the deaths of the rest?

She shook her head, unsure.

"You have an alternative explanation?"

"Arlo told me she got fired from a carpet wholesale warehouse the same year she killed Rogers and DeNato. And she told me that she didn't let men tell her what to do anymore. I think she meant *all* men. I thought, perhaps, her trigger might be losing her jobs."

Fukuda scribbled something on his notepad.

"Did she lose a lot of them?" asked Torrin.

"Yeah."

"Your aunt Donna told us that Arleen's brother, Guy Owen, was in and out of mental institutions."

Uncle Tinsel had a mental disorder?

Why was she surprised? That little nugget fit right in with the rest of the untidy mess that was her family.

"Did he?" She remembered that her uncle came and went from their lives. Her family tree was cringeworthy.

"Did he play a part in your upbringing?"

This conversation made her so uncomfortable, it was difficult not to squirm. Instead, she opened the water and took another sip.

"No. But I remember him visiting." He was one more blurry face among many men.

"Often?"

"A couple of times. He slept on the couch for a while. In between jobs, I think. After my mom's conviction, he contacted Aunt Donna about collecting my mother's things."

Her attempt to locate him via a web search had failed and Demko had found nothing.

"Do you maintain contact?" asked Fukuda.

"No. Have you found him?"

"Not yet."

"Is he a suspect?"

Fukuda nodded as Torrin spoke.

"Your uncle is a person of interest. He left a mental health facility in Alabama twelve years ago and disappeared."

"'Disappeared'? Is he dead?"

Torrin shrugged. "We don't know."

So one of her parents was missing, and the other was on death row. Now add a mentally ill uncle to the stew.

"What was his diagnosis?"

Torrin did not have to look at his notes to answer. "Initially, antisocial personality disorder. Subsequent to admission, his diagnosis switched to schizophrenia."

Like her grandmother, she realized.

"He voluntarily admitted himself in a plea deal to avoid prosecution for sexual assault. Victim was a thirteen-year-old runaway."

Nadine grimaced, the assault and plea deal reminding her of Arlo.

"And he just walked out of the facility?"

"After eighteen months, he set a fire and escaped during the evacuation."

Nadine lowered her head, taking a moment to absorb this new information. Another rotting limb on her family tree.

When she lifted her gaze, it was to find the FBI psychologist scrutinizing her. It was interesting sitting across from another psychologist and watching him do Nadine's job, observing and rendering an opinion on Nadine's mental state.

Actually, it wasn't interesting. In fact, it pissed her off.

Nadine gritted her teeth a moment, bracing. "Arleen told me she killed a man who owed her money and that Guy helped her move the body."

"When did she tell you this?"

"Recently."

She disclosed the rest of their conversation on the topic, which wasn't much. She didn't have a name or a year this might have happened.

Torrin now straightened, his hands folded upon the top of the interview table. His expression was open and earnest. It made her nervous. She suspected that whatever followed, she would not like it. "Nadine, we need your help."

"So you mentioned, yet none of you have asked to see the comparison you requested."

"Fukuda told me it's a geo profile. Our profiler has already established the unsub's—"

"Likely area of residence," she interrupted. "Yes, I know. But as I explain to Special Agent Fukuda, this geo profile is the reverse, delineating areas where the crimes will likely occur. I used it to target Myakka River. Did he not share this with you?"

Now he was leaning forward, listening intently.

"I'd like to see that."

"And here I thought you were more interested in my genealogy."

"Yes. It's relevant." Torrin rubbed his neck. "Let's have a look."

She spent the next twenty minutes reviewing her findings. He never said a word until she finished.

"So, you believe we should search the parks along the coast for the dump."

"But only as far south as Nokomis."

"Hmm. And you associate the use of the cabin by Dun as similar to your mother's use of the houseboat?"

"And the stables. My mother's territory changed with her various jobs. But as you see, Myakka Park is well within this unsub's target territory."

"Yes."

Torrin cleared his throat. And she prepared for whatever wa
sticking there.

"We are prepping to interview your mother again and would
like you to accompany us."

And there it was. Yet another reason they wanted her as an
adjunct member of their team. They needed her help with her
mother. She paused before reaching for the bait, wondering if her
head was already in a snare.

"When?"

CHAPTER TWENTY-NINE

Sharper than a serpent's tooth

The ride up to Lowell on Tuesday afternoon took only forty minutes because the FBI flew them to the Marion County Airport. Ground transportation waited, and soon Nadine spotted the guard tower and then the high chain-link fencing.

Yesterday she had called her aunt Donna's landline and reached her uncle, who confirmed that the FBI had visited and asked her aunt a lot of questions.

Donna returned her call as the prison came into view.

Nadine explained that the Bureau was working on the recent homicides in Sarasota.

"I read about them and it's on the news. It reminds me of Arleen's crimes."

"Yes. It's why I'm involved," said Nadine. "I'm sorry, Aunt Donna, for all of it."

"Oh, honey. None of this is your fault."

Nadine pressed her lips together to keep from crying in front of the agent driving her. Aunt Donna filled the void.

"We'll see you soon. Just as soon as I get back from Dallas. All right?"

Nadine's voice cracked as she spoke. "I'd like that."

She ended the call as they pulled into a separate parking area from the one Nadine had used. She followed the agents through security. The process was simpler when you traveled with the FBI.

They brought Nadine's mother to the interview room. She wore her usual attire of pale blue with a white leg stripe, slip-on sneakers with no laces, wrist shackles and… lipstick?

It *was* lipstick. Nadine tried to remember a time she had ever seen her mother wearing makeup and could not come up with a single occasion.

"Dee-Dee! I'm so happy to see you." She moved forward, shackled arms extended, to hug Nadine.

A guard stepped before Arleen.

"Nope," he said.

"Prick," she said, and took a seat.

Nadine moved to the table, sitting across from Arleen. The agents were already situated in the periphery, against the sidewall.

Nadine cleared her throat. "Hello, Arleen."

Her mother turned to Special Agent Torrin. "She calls me 'Arleen.' Hasn't called me 'Mama' since she was eight."

Nadine hadn't called her "Mama" since Arleen started asking her to take out the garbage.

"Well, Arleen," said Torrin. "Thank you for agreeing to see us today. We hope to gain some insights from you."

"'Insights'?" Arleen laughed and thumbed at the agent as she looked at Nadine. "You hear this guy shoveling it? Wants my 'insights.' Couldn't be bothered to come here during my trial or after my trial or any other damn time. But now he wants to know all about me." She turned to the agent. "Told you last time, you are fifteen years too late."

Her mother folded her arms, lowered her chin, and glared at Torrin.

They had discussed this on the flight. At this juncture, Nadine was to take over and ask the questions that the FBI failed with during the earlier visit.

Nadine lowered her head to remember the first question that they wanted her to pose.

"What's the matter, Dee-Dee? They got something on you?"

"No. They don't. I came because it's an opportunity to see you. I missed last weekend because of this case."

Her mother gave her an appraising look.

"Mama, I want to thank you for all the letters."

Nadine hadn't called her "Mama" in over two decades, and she had not been to the box in Tampa since before her last visit. She was certain it was just stuffed with mail.

Torrin and Fukuda exchanged a look. Clearly, they didn't know everything, and she believed correspondence with Arleen was news.

Her mother's brows lifted, and she appeared both surprised and pleased.

"Be nice if you wrote me back now and then."

"Yes, I know. We've been very busy with this case. If we could get it solved, I'd have more time to write and to visit."

"Maybe I could call you. They let me make calls, if you give me your number and permission."

The thought of her mother being able to call her anytime, to stretch over the miles and land in her cell phone, gave Nadine a chill. She was never checking that box on the application form.

"Yeah," she said. "And if I solve it, I get a raise. Then I could put money in your account every week."

Arleen's eyes lit up, and for just a second, Nadine felt guilty. Then she remembered her mother's victims and the guilt dried up like a puddle in the sun.

The air in the room grew heavier, harder to breathe. She could smell the disinfectant used on the floors and the body odor coming from her mother. The stench made her dizzy.

"Mama, those two on the houseboat. Did you move them?" She was careful not to say those victims *you* murdered.

Arleen's expression brightened at Nadine's interest in discussing murder. "Well, if you mean from the dock, yeah. I took out the boat after they closed for the day. Drove downriver toward Sanford. When I finished with them, I pushed them off the back into the lake and then pulled into the marina down there. Folks leave boats there sometimes. I knew the place, used their hoses to wash out the insides and ditched the mattress in their dumpster. Took most of the night. Then I brung her back, clean as a whistle."

"You cleaned all the boats back then, right?"

"Never cleaned one like that." She cackled, and slapped her knee, making the shackles clatter.

Somehow, Nadine held her "I'm interested" look.

"The marina buys all the cleaning stuff. Air fresheners, bleach and that blue junk for fabrics. It don't take the color, but it gets the blood. Had it with me. Prep work, you know? After you make the kill, it's best to get clear fast as possible. Remember that, Dee-Dee."

Was Arleen really giving her daughter advice on how to get away with murder in front of the FBI? Yes, she decided, and her mother was showing off.

"Were they alive when you took them to the lake?"

"She was. Him, definitely not." Arleen's smile was chilling. Her mother flicked her attention to Torrin. "She never did take much interest in my hobby."

Arleen turned back to Nadine and their gazes locked.

"There's nothing like it, Dee-Dee. Nothing in this world. Maybe someday I'll have more than my opinion on that."

Had her mother just called her out to become a serial killer?

Nadine went back to the second couple with her next question.

"With Lacey Louder—"

"Who?"

"They found her in the St. Johns river in 2000."

Arleen looked confused. Nadine's blood chilled at the clear sign that Arleen couldn't recall the names of the people she had killed. She didn't care enough to learn or remember them.

"The working girl who was with the forest ranger."

"Oh, that tramp." She nodded, following Nadine now. Was it possible that she knew more about her mother's victims than Arleen herself did?

"Why did you kill her separately from Henderson?"

She shrugged. "Seen them together more than once. But then my shift changed. Couldn't get out there on the nights they were fucking, so I improvised."

"Why didn't you drop him in the river?"

"Too heavy and too damn far. You imagine dragging him all the way to the shore through that saw grass. Cut you up like grated cheese, or worse. Strain my back and be out of work? No thank you."

Arleen had just complained about the exertion of disposing of her murder victims. Nadine felt sick with shame at her mother's absence of humanity.

"The initials you carved on the women. That was for 'home-wreckers.' Right?"

Her mother's lopsided grin showed appreciation. She met Nadine's gaze and inclined her chin. Then said, "I ain't sayin'."

Nadine changed tack. "You ever hear from anyone in the family?" she asked.

"What d'you mean, 'the family'?"

"Uncle Tinsel?"

Arleen laughed, a cackling dry thing. "I forgot you called him that. He had that tooth fixed, you know?"

"You've seen him?"

She broke eye contact. "Naw. He wrote for a while. Honestly I ain't heard from him in, oh, *some time.*"

Her smile and the emphasis indicated otherwise.

"Does he visit?"

"'Visit'? Nope."

"Call?"

She smiled and shook her head. "If he does call, I can ask him to look you up," said Arleen. "Just give me your number."

Nadine wasn't doing that.

"He can call me here." Nadine pushed a piece of paper across the table. Arleen didn't take it.

"Not a Florida area code, Dee-Dee. This is up north somewhere." She glanced at the agents standing still against the wall and smiled at Torrin. "Like Washington, maybe?" She pushed it back. "I ain't giving him this."

Nadine took the paper and tucked it away.

Arleen was playing them all.

They stared at each other in silence, opponents once more.

Special Agent Torrin had asked her to use only the questions prepared by the FBI. She fell back to them now.

"I want to ask you about the other man you mentioned to me. The one who owed you money?"

Her mother fumed, her face turning scarlet in an instant. The veins on her neck and forehead bulged and pulsed. Arleen leveled her gaze on Nadine, aiming it like a loaded shotgun.

"You know, Dee-Dee, I always figured you for a smart girl. You got those letters after your name, and all. So, what I'm wondering is, if you're so damn smart, why are you acting as a tool for these gorillas?"

"I'm not a tool. I'm trying to solve a multiple-homicide investigation so I can help you. See you more. Get you more money."

"Ha! This ain't your job, is it? Your job is to figure out if I'm crazy or not. Wading in with the gators to find dead bodies

That's theirs." She twisted her wrist, aiming a thumb at Torrin and making her shackles clank.

"I'm trying to do what's right."

"Because you feel guilty. And you ain't even done nothing." Arleen sneered, her expression full of scorn. "Guilt is the real enemy. It'll trip you up. You can't go back and change the past or who you are, Dee-Dee."

Nadine dropped her eyes as the truth of that struck like buckshot.

"It's your job to survive out there. Get what you need because you can't trust men." She lifted a finger at Torrin, rattling her shackles. "They only want to boss us, blame us for shit that ain't our doing, get in our pants and move on. To survive, you gotta be tougher than they are. Smarter too."

Nadine met her mother's cold stare.

"And you are, Dee-Dee. Trust me on that. You are."

And that was one of the many things that scared Nadine. Her mother was tougher and colder. She knew it. But inside herself, was she her mother's daughter?

Arleen narrowed her eyes on the two agents.

"You think I don't see what you're doing? Using my daughter like a puppet. What is it they say about ungrateful children and serpent's teeth? That surely is my Dee-Dee. My brother ain't forgotten me. My son writes me regular. And my daughter shows up with the FBI. It's a dirty shame."

"Well, Arlo has a lot more time on his hands than me."

Her mother scowled. "Dee-Dee, whether you admit it or not, you are like us. Only difference is, I'm in here and you're out there. If you just stop listening to men, you could be great. You could be free."

"*Free*, like you? Seems to me that you are the opposite of 'free.'"

Arleen tapped her index finger to her temple, leaning in. "I'm free in my mind. I don't let no man tell me what to do. Not no more! Not my father, not my cheating druggie ex-husband. Bastard left the minute he found out I was pregnant with you!"

Was that why he left them, because Arleen had gotten pregnant again? Her mind spun with speculation and she couldn't focus on what Arleen was shouting.

Finally Nadine mentally shook herself, focusing on her mother.

"… Men! They're only good for two things. Screwing and killing. Took me years to figure that out. I don't need no man. Not no more." Arleen stood. "I'm done here."

The guards moved forward as Arleen aimed a finger at her daughter.

"I'm disappointed, Dee-Dee. I surely am disappointed. I ain't given up hope. But I'm getting damned close."

Nadine didn't like being scolded. She lowered her chin and went off script.

"Where's Dad?" Nadine asked.

Her mother's face turned scarlet again. For a moment, Nadine thought Arleen had stopped breathing. Her eyes blazed as she slammed both her shackled hands down on the table.

Both agents straightened, taking aggressive stances. The guard behind Arleen moved forward. Her mother's stare flicked from one to the next and then back to Nadine.

"Shut up about him."

A more cautious person would've dropped the topic. But she had found the pin with which to poke her mother and was not near done.

"He's my father. I have a right to know where he is."

"You were a baby. You have no rights. As for him, he don't want nothing to do with you."

That much was obvious from the decades of absence.

"Why did he leave?"

"That bitch stole him is why. Homewrecker. But I…" Arleen clamped her mouth shut. "I ain't talking about him. He was a terrible father."

That makes them a perfect parenting pair, Nadine thought.

Arleen turned to Torrin. "You find him, you let me know. You have any idea how much money he owes me?"

She turned back to her daughter. Her face was still red, and her mouth twisted in an ugly sneer.

Nadine followed a hunch. She'd heard her mother rage about this other woman for years after their father's abandonment. "The women you killed looked an awful lot like Infinity Yanez. So, I'd say that it did matter."

"How do you know? You never seen her."

Nadine lifted a hand and indicated the FBI agents standing like gray pillars.

Arleen's gaze flicked from the agents, back to Nadine.

"What're you saying? That I killed them others because I couldn't kill her? Well, let me tell you something, missy. She ain't the reason."

"Where are they, then?"

"They run off together."

"Did they?"

"Sure." Arleen flashed a quick smile. Duping Delight, again. It expressed satisfaction from pulling one over on someone. On her.

Her mother knew exactly where Nadine's father was; Nadine was certain.

Was this the reason her dad hadn't been in contact or made any effort to see her in over twenty-five years?

The FBI hadn't been able to locate Dennis Howler. His sister had not heard from him in decades. Suddenly the narrative fixed in Nadine's mind tilted. Had her father abandoned her, or was that what Arleen had wanted everyone to believe?

Her mother had said she'd killed a man with a shovel. Used his truck and his hose and his pool because he owed her money. Was that child support?

Her assumptions crashed into the facts. Either her father had fled ahead of apprehension, changed his identity, and worked somewhere off the books, or…

Is he dead?

Was her father dead?

CHAPTER THIRTY

Darkest before dawn

"Why was the public kept in the dark about the initial murders?"

Nadine caught some of the live broadcast of the press conference on her laptop at eleven on Wednesday morning and was so grateful not to be on hand. But there stood their governor, Neal Eaton, looking polished and confident as always. The man could hold his smile even through a press conference on serial killers. His silver hair and black eyebrows gave him a distinguished flair, and his dark tan made her suspect that this publicly elected official didn't spend a lot of time behind his desk. Eaton had flown in from Tallahassee to stand beside the chief of police, mayor and Special Agent Fukuda, who must have drawn the short straw. From what Demko said, their state's leader wouldn't be behind them for long if they didn't make an arrest soon.

The follow-up was brutal. "Do you feel responsible for Officer Pender and his ex-wife, Hope Kerr, who were unaware that there was a predator in their community?"

The mayor was eloquent in her answer, referencing the need to avoid public panic. The chief of police was less than forthcoming, citing no wish to jeopardize an ongoing investigation.

At this point, Special Agent Fukuda asked the public to be on the lookout for Anthony Dun, possibly driving a white rental van.

Nadine groaned. There were hundreds, maybe thousands, c white vans in the city. She already felt sorry for the police cal center operators and every service provider who showed up at residence or condo in a white van.

She wondered what the reporters would say when they realize that the police department was pulling neighborhood patrols t cover protection and security for the governor's visit?

When the conference ended, she resumed her digital searcl for her uncle, using what she had learned from Torrin, but strucl out again. If the FBI couldn't find Guy Owen, what chance di she have?

They had shared that the prison logs showed Arleen receive few phone calls, but more mail than most inmates. Mail wa opened and checked for contraband. They did not keep a log o callers but would begin doing so at the Bureau's request, alon; with scanning all envelopes and correspondence.

Her mother's implications troubled her. During another restles night, she decided she needed to speak to Arlo again.

She made another call to the chaplain and Arlo called bacl two hours later.

Her brother sounded breathless. "You all right?"

"Yes. Why?"

"Chaplain said you'd been in an accident."

"No. I'm fine. The emergency was more metaphorical."

"You're going to give me a heart attack with this shit." He blev out a breath.

She gave him a second but knew the phone cards used mone and this was burning up his minutes.

"Listen, I upped the amount in your account."

"Thanks, Dee-Dee."

The silence stretched as her heart thumped in her chest. Sh sucked in a breath and launched into her concerns.

"Remember that guy she told me about, the one she said owed her money and that Uncle Tinsel helped her move the—"

Arlo interrupted her. "Dee-Dee, be careful. They monitor these calls."

She paused. Had she been about to say body?

"Okay."

"Uncle Tinsel? Yeah?"

Nadine continued with more care. "He helped her move something... heavy."

"All right."

"Could that have been... been...?" Nadine couldn't manage a word past the lump.

"Dad?" said Arlo.

"I don't know." Her voice rasped. "Maybe. The FBI can't find him. And Mom started to say something and clammed up."

"You think she...?" His words trailed off.

"I don't know. Do you?"

"All the ones after looked like her, like Yanez. Didn't they?" he asked.

She didn't need to ask who he meant. Her victims. And yes. They did.

"We need to find Uncle Guy," said Arlo.

"Are you in touch with him?"

"No. You?"

"No. FBI can't find him, either."

She ended the call more troubled than when she began it.

Nadine made another call, this one to Demko, explaining her suspicion. She asked him to run a search on Infinity.

"I'll let you know what pops up," he promised.

Late in the day, Torrin stopped by to obtain the key to her PO box in order to retrieve the letters her mother mentioned during their visit. Nadine had explained about the PO box and was happy to turn over the job of reading the correspondence to the FBI. Better them than her.

"Do you have any of your mother's personal effects?" asked Torrin.

"My uncle took them after my mother's conviction."

Nadine asked him if Demko had mentioned the Peace River as a possible body dump. He said they were aware.

"I have some additional information on your dad."

"You found him?"

"No. We obtained his military records. They showed a dishonorable discharge for selling drugs on base. He spent time in a rehabilitation facility before returning to Ocala."

"He was a drug dealer?"

"Lots of addicts sell to finance their habits."

Was her father dead or one of a thousand drug-addicted homeless men shuffling through their cities? Both thoughts punched at Nadine's insides.

"Did you find Yanez?"

Torrin shook his head. "She's listed as a missing person since June 1993."

Arleen had killed them both. Nadine was certain, but she had not a shred of proof.

"What about my uncle?"

"Nothing."

"Did she kill him, too?"

*

Torrin had explained that their goal was the apprehension of their prime suspect, Anthony Dun. Her uncle's disappearance was not the focus of their investigation. They didn't know, or seem to care, if either Infinity Yanez or Guy Owen was deceased or had disappeared by design.

On Thursday, she got a message from Demko, telling her they'd been staking out several positions she'd mentioned on the Peace River since Monday night. Where was Carla Giffin right now? The waitress was a married mother of two children, neither her son nor daughter was yet old enough to attend school. And Nick Thrasher might not be the ideal husband, but his job as a manager and cook at the restaurant provided for his wife and baby girl, born with autism. Was that infant now also a child without a father? She hoped they could catch this murderer before the killer dumped the bodies and vanished.

She moved back to her cottage apartment after work on Thursday, partially out of bravado, but mostly because the suite at the airport hotel taxed her budget.

At her place, she installed a curtain on the porthole window and armed her new security system.

Despite the upgrades, she was getting antsy, troubled by the accelerated timeline and in a panic over the pair who had been held at Myakka. Part of her hoped they lived, and another part prayed they were dead. Years ago, her mother had tortured her supervisor Michelle Dents at the marina and Dent's lover, Parker Irwin, keeping them for most of the weekend. After that, it was Nadine's classmate, with her dealer and pimp, Stephen White. Arleen had cut Stephen repeatedly with a carpet knife, before staking him out alive, beside the manure pile, for the ants and flies. When Nadine was a girl, and her mother worked at the stables, she had told Nadine that the flies that bit the horses also laid their eggs on the skin. The larva ate into living flesh, creating open wounds. You didn't have to be dead for maggots to eat at you.

Nadine's stomach heaved at this thought, knowing exactly what White had suffered.

As she crawled into her own bed, her mind fixed on the possibility that the killer had already captured the final pair.

When she finally fell into a restless sleep, images of Sandra Shank woke her in a cold sweat.

On Friday morning, she got a call from Demko.

"We found two bodies. Male and female. Tentative ID is Giffin and Thrasher."

"On the Peace River?"

"No. On Phillippi Creek."

"What? That's west of Myakka." Her profile was wrong.

He did not issue incriminations or tell her that her map had the FBI and local police setting up a dragnet on the wrong waterway. All he said was "Yes."

"I'm so sorry!"

"Not your fault. The bodies have been there several days. They were tangled in debris near the Phillippi Creek Bridge. Found the white van, too, behind one of the outbuildings. The park thought it was one of theirs."

"The van. That's good. Right?"

"Yes, but it looks like Dun sprayed the interior with sodium percarbonate and hydrogen peroxide. Both are hell on organic matter, so we aren't going to get any blood or DNA. I'm assuming he wiped it, but we'll check for prints."

Sandra Shank was next.

"And they didn't find Dun?"

"Correct."

The killer might already have Sandra. She drew a shaky breath. It wasn't Sandra. But it would be a teen, a girl, like her classmate.

"I'll be here processing all day. You want to come down?"

"Yeah. I need to add these victims to my map." The sight of the bodies still upset her, but now for different reasons. Now they infuriated her because each one represented a failure to give the authorities what they needed to catch this killer.

"See you soon then." He disconnected and Nadine tucked her phone away.

What was she missing with her geographic profile? She had entered all the information. The locations were physically similar to where her mother had dropped her victims.

"There's something wrong with it," she told herself, but she could not figure out what.

Nadine headed out, meeting Demko in a beautiful park that she had not even known existed. The divers had ferried the bodies to shore and the ME had already removed them. She jotted down the coordinates for her map, wondering if the tide had carried them into the creek or out?

The FBI had also asked Crean to work as a consultant and she was still on site.

"Anything I should know?" Nadine asked her.

"I saw the remains. This time was different. The male was dead longer. Torrin said the wounds on the female indicate this was not a quick kill. If they were taken together, he kept her alive longer. The multiple lesions seemed designed to inflict pain instead of death."

"Same marks on the left hand and on the female?"

"Yes, missing strip of skin on both, and the slashing marks on her backside. Just the same." Crean glanced at her phone. "I've got to go."

"See you later," Nadine said.

"No. At least not this afternoon. I'm taking half a personal day."

Nadine narrowed her eyes.

"My husband is at a breeders' convention this week and we've got two litters of pups."

That didn't sit right with Nadine, who made no effort to hide her feelings, letting her expression speak for her.

Crean pulled a grim face and then lifted a hand in farewell. They watched as Crean pulled away.

Who took time off at such a time?

*

Back at the office, Nadine carefully added the newest body dum
to her original map and opened the document of her mother
trail of carnage. Then she made a hard copy of each. She set th
printout of her mother's captures, kills and body dumps besid
her updated map and stared at the two. There was no denying tha
the sites were remarkably similar in physical features.

Fukuda visited her office just before five to ask her if she'd take
part in the Sanchez studies.

"I'm not sure that is."

He kept his expression impassive as he answered, "It's a researc
project coauthored by Dr. Margery Crean."

Nadine thought she had read all of her supervisor's research
but this one escaped her.

"Could you give me more details?"

He set a copy of a research paper before her.

"I didn't work on this project," she said, scanning the date. "
would have been too young."

"I'm not asking if you were a researcher. I'm asking if you wer
a research subject," said Fukuda.

This time, when she lifted the carefully stapled pages, her han
shook.

"What is this?"

"A questionnaire used with minors. There is no way for us t
identify the subjects. The study is flawed, according to our researc
team. The subject sample was too narrow and not randomized."

"How did I miss this? I've read all of Crean's publications."

"Not published in the United States," said Fukuda, pointin
to the page. "Germany."

The agent lifted the study from her hands and opened to a pag
containing a questionnaire.

"Look familiar?"

Nadine read the first four questions, and the air left her lungs.

"I took this in high school, senior year."

He collected the pages and thanked her. Nadine was still bracing herself on her desk when he left.

"What the hell?" She retrieved her phone and called Demko.

"Hey there. What's up?"

"Clint, Fukuda showed me a research article. Do you remember taking a survey after your mother's conviction?"

There was a pause. "What kind of survey?"

"All I know is that they called me to the counselor's office and told me I was in a random sampling of teens taking part in a national study. They did not advise me on the nature of the study and, turns out, I was not randomly selected. I'd been targeted as a child of a killer. Crean was one of the researchers."

"How did Crean get permission for such a study?" asked Demko.

"I'm not sure. She was working for a federal mental health agency. Might have used that position to gain access. It's confusing and probably illegal."

"What were the questions?"

Nadine recited the three that she had just read. "Has any member of your family ever committed a violent act? Has a member of your family ever been arrested for a violent act? Has any member of your family been convicted of a felony?"

"Shit."

"Were you aware of your family member's involvement in a violent act? (A) before the crime, (B) after the crime, (C) after the arrest, (D) after the conviction."

"Stop. I remember. We need to have a talk with Dr. Crean."

"Sounds good. You bring the handcuffs. Oh, wait, she's out of the office. Personal day."

"Oh, yeah. Taking care of the kennel. Right? I've been to her place. Picked up Molly there. She lives out on Route 70. Meet you back here?" Demko asked.

"I'm coming with you."

"No. I don't want her to know where I learned about the survey. Your presence will tip her off."

"You're going alone?"

"I'll ask Torrin if he's interested."

Nadine struggled to find a reason to be included and came up empty.

"It's my case, too," she said.

"I know."

There was a long pause and Nadine was about to ask if he was still there.

"Listen, Nadine, could you watch Molly tomorrow? My pet sitter is visiting her grandkids and we are still processing."

Dogs weren't allowed at her place. *You know what they say about rules.*

"Sure. What time would you like me to pick her up?"

"I can drop her off. Is seven too early?"

Of course it was too early! What was she? A distance runner? Saturdays were for sleeping in.

"*Sure*," she said, drawing out the word, not sure.

"Okay, I'll see you Saturday. Bye-bye."

He'd taken that questionnaire, too. It was unethical to include minors without seeking parental approval. Nadine had been too young to give consent. The entire thing needled her.

CHAPTER THIRTY-ONE

Final kills

I spotted them at the championships over a year ago and just knew there were shenanigans going on. There was nothing subtle about the way they were acting. He's a newlywed. His bride, the one financing his Olympic run, is home, too pregnant to travel. And the girl… she's got a live-in boyfriend, who works two jobs to keep her in that skinny rowboat and in the competition. Partners working away so these two can chase their championship dreams and chase tail.

Despicable.

They're now waiting for me in a spot that affords me privacy in an empty building. There's still just the tiny possibility of discovery. That only adds some spice.

I began with him. Arleen's male adulterer lasted four days, but mine is an athlete. Should work in his favor or against it, depending on your point of view. Yesterday, after some bloodletting, I tied and staked him to the ground outside. Nothing draws insects faster, except a corpse.

He's well away from where anyone could hear him scream. Besides, he's given up screaming and begging. Had the nerve to bring up his pregnant wife. Can you believe it?

Telling him what I will do to his whore might have been my very favorite part. When I left him, he kept on shouting threats he is incapable of carrying out. What do they call doing the same thing over and over again and expecting different results? The definition of insanity? I think he is close to insanity now.

When he's done, I'll turn to the girl. This one is more like my usual fare, young, scared… I am giddy with anticipation. She makes me want to tuck her in my trunk and take her back to my place. But it's getting too crowded there and, with all the other bodies, I can't squeeze any more people in. The idea of excavating another room is just too daunting. So it's time to move on.

I wrote Arleen, told her I'll be leaving again and relayed my annoyance that our best prodigy is so slow to answer the call. I'm ready to try Demko or Hartfield. Perhaps that mouse of an assistant, Ruz. Any or all seem better options at this point. It makes me cross. I worry about the next generation.

Today I mount the horns of a dilemma. Do I finish him tonight or do I see if he can make the full four days? I really am much more interested in the girl. And continuing with her lover seems a waste of my time. He doesn't have to be dead before I begin with her. Does he

But that is changing the rules again. I should do this properly.

Nadine is so clever. I would love to ask her how she determined to look in Myakka.

I need to get home. It's Saturday night and I have a big day tomorrow.

CHAPTER THIRTY-TWO

Second wind

Nadine scanned several current news articles. One called her *a killer's daughter* hunting a monster mirroring her mother's crimes. She marveled at Arleen's ability to ruin her daughter's life all the way from a maximum-security prison cell.

Molly rolled to her feet, dancing with joy at the front window, alerting Nadine that Demko had returned. She disabled the alarm and opened the door. Molly rushed out to greet him: The dog gets the first hug. But she gets the kiss.

He looked rumpled. She stepped into his arms and plucked a tiny bit of vegetative debris from his hair and he pulled her in again.

This kiss was full of eagerness and promise. The contact set off a wildfire of heat blazing through her. The yearning to step closer and wrap her arms around him was strong. She deepened the contact as her body danced with arousal. Then she felt him sway on his feet and stepped back to give him a critical stare. The man was done in.

"Hungry?" she asked.

He had to think about it. "Yeah."

She peeled away and into her kitchen as Demko gave Molly a proper greeting.

He followed her to the kitchen as she retrieved the boxed dinner that she grabbed him from her favorite Caribbean barbecue food truck.

"Want me to heat it?" she asked, and opened the lid.

He leaned in to inhale and peer at the Jamaican jerk chicken and rib combo with red beans and rice.

In answer, he relieved her of the container. She offered napkin and fork as he started on the ribs. Then she opened him a beer, setting it beside him on the counter. He gnawed through the ribs and turned to the beer bottle while she watched in amazement.

He spoke between bites of jerk chicken. "We finished processing the Phillippi Creek scenes. Took some searching for where they went into the water. Looks like our guy drove that van right to the boat launch. Afterward, the unsub parked it behind one of the buildings and walked away."

"Surveillance cameras?"

"Only on the main house." He lifted the beer and took swallow before setting it back on the counter. Then he finished the chicken and dug into the rice. "Taking them all the way into the city and to that park adds risk. Any idea why he didn't drop them in Myakka? It's closer. Safer," said Demko.

"I think it has to do with my mother's body dumps. They were all on the river. These are all on the coast."

"Not the last pair."

"She never had a chance to dump the final two. I told you my mom separated capture, kill and dump sites as her series progressed."

After he finished wolfing his food, she led him out to the small living room and he sagged into the couch with a groan, cradling the remains of his second beer. Molly set her chin on his lap and he stroked his dog's head.

"Did you see Crean?" she asked, settling beside him.

"I did. She admitted to conducting the study and categorized it as an unfortunate decision. I told her there might be charges."

He lifted his beer, draining the contents.

"How'd she take it?"

"She told me to speak to her lawyer."

Nadine snorted. That didn't surprise her.

"Anything more on Anthony Dun?"

"Big fat zero. We have a nationwide manhunt going, but the guy disappeared like last week's pay. Everyone in the county has reported seeing a white van, despite our already having found it. Feds think he might have left the state."

"Hmm."

"What?"

"If Dun is our unsub, he can't leave. He has to finish the series." Sandra Shank and Stephen White, the most horrific of all her mother's known kills.

Somehow, she had to stop this.

Demko lifted the empty bottle and attempted to take another swallow, then checked the contents and sighed.

"Would you like another?" She remembered too late that she had no more.

"No, I'd better not. I still have to drive home." His eyes flashed to hers and there was heat there. She sensed his unspoken question. He couldn't have another beer, unless she invited him to stay.

Tempting.

Nadine held his gaze and considered her options. Then she looked at the circles under his red-rimmed eyes. The man needed sleep, and this was a very ill-advised time to become involved with a Homicide detective. Probably the worst period in her life, except the time when her mother was actively murdering people.

Yet, somehow, she was involved.

She recalled Crean's warning to keep her relationship with Demko private. No more sleepovers, she had said.

Nadine fumed. She was not taking directives from *that* woman, boss or no boss.

Demko stared down at the empty beer bottle in his hand.

"Maybe another water." He started to rise, and she pressed him back into the cushions and headed for the kitchen with the empty. When she returned with a cold bottle from the refrigerator, both Molly and Demko were snoring.

"Come on, you two," she said to Demko, and led him to her bed, flicking back the covers.

Demko stripped down to his underwear and stood holding his badge, vest and holstered gun.

"You have a safe?"

She snorted. "No. If it makes you feel better, I promise not to shoot you while you're sleeping."

"That leaves a good portion of the day open," he said, smiling wearily before he set his service weapon on the nightstand and sank to the bed.

"Thanks for taking care of Molly. Thanks for taking care of me."

Had she? She supposed feeding him a cold dinner and giving him a place to forget about the horrific day was care. Intimacy, she thought, the connection that she had longed for, and here he was offering. Nadine didn't know if she was brave enough to let him all the way in.

She knelt before him and kissed him.

"My pleasure," she said, surprised to realize it was true.

He collapsed into the mattress, still gripping his cell phone, asleep before she even covered him. She used her fob to turn off the security system before letting Molly out, watching from the porch, holding her arms across her chest, as she scanned the yard, which had become a dangerous place.

Back inside, Nadine armed the system and folded a comforter on the floor for the boxer, right beside her master.

She slipped into bed, nestling close to him, and felt a sweet mix of longing and contentment. Sometime in the night, she was aware of him using the bathroom, Molly trotting along.

Nadine heard him moving around and assumed he'd let Molly out again. Then she recalled the armed security system and sat up.

Where was he?

And there he was, right beside her, fully dressed.

"Alarm code?" he asked.

She roused to grab her phone and switch off the system.

"Leaving?" she said. "What time is it?"

"Early. Arm the system when I'm out."

*

Later that Sunday morning, Demko called to relay that the FBI had made a positive identification on both Carla Giffin and Nick Thrasher. The families had been notified.

Nadine grappled with the crushing disappointment. Even with all signs pointing to their death, she'd held an unreasonable hope that they might find Giffin and Thrasher in time. Now all she could think of was the conversation the surviving parents would eventually have with their children.

"Daddy died when you were a baby."

"Mommy isn't coming home. Mommy is with the angels."

Actually, Mommy was in the morgue, or all that was left of her. Nadine's emotions warped into fury and iron conviction to catch this twisted killer.

"You okay?" he asked.

"No. I don't think so."

"Yeah. Me too."

"When did you leave?"

"Around five. I had to type up my notes and check if the ID was made. Listen, I hate to tell you this."

Nadine's heart did a little stutter.

"Sheriff called me. They have a missing person. Seems unre lated, but I wanted to update you."

It had happened already?

"A teenager?"

"No. White male, twenty-two years. Name is Elton Delconte An elite athlete. Came from out of the area for the World Rowing competition."

She sagged with relief. "The next were taken together. One teenage girl and her… pimp."

"May be unrelated," he said.

Like the recently missing children, she thought. Not every missing person was one of their victims. She recalled an elderly woman who survived spending the night partially submerged in her car in a canal after making a wrong turn. People disappeared for all sorts of reasons, and, based on the number of Silver and Amber Alerts lighting up her cell phone, they went missing in Sarasota a lot. Still…

"Who reported him missing?"

"His coach. He didn't show up for warm-up and was not at his hotel."

"Was he alone?"

"In his room, yes. But he's traveling with his team."

"Married?" she asked.

"I'll find out."

Her mind buzzed with possibilities. Did this rower match Stephen White, the man who exploited young girls back in Ocala "Check with the other teams. See if there is a woman or girl also missing, or if he's been involved with a lot of them."

"Coach said he's a dedicated athlete with ambitions to make the US Olympic team."

Nadine shook her head, already eliminating him as a possibility

"How long has he been gone?"

"Last practice was yesterday morning, so twenty-four hours."

"Where did he go missing?" she asked.

"Not sure. Benderson Park vicinity."

"The place they do rowing?" she asked. "North?"

"Yes."

"Hotel?"

"Cross of University and North Cattlemen Road. Less than a mile."

"Hmm."

She had added all capture areas to her map, but some of that involved guesswork. The disappearance area fell well within the predicted range.

"I don't like it," said Nadine.

"Well, for now, he's just a missing person," said Demko.

"Could you let me know if he turns up?" she asked.

"Will do."

Nadine wasn't fond of loose ends and anomalies. Things tended to sit where they belong, and having a missing person in the middle of this investigation may have been normal, but it made her anxious.

"Better go."

Nadine waited for him to disconnect, but instead he spoke again.

"Oh, wait. While I have you on the phone, Torrin and his staff have been going through your mother's correspondence. He mentioned that they may need you to visit again. Would you be willing?"

This time, she was not instantly agreeable.

"Let me think about it, okay?"

"I know it takes a toll, but it might be the one thing that puts us ahead of this perp."

Demko said his good-byes and left her alone on a Sunda morning with her geographic profiles and a new missin person.

Had the clock just started ticking again?

*

On Monday, Nadine tackled the tsunami of emails flooding he office in-box. Everyone wanted a piece of the profiler with th serial killer mom. Focusing on other things wasn't working, bu she made it through the day. She finally caved and call Demko

"Any new developments?"

"Yeah, matter of fact. The FBI has made some progress o finding Anthony Dun. Word is that they have confirmed a ti The governor is back in town, and they are setting the stage scheduling a press conference."

"Don't they have to catch him before they can put him in fror of the TV cameras?" she asked.

"That's the way we do it down here. But I have no idea wha goes on in Tallahassee or DC. They already called the local new Want them on site to get footage of Dun's arrest."

Nadine shifted the office phone to her shoulder and jiggled he cell phone awake to glance at the time. It was 5:15 p.m.

"You free tonight?" she asked.

"For…?"

"I wondered if you would like to have dinner with me."

"You cooking?" he asked.

Nadine affected a tone of shock. "Don't even joke about it."

He laughed and then there was a long silent pause.

"I wish I could. Unfortunately, it's all hands on deck fo the dragnet around Dun. The FBI has 'eyes on,' and we're ju coordinating the takedown."

"Well, good luck."

"You have any interest in coming along?"

Nadine was rejecting the offer before he finished the question. "I don't want to upstage the FBI's party."

"They'd never know you were there."

"Thanks, but no. If I never see Anthony Dun again, it would be too soon."

"You'll see him in court, if nowhere else."

He was right. She would have to testify to her interactions with Anthony Dun. She wondered again if he was the man who had been in her house. The FBI said he was there but had yet to produce any evidence to prove their allegation. Also, why would Anthony Dun write *Legacy* on her bathroom mirror? Did he mean that they both had the legacy of incarcerated parents who had committed terrible crimes?

Demko spoke to someone else, his words muffled and then back to Nadine. "Gotta go. SWAT team just arrived, and we already have county sheriffs, city police, FBI and ATF."

"ATF? How did they get involved?"

"I'm not sure. Something about unregistered weapons linked to Dun."

The possibility of a house being booby-trapped exploded in her mind. She squeezed the receiver.

"Please take care!"

"Yes. I will."

"Did they find the young rower?" she asked.

"No. Not yet. But you were right about the girls. A teammate told me he has a reputation. Promiscuous."

"Anyone else missing?"

"None reported."

She released a breath. "Be careful."

He made a humming sound. A laugh? She wasn't sure.

"Always," he said.

He did this sort of thing as part of his job. But it didn't make it any easier. When had his safety become so vital to her?

"I'll call after it's done."

After it's Dun, she thought.

*

Nadine made it home before six and set out the hard copies of the geo-map renderings on the dinette, hoping they might spark some insights.

She worried about Demko and hoped he'd be back soon. With that thought in mind, she headed to a local gourmet market on Osprey.

At home, she juggled the bag holding hot calzones, meatballs, tiramisu and her keys. She kicked the front door shut and locked it. With arms full, she passed the dinette, where her laptop, files and the geographic maps sat, and growled, her frustration close to the surface. What was she missing?

But there was something. She paused and cocked her head.

No… nothing. But she thought…

She blew out a long breath and left the maps, heading for the kitchen and putting away the food. When she returned to the dinette, she studied the map again from a distance. From several feet off, the marks of her mother's victims made a pattern, of sorts.

Nadine turned one of the maps at a ninety-degree angle. Then she stepped back to compare the two.

It clicked in her brain, a corresponding configuration. She snatched up the maps, placing them side by side, but with the local map upside down. A shiver of awareness traveled along her spine. This was what she had been hunting for, something more than topographical similarities. This was the detail that her subconscious had registered, giving her that sense of something missing. Now insight had finally reached her conscious mind.

She only had to turn the local map 180 degrees to align the directions of each body dump with those of her mother's known victims. East was West. North was South. So simple!

Nadine placed one map on top of the other and held them to the dining room light. The points were a near-perfect match.

The map of Sarasota, Desoto and Manatee Counties was larger than the one of Marion, Volusia and Lake, but her mind made the readjustment. She finally understood why the unsub used Myakka and why he dropped the bodies in Phillippi Creek: because the kill and dump sites now aligned perfectly with her mother's.

The small hairs on her arms and neck lifted as she stared at the blank spot on her map, where the kill site of her classmate showed through from beneath. They recovered Sandra and Mr. White's bodies where she had held them captive for days. There was no body dump because the police arrested Arleen before she could move her final victims.

And just like that, she knew where they'd be. With that information came the possibility that she could save them.

The sheriff had said there was only one person missing. But there were two. She was certain. They'd figure that out, but by then, it might be too late.

She made a circle on her map. The FBI could set up a dragnet. They could rescue them and catch this killer.

Nadine snatched up a lamp from beside the couch and tossed the shade away. She placed that light under the dining room table. The bare bulb glowing through the glass surface made it easy to trace one map on top of the other. She checked the Sarasota map against the small black X marking her classmate's body found all those years ago. She checked it again. Then she opened her files on her laptop, rotated one, overlaid them and made the top one more transparent. It required only reducing her mother's map slightly to make a perfect match. Finally she opened Google Maps and went to the satellite view.

There was no mistake. The area on the map was a match for Dr. Margery Crean's home residence, a five-acre plot that included several outbuildings and a dog kennel.

How had she missed this?

Crean's husband's business was similar to the horse stable where her mother had worked, doing terrible things to Sandra and Stephen White.

What had Crean told her? Her husband was out of town on a breeders' convention? She was home alone, taking care of all of the dogs and their pups. Was she also taking care of other business—personal business?

This had been under her nose the entire time!

Dr. Margery Crean, noted expert on serial killers, expert of aberrant psychological behavior, was not just an unethical researcher. She was a killer. And not just any serial killer, *their* serial killer.

Nadine lifted the phone and called Demko. He picked up on the third ring. She heard men's and women's voices and the rumble of large equipment, alerting her that he was in the field. He answered her call, despite being in the middle of a joint department operation to capture Dun.

"What's up?"

"You're in the wrong place."

"What? Nadine, what did you say?"

Behind him came the mechanical beeping of a large vehicle traveling in reverse.

Nadine raised her voice, shouting into the phone, explaining in rapid, broken sentences. Her words tumbled, one over the other, like gravel poured from a dump truck.

"He's not the guy. He's a decoy. Or a mistake. Just the wrong guy, in the wrong place. He's like me. Caught up in the whirlwind. I overlaid the maps. Put one upside down. They match!"

"Nadine, slow down. I can't understand you. What are you saying?"

"It's not Dun! I'm certain."

"How do you know?"

"He stands out. He's odd."

"That's right."

"And people notice him." It was so obvious to her. Why couldn't he see it?

"Because he's a psychopath. Their profiler said so."

"They're wrong. He's not a psychopath and he's not our killer. Demko, listen. They'll be out there on or near Route 70. Something like a horse farm." She told him the address.

"You just going to drive around looking for horses?"

"You have to go to Margery Crean's dog-breeding facility."

He went silent. She waited and then spoke.

"Demko?"

"Nadine, listen. I have to tell you something. But you have to promise me you won't do anything crazy."

"Tell me what?"

"That rower, Elton Delconte, snuck off to see a girl. His teammate finally got worried enough to alert the coach."

A quicksilver stab of premonition ripped through her.

"Where is she?"

"We haven't tracked her down yet. She told her boyfriend she had a competition. She's a sculler. It's like a two-oar versus one-oar thing. But she's not competing. She came here to see Delconte."

"Her boyfriend didn't know she was missing?"

"Right. Not until she didn't check in. Then he called her coach. I guess they've been doing this awhile."

"Name?"

"It's Joanna. Joanna Silver. She's an Olympic hopeful."

"How old?"

"Nineteen."

"That's her."

The killer had them. Both. She felt it in the marrow of her bones and in the throbbing of blood in her veins. She would not let this happen again. Not again!

"I'm going out there," she said.

"Out where? To the dog kennel?"

"I'm going."

"Nadine—"

"You want to stop me? Come and get me."

She disconnected the call, grabbed her purse and key fo and headed out to her car. She reached Fruitville Road and w. heading for the interstate when the phone rang again throug the car's hands-free system. Demko's number lit up the displa She took the call.

"You sure about this?" he said.

"It's not Dun. True psychopaths have learned to blend. Yo don't notice us, will never notice us. That's why we're successfu We seem normal."

"Nadine?"

"Are you coming or not?"

"You said, *'we.'*"

"What?"

"You said, 'we're successful' and 'we seem normal.'"

She had. Her foot slipped from the accelerator. What ha she just done? Had she just told a Homicide detective that sl considered herself a psychopath?

Nadine swerved to the shoulder, gripping the wheel, pantir like a long-distance runner.

"Nadine? Are you there?"

She tried to regain her equilibrium as she stared out tl windshield. Her mouth was filled with the sour taste of disgus

"Nadine! Answer me!"

The world had gone quiet and bright. Everything shifted to pinpoint focus. This time, she would save Sandra.

She turned toward the speaker on the overhead console.

"I'm here."

"This is crazy," he said.

"Crean's husband is out of town," Nadine said. "Breeders' event. She's been alone since—"

"Friday," he said, interrupting. "I was just out there."

"Did you search the outbuildings?"

"No."

Delconte went missing on Saturday morning. Their perp had already had three days to enjoy these latest living toys, and when Stephen White was dead, this monster would turn to Sandra.

"It's her, isn't it?" Demko asked.

"Follow if you can. Good-bye, Clint."

CHAPTER THIRTY-THREE

Every dog has its day

It occurred to Nadine, en route, that she didn't have a gun or knife or any weapon at all. But the world was full of useful tools and she had something more valuable—the mind of a killer.

Nadine stepped on the accelerator, flying up I-75.

Crean had been in every federal correctional facility holding their parents. She'd had access to their mothers, likely interviewed each one. Had she asked about their families and noted who had entered law enforcement?

But what was the purpose of bringing them here and then re-creating her mother's crimes? The word scrawled on Nadine's mirror came to mind: *Legacy.*

If her supervisor wanted to see her break, Crean wouldn't survive it, because evil didn't just live among them. It lived within them. Didn't interviewing Arleen Howler teach Crean that much?

She'd ask Crean all her questions after they rescued that girl, because she was not letting her kill that teenager. Nadine could not, and would not, live with her death on her conscience.

The descendants of killers understood, more than most, the scars left by their foul deeds. Murderers didn't just kill people; they killed all their unborn descendants, whole generations, and scarred the surviving families.

Somehow, Demko beat her there. When she arrived at Crean's home, she found his vehicle parked on the shoulder before the long curving drive. She pulled in behind him and he appeared at her driver's-side door before she even had her seat belt off.

Nadine stepped out of her car and they stared across the road at the Crean family residence. Under the shade of several large live oak trees sat a ranch-style home, painted barn-red and decorated with country charm with wagon wheels and flowerbeds brimming with colorful blooms. Crean's car was parked before an enormous garage that had an additional bay door large enough for an RV or boat. This structure was a likely spot to hold two captive victims, but it was the kennels that Nadine itched to visit.

Beyond the garage stood two barnlike buildings, one new with green siding and a metal roof, and one that seemed near collapse. The new building was flanked with chain-link exercise pens and a row of individual outdoor kennels. The sound of yapping and barking told her that the Creans did have some canines housed here.

The second building looked older and the roof sagged.

"Judging from the vehicle, I'd say she's home." Demko's voice came out as a threatening snarl. He had his target and morphed into the hunter she had long recognized him to be.

Nadine shifted from side to side, uncomfortable in her own skin; she was reluctant to access the predator lurking within. "What do we do now?"

Demko grimaced. "'We'? *We* don't do anything. You stay here and hold on to your phone. I'm going to check out the kennels."

"Which one?"

"Both."

"Can you just enter her property?"

"Your maps give me probable cause. We have two persons in danger. That's all I need to investigate. If I find something, I can pull Florida Highway Patrol from the manhunt."

The troopers were experts at high-speed chases, but when facing a serial killer, she would prefer the sheriffs. Unfortunately, they were protecting the governor or tied up in the capture of Anthony Dun.

Demko tapped on the phone that was still under her bra, the screen glowing.

"Keep that in your hand. Call 911 if anything happens. I'll call if it's all clear."

"You could turn on the video chat. I could watch what was happening."

"Nadine, I need both hands."

"Of course. Of course you do." She leaned in and kissed him on the cheek. His eyes rounded in surprise. Then he kissed her back, the contact hard and possessive. When he drew away, she was breathless.

"Good luck."

He made a growling sound in his throat and took off at a lope, gun drawn, staying low to the ground. She watched as he circled behind the garage and continued toward the kennels, then out of sight.

The hum of the insects in the tall grass at the roadside filled the air. A tuft of white hair was caught on one of the barbs of cattle fence skirting the road. Inside the pasture, the grass was shorn down to stubble and clear cattle paths zigzagged the wide-open stretch of yellowing grass.

She listened, but all she heard was the rattle of the wind in the palmetto palms above her head, the insects and the incessant barking of the penned dogs.

Their frenzy made her pause. Was that normal barking? Or had something caused them to bark?

What was taking him so long? He had to have reached the kennel by now.

Nadine waited, phone in hand, for something to happen. But nothing did and the minutes stretched out.

She realized that, should Crean glance through her windows, he would see two vehicles parked across the street and Nadine pacing along the shoulder.

Nadine stopped and squared her shoulders. She was done waiting. Crossing the road, she moved behind the barn, out of sight of the house, hoping to catch a glimpse of Demko.

Her phone vibrated and she jumped. Startled, her fingers were clumsy as she checked the cell phone and saw an incoming text.

Demko's name appeared on the glowing screen. The message read:

Second kennel. All clear.

Relief made her shoulders sag. She moved around the barn at a trot, hurrying to the older kennel and opening the door. Electric lights illuminated the interior and she was struck by the odor of urine and feces. There was also the smell of straw and dust.

"Demko?" Nadine's voice was somewhere between a whisper and a call. She inched forward over the stained concrete, through the area that held dusty grooming tables, trophies and faded ribbons. There was a hole in the rusted tin roof and pigeons roosted on the rafters. She inched toward the inner door before her. Beyond, all was quiet.

The sense of danger sparked inside her and she backed away from the inner door. Then she grabbed the nearest weapon. It was a large flat shovel, the kind, she assumed, that was used for removing dog waste. Then she retraced her footsteps, inching forward.

She readjusted her grip on the wooden handle as she entered the kennel. Some rodent scuttled along the wall and out of sight.

The first kennel was empty and so was the next enclosure. Th
structure seemed abandoned.

"Demko?" She looked down at her phone clutched in her le
hand and saw no further messages.

It was then that she remembered him telling her that he woul
call her. *Call.* He said, *"I'll call if it's all clear."* Not *"I'll text you.*

A text message had summoned Juliette to her home. This coul
be the same trick. But if it was, the killer had Demko's phone, an
that meant their killer had Demko.

Nadine stared at the text. Definitely sent from Demko's phon
She stowed her phone back under her bra strap and placed bot
hands on the shovel handle as she crept forward. The text on
gave her more reason to continue.

Demko was in trouble. She sensed it.

The dogs barking in the adjoining building made it difficu
to hear anything else. But it also made it impossible for whoev
had Demko to hear her. The sound changed and she recognize
the drum of heavy rain on the metal roof.

She spotted blood on the floor and lifted the shovel highe
readying her swing, and followed the blood smear.

Something had been dragged along the center aisle and int
the cage to her right. The door was shut. Inside, slumped on t
dirty straw, lay Detective Demko's unconscious form.

Terror over his condition tore at her throat with needlepoin
claws and she could manage only a strangled cry. He wasn't movin

"Clint!" She rushed forward, shifting the shovel to her le
hand and opening the kennel, searching for the rise and fall o
his breathing, but saw none. His complete stillness struck a bo
of dread up her spine.

How badly was he hurt? The alarm siren in her brain shrieke
until she could hear nothing else.

She was about to step inside when she hesitated. Once in th
pen, it would be easy to lock them both in. She stepped back an

glanced the way she had come, then continued to the exit that led to the deserted exercise pens.

She reached for her phone when a door banged.

Someone had opened the inner door to the trophy room. Nadine stowed the phone back in her bra, gripping the shovel with both hands as she turned. There stood Margery Crean. She held the doorknob with one hand and a dripping golf umbrella in the other.

Poor choice of weapon, Nadine thought as she faced Crean.

All the questions she wanted to ask dissolved, sugar in hot water, as blinding red rage descended. She lifted the shovel like a bat and charged, screaming down the corridor, at her opponent.

Crean screamed, too, staggering backward, and threw the door shut. The lock engaged as Nadine hurled herself into the barrier. It held. So, she used the handle, repeatedly bashing at the rectangular section of glass above the knob. Through the window of the door, Crean gaped at her with wide-eyed terror.

"I'll kill you. You hurt him, you die."

She delivered her words with clinical detachment as she continued to attack the safety glass, which now showed signs of imminent failure. Crean lifted her phone and fled out the main door.

The glass shattered like a car windshield. Tiny cubes rained down, but Crean was out of sight. Nadine paused. Crean's panic confused Nadine, because it did not fit the cool calculation and foresight of a serial killer trapping prey or the blind rage released on victims.

Where was the girl?

Nadine backtracked past Demko, stepping around the smear of his blood, as she headed for the exit leading to the caged exercise area. At the last indoor kennel, she saw her huddled in the shadows.

Sandra.

Red welts covered her back and open sores oozed clear fluid. She did not move or rouse as Nadine squatted beside her enclosure.

"Sandra!" she called.

The teen remained motionless.

"Sandra!" She laced the fingers of one hand through the wire of the cage and shook the door. And then she remembered something. This was not Sandra Shank. This was a new girl. What was her name?

"Joanna!"

The girl groaned, then gasped in pain.

Nadine raised her voice to be heard above the barking.

"I'm here to help you. Getting help. Help is coming."

She sounded demented. Was she here to help? Was help on its way?

Only then did she recall the phone. She plucked out her cell.

That was when someone began clapping.

Turning, she saw Gary Osterlund standing only a few feet away, applauding. For a moment, she was filled with a mixture of relief and giddy joy.

Help had arrived.

But her elation wavered. His expression was wrong. It seemed like triumph.

And how had Osterlund known where to find her?

He was smiling, and for just an instant, he looked familiar, like someone else.

Then he stopped clapping and the smile was replaced by a cold, unreadable mask. She'd seen that look on her mother's face and it made her shiver. Nadine was now sure of one thing. He was not here to help. What he was here for was exactly the opposite of help.

"Put down the phone, Nadine."

He drew a pistol from his belt. The black plastic gun looked like a toy, but she was certain it was not.

"Now," he said.

Nadine did as instructed, placing her phone on the concrete, but she kept possession of the shovel handle.

"Head of personnel," she muttered. "You hired us. All of us."

"My maudlin offspring of murderers."

"Why?"

"Hobby. Honestly, I expected them to be made of sterner stuff. Thought to kindle them into something more. They failed, one and all. But not you, Nadine. You've got it. I see it in the grip on that shovel and the way you went after Crean. Honestly, I think she wet herself."

Crean! She'd escaped. Surely, she was calling for help right now.

"Or she may have just wet herself after I shot her."

There would be no help from Crean.

Beside Nadine, the girl moaned.

"That one is a lot like Sandra. It was why I picked her. An athlete. So fit. Strong too."

"How do you know about Sandra?"

His answer was a sinister smile. Their gazes locked and then his attention drifted back to Joanna. "She's already taken so much. But without water, she won't last."

"Where's Delconte?"

"Out past the piles of dog shit. It draws flies and so does he."

"Dead?"

"Probably."

Joanna began to cry.

"Do you want to see him?" Osterlund's eyes glittered.

Go out alone in the woods with a serial killer? No, definitely not. But it would get him away from Demko and Joanna. And it would give her more time for help to reach them.

How long after he didn't check in would they send someone?

Nadine remembered the governor and his protective detail and the joint operation to take down Anthony Dun. Her hope lagged. It would be too late.

"Sure," she said, belatedly adding, "Let's go."

He smiled. "Yes, that would be one way, but selfless. You need to think more about you, Dee-Dee."

The way that he said her name made every hair on her hea
stand up.

"Why did you call me that?"

"You don't remember me. Do you? Because you were so youn
when I left. And after the conviction, well, you were distraught.
He swept his free hand to his receding hairline. "I had more ha
then. But the family resemblance? You noticed, I think."

Nadine shook her head, at a loss.

"You recognized the photo in my office, didn't you? The on
of your mother?"

She remembered the school photo of the girl she had seen weel
ago, when she had sat in Osterlund's office filling in forms. Th
photo had looked familiar. Had that been her mother? Nadin
blinked at him. Where did he get it?

"The last time I saw you was after the verdict, when I came b
for her things."

The only one who came by after the conviction was…

"Uncle Guy." She gasped the words.

"Yes! You used to call me Uncle Tinsel." He tapped a from
tooth. "Got that one capped."

Her mother's brother, in and out of mental hospitals. Sexu
assault. Schizophrenic. Escaped, according to the FBI.

"Guy Owen?"

He nodded vigorously, the grin splitting his face, making hi
even more terrifying. "Yes. Uncle Guy!"

"Why are you doing this?"

"Help you embrace our family legacy, accept what you ar
Teach you to use your killer instinct."

"You were in my place."

"Yes."

"And the second time, the attempt?"

He laughed. "That was Dun. I told him about your break-i
Told him that a half-full garbage bag of clothing was one of you

buttons. Gave him a nudge, and he nearly walked right into the FBI's arms."

"You set him up?"

He chuckled. "Always good to have a fall guy, Nadine. I told your mother that many times."

"You've been to see my mom."

"Not for a long time. Not since before I killed the real Gary. Needed a fresh start, you know? After she went to prison, I sent his résumé to Lowell Correctional. I worked in personnel there for years, before coming here. Gave me free rein to visit her. I was with Arleen every day while we laid out this plan. She wanted me to find you. Help you finish what she started." He was babbling now, his words tumbling together in his haste. "I even hired you. Great job, isn't it? Perfect for you, hiding in plain sight."

"That was her photo on your desk. You and her."

"Yes. I moved it because you seemed to recognize us."

"You'll get caught," she said.

"Not necessarily. You know the trouble with the FBI research on serial killers?"

"No women in the studies?"

"No." He laughed. "That's Arleen's thing. She's a broken record on that point." He rolled his eyes. "The real problem is that they only have data on the ones they catch. What they need is data on the ones they never catch. The ones like me."

"They'll catch you."

"They haven't. I'll leave the ones in my house for them to clean up when I go. You should come with me, Dee-Dee. You can follow after you finish up here."

Nadine stopped herself from telling him that she wasn't following him. "Why should I trust you?"

"I'm family. And I'm gifted. Do you know how many bodies have buried in my house? Twenty-two. No, twenty-three. Yes. I

think that's right." His smile seemed triumphant. "So, don't te
me what I can and can't get away with."

"Let me go."

"Of course. I plan on it. They'll pin these deaths on me." H
waved his gun casually in the direction of Joanna. "But I'll be gon
and you won't tell. You didn't tell on your mother. Just bad luc
the garbageman noticed the blood on that bag. Careless. She w
drinking too much. Murder and mojitos. Bad mix."

Nadine inched toward the rear exit. Why hadn't her moth
told him that she had been the one to turn her in? He hadn
been at the trial. Had he been in the hospital then? But the new
reported it all.

"I testified against her."

"Yes. But you had to. No one blames you. We all understar
protecting yourself. It's the first rule."

Nadine glanced toward the back exit.

"If you leave, I'll kill them."

She tried a threat. "I'll tell them who you are."

"I considered that. A disappointment. But I'm leaving. Alrea
have a new identity prepared. One of my victims. We have simil
features. Well, not now, of course." He grinned.

"Your face will be on posters."

"This face?" He pointed the barrel of the gun at his cheek. "N
one remembers it. But I've scheduled plastic surgery. Prepaid. S
run along. Break your mother's heart and mine. When you con
back, I'll be gone, and Crean, the girl, her lover and that one"—I
waved the gun in Demko's direction—"will all be dead."

She had to prevent that.

"What do you expect me to do, exactly?"

He smiled and she saw her mother in the shape of his ey
"Embrace who you are, accept your legacy. And… I want
witness your first kill." He sucked in a breath and shivered wi
delight.

Nadine thought she might be sick.

"I can't kill that girl."

He snorted. "Not the girl. She's mine. The detective."

For a moment, she just stared.

"Why should I? You already said that you'd let me go."

"But you are here to save the girl. Right? Kill the detective and I'll let you have her. Do what you like. Save her. Kill her. Up to you to play God."

Uncle Guy held out a familiar carpet knife. The one her mother had used. The one the police could never find. She recognized it instantly by the flecks of pale blue paint splattered on the handle.

"Go on," he urged. "Take it."

And there it was, the devil's choice. She could walk away and let them all die or kill Demko and save Joanna.

Nadine prepared to do something that she had resisted her entire life. To save the girl, she needed to release her darker inner self.

CHAPTER THIRTY-FOUR

The lady or the tiger?

It wasn't hard, liberating the monster inside her, not as hard as holding it in for all these years.

Good old Uncle Guy stood, smiling, holding out Nadine's mother's knife to the tiger, raised in captivity, ready and eager to maul its owner.

Her family legacy. He was polite, passing her the weapon, handle first. But he was no fool. Such a successful killer had not survived so long by taking chances. He kept his pistol pointed at his niece as she set the shovel aside and took the blade. She wrapped her fingers around the grip. The object seemed to radiate evil. How many had died by this weapon?

Nadine tightened her hold.

"I've been waiting for this. Oh, Arleen will be so pleased. We talked and talked about you. Your potential. And to be here for your first kill! After your debacle with Hartfield, I harbored doubts."

"You're the one who set up Juliette. Right? The fingerprint on the seltzer can?"

"Lifted it from the trash at her office after a visit."

"The text message she received. You sent that, too!"

He grinned and inclined his head, pleased now, as he took a bow. "Guilty."

"And the grave at Tina Ruz's place and the clown mask for Demko?"

"Yes. All me!"

"And you set up Demko. How did you arrange for me to find that article?"

He seemed confused. "Article?" A look of delight lit up his face. "Wait. Did you almost kill him already? And I might have missed it. That was not me. But I did send Crean down here. Thought you might kill her with that shovel." He waved the barrel of his gun back toward the trophy room and grooming station. "You know I think she might be going deaf. All the dogs barking, and she didn't even hear… but, anyway, I had to call her house from a burner and tell her I saw one of her dogs on the road. That got her down here."

The knife handle was a perfect fit in her hand. Nadine glanced at the wicked curved blade and pictured all the people killed with this very weapon.

"You should have killed her. She's a coward. Not one of us. Just a voyeur like the men who write your mother, getting a thrill from thinking about it, but never getting the guts to act. And your detective. I thought his mother's blood would be stronger in that one. But he's just the sanitation crew, there to clean up the mess."

He was too far away for her to strike with the blade. For the briefest second, she considered using the knife on herself. It was a coward's solution. All she would accomplish was not having to watch him kill the girl and Demko and, likely, Crean.

"Make your first cut," he said.

How many did he expect her to make? She stepped toward Demko, still locked in the dog kennel, and laced the fingers of one hand through the wire mesh.

She lifted a brow and gave her uncle an impatient look. "Open it."

He smiled, tasting victory, as Nadine bit her lower lip to keep it from trembling. This was not the time to show weakness or fear.

She remained where she was, but he motioned her back with the barrel of his pistol, and she retreated.

"Farther," he ordered.

She inched back as her chances to overpower him slipped away. When she was against the opposite wall, he turned to the latch and tugged it free. He opened the door wide and pulled it before him, using it as a shield.

"Go on."

She looked at the open door to the cage and Demko's inert form beyond. His torso rose and fell in short shallow breaths. He was still alive. How badly was he injured?

Nadine's gaze traveled over the opening and then back to her uncle.

"I'm not going in there."

He nodded again. "Very good. It's our nature to suspect a trap and avoid it."

"Speaking of avoiding a trap, if I kill Demko, how am I supposed to avoid going to jail for the rest of my life?"

She was trying the bit where you keep them talking until help arrived, but, really, she'd given up hope that law enforcement personnel would come speeding in and surround the place.

They were all capturing Anthony Dun with the news cameras rolling.

"You won't go to jail. This is perfect for your first. You don't have to dispose of the body or even dump it. You just have to call it in. The big bad serial killer has struck again. You kill Demko, kill the girl and we both walk away. Then I can go back to my way of hunting, knowing that you are on your own path. You can join me after you fulfill the terms of your contract. Our legacy lives on."

"You said you'd let the girl go."

"I did say that. Yes. I will."

He was lying. She understood now. She and Uncle Guy killed them all and walked away, or she killed her uncle.

Him or her. Easy choice.

He was an experienced killer. This latest run of death was only him trying to stir her instincts, as he called them.

"Do you really want him to go free, or do you just want deniability?" asked her uncle.

She knew what he wanted to hear and gave it to him.

"Deniability."

"Perfect." He sighed.

Nadine remained where she was as he smiled, encouraging.

"I've been looking forward to this. You don't know. It is as close as I will ever come to reliving my first kill."

Except the only one she wanted to kill was him.

"I'm not going in that cage."

He swung the door clear and stepped into the pen, giving her his back for an instant. She took a hesitant step. Where should she cut? The throat or stab him in the back?

Her hesitation was costly. Uncle Guy already had Demko by one leg and easily dragged him out into the corridor.

"There. No cage. Now make your first cut." For incentive, he stepped before the cage holding Joanna and pointed the pistol at the girl. This brought Uncle Guy even farther from her. If she ran at him, how fast could he swing that pistol around and shoot?

Nadine circled Demko, pretending to decide where to begin. Behind her, she could hear Uncle Guy's breathing accelerate. The sound made her sick.

He wanted this. Wanted to see her do this terrible thing. And once she did, would she be forever changed?

He'd still kill the girl. Offering his captive's freedom was just a way to soothe her conscience. But Joanna was a witness. The girl could identify him, so her uncle couldn't let her live.

But he wanted to watch her cut.

That desire gave Nadine one advantage. She moved to block his view of the knife in her hand with her body. She stooped and then squatted over Demko, who now lay on his back, arms stretched over his head, eyes fluttering. A large purple welt bloomed on Demko's forehead, and a trickle of dried blood had run down his temple and clotted in his hair.

Nadine had turned her back on a killer, leaving herself exposed. But he couldn't see her cut. Would he come closer?

Behind her came the rasp of Guy's footsteps.

She leaned in, holding the knife to Demko's throat, blocking her uncle's view.

He moved again. The sweep of his feet whispered across the concrete. Beyond, empty cages sat. And then, in her periphery, she saw it. His leg, the hem of his dark gray trousers covered with bits of straw bedding and the brown leather loafer.

Nadine lifted the knife. He sucked in a breath as she swept her arm across Demko's throat, overreaching and slicing, hard and fast, at her uncle's calf.

He howled with pain, lifting his wounded leg as she dove into the other one. Her shoulder struck his shin and the pain of the impact sent stars exploding behind her eyes.

Uncle Guy hit the concrete, emitting a grunt as she used the knife like a grappling hook, jabbing it into his thigh and heaving herself on top of him.

He screamed as the blade bit into his shoulder. She straddled him now. His pupil was learning, but not as he expected. One quick cut across the neck would end him.

With widening eyes, her uncle perceived the murder she intended. This was her first kill, and he wanted to watch. And here it was.

She hoped he enjoyed the view.

He had inadvertently brought her to the choice. Kill him or spare him. The third outcome surfaced as he lifted the pistol. He might kill her.

Nadine swung the knife. The arc narrowly missed his throat on its way to her target. Her mother's blade was still so sharp. It sliced through the thin fabric of his shirtsleeve and carved deep into the muscle of his upper arm. She felt the resistance as she hit bone.

The muzzle flashed.

The vibrations of sound and bullet reached her in the same instant. There was no immediate pain, just the sensation of being punched in the midsection. She was too focused on finishing this. She lived in the seconds it took for the blood to jet from the deep laceration parting muscle and vessels in his bicep.

The spray of blood told Nadine that she had compromised the brachial artery. Their eyes met. She saw the fear in his.

The pistol clattered to the floor.

He was bleeding from his lower leg, thigh, shoulder and arm. He had become a soaker hose of blood. The last lesion might prove fatal. He made his only choice, grabbing the wound with his one good hand and pressing hard. Blood spurted between his fingers, but the flow slowed.

Blood dripped from her face and onto his chest. She pushed off the floor and rose above him, only now registering the pain in her side. She used the hand not clutching the knife to press her stomach. Her shirt was sodden, stained with his blood. His blood, but also hers.

He'd shot her.

Uncle Guy used his one good leg to push off, inching backward and away from Nadine.

"What have you done?" he shouted.

"What you asked. You got to watch."

His eyes widened and then narrowed to slits, going cold as a reptile's.

"I'm not going to die."

"Your choice," she said. "Let go of that arm and you'll bleed out or hold tight and go to prison."

Nadine groaned as she took a step closer to the pistol he'd dropped. Drawing her leg back caused such pain that it brought tears to her eyes. But she kicked the weapon, giving a cry of agony as every muscle in her stomach cramped.

The pistol skidded over the concrete, like a sled on ice, coming to a stop between her and the exit to the kennels.

He fumbled at his belt buckle as she staggered toward Demko. Before reaching the detective, she saw the glint of something shiny on the floor.

Her phone.

Nadine needed to grip the chain-link fencing of the kennel to keep from toppling over as she stooped. Her knee banged the ground as she reached and used her thumbprint to unlock the device.

Despite her mind's command to rise, she slumped against the aluminum cage. Demko was stretched out before her. Dust motes swirled through the air, growing thicker.

And then a sharp stab of terror startled her back to alertness. It wasn't dust motes. It was her vision, failing, as she… what? Was she drifting into shock?

Uncle Guy had his belt around his upper arm. If she lost consciousness, he'd kill them all, and then walk out of here. She knew it. She could see the plan forming in his mind. He watched her, like a hungry dog, just waiting for his chance.

Nadine lifted the phone.

His gaze flashed to the pistol. He would have to get past her and the knife to reach it. Already, he was rising, somehow ignoring the wounded leg, as he balanced, storklike.

Nadine wanted to live. She wanted the girl and Demko to survive this ordeal. But more than either, she wanted this evil stopped. If she could do this one thing, it would be enough.

"They won't get here in time," he promised.

Nadine just smiled as she punched 911 into her phone.

"Hang up, Nadine. We can still walk out of here."

She shook her head, refusing his offer. "My job is to catch our killer."

Her uncle might still murder them all. But they would be the last.

The voice in her ear sounded far away.

"911. What is your emergency?"

"This is Dr. Nadine Finch. I'm a criminal psychologist for Sarasota County. We have an officer down."

"Ma'am, could you repeat that?"

"I need help. I'm at the home of Margery Crean, inside her dog kennel with an officer down. Detective Clint Demko. I've been shot by—"

"No!" her uncle shouted, wobbling now. He and she both knew that 911 recorded all conversations.

Once she spoke, there would be no way to erase her words or his recording.

"Do you have an active shooter?" asked the operator.

"Yes." She had to get this into the record. "I've been shot by Mr. Gary Osterlund. His real name is—"

Her uncle fell forward, one palm and one foot on the ground as he scuttled toward her.

"Name is Guy Owen. He shot me and is holding three others hostage. Joanna Silver is here with us in the kennel. We need EMS and police..." The arm holding the phone dropped away. Nadine's knuckles knocked the hard floor. Her fingers relaxed.

"Dr. Finch, are you there? Help is on the way."

Uncle Guy had nearly reached her, but she smiled.

"I'm not like you."

CHAPTER THIRTY-FIVE

You and me and the devil make three

Nadine awoke in pain, with two strangers in blue-and-white uniforms looming over her. They moved her from her resting place crumpled against the dog enclosure, to the cold concrete floor.

What is all that barking?

"Where is the blood coming from?" asked the one with the earbuds and man bun.

It's my uncle's blood. She thought she had said this aloud, but then she realized she had not spoken.

Both men had strange halos of light around them. It reminded her of when she was a kid and she spent too much time in the public pool. A rainbow surrounded them as they leaned in.

"Here," said the heavier of the pair. "Bullet wound in her lower left quadrant."

"Dr. Finch. Can you hear me?" said the other paramedic.

I'm nodding, aren't I?

She lifted one hand and pointed toward the cage where Joann sprawled. But when she turned her head, she realized the kennel was empty.

Nadine blinked and spotted the familiar shiny black shoes and navy pants of the police. Three more people surrounded her

One squatted, and she recognized the young patrol officer who worked protection one night at the hotel.

"Dr. Finch, Gary Osterlund and Margery Crean are en route to Sarasota Memorial. Joanna is outside with the EMTs. They're taking her now. You are going in that ambulance."

"Demko?"

"He's gone."

Her heart twisted. "Dead?"

"No, ma'am. En route to Sarasota Memorial."

The heavier EMT crowded in beside her. "I'm putting a bandage on this. Then we'll get you on the stretcher."

Both the bandage and the transfer hurt more than she expected. Now she was sweating and freezing at the same time.

Outside the world had turned dark. Overhead, the web of live oaks twisted, black and dense. Lights flashed blue and red on the branches. The white strobe hit her eyes like an ice pick.

There was something nagging at her. Forgetting something. What was it? Something else she needed to do. But what?

"I'll take that now," said a familiar voice.

She squinted at the man who stood above her. Special Agent Torrin pried the carpet knife from her fingers with a gloved hand and dropped it in an evidence bag.

"It's hers. My mother's."

"Let's get you to the hospital."

She pointed back to the rear door. "Gun?"

"We got it."

And she remembered.

"Wait! He's out there."

"Who?" he asked.

"The rower. Delconte. Uncle Guy said he's past the dog waste."

Torrin leaned in, as if he couldn't hear her.

"Say that again."

"Elton Delconte. In the woods. Past the kennel."

The agent straightened and shouted something, disappearing from her line of vision.

Nadine remembered the ride, mostly because each bump caused a stabbing pain to streak from her stomach up her spine. The emergency room staff met her before she even cleared the ambulance and everything from then on went fuzzy. They said "surgery," and she said, no, she didn't want that.

But when she woke up, she was lying on her back in a hospital bed, freezing cold, with her arms lying neatly at her sides atop the thin cotton blanket that covered much of the blue-and-white hospital gown that she now wore.

Disconcerting.

Nadine groaned. The effort of making the sound caused her stomach muscles to twitch and the pain to rouse with the rest of her. If she didn't know better, she'd say someone had shot her again.

She threw off the blanket and tugged up the gown, revealing the thick white dressing and bandage wrapping her middle and the catheter threading over her thigh. There was a large tube in her nose.

So, he hadn't killed her. But had she killed him?

The need for answers and pain meds had her groping for the call button. But she changed direction, trying to tug the tube from her nose. A clean-shaven young man in purple scrubs appeared.

"Uh-oh. Don't do that. You need that so your intestines can heal."

She released her hold on the tube. He smiled down at her.

"Hey there. Welcome back. You with me this time?"

His question made her wonder how many times she had replayed this exact vignette.

"Maybe."

He laughed. "Need something for the pain?"

Nadine nodded. "Detective Demko?"

"Right over there." He pointed to a drawn curtain. "Five of you came in last night."

"Who?"

"Rest now. I'll get your medicine."

He returned and added something to her intravenous line that dropped her like an elephant gun.

The next time she came around, it was to find Special Agent Torrin and Special Agent Fukuda standing at her bedrail, side by side, in matching gray suits.

"Twins," she said, and giggled, which hurt, so she groaned.

The men glanced at each other. They were both male, and that was where the physical resemblances ended.

"The gray," said Fukuda, pointing from his lapel to Torrin's.

Torrin nodded. "How do you feel?"

"Like somebody shot me."

"Yeah. Your uncle. We didn't see that coming."

"Family biz," she said, and grimaced against the pain that built with each second. "What happened?"

Special Agent Fukuda took that one. "You were shot in the stomach. The bullet punctured your bowels but missed your kidney. You had surgery and are on antibiotics to prevent infection."

A bowel puncture? She pictured the contents of her lower intestine leaking into her abdominal cavity. That could not be good.

"TMI, Fukuda." Torrin patted her cheek. "Through and through. You're okay, kid."

"Demko?"

"He has a fractured skull. Guessed he's not as thickheaded as he appears. There was bleeding. A subdural…" Torrin's words failed and Fukuda took over.

"Hematoma," supplied Fukuda.

"Right. They had to relieve the pressure."

Nadine winced. Relieving pressure on your brain meant Demko had a new hole in his head. Suddenly her hole seemed preferable.

"Brain damage?"

"No. They don't think so. They put him out for a while, so he can heal."

Out? That sounded dismal.

"You up to making a statement?"

She shook her head. "Tell me what happened after..." She needed that pain medication. A whimper escaped her lips.

Fukuda stepped closer. "Sheriffs were first on scene. They got Owen. Found him at his vehicle."

"Why didn't he shoot me? Again, I mean."

"Said he had to get past you and the knife to reach the pistol. Decided to run. Back exit."

Had she been conscious enough to threaten him? She didn't remember.

"But he shot Dr. Crean in the face. The bullet went through her hand and then her cheek. In one side, out the other. She's having reconstructive surgery, but she'll live."

Shot by a serial killer. She imagined that would boost Crean's reputation as an expert. It was an unsettling way to become an authority.

"Sandra?" Tears were rolling from the corners of her eyes.

Fukuda turned to Torrin. "Get the nurse."

Torrin peeled away and out of sight.

She tried again. "The girl?"

"They moved her to a regular room. Dehydrated. Wounds and bruises are healing. She'll come through all right."

Because Uncle Guy had been saving her for last.

"And the rower?"

"What's that?" Fukuda leaned closer.

"Del-con-te?"

"Oh, well. That's the miracle. Sheriffs brought their rescue dogs. They started behind the kennel because of you and found him."

"Alive?"

"So far. He's in bad shape. But holding on. His wife is with him."

Nadine closed her eyes tight and let the tears come slipping down her temples from behind closed lids.

Her nurse appeared. She felt a burning at the crook of her arm and then the pain receded, drawing back to a place where it could not reach her.

*

After nine days, they removed Nadine's nasogastric tube and catheter, and moved her to her own room. Demko was still in a drug-induced coma, but the swelling of his brain had abated. His nurse told her that he should be returning to the world of the living soon. She almost envied him.

He didn't have to give statements and depositions. He didn't have to be wheeled into Uncle Guy's hospital room under heavy guard or formally identify his own uncle as the man who had shot him.

That was her afternoon agenda. Her poor healing intestines did not need her clenching the muscles of her stomach. But the anxiety of seeing her uncle built like two colliding tectonic plates. Eventually something inside her would break loose.

She now sat in her wheelchair, thanks to her nurse, who was excellent. He would not allow her to dress but had tucked a blanket around her legs, swaddling her like a newborn.

"All set?" asked Torrin from the doorway.

Nadine sighed, pushing away her uneaten lime Jell-O. How could anyone be ready for such a thing?

The FBI had confirmed that her uncle had murdered the real Gary Osterlund, allowing Guy to secure a job at an Orlando theme park in human resources, using Osterlund's credentials. Six years after his sister's conviction, he'd secured a position at Lowell

Federal Corrections in payroll, where the siblings had hatched
this scheme. His success securing employment from the city of
Sarasota, two years back, initiated their plan.

Since then, he'd targeted Dun as a fall guy and recently created
fake identification at work that he used to rent the van and the
cabin. He had been writing Arleen, and the FBI had intercepted
two letters and a postcard.

"Did you ever find Anthony Dun?"

"Yeah. We got him that night, staying with a friend from work.
He's under arrest, charges pending."

That was good. She was glad they found him, and glad he wasn't
wrongly accused of her uncle's crimes.

Torrin took her down the hallway. She and her uncle were
floormates. But soon he would be changing locations. That, at
least, gave her courage. This was only the first step. She had been
down this road before. There would be a trial and she would have
to testify against him, just as she had against Arleen.

The guilt she expected didn't arrive. Instead, she felt a kind of
satisfaction, knowing that she would be helping protect the world
from the danger that ran in a wide streak through her family tree.

She caught sight of the nurses' station. Her nurse, Ross, lifted
his gaze and then his hand in greeting as she rolled by.

And there she was, at the door to her uncle's room, identifiable
by the police officer stationed outside.

Torrin guided her wheelchair past the officer and through the
doorway. Inside, Special Agent Fukuda stood at the footrail of
Guy Owen's bed.

Nadine's uncle sat propped up on pillows, a slight smile lifting the
corners of his mouth. He looked as placid and harmless as a beloved
grandfather. The perfect chameleon. The jurors would struggle to
believe that this small docile man could do all the things they would
charge him with. And the list was long. Torrin had told her that her
uncle's claims of bodies in his home were no exaggeration.

"Hello, Dee-Dee. How's my girl?" asked her uncle.

Unlike him, she did not shield her expression. She had no reason to hide. So, she let him see it there in her eyes, the disgust.

"Is this the man who shot you?" asked Fukuda.

"Yes."

"Do you have any doubt that this is the man?" he asked.

"I do not."

"That's all we need," said Torrin from behind her, and began to roll her out of the room.

"Wait," said Nadine.

Torrin paused.

Nadine held her uncle's gaze as he lifted a brow in anticipation.

"Did you kill my father?"

Her uncle laughed, as if delighted, then recovered, still holding his smile, that smile of a man duping someone.

"I would never hurt your dad."

"But you helped her move his body."

"I helped her move two bodies." He directed this comment to Torrin.

"Dennis Howler and Infinity Yanez?" asked Nadine.

He said nothing to this.

"Where are they?" asked Nadine.

Her uncle looked delighted. His eyes sparkled and his grin was as wide as a hyena's.

"Oh, that's the sort of information that might help me avoid that needle," he said, referring to Florida's current method of capital punishment.

Nadine had had enough of his smug, self-satisfied face, so much like her mother's.

"Take me out," she said.

Torrin rolled her from the room.

Her uncle called after her.

"Just inexperience, Dee-Dee! You'll get better with practice."

It wasn't inexperience. If she had wanted to kill him, he'd b
dead. But she didn't endure any such craving. And that truth gav
her hope. Hope for a future that did not include hiding for fea
of discovery. The entire world now knew who she was, and sh
was surviving it.

Best of all, she was not like her mother or uncle. Nadin
believed that now. Never had been and never would be.

Because of them, she had been given the chance to kill an
turned it down.

So, not a killer. But was she brave enough to let others get clos
see the terrible parts of her past?

Perhaps.

Nadine's family tree grew monsters. That kind of legacy left sca

Special Agent Torrin accompanied Nadine back to her roo
and waited while the nurse helped her transfer to the chair besid
her bed.

"Thank you for the identification, Nadine."

"Glad to help."

He didn't leave and his expression put Nadine on alert.

"Your profile was correct, Nadine. Nearly perfect, in fact."

That gave her little satisfaction, because despite her effor
her uncle had murdered six people. "He almost completed t
series," she said.

"But he didn't." That was true. "I'd like to show you somethin
if that's all right. We found this in your uncle's house. A yearboo
Your mother's yearbook."

Whatever it was, she was certain she did not want to see. B
not knowing would be worse.

"Yes. All right."

He drew the book from his bag and opened it to the pag
containing senior photos. First, he pointed to the one identifi
as Arleen Howler.

"This and her homeroom photo are the only shots of your mother in the entire book."

Nadine studied the black-and-white image, seeing the resemblance between her and her mom. But her mother's hair looked to have been hacked with scissors and she had a wide-eyed, haunted expression.

Torrin offered a five-by-seven color photo, laying it on the open page.

"This is Gena Heilman. Gena was captain of the volleyball team and homecoming queen."

Nadine studied the photo of the teen. Her head was tilted just so. She had a bright smile, perfect teeth and dimples. Her dark eyes sparkled, alive with mischief, accentuated by carefully applied liner. Her dark hair cascaded over her shoulders.

"According to the teachers and staff we interviewed, Gena was very popular."

Nadine picked up on the vibe. "'Was'?"

"She went missing senior year. I had my agents do some digging. Spoke to retired teachers and administrators and some of Gena's friends. From that, we gleaned that your mother was involved with a boy, well, lots of boys, but one in particular. He ended up dating Gena. They were one of the most popular couples. He was Gena's date for prom."

Torrin flipped to an image of a handsome boy. Someone had drawn a heart around his senior photo.

He'd either dumped her mother or used her.

"Is he…"

"He's alive. Still resides up in Ocala. We're sending someone to speak to him."

Nadine's skin stippled and she shifted on the plastic chair as she stared at the photograph of the girl who disappeared.

"Was Gena my mother's first kill?"

"We have no evidence of that. But there's this." Torrin flipped to Gena's senior photo. Someone had scratched out her eyes. Torrin turned to the homecoming page and there was Gena, standing beside the prom king, whose arm encircled her. Gena wore a long halter dress and her crown; she looked perfect except for one detail. Her eyes had been scratched away until the page had torn. In the sports section, Gena dove for a volleyball. Again, her eyes were scratched away.

"They're all like this. All eleven photos."

"It doesn't mean she killed her."

"It doesn't. But we suspect that she did. This high school student, Heilman, matches your mother's profile for female victims."

"What happened?"

"She went missing after a party at a local drinking spot favored by teens. Police thought she could be a runaway. Apparently, her home life was not as ideal as her image."

"Where was the party?"

"Hontoon Island State Park."

Nadine's stomach cramped. Torrin closed the book.

Hontoon Island. The place she, Arlo and her mom had so often visited. The place they had found Lacey Louder, the third victim in the series.

"Arleen has been uncooperative when questioned."

Nadine set her teeth. She'd get her mother to cooperate. That much she was sure of.

"I'd be happy to help with questioning, Special Agent Torrin."

"Thank you, Dr. Finch. I'm sorry to burden you with this now. But there are families who deserve closure."

"Yes. Of course." She thought of something else. "Can I ask you about Dr. Crean?"

"Sure."

"Why didn't she know that those two were in her kennels?"

"That second building isn't used. She told me it was scheduled to be torn down this month."

"So, she never checked it?"

"No reason. Dogs were all in the new kennel."

"I see."

"Gotta run. I'll be in touch," said Torrin as he tucked the book back in his bag and headed out the door. There he paused to glance back at her. "Nadine? I've asked our BAU to reach out to you. I have told them you'd be an asset."

"Uh, I'm flattered."

"Don't be. You've got the education and the experience. But more important, you're a natural."

He left her, and she thought about what it might be like to work for the FBI. Gradually her mind turned to her uncle's admission of moving bodies and her mother's slip that she had killed a man who owed her money.

She sat back and wondered if she should tug this thread. Should she try to find her father's remains, join the hunt for Gena Heilman or duck back into her shell? There was so much horror in her family. So much death.

Nadine's phone chimed with an incoming call. She glanced at the screen, seeing the image of her aunt Donna, and collected the phone from the nightstand.

"Hello?"

"Nadine? Sweetheart, I just heard. I'm still in Dallas at the law conference. I'm flying out tomorrow. Stewart and the girls are picking me up in Orlando," she said, speaking of her daughters and husband. "We're coming straight there."

Nadine's lip quivered. She already had a family. Why hadn't she ever let them in?

"You don't need to."

"Oh, honey, don't be silly. When I heard, I booked the first flight. Why didn't you call me?"

There was a pause.

"I'm sorry. I… it's been a lot."

"We'll be there sometime tomorrow afternoon."

Nadine squeezed her eyes shut as she realized she'd have to tell her aunt that there was a real possibility that her brother, Dennis, was dead.

"Thank you."

"Oh, darling. Don't thank me. We'd do anything for you."

And they had tried. She had never let them, but that ended today.

"Aunt Donna? I need to tell you something." Nadine let the words tumble out, what she learned, what she feared, what the FBI suspected about her father. Finally she wore herself down to a stop. "Are you still there?"

"Of course I'm here. The FBI already told me about Dennis. I've felt he was gone for a long time now, Nadine."

"How can you even stand to look at me?"

"Oh, sweetheart! None of this is your fault. You hang in there. We're coming."

Nadine sniffed. "I can't wait to see you all."

CHAPTER THIRTY-SIX

Friend indeed

Nadine called Juliette on Friday morning to ask if she would pick her up and bring her to her place. Nadine could barely walk, but he had met the low bar required for discharge.

While she'd been in the hospital, August turned to September, which in Florida meant absolutely nothing. Fall felt like summer, ut with less rain and more school buses.

"You have prescriptions?" Juliette asked, after Nadine was ettled in her vehicle. Clearly, she knew the drill.

"Yup."

They stopped at the pharmacy drive-through and they waited or what seemed a lifetime for the three prescriptions, each wrapped in their own white paper bag and stapled together.

"Listen, I swung by your house. The news teams are camped ut there. You want to head to my place?"

"Juliette, I am so grateful."

So, this was what it was like, to have a friend you could trust nd one that had your back.

"And about the way I treated you, at the restaurant and at my ouse, I'm so sorry."

"I know. I know. People like us have to be more careful than most folks. I get it." She gave Nadine a generous smile.

"I don't think I deserve you."

Juliette offered Nadine a sympathetic pat on the forearm an a bottle of water to take her pills. "I used to feel that way. But I' a good person. My job is off-putting to some, but I'm not m mother and you aren't yours."

"That's true."

"So, let's start again. This time with some honesty," said Juliett

"I'd love that, really."

"Okay, then." Juliette set them in motion. "Did you hear abou Osterlund's… I mean your uncle's house?"

"Yes. Some. Torrin said they had found many of the victim wedding rings in his bedroom."

"I didn't know that. I meant about the excavation."

"Torrin said something about bodies and a pit." She brace for what they might have found, remembering her uncle's claim

"In his guest room. It's a mass grave. He kept his victims i there and buried them when he was done with them. Evidence that he was still taking victims during this latest string of murders

"How?"

"Runaways, young ones judging from the skeletons."

"Skeletons? How many?"

"Two dozen so far."

Nadine dropped her head to say a prayer for his victims Juliette rolled to a stop at the traffic light.

"We've got a team of forensic anthropologists down from t museum up in Tampa and have requested another team fro Miami-Dade. It'll take months to recover them all."

*

Her family arrived on Friday afternoon and her aunt had chas the news teams off with threats of legal action. Nadine had n lifted a finger since they'd swarmed her cottage and felt gratef and relieved.

The call from Special Agent Torrin came the next day. The doctors planned to wake Clint Demko from his induced coma, and he thought Nadine should be there.

Apparently, the process was like turning on an intravenously delivered switch. Or it wasn't. Nadine's internet search told her that, after this procedure, some folks popped awake and others never did.

Protecting the brain was a dangerous business. Demko might have permanent impairment. The blow he took damaged the frontal lobe, which controlled movement, problem solving, thinking and personality. All qualities she was sure Clint Demko would wish to retain.

As she was not yet cleared to drive, Juliette agreed to get her there. She had managed to convince her family to take advantage of her absence to visit the botanical gardens, promising not to do anything strenuous until they returned.

She was walking now, but so slowly that she opted for the wheelchair at the hospital, and then Juliette helped her transfer to a seat at his bedside.

There were already two other visitors who introduced themselves as Demko's sister and brother, Carlie and Danny. She remembered Demko telling her that Carlie, born Caroline Nix, was his sister and that they were adopted after his father's murder. That made Danny the cousin.

Juliette left them to move the car and said she had some business at the hospital.

"I'll be back soon, but text me if he wakes up." She offered a wave.

Carlie looked like Demko, with similar deep blue eyes and hair slightly lighter blond than his. Danny didn't resemble him. He was thinner, with a slighter build, a thick bushy black beard and light brown eyes. His nose was narrow and with no characteristic bump, like both Demko and Carlie. His cloudy eyes and the thick lenses in his glasses confirmed he was the one losing his sight.

"Doctor's on his way," said the nurse.

They passed in the entrance, causing the nurse to reverse course back to Demko's bedside.

The neurologist explained that Demko had come off the respirator early this morning and the mask he now wore administered just oxygen. His doctors had halted the medications to sedate, and they were just waiting.

So, they waited. Not the neurologist, of course. He left almost immediately.

She took her pain pills at his bedside and chatted with Carlie. Danny had missed lunch, so after ninety minutes, he and Carlie headed down to the cafeteria, promising to bring her a cup of coffee.

Nadine moved to Demko's bed, sitting by his side, and taking hold of his hand. He didn't squeeze back, and his fingers were icy and pliant as wet clay.

It didn't matter. He was alive. He'd wake up, and this time, she'd tell him how important he was to her. And she'd show him.

But he didn't wake up, and as the seconds turned to minutes, Nadine battled a rising panic.

She brushed his hair from his forehead, stroking his wide brow as she spoke.

"Clint? Can you hear me? It's Nadine. Your family is here. We want you to wake up."

He didn't.

She did her breathing exercises and tried to read on her phone. But she kept losing her place. Finally she just stared at him, praying for some sign that he was coming out of the coma.

Nadine leaned forward and kissed his cheek, then whispered in his ear.

"Come back to me, Clint. I need you."

She drew away, watching for any reaction and tried to stem the disappointment when she saw none. She needed to be patient and believe he'd fight his way back to her.

From the corridor came the aroma of food and the rattle of
he lunch service. Nothing smelled good; in fact, the odor turned
ier stomach.

The twitch of a finger drew her full attention. He exhaled in
vhat sounded like a groan. She stroked his cheek. The bandage
on his forehead hid the place where surgeons had bored into his
kull to remove the blood clot.

Demko's eyeballs moved beneath his lids. Was he dreaming?

Then he pinched his eyes closed.

"Clint? Can you hear me? It's Nadine."

He opened one eye, and he peered at her. She waited, recalling
ier own disorientation waking from anesthesia.

"Hey there. Welcome back," she said, and smiled.

His first try at speaking was a dry sound.

Nadine offered him some ice chips. After crunching and swal-
owing, he tried again.

"Hospital?"

"Yes." She explained about the medically induced coma,
iead injury, subdural hematoma and how long he had been
inconscious.

He listened, eyes closed, hand gripping hers.

"Your sister, Carlie, is here with Danny."

Demko smiled at that.

"Did we get him?"

She didn't need to ask who he meant.

"Yes."

"Tell me."

She took a long breath, then filled in the missing pieces of
vhat had happened.

"Torrin said that Uncle Guy ate with the crime techs and others
n the police department. That's how he knew how to destroy the
vidence in that van. And he sat in on criminal trials. He studied
t all from the inside. He told me, himself, that he planted that

seltzer can in order to frame Juliette and admitted he sent the te[
to lure her to my place."

She paused when he began snoring. This time, the unconsciou[
ness seemed natural. She moved back to her chair just before h[
family came in.

"Did he wake up?" asked Carlie.

"Not yet." She was still a fairly proficient liar.

"Oh, phew," said Carlie.

No one, especially not a sister, wanted to learn that they[
missed their loved one waking up from a coma.

Carlie's brow knitted. "Shouldn't he have woken up by now[

"He seems to be sleeping."

She still sat with his family when Danny's two siblings, actual[
Demko's cousins, Bobby and Kaylee, arrived.

The four chatted together in hushed voices as they waited f[
Demko to rouse and join them.

When he did, it was to find Nadine and his family all around hi[

"Hey. The gang's all here," he said. His voice was weak, b[
his smile bright.

Carlie began to cry, but soon Demko and his family we[
chatting away. After a bit, he turned to Nadine, extending h[
hand. She took it and he squeezed.

"You look happy," he said.

"It's nice to see a big normal family."

He met her gaze. "What about yours?"

"My aunt, uncle and cousins are here in town visiting."

"Nice. Good to have some backup."

"Yes."

"I'd like to meet them."

She took his hand and squeezed, then laced her fingers with h[

"I'd like that. Aren't we lucky to have good friends and[
supportive family? People we can count on. It makes all t[
difference."

Carlie went out to fetch the nurse and Nadine sent Juliette a
text. She replied with a thumbs-up emoji. Finally Nadine sent
another text to Tina.

His sister returned with a nurse, who checked Demko's vitals
and raised the head of his bed so he could sit up. That made him
dizzy and the nurse said that was normal, then left to get him a
lemon ice.

Juliette burst into the room, arms outstretched.

"Hey!" she said. "You're awake!"

She stepped forward to gently hug Demko. He patted her on
the back, and she used his bedsheet to dry her eyes. She bobbed
her head as he introduced her to Carlie and his cousins.

Juliette perched on the window ledge as they waited for the
nurse.

"What's new, Juliette?" Demko asked. "I know I have some
catching up to do."

"Well, did you hear about Dr. Crean?" asked Juliette, her eyes
twinkled, and she had a smile that told she had a delicious bit of
mischief to relay.

"She was released from the hospital," said Nadine.

"Yes," said Juliette. "But she's submitted her paperwork. She's
retiring."

"Really?" said Demko.

"Yeah. And she's got a book deal." Juliette cast Nadine a glance.
"A big one."

"Are they interviewing for her position?" Nadine asked.

"Word is that they'll offer it to you."

"Me!" She gasped and immediately turned to Demko to see
his reaction.

He beamed at her, nodding. "You'd be a natural."

"Will you take it?" asked Juliette.

Nadine thought about that and about the conversation she'd
had with Torrin. "I don't think so."

Juliette frowned and Demko looked confused.

"Torrin said they want to recruit me."

"Who? The FBI?" asked Juliette.

"Yup."

Juliette gave a low whistle. "That's badass."

"You going to take it?" asked Demko.

"Not without discussing it with you first."

"You should take it. Huge opportunity. And they'd be cr. not to want you."

Something about the way he said "want you" made her stoma flutter.

"I'd like to see this case through, but I was thinking of accep ing their offer. And the Bureau might be able to help me find father," said Nadine.

Demko nodded. "I'll help you."

"So will I," said Juliette.

She took both their hands as her heart filled with an upsw of joy.

At that moment, Tina dashed into the room. She took o look at them and burst into tears. She cried on Juliette's shoul and hugged Demko so tight his eyes bulged. Finally she wrapp Nadine up in a warm hug, tears pouring down her cheeks.

"This is my assistant, Tina," said Nadine to his family.

Tina hugged them, too.

Danny laughed at Tina's exuberance. "I think I have the wro assistant. Mine might like to see me in a hospital bed."

Juliette chuckled. "Well, we're more like a family."

A LETTER FROM JENNA

Dear Reader,

First, a great big thank-you for choosing to read *A Killer's Daughter*. I'm delighted and grateful that you joined me in Nadine Finch's exciting world! If you want to be the first to know about all my latest releases, just sign up at the following link. Your email address will never be shared and you can unsubscribe at any time.

www.bookouture.com/jenna-kernan

A Killer's Daughter has undergone many changes since concept. I loved the idea of the daughter of a serial killer confronting her mom's dark legacy and surrounding her with adult children of killers. The concept lifted the hairs on my neck, and I knew I was onto something.

I hope you enjoyed *A Killer's Daughter* as much as I enjoyed writing it. If you did, would you leave a short review on Amazon or the review site of your choosing? By doing so, you help new readers find this story. Even a line or two can make an enormous difference in the success of this book.

I'd love to learn what you thought about Nadine's unfortunate upbringing and her successfully solving, and surviving, her first case. During the rewriting process, I did consider killing her once or twice!

Please look for the second Nadine Finch book in May 2021 where Nadine, Demko and Juliette will be heading to Central Florida and Arleen's old stomping ground. Bring your bug repellent and watch out for gators!

I love to hear from readers. Please get in touch on social media, GoodReads, in an Amazon review or on my website www.jennakernan.com.

Be safe. Stay well.

Happy Reading!
Jenna Kernan

authorjennakernan

@jennakernan

@jenna_kernan

www.jennakernan.com

ACKNOWLEDGMENTS

This book grew from a poorly crafted brilliant idea into a manuscript worthy of presenting to editors largely because of the advice, editorial input and support of my agent, Ann Leslie Tuttle, of Dystel, Goderich & Bourret. Ann Leslie worked on my first book and has been a constant support and one-woman cheering section for me and my writing for nearly twenty years. I'm so grateful for her friendship and encouragement.

My Bookouture editor, Ellen Gleeson, again elevated this story through excellent editing and advice. She flagged issues and offered insightful suggestions to make this story shine. I'm so grateful for her belief in this story and in me!

I'm appreciative of Bookouture for their faith in my story and for the opportunity for me to hop genres. From the art team for crafting this striking cover, to contracts, to production and to the marketing team for putting this story into the hands of readers—this is one classy operation, and one with which I am happy to be included.

In addition, I offer my appreciation to the writing organizations that continue to provide quality education to mystery, thriller and police procedural writers. Thank you to Sisters in Crime, Mystery Writers of America, Mystery Writers of Florida, Thrill Writers International and Writers Police Academy. Also my gratitude goes to Novelists, Inc., a group of professional authors with

unmatched commercial acumen who are always on the forefro
of the business of writing.

It is important to have professional support and expertise a
equally vital to have emotional support and love. My family h
always been generous with praise and encouragement. Thank y
to my siblings, Amy, Nan and Jim, for cheering me on and
my mom, Margaret Cunningham Hathaway, for her faith in m

The final acknowledgment goes to my husband, also nam
Jim, who allows me the time needed to write, and gives consta
love and encouragement. He is always ready to offer practic
advice on a range of topics from "Should I hire a branding expert
to "Who would you call to help you move a body?" I'm so luc
to share this journey with you!

Finally I am grateful to my readers, both longtime and bran
new. A story doesn't live until it is in your hands!

Made in the USA
Coppell, TX
12 June 2021